The Time Philosopher

Susan Whiting Kemp

Published by Susan Kemp, 2024.

THE TIME PHILOSOPHER

First edition. May 24, 2024.

Copyright © 2024 Susan Whiting Kemp.

ISBN: 978-1733645249

Written by Susan Whiting Kemp.

Acknowledgments

Thank you Nancy Bonnington and Evelyn Arvey for reading and critiquing the early versions of *The Time Philosopher.* You have my eternal gratitude for your knowledge, enthusiasm, and support along the way. I couldn't ask for better friends and literary buddies.

Special thanks to my editor, Kara Aisenbrey of Just the Right Words. Your astute feedback vastly improved this novel. I truly appreciated your time and attention to detail.

I'm also thankful for my husband and children. Your love and encouragement sustain me.

Prologue

The Aguageddon began in western Washington State. No rain fell in the spring, when Seattle should have been drenched. By July the drought had spread south through Oregon and California, and north into British Columbia, then accelerated suddenly, with Washington's lakes and rivers emptying in one day. When people realized their precious fresh water might be gone forever, turmoil erupted throughout the Pacific Northwest. The next day the seas began to recede, turning a local disaster into a worldwide catastrophe.

Marella Wells journeyed by foot on the ocean bed to stop the cause: Project Athena, a machine that had been built to reduce climate change by removing carbon dioxide from the atmosphere, but which also removed water from the Earth. With her mentor-boss Elizabeth Fehr and college student Noah Mburu, she battled her way through windstorms, sandstorms, fire, and other life-threatening disasters, with a violent religious cult at her heels.

By reaching Wisdom Island and shutting down Project Athena, she made the water return, but only after the world had endured ten days of turmoil. With no water to quench the fires, most of western Washington burned. Fifteen thousand square miles of cities, farms, and forest were incinerated.

As if that weren't enough, when the oceans drained away, the atmosphere lowered to take their place, leaving mountainous regions without oxygen. Millions of people suffocated.

In the end, a billion people died. But now the water was back. It was time to rebuild and start anew.

However, Project Athena wasn't done with Marella.

Not yet.

Chapter One

M arella Wells now knew that guilt had a taste. A blend of warm iron and wet mold, reminding her of the choice she'd made.

On the teak deck of a tree-house home, she leaned on the railing, soaking in the view. The disaster—now over—had dried up many of the leaves that would normally be there in August, and so the Hoquiam River's East Fork was visible a few miles away. It was reassuring to see it flowing. Perfectly normal. Everything as it should be.

The sight undammed a reservoir of memories. Being stranded with Noah on Wisdom Island, rain pouring down as water returned to the world. Holding each other for warmth. Falling in love but not knowing whether they would live or die, although they had hope, if not for themselves, for their families back on the mainland.

They had survived the Aguageddon. She should be proud of stopping the water from disappearing from the Earth. Maybe when her head felt better she would be able to move on. That might take time; it had only been a week since Marella had nearly died from dehydration and the effects of Project Athena, a machine built using dangerous new technology. Her thoughts were still foggy. She imagined her head stuffed with insulation, pink and dry to the touch.

There was a task she needed to take care of: to tell Belinda Waverly, HemisNorth's CEO, that Project Athena had caused the Aguageddon, so its design plans needed to be destroyed. She wished she could call, but cell phones—even if she had one—weren't working after the disaster, and the internet was also down in western Washington. But then, it was a conversation better held in person anyway.

It would be a difficult one. She didn't know Belinda personally, but she admired her. There were many stories of random generous acts, such as giving the coat off her back to an unhoused woman. It had been Belinda's idea to set up an emergency fund to help HemisNorth employees. She had approved the development of Project Athena in the first place to help reduce climate change effects. To find out it had killed countless people and animals would be devastating to her, but she had to be told, so that she could make sure it would never happen again.

She'd heard from the neighbor that Belinda was staying at the Bandouer Hotel in Aberdeen, which was ten minutes away by electric bicycle. Perhaps soon she'd feel up to such a meeting, but not this morning. It could wait just a little longer.

Marella looked back at the Jorgen tree house where she, her mother, and her sister, Brielle, were staying. Marella didn't deserve to be in a beautiful place like this, not after what she'd done to Elizabeth. She didn't merit the comfort of an award-winning architectural marvel, its one thousand square feet wrapped around a giant cedar, with round windows that added to its charm.

She couldn't change the past, as Mom always said, but she could change the future. And so she should enjoy being up here. It did feel a little like an escape from the troubles of the world below.

She went inside, crossing over a large red Persian rug, every square inch woven with roses, grapes, and vines. The lush colors made her feel pampered. She'd never lived in a place where something you walked on was that artistic.

A two-story bookcase was filled with books grouped by color. White spines were on the bottom, greens hip-high, then blues, oranges, reds, purples, and blacks, which were reachable from a sliding ladder. It gave the room an air of a children's play space, perky and fun.

Her mother straightened the elastic sleeve on her daisy-pattern blouse, then handed Marella a steaming mug of liquid that smelled like sawed wood. "I found a ginseng-blend tea in the cupboard. It's good for memory, so maybe it will help your head. I think it's cool enough now." She pushed her auburn hair behind her ears and pursed her lips, giving her the expression of a scientist hoping her experiment would bear results.

Marella sipped. Although it tasted like mothballs, she downed it in the hopes that Mom was right.

Her mother wiped her hands together, then fluffed the cushions on the built-in bench at the bay window. Her busyness would have been reassuring—that was just Mom—except her movements seemed effortful, as if she was running on empty and might sink to the ground with exhaustion at any moment.

Because of the modern open floor plan, Brielle was visible in the kitchen, where she was filling a bottle in the sink. That still seemed miraculous a week after the water had returned. She had lost weight; her tie-dyed T-shirt and purple jogger pants didn't fit like they used to, but she seemed almost back to her usual buoyant self as she capped a bottle and held it up like a trophy.

Marella sank onto a bench next to the tree trunk, which reached from floor to ceiling, as if it had grown through the house on its way to the sky. She leaned back against the rough bark.

Mom brought Brielle another container to fill, then stopped and stared at the wall, as if her thoughts had ground to a halt. She could be distracted at times, but this seemed different.

"Are you all right, Mom?" asked Marella.

She broke out of her trance. "Fine," she said, almost brightly. "Just a little tired."

Marella got the feeling they hadn't told her everything about their race down the slopes of Mount Rainier when the atmosphere was lowering to take the place of the disappearing oceans. She did know one thing—that Brielle and Mom had saved the life of the owner of this tree house, and that was why they could stay here for free and use the owner's electric bicycle. They didn't seem to want to talk about it beyond that, not yet, and they hadn't pestered her for the details of her journey either. That was all for the best. Marella would rather not dwell on it.

"You look tired too," said Mom. "You need to rest."

Marella shook her head. She'd had plenty of sleep.

"Eat something then."

They were trying to ration the few cans of food and the stale crackers that had been in the cupboard. They hadn't been able to access their bank accounts because the banks hadn't reopened yet, so they had little cash. Food costs had become exorbitant. Grocery stores—the few that were open—were sparsely stocked and had armed guards.

Brielle, a survival show fanatic, had gathered dandelion leaves—dried out, of course—and a few edible roots Marella had never heard of. Marella picked a root from a plate and took a bite. It was small and bitter, but she chewed and swallowed it anyway.

Brielle beamed with joy watching her eat the results of her foraging. She had also made snare traps to catch a rabbit, squirrel, or bird, but Marella had seen no wild animals since the Aguageddon and wasn't sure how many might have survived.

"Where's Noah?" asked Marella.

"The neighbor is an architect," said Brielle. "He went over there. He said he might be a while."

That was excellent! Noah had been going to school at the University of Washington to learn building development. She was happy that he'd found somebody to talk shop with.

She looked forward to his embrace when he returned. They could continue planning the new life they would all share when they moved to Spokane to join his family. It would be a total reset: new place, new life. The past behind, the future ahead. She would have the extended family she'd always wished for, including his parents, who sounded sweet and fun, and his siblings and cousins, who apparently all had a great sense of humor.

In eastern Washington, they could have phones and internet. She felt cut off without them, unsure of what was happening locally as well as around the world. They could get news on the TV here, if they could only get it to work.

Brielle filled another container with water. Where had she gotten them all? Two dozen now sat on the counters and the floor.

"I think you have enough water stashed," said Marella. "The Aguageddon's over."

She shook her head. "There might be an earthquake or another disaster. We have to be ready."

"We can't take all that to eastern Washington on a bus," said Marella.

"Go lie down," said Mom abruptly. "You look terrible. I've never seen you with rings under your eyes."

Marella suppressed an annoyed retort. Who cared what she looked like? Her head was the problem. Her brain felt heavy in her skull, and her thoughts... She would prefer not to think at all. A memory: crawling through sand on the empty sea bottom, begging for water. *Think about something else.*

Would her brain ever feel clear? The words *permanent damage* repeated in her mind. Had Project Athena done this to her? She remembered its slow-motion lightning bolt searching for her, finally finding her, making her head feel split in two.

At least the pain of that was gone. She should be grateful. But now that she'd finished drinking the ginseng tea and eating the root, the taste of guilt—warm iron and wet mold—had returned.

Brielle crossed to one of the large porthole-like windows. She gazed out, like a youthful deckhand eager for a sight of land. "HemisNorth is doing something big near their plant."

Marella and Mom joined Brielle. She could see the plant's buildings and tall towers several miles away, at the bottom of the hill. The Grays Harbor area had been lucky. The Western Inferno, which had decimated half of Washington State, had stopped just north of here, sparing Aberdeen and the HemisNorth plant.

Dozens of trucks flung dust from dirt roads. She couldn't see the land on the other side of the river, but dust rose from there as well.

"When we were downtown I heard somebody say HemisNorth is going to rebuild all of western Washington," said Brielle.

"I hope they do. Then maybe things will get back to normal sooner." Mom put her arm around Brielle, and they exchanged a look of hope.

How odd. While Marella and Noah had agreed to keep HemisNorth's culpability quiet for now, they had told Mom and Brielle. So then why would they speak well of HemisNorth, knowing the company had caused the Aguageddon? Mom wasn't the type to forgive a corporation its failings.

Never mind. She didn't want to think about the disaster. She was proud she'd averted it, but her success had come with a cost. She would never think of herself in the same way again.

Marella felt a wave of nausea. The landscape outside wavered like a mirage, then dissolved into a swirl. Patience. This would pass. It was just a delayed symptom of overexertion, heat stroke, and malnutrition. Sometimes you got worse before you got better.

The windowsill felt grainy. It turned brownish-black, then disintegrated under her hand. She smelled ammonia.

All went dark. She couldn't feel the ground under her feet. Couldn't tell which direction was up. Her skin, porous as netting, was no protection against a sudden wave of freezing air. A frightening feeling of eternity stretched out from her on all sides. She was falling into it, even though she was already in it. How could that be?

It felt as if her body was being stretched, every particle of her extending to fill that eternity. She tried to shriek for help, but her parts were too scattered. She was becoming nothing.

· · · ·

OVER AN INSANELY LONG period of time, her particles seemed to snap back together. She saw yellow-and-black patterns, then fuzzy shapes. Gasping, she reached for the wall, but it wasn't there.

Her vision sharpened. She wasn't in the tree house; rather, she was in a long room with small tables. People occupied those tables, which held white mugs and plates of food. It smelled like fresh bread, making her mouth water. There was a background murmur of conversation.

A restaurant? A coffee shop? Yes, a coffee shop. The front counter just visible, way on the other side of a long, narrow room. How had she gotten here? She hugged herself, partly from cold, partly from confusion.

"Are you all right?" asked a woman wearing a knit cap.

No. Something is terribly wrong. "Fine," she tried to say, but her lips and tongue wouldn't form consonants, and the word erupted as a grunt. She turned away, embarrassed.

She was next to a sideboard with business cards and flyers. To appear purposeful while she gathered herself, she leaned on it, eyeing a flyer, unable to read its blurry words.

Through the window she saw a dusting of white on the bushes. She blinked, uncomprehending. It was August. Had a new disaster occurred? Had dormant volcano Mount Saint Helens come back to life, spewing ash into the air? Probably not, since heavy wool coats were draped over the backs of chairs, so it was cold outside, making that more likely to be snow. But nobody seemed concerned that it had snowed in summer.

She had a sudden, dreadful thought. That she had Alzheimer's and was an old person returning to a favorite haunt. She gazed at the back of her hand, half expecting it to be crisscrossed with blue veins, but no, she was still nineteen, still wearing her only clothes, black leggings and a slate-gray short-sleeve blouse, both faded and shabby, given to her by a volunteer on her arrival in Grays Harbor.

"Where am I?" she whispered to herself, finally able to form words.

The flyer came into focus, telling her Shakespeare's *As You Like It* was playing January 10 through February 25, 2002. But it wasn't 2002. That was a typo. She reached for a want-ad newspaper. Its date read *January 14, 2002.*

That was wrong too. It was 2023, not 2002, which was twenty-one years ago. Two years before she was born.

Everybody was dressed vintage. Baggy pants. Velour tracksuits. Newsboy hats. Belly shirts, in spite of the cold.

The old-fashioned clothing. The dates on the page. She had to be dreaming. If so, her dream brain had gotten everything perfect. None of the patrons had laptops. Nobody gazed at a phone. A few people held hard-copy books, while the rest chatted enthusiastically. She could see every detail in the art on the wall. Smell the coffee and mochas. Dreams didn't have smell, did they? She ran her fingers over the sideboard, feeling the texture of an uneven knot in the wood. This was real.

She shuffled to one of the tables and asked a woman with a big-tooth horsey smile, "What's the date today?"

"January fourteenth."

"What year?"

"2002."

Marella's mouth hung open. The woman nodded conspiratorially. "Yes, 2002. I know, it's hard to believe." For just a moment Marella thought the woman would tell her she'd time traveled. Instead she said, "I keep writing 2001."

Marella nodded dully and turned away. Was it nostalgia day at the coffee shop, everybody pretending to be in 2002? That seemed unlikely, especially after a massive disaster. And for that matter, food and coffee had become scarce and expensive; how could all these people be here, enjoying such luxury?

One aspect of this place seemed especially strange: everybody was laid-back, not watching each other warily like the people she'd seen in downtown Aberdeen. Not a single person had the hollow-eyed stare she'd seen in many of the survivors. They all seemed well-fed, well-hydrated, well-adjusted.

Perhaps she'd had a blackout and was somehow missing a span of time. She and her family must have left Grays Harbor, and she just didn't remember. And so now she must be in the Cascade mountains. That would explain the early freeze.

What town was this, then? She launched herself out a side door, onto a sidewalk. Her breath hung in the frigid air, and the cold wrapped itself around her bare arms. A car had a Washington State license plate. But—it couldn't be—its tab showed it would expire in 2003. Anxiety made her gut churn.

Pushing away from the icy metal of the bumper, she strode clumsily around the side of the coffee shop and onto the main street. She passed the coffee shop's storefront, continuing on to a restaurant, where she stopped abruptly. A banner in its window boasted *Seattle's Best Pancakes!*

She was in Seattle. Impossible! Seattle had burned down during the Aguageddon. It was gone. And yet here she was.

She spotted a news shop, its window displaying racks of magazines and newspapers. Heart pounding, she pushed open the door, which made a tiny bell tinkle. From a tall stack, she scooped up a hard copy of the *Seattle Post-Intelligencer*, dated January 14,

2002. Then a *Seattle Times*, dated January 14, 2002. She ran to the magazine racks. All were dated January or February 2002.

It seemed undeniable now that she had gone back in time. The only reason that was at all plausible was that another impossible event had just happened. The water had almost vanished from the world.

Now it seemed she was time traveling. She didn't have a better explanation.

She and Brielle used to talk about what they would do if they went back in time. There were the obvious things: Stop Hitler from carrying out the Holocaust. Pick a winning lottery number. Interview a famous person from centuries past.

And of course, keep their father from passing away. She'd always wished he hadn't died on that camping trip when she was five.

Although she had been so young, one fond memory of Dad was very clear. They were placing chocolate chips on a pancake to create a face. One side of the mouth frowned while the other smiled; they'd made their own mouths half frowny, half smiley. Their kooky expressions made each other belly laugh.

To go back in time and save her father had been an impossible fantasy. That it could even be remotely possible made her stomach flutter.

Now there was another item to add: stop the Aguageddon from ever happening.

What if this was her chance to do so? And if so, how? Could she warn somebody?

She stumbled over to the counter. A big-haired woman standing behind it raised her eyebrows, looking her up and down. "Are you all right?"

Marella must have looked as anguished as she felt. She blurted, "Two decades from now, HemisNorth will develop a secret technology that will take all the water away from the Earth. We have to stop them."

The woman leaned back, as if Marella might be dangerous. She felt her face redden. Wearing shoddy clothes, spouting nonsense, acting frantic. The woman thought she had mental issues or was a drug addict. This attempt was ridiculous. She started to turn away.

"Wait." The woman reached behind the counter, then handed her a lemon-colored card. "Call this number."

For a split second, she imagined the woman was somehow familiar with time traveling and knew how to help her. But of course that couldn't be, and the card had a telephone number for a crisis line. The woman continued. "They can direct you to treatment, counseling, job training, and so on. Everything you need to get your life back on track. All you have to do is call." She fished change from a pocket and handed it to her. "There's a phone booth across the street."

"Thank you." Marella took the card and the money, which barely fit into the tiny pocket in her leggings, then walked woodenly out the door.

Disappointment turned to hope. This was her connection. She could call somebody on a landline. But who? She didn't know her mother's telephone number from 2002. Even if she got ahold of her, what would she say? *Hi Mom, I'm your unborn child who has come to warn you about an upcoming apocalyptic disaster.*

Still, she scurried to the phone booth, which wasn't much of a booth, just a glass bay open to the elements. A phone book hung on a metal binder that swiveled up when she lifted. She turned the thin pages, looking for her mother and father, but neither were there, even though they'd each lived in Seattle in 2002. Was it because names could be unlisted back then? Not back *then*, back *now*. She looked for her former boss, Elizabeth Fehr, but her name was also missing.

She let the book swivel back down. Where should she go? What should she do? She rubbed her arms briskly, shivering so hard her hands skipped over her skin. The cold was nearly unbearable.

But it was more than the cold of the weather. It was a cold that infused her soul. The cold of eternity, stretching her. It was happening again.

All went dark. She reached out, but there was nothing to hold on to. She was plunging into eternity, being stretched, then scattered. This would never end.

· · · ·

PIECES OF HER MIND searched for one other. Thoughts consolidated, like Lego pieces snapping together. Bit by bit, they connected and she knew who she was, but not where she was.

When her body, too, consolidated, she was inside. The blurry red surface on which she stood came into focus, revealing large floral shapes alternating with triangles and squares. The tree house's Persian carpet.

Mom and Brielle were there, watching her, eyes wide with alarm. Marella tried to speak, but her words came out as a garbled muddle. She was shivering so hard her mother wrapped her arms around her. Brielle took her hand.

Finally Marella managed to speak actual words. "How long was I gone for?"

Brielle's breathy answer revealed her fright for her sister. "You didn't actually lose consciousness, but you were babbling for a minute. You didn't make any sense at all."

"But how long did I disappear for?" asked Marella.

Mom squeezed tightly, as if to make sure she didn't fly away. While her voice was calming, there was an undercurrent of distress. "You didn't disappear. You had some kind of episode, sweetie, but you're better now."

Didn't disappear? Why wouldn't she acknowledge that Marella had been gone? Marella was still trying to make sense of things—what was she overlooking? "I time traveled to the past. For about a half hour."

Mom guided her toward the couch, saying, "Oh my, oh my" under her breath.

"Mar-Mar, you're delirious," Brielle whispered, as if saying it too loudly might trigger worse.

Marella allowed herself to be led, words spilling out in her hurry to describe her amazing journey. "No, it really happened. I was in Seattle in 2002. I was in a coffee shop, and there were people sitting at the tables. They wore clothes from the 2000s. And the newspapers and magazines said 2002."

Making a noise of dismay, Brielle looked at Mom for direction.

Mom put on her "everything will be all right" mask: a slight smile and serene eyes. "Marella, you didn't go back in time. You're ill. More than I thought."

Marella sat, wondering how to get them all back in sync. They were such a close family, and yet she could feel how her supposed mental illness was dividing them. They saw her as the sick one, not the one who had just done something bizarrely fantastic. Plus she needed their help to figure out what to do next. "You don't believe me, but it's true! Feel how cold I am. It was January, there was snow." She was still shivering.

Mom gave Marella's arm a diagnostic rub. "You're in shock. The body pulls all the blood to the core. Get her a blanket."

Brielle rushed to a linen closet, retrieved an orange blanket, draped it around Marella, and patted it, looking relieved to have helped.

Marella reveled in the blanket's warmth. It made sense that they thought she was having mental problems. She had jabbered without taking a breath between sentences.

But then, could it actually have been a hallucination? She seriously considered whether that was the case. After all, they said she hadn't disappeared. The thought made her feel untethered. Had the Aguageddon given her severe enough brain damage to have such detailed hallucinations? The sweet smell of mocha, the variety of people at the tables, the detailed printing on the newspapers, the glossy feel of the magazines. How could she believe anything her brain told her, if that hadn't been real?

She breathed in sharply, realizing exactly how to know one way or the other. She fished in the pocket of her leggings, nervous that it would be empty. It wasn't! She brandished the lemon-colored card and the coins triumphantly. "A woman handed these to me in 2002. It's proof. I traveled back in time and returned with these. Look!"

Brielle looked at the card. "It's for a crisis line."

Mom tightened the blanket around Marella. "That must have been in the pocket when the Red Cross gave you clothes. Your mind is playing tricks on you. You need to rest."

Marella looked at the dates on the coins, announcing, "These are 1995, 1992, and 1997. All before 2002."

"That's not really proof." Brielle seemed conflicted at having to contradict her.

Of course it was proof. Why didn't they believe her? "There was nothing in the pocket when I got these leggings. I need to understand why I time traveled."

"Marella, stop," Brielle said. "See what this is doing to Mom?"

Mom's "everything is all right" mask had disintegrated. She wrung her hands; a tear spilled down her cheek.

It was hard to watch, but Marella couldn't back down now. Something extraordinary had happened, and they needed to know that. What if it happened again? What should she do? It would be too overwhelming to sort this out on her own. "Mom, I know this sounds unlikely, but think about how unlikely it was that Project

Athena could take so much water from the world that the oceans would lower."

"No." Mom looked shamed, as if admitting to a transgression. "Project Athena didn't take the water."

"Wait. You're telling me you don't believe Project Athena caused the Aguageddon?"

Mom pulled up to her full height. Seeming to decide to be candid with her daughter, she spoke resolutely. "No, Marella. It didn't."

This was the real reason they hadn't asked for more details about her journey to Wisdom Island. They hadn't believed her then either. How could that be, when they'd almost always given her the benefit of the doubt? She felt unstable, as if each foot occupied one side of a teeter-totter. "You never said you didn't believe me about Project Athena."

"You've been so muddled." Brielle lowered her eyes. "Mom didn't think it would be a good idea to argue with you."

So they had teamed up against her. Talked about her behind her back. Placated. Pretended. This wasn't how her family did things. The hurt she felt made her louder. "But the oceans disappeared. You know that. The lower water level made the atmosphere drop to fill the empty space. There was no oxygen at high elevations. That was why you had to leave Mount Rainier. You would have suffocated if you hadn't. The people who didn't leave died."

"True," said Mom, palms together, the earnest negotiator. "But Project Athena didn't do it. Concurrent Alignment did. The perfect storm of cosmic events. Solar flares, alignment of planets, alignment of galaxies."

Everybody they'd talked to after the Aguageddon believed its cause was Concurrent Alignment. The people from the Red Cross, the neighbor, the bank teller, and others they had come across downtown. Everybody believed this theory, except for the few who thought outer-space aliens had siphoned the water from the oceans but then returned it because it was salty. To Marella, it seemed unlikely that distant planets and galaxies would affect the Earth so abruptly, but maybe that was because she knew better.

It was unnerving to find out her own family believed others when they spouted such nonsense, but not her when she told them the truth.

Mom rubbed her forehead with her fingertips, like she did when feeling stymied. She tried to speak soothingly. "We can't go to eastern Washington. You shouldn't travel when you're so sick. And anyway, we don't know how safe it is between here and there."

Marella bowed her head in dismay. Her hope of combining her family with Noah's was in jeopardy. How ironic that her mother always wanted to pull up stakes and move to another city, yet now wanted to stay put. The world had definitely turned upside down.

Mom and Brielle seemed like strangers; their lack of belief in her filled the house to overflowing. Marella tossed away the blanket. She needed to get away from them.

She also needed to inform Belinda about Project Athena. Might as well do that now and get it over with. There was no time like the present.

Chapter Two

Riding the e-bike gave Marella a sense of freedom and release, until she reached a shantytown alongside the road. Hundreds of shacks were made of wood, oiled cardboard, corrugated iron, and other materials. It smelled of urine, feces, and rotting garbage. The place seemed populated by sleepwalkers: disaster-addled survivors with hollow eyes, their thin arms dangling as they watched her speed by. She guessed that some of them might be desperate for the bike or anything she might be carrying, and she watched carefully for potholes; this would be a bad place to take a spill.

A half hour after leaving the tree house, Marella was in the Bandouer Hotel lobby, striding across a marble floor streaked with veins of gold and azure. It was a stark contrast to the hovels she had just passed. A large bulletin board held a mosaic of handwritten notes, mostly of people searching for missing loved ones. A fretful woman in a soiled tank top was about to add to it when she spotted Marella and brought the note to her. *Theodore Milton, five years old, has a red birthmark on his forehead, last seen in Ellensburg, WA.* "Have you seen Theo?"

"No, I'm sorry."

The woman deflated as if Marella had been her only hope. She walked away.

A couple of people crossed the lobby, giving Marella a wide berth. She didn't take it personally. People avoided each other more now. There was mistrust all around.

Upstairs, she took a deep breath, then knocked on the door of the executive suite. How would Belinda take the news that the company she ran had caused a global disaster that killed a billion people and nearly desiccated the entire planet? Although Marella didn't know her personally, others described her in reverent terms, labeling her a visionary. For that reason, she hoped Belinda would listen without prejudice.

Belinda opened the door. With her prominent jawline and intelligent eyes, she reminded Marella of a midcareer Katharine Hepburn, wise and energetic. She raised her arms in ecstatic joy, as if she'd found a long-lost sister.

"Marella Wells, it's really you!"

To her surprise, Belinda rushed forward, wrapping her in a warm, honeysuckle-fortified hug. After a split second, Marella realized she should hug her back, and what could have been an awkward moment became agreeable. Two people celebrating connection after a catastrophe.

They pulled back, both smiling large. "I'm so glad to see you," said Belinda. "You're the only Seattle employee I know of who survived. Everybody else is dead or missing."

Marella's smile faded. The only one—out of the two hundred employees in that office.

Her chest felt tight. She had suspected many of her coworkers had died. But nearly all of them? Her mind flipped through faces she used to see every day at the office. The chemist who paddled her kayak to work, the accountant who was patient with Marella's time sheet mistakes, and so many more. Dead. Gone. The water had returned, but they never would.

And of course there was Diana Brinkhauser, who had been Marella's neighbor, a chemical engineer who'd helped her get the job at HemisNorth. Marella prayed that she was just missing, not dead, and would be found, but she couldn't bring herself to ask Belinda. She didn't want to break down in front of her and risk losing sight of her goal.

Lightly touching Marella's elbow, Belinda guided her to a nubby white couch, then poured them coffee from an urn on a side table.

The upscale room made Marella feel a bit out of place. Three artillery-shell-shaped vases graced one end of a fireplace mantel. A brass javelin thrower balanced on the other. Champagne glasses were lined up in a glass-fronted cabinet over the wet bar.

Belinda set two mugs on a glass coffee table designed to look like a slab of Arctic ice. Marella surreptitiously overloaded her coffee with cream and sugar, thankful for the calories.

Belinda lowered herself to an easy chair, smoothing her pinstripe suit. Her eyes crinkled with gladness, making Marella feel exceptionally welcome.

"I was in Texas when western Washington burned," said Belinda. "But you were in Seattle. How did you survive?"

"By driving out onto the seabed." Flickers of memory sprang up. Smoke and heat. Desperate people fleeing the flames.

"Were you with your family?" asked Belinda. "You have a mother and a sister, I remember. Please tell me they survived too."

She shouldn't have been surprised that Belinda knew about her family; she'd heard the woman made it a point to know about her employees. Still, there were fifty thousand of them around the world, so it made her feel appreciated.

"They survived too, but I wasn't with them. I was with Elizabeth Fehr."

Belinda jumped up, making her coffee slosh. "Elizabeth is alive? Where is she?"

"No. She uh... she's not. She didn't make it."

The CEO's shoulders slumped. Elizabeth had not only been a valued leader in the company, but also Belinda's friend. She sat back down and put her mug on the table carefully, as if it were made of eggshell. After absentmindedly wiping the coffee from her hand with a tissue, she dabbed her eyes with it. "I thought it was a possibility, but to hear it as a certainty... it's hard."

"I'm sorry." Marella had an urge to enfold her in a comforting hug, but she held back. Belinda hugging her was one thing. Marella hugging her was another. Marella had been a lowly former project assistant. Even though she'd saved the lives of everybody in the world, nobody knew it, and she still considered herself low-ranking. Besides, she needed distance—even if only a few feet—to inform Belinda of her company's terrible part in the Aguageddon.

"How did Elizabeth die?" asked Belinda.

How did she die? By my own hands. Marella could still feel the roughness of her former boss's lips on her palm, the wetness of Elizabeth's blood and spittle. Determined to keep her composure, she rubbed her hands on her thighs to dispel the ghastly sensation. She needed to convey how dangerous Project Athena was and that it had not only failed in its intended function, but had also caused enormous tragedy.

Belinda's face was draped in grief. Marella needed to tell her something comforting so they could move on to the next bombshell. *Elizabeth died through mercy.* No! That would give it away. She needed to compose an answer that wouldn't invite suspicion.

To buy time, she sipped her coffee. She tried to lean back, but the couch's artfully minuscule back was too short.

Just tell her. Move the conversation forward. Only the basics. She doesn't have to know all the details. Without looking into Belinda's eyes, she spoke. "We were on our way to Wisdom Island when the ocean drained away from under us and the raft grounded. We had to walk on the dry seafloor. There were stone towers. An earthquake shook them. Rocks dropped on Elizabeth." Marella's voice caught. She could almost hear Elizabeth's groans once more.

Belinda put a hand to her heart. "It makes no sense. Why would Elizabeth try to take you to Wisdom Island? Why not go to Mount Rainier, where there was still ice and snow?"

Here's your opening. Tell her. "We went there to shut down Project Athena."

Belinda grasped the armrest so tightly her fingernails made valleys in the cloth; her voice lowered an octave. "Project Athena is highly confidential, and you don't have clearance..."

Marella steeled herself against what she thought would be rage, but Belinda controlled herself so quickly that whatever had been beneath the surface remained hidden. She relaxed her hands and spoke sadly once more. "Never mind. Why did Elizabeth think that was so important?"

Now Marella just had to spit out the words, but it was hard, so hard, to give sorrowful Belinda this double whammy. "Because it was causing the Aguageddon."

She went rigid, which made Marella babble to get it all out before Belinda stopped her. "Project Athena was taking all the water away from the Earth. And we had to fix that. Because we couldn't get help. We couldn't get anybody on the phone. And we were alone at the HemisNorth office when we confirmed it."

Marella remembered the feeling of desperation so clearly. If only she could have effected change while time traveling to 2002. The Aguageddon would never have happened, and life would be normal. Would she ever have another chance? Would she time travel again? She told herself not to be distracted by that now. She still had a mission to accomplish.

Wrapping her arms around herself, Belinda spoke softly. "Oh my god. How could Elizabeth have thought Project Athena was responsible? She might be alive now if she hadn't."

"But Elizabeth was right," said Marella.

Belinda stood, shaking her head and fanning her hands to emphasize how ridiculous the notion was. "I'm sorry you suffered because of this... this... delusional idea. Project Athena didn't cause a worldwide disaster. Scientists have determined it was Concurrent Alignment."

"Yes, I've heard that, and it's just not true—"

"It's true." Belinda projected the confidence she embodied as the leader of a global company. "We were incredibly unlucky that all those cosmic events happened at once, but it's over now. We can move on, knowing that we need to be better prepared for the next disaster."

It wasn't surprising that she didn't believe right away that HemisNorth's Project Athena had caused the disaster, but her tone made Marella nervous their meeting would end abruptly, before she obtained Belinda's assurance to destroy any plans.

She stood too, heart racing. "It wasn't just Elizabeth. I used humidity data. I made a diagram. With circles. It showed that every time a new Project Athena module got turned on, the drought spread."

Belinda huffed disagreement. Marella needed to explain it better. She spoke quickly and insistently. "We called Victor, the scientist who was on Wisdom Island monitoring Project Athena. He had altered the data. On the instruments that took the readings. So you couldn't see that Project Athena was taking water away from the world instead of carbon dioxide. Victor was dying from dehydration, because of Project Athena, and we couldn't get any help to get to him and save him and turn it off. No police. No military. No helicopter companies. No nothing. So we drove on the seabed, then rafted, then walked. I made it all the way to the island. Noah and I—"

"Noah? Who's that?"

"Noah Mburu—a college student we met on the way. We shut Project Athena off, or the Aguageddon would have kept going forever. And there was something wrong with the design, so that shutting it down made it explode."

Belinda gestured for Marella to stop. "You're correct that it's destroyed. We sent a supply drone to the island after the water returned, so we've seen the images. However, shutting Project Athena down wouldn't cause an explosion, and certainly not such a massive one."

Desperation made Marella sound like a spoiled child trying to get her way. She kept on, regardless. "Belinda, I was there. We shut it down and it exploded immediately. We barely escaped. It's just like the prototype. That exploded too."

Belinda spoke quietly yet firmly. "I'll tell you in confidence that it was sabotage. We think we know who was responsible. I won't go into detail, except to tell you the danger is past. However, you need to understand that shutting down the machine did not cause that explosion."

Marella felt flustered at Belinda's adamant declaration and her seeming belief that the matter was settled, but this wasn't about explosions. It was about the machine's failure. She needed to get the discussion back on track. "My point is that Project Athena took the water away. It caused the Aguageddon! Delete the plans. The design plans. Any data. Whatever you have that describes how it works. Destroy them."

Belinda's head pulled back, though her voice remained level. "You're wrong, absolutely wrong." She sounded so sure of herself. The expert in all things, especially this one. Marella would have almost preferred an angry reaction, rather than this assured calm. Such conviction could be impossible to overcome.

She felt terribly powerless. Her family hadn't believed her about the machine—or the time travel, for that matter—and now Belinda doubted her as well. She felt a ridiculous urge to turn snarky. *Fine! Have it your way, and then don't be surprised when the disaster returns and everything goes to shit and more people die and you shrivel up like beef jerky...* She blocked the train of thought. She would have to find a reasonable way to get through to her. She looked down at the parquet flooring, trying to gather the right words.

Belinda strode to the window, looking out at the bare branches of a maple tree that had died after the three-month drought and ten-day disaster. She patted the sill as if she had made a decision, then turned.

"My home in Seattle burned down while I was at the Texas facility, so I lived. My children did too—luckily they and their families live on the East Coast. But others didn't escape with their lives. My husband was one of them."

Marella released a breathy noise of distress. "Oh Belinda, I'm so sorry."

Belinda took some catch breaths, as if she might lose her composure, then got hold of herself. She nodded acceptance of Marella's consolation. "I also lost good friends. Everybody lost somebody, and those who survived are scattered, and the businesses where they worked have burned down. But HemisNorth can help make the recovery more than a recovery. We can come out of this better than before."

Belinda held herself heroically tall, seeming larger than life. Marella wouldn't have been surprised to hear inspiring music play as she continued to speak. "There's turmoil throughout the rest of the world. Most of the world's fish have died, along with many land animals and crops. Because our offices are so widespread, HemisNorth—along with our HemisSouth subsidiary—is in a unique position to support government efforts and provide stability all around the globe. Let's not get distracted from the real need here. We need to help all these people. Forget about Project Athena, it's no longer relevant."

Belinda's attitude implied that that matter was closed. Marella fished desperately for a way to reopen it. "Humor me. What if I'm right? If Project Athena isn't relevant, just destroy the plans. Do it for Elizabeth. It's what she would have wanted."

It sounded so ridiculous as the words came out of her mouth. *It's what she would have wanted.* What kind of persuasion was that?

Belinda sat back down, looking somewhat deflated. Marella sat too, wincing inwardly at her own incompetence. If the discussion turned back to Elizabeth, Marella was sure to break down.

Luckily it didn't. Belinda responded, "There are no design plans left. All of western Washington State burned down. The corporate offices in Seattle are gone. Everything was destroyed in the Western Inferno."

"But HemisNorth backs everything up to out-of-state servers."

"Not those plans. They were too sensitive. They were in closed systems—one on the island and one in Seattle. So since Project Athena is destroyed, it's a complete loss." She pressed her lips together and shook her head sadly.

Marella wiped sweat from her hands, feeling a sense of relief. It made sense. The fact that Project Athena's program existed only in a closed system had forced her and Elizabeth to go the island personally. "Okay, okay, that's good, but we have to make sure that people who worked on the project don't try to recreate it."

"Len and Eshana were the only ones who understood Project Athena completely, and they're dead. We couldn't build another one even if we wanted to."

Marella had known that Eshana Collins and Len Janderson, the machine's inventors, were dead—that had happened before the Aguageddon. She hadn't understood that their genius was so irreplaceable. She perked up. No Project Athena plans. Nobody with enough knowledge. Had she indeed achieved what she'd come for?

"Besides," said Belinda, "our priority is the millions of people who are unsheltered and unemployed. The local and national governments are stalled, and nothing is getting done, so

HemisNorth is going to rebuild Washington. A much improved Washington." Her enthusiasm mounted. "We're doing great things. Imagine how magnificent our planned cities will be. Using 3D printers to build structures will speed the work enormously. We can build an entire building in only twenty-four hours."

HemisNorth had caused the Aguageddon. Was it a good thing that nobody knew, so that they could now fix their mistake? Was that even possible?

Rebuilding Washington seemed like a tall enough order, but Belinda had also said they would help with world stability. How would a corporation like HemisNorth support that?

Belinda touched her shoulder in solidarity, her face radiating care and concern. "I'm sorry Elizabeth encouraged you to go on such a dangerous trip. I apologize on her behalf, and I'm thankful you survived. But she was completely wrong about Project Athena. It was built to remove excess carbon dioxide from the atmosphere, and that's what it was doing. It did not take away water. Concurrent Alignment did."

Marella hesitated, fighting an impulse to correct her. Belinda seemed to see her resistance. She added, "Trust me on this. I wouldn't steer you wrong, not when you're so special. My only link to Seattle. It tears me apart that Elizabeth misled you so badly."

Marella had mixed feelings: a tinge of pleasure—she was special to Belinda—along with dismay. Elizabeth had been a hero, not a delusional fool.

Yet if they couldn't build another Project Athena, what was the point of insisting? If HemisNorth was going to construct housing, they would succeed faster if they weren't sidelined by protests, lawsuits, or other distractions. Getting the truth out was important, she supposed. Although that could happen later.

Marella's throat was tight. She didn't want to lie, but it seemed like the best thing to do at that moment. "I guess you're right. I just... Elizabeth sounded like she knew..." She felt hot with shame, throwing Elizabeth under the bus.

Belinda's smile was filled with relief. She regarded Marella compassionately, then looked away, as if surfacing from a dream. She glanced at her watch. "I was about to leave for our Grays Harbor manufacturing facility when you surprised me with this visit. I'm glad I was here, but I must get going." She downed her coffee all at once, like a heron gulping down a fish. "Where are you living? Do you need a place to stay?"

Even after this difficult conversation, Belinda was looking out for her. It bolstered Marella somewhat. "In the Jorgen tree house on the hill. My mom helped the owner. He said we could stay there."

Belinda nodded approvingly, seeming surprised. "Ah! I know that one. I saw photographs in an architectural magazine." She clasped her hands. "All right then, the next step is to find you a spot in the Grays Harbor facility so you can return to work. Check with reception there in two days and we'll be ready for you."

It was surprisingly tempting to consider going back to work. Belinda's comment about fish and animals dying and crop failure reminded her of her empty belly. She could use the money. But to return to HemisNorth, knowing what Project Athena had done to the world, to her, to her family—that would be wrong.

It seemed she had accomplished what she'd come for: to make sure that nobody would ever build another Project Athena. The plans for the deadly machine no longer existed anywhere, and Project Athena itself—both the prototype and the actual modules—had exploded into thousands of twisted pieces, many of which now lay on the sea floor, scattered in the Pacific Ocean around Wisdom Island.

And so, did anybody ever need to know the truth? The Aguageddon was over. Its true instigators were dead. And what was more, it was best that nobody knew that a machine like Project Athena was feasible, since it was so dangerous.

The two fellow survivors hugged once more, and Marella felt a kinship with Belinda, almost as if they had struggled through the Aguageddon together. She left the hotel room, shutting the door behind her. She half turned, thinking to knock on the door and ask, "Is there anything we missed? Are the plans really and truly destroyed?"

She didn't. She would only get the same answer. Besides, Belinda was right. It was time to move forward, into a better life.

Chapter Three

Marella locked up the electric bicycle after her return from HemisNorth, then Noah Mburu came through the gate from the neighbor's house. On his arrival, the midday sun broke through the clouds, making it seem as if his smile lit up the yard. The light rimmed his curly dark hair with golden brown and made shadows under his high cheekbones.

His inquisitive gaze always seemed like that of a world explorer, just arrived in a new land to track down enchanting places nobody else had ever seen.

Marella was suddenly sure that together they could accomplish anything, even discover why and how she had time traveled to 2002. After all, they had defeated the Aguageddon. At that moment, every other challenge seemed to pale in comparison.

His stride was somewhat awkward; his feet had been cut while walking barefoot on shell and rock-covered ground. But at least he seemed to be healing fast. He also had a burn on his back the shape of Antarctica. It was healing well, even though it had been so bad that the doctor said his skin there would always be white rather than brown.

They embraced. With their arms clamped tightly around each other, they fit as snuggly as two halves of an oyster shell. Marella didn't want to let go. She had made it to the bottom of the Pacific Ocean and back with him. He, too, seemed to not want it to end.

Finally they pulled apart and sat together, easing their feet into a stream that ran alongside the yard. They held hands, fingers interlaced, knuckles alternating, his skin beautifully contrasting with hers, like zebra stripes.

Tell him about the time travel.

She couldn't bring herself to do it yet. What if he didn't believe her?

Noah stroked the side of her face. "Someday I'll build you a house. How about Craftsman style?"

She beamed. To live together with Noah, in a house of their own, was a beautiful dream. "What's Craftsman style?"

"Big porches, fat rafters. Next to a stream like this one."

"If you're going to build it for me, shouldn't it be a Taj Mahal?"

His laugh was a sweet rumble that warmed her, even with her feet in the cool stream. "Then you'll need to help build it."

"That's a given."

"I'll have to learn how to make domes."

"I'll make them," said Marella. "I once made a Saint Basil's Cathedral out of papier-mâché."

"The one in Moscow? With the stripes and things? That's impressive."

"Not so impressive, now that I think of it. It was kind of lopsided." She flipped her hand, a nonchalant gesture. "You can make the domes after all."

"So then what's your contribution?" asked Noah with pretend outrage.

"I'll pick out the furniture," said Marella in a posh accent. "Tell the movers where to put it. It's a hard job, but somebody's got to do it."

He chuckled, then deepened his voice comically. "I'll need a man cave."

"In a Taj Mahal?" She laughed. "I can't even picture it." She could, however, picture a future where they laughed together, just like this, over silly things. A future that was lighthearted, loving, sexy, and exciting, and all those things that a perfect partnership brought.

They sat for a while, watching the light play on their feet and the rocks in the stream. A small caddis fly larva, its shell fashioned of tiny stones, crept along on spindly legs. Like them, it had somehow survived for a time without water. It had beat the odds.

She spotted a plastic toy in the stream. A small purple-and-green figurine of a superhero she didn't recognize, muscles bulging, cape rippling.

People said time was like a river—or perhaps like this stream—flowing ever onward. She imagined herself as the figurine, with the power to move through time at will. The figure's knees were bent, its arms raised in takeoff mode. She took it as a sign. She, too, should be powerful. Wallow less in her own guilt. Easier said than done, since it involved more than just Elizabeth's death. She'd also killed a teenager, Olivia, a cult follower who'd been trying to kill her. It was self-defense, but she still blamed herself. If she'd only discovered the girl's untrustworthiness sooner, it wouldn't have come to that.

She spit, trying to expel the taste of guilt. It didn't work. No matter what she did, she still tasted warm iron and wet mold. *Just don't think about it.*

She moved her foot. The water flowed around it, not stopping, seemingly unaffected. Her recent experience of time wasn't like a river. If time wasn't a river, then what was it?

She needed to tell Noah about the time travel, yet it was hard to find the right words. Mom and Brielle had thought she was crazy because of it. She would be crushed if Noah did too. After all they'd been through, it seemed like he would believe her, but she'd misjudged his reaction before. She'd told him what she'd done to Elizabeth, hoping for understanding, but getting none. It had torn them apart for a time.

Would this be the same? A confession, then condemnation?

Instead of telling him, she kissed him. The world disappeared. It was just Marella and Noah. Just this moment in time.

Time, which couldn't be a river or a stream. So what was it?

He pulled back, taking both her hands in his. Could he feel her distraction?

"It's funny you mentioned the Taj Mahal. Because there's something I've never told anybody about." Ah. He was distracted by something too. He was smiling shyly, so it was something good. Marella was relieved. She could put off telling him, though she vowed to speak up when he was done.

He swished his feet in the water. "I have this dream. Someday I want to build something big. Like the Seven Wonders of the Ancient World, or of the modern world."

She loved his drive. In high school he'd founded a group for students with disabilities. At the university, he'd been looking forward to learning about real estate development that incorporated accommodations for differently abled students. She perked up. "Tell me more."

He grinned, seeming thrilled with her enthusiasm. "My new wonder-of-the-world would combine the mystery of the Great Pyramid of Giza with the beauty of the Hanging Gardens of Babylon, the majesty of the Colossus of Rhodes, and the vastness of the Great Wall of China. But it would be different than all of those."

Marella envisioned an enormous statue coming to life and stepping over the great wall on its way to a pyramid. "What would it be?"

"I don't know yet. I still need to figure that out, but for sure it needs to be something that draws humanity together. It wouldn't just be big for the sake of being big. Not just a monolith. Definitely not a barrier. And real, not virtual reality."

She loved this about him, that there was always more to discover. She loved his energy, his certainty.

"That's all," he concluded. "I just wanted you to know what you're getting into by being with me."

The break in the conversation gave her the opening she needed to bring up the time travel. She needed to tell somebody who would understand, who could give her advice. She'd solved a problem with his help before. She could do it again, if she would just try. She took a deep breath. *Just get it over with.* "There's something I wanted to tell you about too."

He looked as if he expected something delightful. Marella warned, "It's not the same kind of thing as what you were just talking about."

Looking serious now, he gestured for her to continue.

She rubbed a smudge on her leggings. "When we were on the island, just after we shut Project Athena down and we ran outside, remember when the module's big loop zapped me?"

He seemed confused. "No."

"It was like a slow-motion lightning bolt. It came at my head and struck me, and it seemed like it was attached to me. It would have kept on zapping me, but you pulled me away from it."

"I didn't see anything like that." He tilted his head, as if this was a joke that he wasn't getting.

Marella was taken aback. How could he have missed seeing that bright bolt? She had been sure he had witnessed it and would corroborate it to her family. Now it would be harder for him to believe her.

She'd already started to tell him. If she didn't continue, she would remain isolated with the knowledge. "Well... it happened. And for those moments, it was cold. And I felt like I was being stretched out across all of eternity." Her throat tightened, making it hard to speak.

"Okay." He stroked her hair encouragingly. "Go on."

"Just a little while ago, I felt that same feeling. Exactly the same. I felt cold and stretched out. And then I traveled back in time. I spent a half hour in 2002. I was in Seattle."

He squeezed her hand. "You were dreaming."

Marella took her hand away from his, to show how serious she was. He didn't believe her, but the more he knew, the more likely he was to get it. He just needed to experience it from her point of view. "No, I was wide awake. I know it sounds crazy, but it actually happened. Everything was so clear." She described the event in detail. The flyer with the date of 2002, the snow, the car tab, the lady in the news shop handing her the card. "And I have proof. These weren't in my pocket before I time traveled. But I've got them now." She showed him the lemon-colored card and the coins.

He took them, examined both sides of the card, then handed them back. "This is—wow. I mean... I don't know." He looked at the stream for a moment, then spoke, still gently, as if talking to an invalid. The love was there, but not the belief in her. "Project Athena dehydrated me so much that I hallucinated. So did you. You thought you saw sharks circling in the air. This is a holdover from that. You're still healing."

Marella's heart sank. Where was the trust they had in each other? "This is different. It wasn't a dream, and it wasn't a hallucination. I need your help to figure out how I time traveled. I think it might have been triggered by Project Athena. The feeling was so similar, it must be related. But why? How would Project Athena have made me time travel?"

"It didn't. Project Athena is gone. It exploded into smithereens, and so it's not affecting you." He was looking at her oddly now. As if she were unwell. It made her feel like he had discovered a flaw in her. Did he wonder if there were more flaws to come? She wanted to agree with him to get him to stop looking at her like that, but was angry with herself for thinking that way. Relationships were about truth. And besides, this was about so much more. She had time traveled! It was fearful and crazy and strange and fascinating!

"But before Project Athena exploded, it could have affected me. It's that same feeling of eternity that I had when I was looking into the module loop. Everything so endless and stretching into forever."

Noah's brow knitted, then smoothed as he hid his anxiety, possibly for her benefit. He was good at acting calm under pressure. He spoke matter-of-factly, like a teacher explaining a math problem. "Time travel isn't possible, because even if you could go back in time—which you can't—nobody would survive it." He scooped up a rock and a stick. "Say you're this stick. And this rock is the Earth. At this moment in time, the Earth is here. But it revolves around the sun." He moved the rock forward but held the stick in place. "So if you went back in time, you'd be where the Earth used to be, but it wouldn't be there anymore. You'd end up in empty space, in a vacuum."

He had an expectant look, as if his explanation would convince her and then everything would be okay. He truly wanted to help her. He did love her. It was just that he was so sure he was right, he wouldn't allow that she could be.

Marella took the rock and stick out of his hands and tossed them away, which made him look puzzled. Her tone was more surly than she intended. "It doesn't work that way because I survived it. I went to the past and came back."

He leaned back with an attitude of frustration. He spoke slowly and distinctly, as if she'd merely misunderstood his words. "You didn't go back in time. It was a flashback or something. It wasn't real."

She was desperate to convince him now. She needed an ally, not this person who had stopped believing in her. She squeezed his hand with each phrase and spoke lovingly. "I did. It was real. I smelled coffee. I touched snow. I brought that card and the coins back with me."

He gazed steadily at her, still seeming to wait for her to give up this nonsense.

This wasn't working. She needed to change tactics. "Remember how at first you didn't believe that Project Athena caused the

Aguageddon? But you know now that it did. You need to trust me that this is true also."

"That was different. Everybody could see the water was gone. And as soon as we shut down Project Athena, the water came back. But this is just you. I don't time travel even though I was on the island with you."

He spoke gently, so she knew he didn't intend to be mean, but it hurt all the same. She set her jaw and crossed her arms. "I'm not crazy."

"Oh, Marella!" He embraced her, crossed arms and all, speaking in a soothing voice. "Nobody's calling you crazy. We went through some horrible times. A phenomenally major disaster. People tried to kill us. I'm having trouble with it too, just in a different way. I'm jumpy. Nervous. This doesn't reflect badly on you. It's normal after a disaster. We can find a counselor in town. Or a minister. I'm sure they could help us both sort things out."

His embrace felt controlling, as if he were trying to contain her, even though she knew he meant well. Arms still crossed, she pulled away, speaking gloomily. "I thought you of all people would believe me."

Noah laced his fingers over his forehead, elbows lifted. He seemed perplexed, as if working out how to fix things between them. He dropped his arms as an idea came to him. "I was just talking with Alphonse, the next door neighbor. He's set up a company called Rebuild Washington, and he wants to hire me. I think I should take him up on it. He wants to meet with some people later this week. Planners, architects, lawyers. We would help the people left unhoused after the Western Inferno. Work out the logistics. You and I could both get involved. You're exactly the kind of person they need. There's a lot to work out, and it'll distract you from all that. Help you move on."

This was a blow she couldn't have seen coming. Not after he'd described his family so thoroughly, and how much they would love her and accept her, Brielle, and Mom. Not after he'd described Spokane in such glowing terms—its rushing river and tumbling falls, its great parks, its fun hangouts. She'd spent days talking it over with him, and now suddenly their goal was vanishing like a thin trail of cigarette smoke.

"But we were going to go stay with your family. Get a fresh start in Spokane."

"I know, but this is even better. Think how much I could learn about real estate development. And you too—you could have a great career like you wanted. There'll be so much opportunity once we get the funding figured out."

Marella bent her forehead to her fist. She felt betrayed, as if everyone else had jumped off the boat, leaving her to navigate the rapids alone.

She had to admit that this wasn't the first time she'd felt betrayed by Noah. When she had confessed to him about Elizabeth's mercy killing, hoping for comfort about the difficult choice she'd made, he'd reacted badly. So much had happened in the meantime that it was glossed over. But it remained in Marella's thoughts, like a mud splatter on a side fence.

Did he still think of her as a murderer? He didn't act like it, but things like that had a way of coming back to haunt you. She already felt guilty enough without his judgment.

He spoke softly. "Project Athena couldn't make you travel through time. The modules are gone forever."

Gone forever? Maybe not. An idea popped into her head. "The ones on Wisdom Island are gone. And so is the prototype. But maybe there's a backup Project Athena. Maybe that's what's affecting me."

"No. Another machine can't be running because there's no drought."

She should have thought of that. It made perfect sense. And of course, Belinda had called Project Athena a complete loss.

"Try to be open to the idea that you're having delusions," said Noah. "Just don't count it out. Would you do that for me?"

I'm not delusional. She nodded, staring at the caddis fly struggling against the current. Struggling against time? A tiny kindred spirit.

"I talked to Belinda Waverly," blurted Marella. "I just got back."

He looked worried. "You should have waited for me to go with you. Alphonse told me people are getting carjacked. It would have been easy for somebody to knock you off that bike."

She grunted noncommittally. He was right, but he'd been gone when she left. And anyway, it frustrated her that the topic had turned back to her. Judging her actions. "I told Belinda that Project Athena caused the Aguageddon."

"How did she take it?"

"She didn't believe it."

Noah sighed. "I'm not surprised. Even if she did believe you, she wouldn't admit to it. But HemisNorth really fucked up. Millions of people are dead. Did you ask her about the Project Athena design plans?"

"She said they were all destroyed in the Western Inferno."

"I don't know that we can take her word for it."

"She's probably right. That's why we had to go to Wisdom Island, remember? It was a closed system. And so there was no off-site backup except in Seattle, and that burned in the fire."

"Well... we can't make it public until we're sure."

"Maybe we don't need to make it public."

Noah raised his eyebrows in surprise.

Marella explained further. "It's like we said: we don't want cult leaders and terrorists to know that a thing like Project Athena is possible. But also, Belinda was so good to me. We're the only two Seattle employees we know of who survived. I don't want to hurt her."

Noah spoke sympathetically, as if he didn't want to say it, but felt he must. "Marella, she's the CEO of HemisNorth, so she's more culpable than anybody else alive. She approved Project Athena in the first place. Don't let your feelings for her get in the way of what's right."

"It's more than that. HemisNorth has big plans to rebuild western Washington, and since they have so many offices around the world, they can help more than just local people. I don't want to interrupt that. Plus, I don't want the world busting in to grill us. I just want to move on..." She felt herself at the breaking point, but took a deep breath and finished. "And be with you." She pleaded silently for him to be on her team.

He stroked her fingers with his thumbs. "Yeah. That would be a shit show for real. I don't want that either." He thought a moment, then said, "Don't worry about it right now. There's no rush to make any decisions. We can deal with all that later on."

Marella's feet felt numb, too cold from the water. The cold traveled up her legs, through her hips and groin, to her heart, which felt like a block of ice. She smelled ammonia.

The sunlight faded. She tried to move, but didn't seem to be touching anything—there was nothing to push against. A feeling of eternity stretched her very being, outward, inward; and then there was no such thing as direction.

• • • •

AFTER WHAT COULD HAVE been minutes or eons, Marella felt her particles snapping back together. Thought returned, bit by bit. She could feel her body; she was sitting on a hard surface, shivering. She couldn't see. Had she gone blind? But no, outlines were starting to take shape. Of people. Two of them. She was inside, but couldn't make out where she was. The people were speaking, but they sounded fuzzy, as if projected from an old-time radio.

In spite of the pain she'd endured, a shiver of excitement ran through her. Was she time traveling again, and if so, what time period was she in? Was it 2002 again, or some other time?

She felt hands on her face. A gentle touch. A female voice that sounded familiar. Finally she could understand what the person was saying. "Remember this number. Three-seven-five-three-seven-eight-nine-two-eight-one." The voice said the number over and over again.

Brielle. That was Brielle's voice.

Everything went dark once more. She felt even colder than before. She tried to reach out and grab hold of something, anything, to ground her and keep from going through the same torture she'd barely surfaced from, but her arms no longer existed. Her body dissolved. She felt nothing.

• • • •

AFTER A NAMELESS PERIOD of time, the particles of her body began to return, forming fingers and ears, then eyes—which she squeezed shut. She also had insides—made of ice—but her skin was warm. Was that the sun? She tried to ask for help, but her lips couldn't shape words.

There was a voice. She couldn't make out who it was or what they were saying. She felt an arm around her. The voice became familiar, though she couldn't quite place it. Pieces of energy fell through her skin and into her body, like hot pebbles dropped into water.

Now she recognized Noah's voice. He was saying, "It's okay. I've got you."

She opened her eyes. It was blurry and bright. She could move a little. She pulled her feet from the stream. She fought to speak, but her mouth and tongue felt swollen. When she could finally talk, the words came out as if she was drunk. "Three-seven-five-three-seven-eight-nine-two-eight-one."

"Just relax."

"Write it down. Three-seven-five-three-seven-eight-nine-two-eight-one. Brielle told me."

"Don't talk. Wait until you get your strength back."

"Write. Write!"

"Okay, okay." With a twig, Noah wrote the numbers in the dirt, then squeezed her gently. "Your skin is so cold." He rubbed her arms and back briskly. She leaned into it, feeling the surface warmth, her chicken skin smoothing out, the inner chill beginning to fade.

"I'm doing better now," she said.

Noah looked focused, as if he had something important to say. She had a feeling she wasn't going to like it. "Marella, I think you have epilepsy. We need to get you to a doctor."

"It's not epilepsy. I time traveled again."

"Don't be so stubborn. Your head has been feeling weird, and now this. We have a chance to make our lives better—together—and we need to get you well so we can do that."

She didn't argue. She knew that this wasn't an ailment, but had no further means of convincing him. When she recovered, they went into the tree house and she wrote the numbers down.

Noah's disbelief was devastating. It meant nobody would come to her rescue and determine what was going on and what to do about it. She was alone with this mystery. She couldn't help imagining herself abandoned in a melodramatic scenario: a barren plain at twilight, the wind pummeling the sickly grass, with wolves howling and thunder in the distance.

She gave a grunt of annoyance at her ridiculousness. Enough feeling sorry for herself. If she had only herself to count on, then that was that.

She'd been in this situation only recently. During the Aguageddon, she had come to understand that she was just as responsible for climate change as everybody else. She had contributed to landfills, soil pollution, greenhouse gas, ocean microplastics, and so on. Sure, other people had too, but the only person she truly had control over was herself, and so she was the reason scientists at HemisNorth had been compelled to create Project Athena. Therefore, when it failed she had taken responsibility for shutting it down.

Now she had to take responsibility once more, without relying on anybody else. So far the time travel experience had felt like something that was being done to her, but she was finished being the victim.

A feeling of defiance pushed away all traces of anguish. She was going to figure out how her time traveling worked. If she got help along the way, that would be gravy, but she couldn't let herself be held back by the disbelief of others.

She was going to take charge of this problem. She was going to find out what was happening to her and do something about it.

Chapter Four

On the tree house porch, Marella sprawled in a wicker chair, where she had retreated after her frustrating conversation with Noah.

The time travel jaunts had been about three hours apart. It was three o'clock now. If they were going to happen at regular intervals, the next would be in two hours, at five o'clock. That might not be the case, but if it was, she now had two hours to anticipate the sheer agony, the ripping apart of her being, the unending darkness.

The waiting was torturous. The mere thought of it made her huddle into herself. If only she could do something about it. If only she knew why it happened.

Since it felt like there was a connection between the time travel and the zap she'd received from Project Athena, she wished she knew more about the science behind the climate machine. That might give her control over when and where she time traveled, and allow her to go back in time and warn Eshana and Len not to launch Project Athena in the first place. Then the days of fire, smoke, and death would never have happened. How awesome that would be! It would be like snapping her fingers and making her troubles go away.

Although, if she somehow canceled the Aguageddon, she would never meet Noah. The thought made her miserable. She might be disappointed with him now, but that would pass.

If she succeeded, she would never know about such a sacrifice. Still, the possible loss of his smile, his touch, his warmth, made her feel lost.

She was getting ahead of herself. She wasn't about to lose Noah because she couldn't control the time travel.

Or could she? What if it was as simple as visualizing a specific place and imagining herself there?

The thought made her tremble. It would be like making herself jump into molten lava. Which would be worth it, she told herself. The Aguageddon had killed a billion people. Undoing that was worth any hardship she would have to endure.

Closing her eyes, she visualized the kitchen at HemisNorth where she'd once seen Len and Eshana getting coffee. With his white beard and piercing gaze, Len had reminded her of a tall Sigmund Freud. Eshana could have played Nefertiti in a movie, except for her round glasses.

She shifted in the creaky wicker chair, but couldn't get comfortable. She concentrated for minutes, but doubt got in the way. She wouldn't be able to gain control so easily—things were never that simple. But then, of course it wouldn't work, not if she didn't believe it would. She needed to be sure beyond the shadow of a doubt that it would happen. Visualize herself succeeding.

Maybe she was too relaxed. Perhaps it required effort of some kind. She tightened her elbows against her sides and squeezed her lips together. It was her second day of work. In the kitchen, she held a green mug with the blue-and-purple HemisNorth logo. The waistband of her secondhand clothing store slacks scratched her, and she'd wondered if she'd removed the price tag and its plastic attachment. She hadn't. She'd taken it out in the bathroom a few minutes later. And then she'd returned to her desk, nervous that she'd taken too long at her break.

Concentrate. Not her desk, but the kitchen. Eshana had said she liked the new coffee brand better, and Len said it had a woody flavor reminiscent of whiskey barrels. Eshana said she'd take his word for it, as she hadn't eaten many whiskey barrels lately. Len had pointed a finger at his nose and then her. *You got me.*

She replayed the moment over and over, willing herself to slide into it. To be there. Make the moment real.

Nothing happened. She only felt a sense of sad nostalgia for a life that was gone forever. But at least Marella and Noah had brought water back to the world.

Without meaning to, she thought again about getting zapped by Project Athena, back on Wisdom Island. Project Athena had been giving off a screech that seemed to pierce her eardrums; its modules were about to explode. She and Noah ran for their lives.

She felt a pulling. Like she could go to the island if she just allowed it to happen. She was terrified. She smelled smoke and felt the heat of fire. She imagined sliding onto the island right into the midst of a fireball, her skin scorching, blistering. Taking a breath only to suck in flames. Her lungs sizzling, melting, crackling.

Her eyes flew open and she jumped up. The tree house deck seemed to wobble under her feet. She stood still, making sure to pay attention to her surroundings, be there in the moment, rather than the past. The breeze nudged the bird feeder, bringing the smell of spruce.

Shaken, feeling as if she'd averted a disaster, she went inside. Brielle was looking out the window. Mom and Noah, who were hunched over the kitchen table, shut up the second she came in. Probably talking about her. Her mother wore a worried mom type of smile. Marella tried to look as if nothing were wrong.

She felt a prickling feeling, like needles lightly touching her skin, all over. She rubbed at her arms. What now? It was as if somebody was watching her. Somebody behind her, or above her. She glanced back and around. Nobody there. Her skin began itching.

Brielle pointed out of the window. "What's that oozy-looking stuff?"

"Pine pitch," said Mom.

"No," said Brielle, "it's like a cloud, but below us."

Mom and Noah joined her. "That's weird," said Mom. "It looks iridescent and flowy, like when you pour oil in water."

"I've never seen iridescent fog before," said Brielle.

"That's not normal," said Noah. "It's some kind of chemical fog."

"Could it have come from the HemisNorth plant?" Mom's voice was husky with concern. "They make so many different chemicals. Somebody could have mixed the wrong ones together."

Marella trotted to the window. Down below, a cloud the size of their tree house was flowing along the ground. Hints of purple and indigo percolated through its dense whiteness, like hidden soap bubbles. The fog's movement seemed oddly sensual, as if it were searching for a mate to seduce. But that couldn't be so. It was just a fog, looking too beautiful to be real.

The fog flowed away from the base of the tree house and into the bushes. It kept moving until they could no longer see it among the trees.

The prickling on her skin stopped, leaving Marella feeling heavy. Life was too strange, full of unanswered questions, and here were more. Was it an innocuous fog or a dangerous chemical fog? Where had it come from? Why did it feel oddly familiar? Not knowing felt like a tipping point. Too much to bear.

• • • •

AT SIX O'CLOCK THAT evening, Marella woke up from a ten-minute nap in the loft feeling a little refreshed, though her head still felt like an overpacked suitcase. It had been four hours since she time traveled, and it hadn't happened again. Maybe it never would. From a pain standpoint, she fervently hoped so.

She pondered what to do about her head. Could the stuffiness be related to time travel? She'd seen a doctor about her ankle and was using an ankle wrap, but had been told her head stuffiness would clear up on its own with food and hydration. If she went back, what could they do? She imagined a doctor handing her a prescription. "Your CT scan revealed kelp on the brain. You must have picked it up in the ocean. Take these pills twice a day for two weeks with a full glass of water, and it'll dissolve over time."

She peered over the loft railing. Noah and Brielle were inspecting the TV's backside, trying to get it to work.

"Marella's awake!" said Brielle, as if it were the most wonderful thing that had ever happened. Trying to get back on Marella's good side, it seemed. It would probably work, given time.

Time! So incomprehensible.

Marella started down the spiral stairs, and Noah rushed to assist. He kissed her hand like royalty, then kept hold of it until they reached the bottom. He seemed to be trying to make up for their rift. It was sweet, but she was still distressed that he didn't believe her, and it was also unnerving that he thought her so frail.

Mom waved them over to a bench next to the cedar tree trunk. Although the house had been built around it, Marella imagined the tree bursting through the floor, then the ceiling, letting nothing stand in its way. Just like Marella should do, she supposed, except she didn't really know what was in her way. How could she overcome something she didn't understand?

Mom seemed cheerful. She, too, was trying to mend fences with Marella. She rested a palm on the tree's crinkled bark. "I like that this tree is a living part of this house. I can feel its consciousness infusing this space."

Marella glanced at Noah, a devout Christian. How would he take Mom's brand of spirituality? He raised his eyebrows slightly but kept quiet.

"You don't believe a tree can have consciousness?" asked Mom.

Noah shrugged, clearly not wanting to get into a debate with his lover's mother.

Mom tapped her head. "Our minds are not just our physical brains. Consciousness is a force that we draw from. Think about how perfect it is—we're a part of everything instead of a lone, wandering piece of it. What? You don't believe me?"

Noah sighed. "I just... have a hard time with the idea of a tree being conscious."

"Why?" asked Mom, hands on hips.

"It doesn't have a brain, for one thing." Noah playfully mirrored her, placing his hands on his hips as well.

"Who says you need a brain? I'm not talking ability to do calculus. I'm talking awareness. Is a dog aware of what's going on around it?"

"Sure," said Noah hesitantly.

"And so is a caterpillar. It's aware."

"I guess." Noah was smiling. Good. He wasn't offended by her mini assault.

"So what's different about a tree?" Mom gestured at the cedar with the grace of a game show model. "It's a living being even if it's rooted to the ground. It has a connection to the Earth and to other trees, to fungus even. Trees send each other distress signals when insects attack, or when they have a disease, and other trees get those messages and then change what they do. They send each other healing powers."

"Sending messages to one another isn't the same as consciousness," said Noah amiably. He'd been drawn in now, but seemed to be enjoying it.

"If you don't believe me, feel for yourself. Place your hands on it. You and Marella do that together—that will make it work better." Mom illustrated, placing her palms on the cedar and closing her eyes. "Be open to it. Allow the energy to infuse you."

So that was what this was all about. Mom thought the tree would send its healing powers to Marella if she touched it. Marella usually resisted her meditative remedies, since they didn't work for her. By getting Noah involved, Mom hoped Marella would try too. She could be weird, but she was no dummy.

Marella sighed inwardly. Mom meant well. She placed her hands on the cedar. The rough bark felt pointy; its smell reminded her of HemisNorth floor cleaner.

Noah put his hands next to hers and closed his eyes.

After shaking her arms lightly as if prepping for athletics, Brielle touched her fingertips to the tree; her hands made Marella think of two bald tarantulas on their way to the canopy.

Brielle closed her eyes. She believed in Mom's therapies, and they sometimes worked for her.

"Be very quiet and concentrate," said Mom. "You'll start to sense the life force."

Marella tried. Closing her eyes, she "opened her channels," but felt no life force, no consciousness, no healing. Mom and Marella breathed through rounded lips, sounding like the wind gusting through cracked windows.

After two minutes, Mom asked, "Did you feel it?"

They all opened their eyes, removing their hands from the tree. Noah pursed his lips, seeming to look for the right answer. "I suppose I felt God's love."

Mom sat on the bench, triumphant. "You see? What about you, Marella?"

She smiled wanly back. *Let's keep the peace.* "There might have been something. A little."

"I felt it," offered Brielle. Somehow she appeared less thin, as if the tree's consciousness had returned her to health. If only it were that easy for Marella. Life would be so much simpler if touching a tree made everything better.

Marella was relieved that Noah was accepting of Mom's weirdness. And it was just as well it hadn't worked. She had enough distractions right now. Adding tree voices in her head or whatever Mom was anticipating would probably send her over the edge.

There was a grunt behind them. Marella jerked, startled. A person was standing by a living room window, where moments ago there had been empty air. The woman looked exactly like Marella. Same shoulder-length hair, same diamond-shaped face. She was wearing the same clothes Marella had on now—leggings and a slate-gray blouse—but had a three-inch-long cut on her forearm.

That's me. I just appeared out of nowhere. Marella blinked several times. How could it be?

It wasn't possible. She had to be hallucinating. Her mind was damaged, severely damaged, and it was creating false visions. She definitely needed to get to a doctor, and soon. An emergency room, even. What if she had a brain tumor? Something was very wrong. She closed her eyes, willing the apparition to be gone when she opened them.

But it wasn't. And now the other Marella was trying to move, stuttering and gasping.

"Oh my god," said Noah. He rubbed his eyes, not seeming to believe what he saw.

"There's two of you," said Brielle. She seemed focused, as if watching a stage show, determined to expose the trapdoor in the magician's boxes.

Mom jumped up. "What's going on?" She sounded aggravated.

They all looked back and forth between Marella and the doppelganger, whose mouth worked as she tried to form words.

If Mom, Brielle, and Noah could see this, then it wasn't a hallucination. Marella's heart was pumping so hard she could hear it.

"I don't know how you kids did this," said Mom, "but it isn't funny."

Marella addressed the new version of herself. "What's going on? How did you get here?"

The second Marella moved stiffly, like a fawn taking its first step. Marella had been incapacitated after she had time traveled, and that seemed to be what was happening to the other Marella now. She probably had come from the future and was now trying to recover, squinting, grunting, and clutching at the air. It was painful to watch. That was her, suffering and helpless.

"I'm dreaming," said Mom. "That's what's going on. I need to wake up." She slapped her cheeks.

"You're not dreaming," said Noah. "I see it too, but I don't know how."

The second Marella, still framed by the window, thrust her head forward, working her lips, like a fish trying to take the worm from a line but unable to get its mouth around it.

Marella felt strange. Compressed. As if there was only room for one Marella, yet somehow the two of them were here. It made her think of a helium balloon being held underwater.

Finally some words emerged from the second Marella's mouth, slurred but clear enough to understand. "What... is... shape... of time?"

The shape of time? Marella had thought of time in terms of direction, not shape. What did it mean? This only added to her confusion.

"Look!" said Brielle, pointing up to the loft.

A third Marella was there, hand on the railing. This Marella didn't grunt or appear disoriented. Rather, she stood straight and still, gazing down at them with a look of longing. As if standing on a widow's watch as a ship sailed to sea, never to return.

The feeling of being compressed became stronger. The three of them were not supposed to be here, not all in one place. A shiver twisted its way down her spine. It felt like something terrible was going to happen.

"What's going on?" Marella asked the third Marella, her voice breaking.

The third Marella gazed lovingly from the loft, voice full of sorrow. "I can only tell you one thing. You're right about Project Athena."

Mom stomped in frustration. "One of you darn kids tell me how you did this."

"I didn't do anything," cried Brielle.

"This is not happening," said Noah, as if trying to convince himself.

Yet another Marella appeared, the fourth one in the room, increasing the feeling of compression until she felt like a balloon about to pop. This Marella was sprawled on the carpet like a person who had fallen from a great height.

That unlikely position. Twisted, unmoving. Eyes open and unseeing. Mouth slack. That Marella was dead. Dead! It looked as if she'd been there a long time, as if the life had seeped out of her weeks earlier. The carpet's red flowers looked like blood draining from her sides, although a cut on her arm wasn't bleeding that profusely.

"She's dead!" Brielle's face was twisted with anguish. "Mom, Marella's dead! What's going on? Why is she here, and there, and there, and how could she be dead?"

"God, no, please!" Noah addressed the heavens. "What does this mean? What are you trying to tell us?"

Mom rushed to the fourth Marella and kneeled beside her, wailing, "My baby. What happened to you?"

The fourth Marella was dead. So was she herself dead too? Near-death stories often described the victim as being outside of herself, looking down from above. Marella half expected to begin rising like smoke to where she could see the tops of everybody's heads. Then a bright light would appear for her to walk toward. And then she would be gone from this world. Anguish, along with the feeling of compression, made her want to wail.

"This can't be real," said Mom, looking from Marella to the dead Marella and back again. "You're over there, so you can't be here." She reached out to touch the dead Marella. Finding her solid, she gasped and pulled her hand back.

Everyone was still. She couldn't look at her lifeless self, so she stared at Noah, who was breathing hard. He seemed to want to take action, without knowing what that might be.

The feeling of being compressed made her disoriented. She could see which way was up and which was down, but it didn't feel correct. The pressure built.

The third Marella shouted from the loft, "Save her."

Marella's gaze snapped back to the fourth Marella. It didn't look as if the inert figure could be saved. There was no life in her. The spark long gone. No existence to retrieve.

As if shot from a gun, Noah rushed to the fourth Marella, grasped her ankles, and pulled until she lay flat on her back. Brielle placed her hands in CPR position, arms straight, and pumped the dead Marella's chest, quietly chanting the words to "Stayin' Alive" to keep the correct pace.

"Come on, girl, come back to us." Mom squeezed the words through a tightened throat.

Noah's voice resonated with anguish. "You promised me we would be together. Don't leave me now, after all we've been through." He was talking to somebody else, yet it was her.

Marella felt her gorge rising. She swallowed over and over, clenching her fists against her thighs. She was dead. But how? The cut on the fourth Marella's arm didn't look lethal, and there were no other visible wounds. The pale green blouse she wore—which Marella had never seen before—seemed clean and crisp. Otherwise she looked the same as Marella did now. Same age, same hair length.

If all these versions of herself had time traveled, then she was watching her own future. That meant that she herself would be lying there soon, getting her chest pumped. It could happen anytime. In a week. Tomorrow. Today.

She felt less compressed than before. The Marella by the window had disappeared, as had the one in the loft. The fourth Marella, however, remained.

Brielle began to flag and Noah took over CPR.

Mom's hands covered her mouth. Marella's eyes watered, seeing her mother's anguish. Ironically, she would rather die than put Mom through something like this.

"Come on, Mar-Mar!" said Brielle to the fourth Marella. "You can do it. You told me anything is possible. Make it true."

The fourth Marella's eyes blinked. An arm jerked. She sucked in a desperate breath. Noah lifted his hands; she jackknifed to the side.

The original Marella cried out with relief. Finally she rushed to the newly revived Marella, though she stopped short of touching her. She had some notion that it would make them both poof into nothingness. In science fiction, a paradox like this would cause all kinds of dangerous events. You were supposed to avoid that. She leaned over the struggling fourth Marella. "What happened to you?"

The fourth Marella panted, reaching out for Mom, who held her hand. Marella felt even more disoriented watching her mother clutch onto a version of herself. The fourth Marella attempted to speak, moving her mouth and grunting. "Heth."

"Hell," interpreted Brielle. "She said 'hell.'" She clapped her hand over her mouth, seeming to realize the implication of what she said. Her sister had gone to hell and back.

"Quiet, Brielle," said Mom firmly. "Marella, what is it?"

The fourth Marella worked her mouth and lips, trying again. "Hathen."

"Heaven!" Brielle straightened her shoulders, relieved by this much better alternative.

Abruptly, the fourth Marella disappeared, leaving Mom's hands empty.

"She's gone!" Gingerly, Mom felt the air where she had been, then looked around, as if she might materialize elsewhere in the tree house.

With the feeling of compression gone, Marella knew that there were no other Marellas. Only Noah, Mom, and Brielle remained, forming an odd, frozen tableau on the carpet.

The time-travel mystery had deepened, and the only person who could solve it for her—one of her other selves—had refused to do so. Why? What had kept her quiet?

Noah sprang up, rushing to her. Her expression must have been wild, since he began speaking soothingly. "It's all right, love, it's all right."

Mom leapt up next. Looking a little dazed, she clutched Marella's arm, touching her hair, her shoulder, her chin, as if to assure herself she was real. "What just happened?"

Brielle seized Marella's hand. She spoke reproachfully, as if Marella was hiding a secret from her. "What are they? Why did they come? Why did they disappear?"

Marella squeezed Brielle's hand back. In spite of her sister's petulance, it felt like a lifeline. "I think they're me from the future, time traveling, but I don't understand how."

"This is all just too weird." Noah spoke slowly, with a sense of awe. "People don't just time travel. But I think you really did. It was just like you tried to tell me. And I was so sure you weren't."

"I don't know how else to explain it," said Marella.

"Mass hysteria," said Mom resolutely. "That's a thing."

Marella made a noise of frustration. She didn't need stubborn Mom right now, she needed practical Mom.

She glanced at the loft where the knowledgeable Marella had been. What if her future was to endlessly jump from one time to another, remaining only a short time in each one? Was that why the third Marella had looked so sad?

Suddenly something dropped from the ceiling, landing with a cracking noise, making them jump. They all backed up, as if it were a grenade.

It was a fist-size rock. Black, girdled with two white stripes of quartz.

"Where'd that come from?" asked Brielle. There were no rafters above. No nooks, no holes, no places where the rock could have been lodged, yet there it was.

Marella finally stepped forward. "Wait!" warned Mom, but she had already scooped it up. It felt smooth. The quartz was somewhat transparent, without breaks in the bands. She wasn't particularly superstitious, but it felt like a sign. What would the black-and-white rock's message be? Black and white. Noah and Marella? Yin and yang? Right and wrong? Guilt and innocence?

"It's a sign," said Brielle, as if speaking a fact.

If this was a sign, it was indecipherable. Marella felt like throwing the rock, but instead set it on the coffee table.

They all looked around as if waiting for more to happen. A tree creaked outside. A seagull landed on the deck. For a bewildering moment, she wondered if the bird was a fifth Marella, transformed or reincarnated. Nothing seemed impossible.

The tree house had been a place of refuge and comfort, but now it felt like a paranormal vortex where strange happenings converged. "I'm a little dizzy." Marella reached out.

"Got you." Noah took her arm and led her to a chair, murmuring comforting words, which she appreciated more than she could say right then.

Brielle went up to the loft, apparently looking for more Marellas. She peered around, then returned and flew from one window to another. Marella imagined a hoard of doppelgangers popping in and out of existence outside on the ground below, but Brielle reported none, instead saying, "That was just insane. How are you time traveling?"

"I don't know. It just happens. This is the third time."

"I don't believe it." Mom twisted her fingers. "There's got to be some other explanation. Like... like there's something in the water. That's it. It's making us all crazy." She rushed to the kitchen and held up a jar of water, squinting at it.

"Mom," said Marella pointedly. "I time traveled. It wasn't the water."

Mom dumped the water into the sink with a flourish, as if saying that Marella shouldn't argue with her mother.

"But... why would it just suddenly happen?" asked Brielle, emphasizing each word, as if asking insistently would get her a solid answer.

You tell me and we'll both know, thought Marella, but that wasn't helpful. She had been given a clue though, she now remembered. "The one of me that was in the loft just now said I was right about Project Athena. I think that means that Project Athena is causing me to time travel." She wished it had been hallucinations after all. Because now she had a mystery that seemed unsolvable. "And so I know that in the near future I die."

"You didn't die," Noah said quickly, as if allowing her statement to remain uncontested would give it strength. "You stopped breathing."

"And we saved you," said Brielle, rushing to embrace her. Any trace of frustration or accusation was gone. This was the sister that looked up to her, loved her, cared for her.

Marella wasn't alone with this anymore.

"Yes. You did save me. Thank you. Thank you." Marella hugged her back, feeling the enthusiasm of her support. Brielle had saved her life. And so had Noah.

"Except..." Noah turned away slightly, as if he didn't want to continue.

"Except what?" asked Brielle.

He looked stricken, eyes focused inward. "The Marella we revived—the future you—might have gone back to the same point in time where she stopped breathing. Whatever caused that will still be there. It could stop her from breathing again. And then she might really die."

Marella swallowed hard. He'd spoken in the third person, as if it were somebody else. But it wasn't. It was she herself who might really die. And it would happen soon.

Chapter Five

After Noah pointed out that Marella could stop breathing permanently, Mom began pacing the way she did every few months when she got overly restless, staring at the floor and pulling her lips in. From the sink, to the bookshelf, to the window, then back to the sink. Normally Marella would try to distract her from it, but she was too overwhelmed. Why did she have to start that up now? She needed Mom's brain power. Again, she needed practical Mom, not off-kilter Mom.

"We won't let you stop breathing." Brielle's voice trembled. "There's something we can do to stop it. I don't know what it is, but we'll figure it out, because we have to, there's no way we're going to let that go down, so we have to keep it from happening..."

Marella spoke up to get her to stop, otherwise she would keep saying the same thing over and over. It was just what she did when mystified. "Thanks, Brielle. I'm glad you're here for me."

Brielle made a long, drawn-out sigh. It was comforting that she cared so much, even though she was just as confused as Marella.

Noah marched to Marella's side and spoke with confidence. "We will figure this out."

She was glad for his sudden poise. It gave her the strength to dive in, even though she would have preferred to hide in a cave until this all somehow blew over. "How do we figure out what caused me to stop breathing? I mean, what *will* cause it."

Noah and Brielle concentrated, as if solving a tricky crossword puzzle. Mom continued to pace.

Marella stood slowly to keep from getting dizzy again, then shuffled to the sink, poured some water, and downed it. An idea struck her. "The dead me was wearing a sea-green shirt. I'll never put that on."

"It's a start, but the shirt didn't stop you from breathing. We still have to keep you away from anything dangerous." Noah joined her at the sink, putting his hands on her shoulders as if that could shield her from harm. His hands felt warm, and she felt safer—just slightly—after his declaration.

"Yeah, but what are we saving her from?" asked Brielle. "I know! We can rule out drowning because you weren't wet."

"What causes somebody to stop breathing without leaving any sign?" Marella pressed her palms to her temples in a failed attempt to ease the stuffed feeling in her head. The situation was so bizarre she wouldn't be surprised if a magician suddenly appeared and pulled an endless stream of colorful scarves out of her ear to relieve her suffering.

"Lack of oxygen." Brielle sounded fearful. "Like when the atmosphere lowered on Mount Rainier. Don't go to the mountains. Stay at sea level."

Marella felt a surge of distress, along with compassion for her sister. Brielle and Mom had escaped from just such a scenario. But it couldn't happen again because there was no Project Athena. The atmosphere would stay where it was. Still, she didn't want to block the flow of ideas. "No mountains," she repeated. "Agreed."

Mom passed the couch, went to the window, and then back to the bookshelf, still looking at the ground and now chewing on a nail. Marella grew irritable. This wasn't the time for that. This was the time for serious reasoning.

Noah snapped his fingers. "Hey! If you time traveled, then that number Brielle gave you means something after all."

"What number?" asked Brielle.

"I time traveled to somewhere dark, and you kept repeating a number," said Marella. "Three-seven-five-three-seven-eight-nine-two-eight-one. Do you know what that is?"

"No, but it's got to be a telephone number." Brielle jumped up and down. "Call it!"

"No phones and no service," reminded Noah.

Brielle made a face of annoyance. She'd momentarily forgotten.

Mom stopped on the edge of the carpet and waved her hands wildly. "Forget the numbers. She didn't time travel."

"She did too." Brielle squared her shoulders in a stance she'd acquired during a stint on a debate team. "You and I both touched another Marella when she was lying on the floor. It was real." She pointed forcefully at the carpet at Mom's feet.

"No, no, no!" Mom waved harder and made a face like something stunk.

The stuffiness. The pain. Mom's unwillingness to believe her. Marella burst out, "It's right in front of your eyes. Everybody saw it, and you're the only one who thinks I'm delusional. You're always telling us to believe in each other, but you won't believe in me."

Mom's jaw trembled. "You can't be time traveling. We're all seeing things because otherwise everything else you told me is true. That cult leader chasing after you, the machine exploding, all that." Her words became strained, as if she were being punched in the gut. "If what you told me is all real, it means I almost lost you over and over, and you're in danger now, and I don't know how to help you. You're my child and the world was crazy and I thought it was better but now it's not and why can't the catastrophes just stop already!"

Brielle raced to embrace her. Marella stayed where she was, anger fading but still alight. She was the one who needed comforting, yet suddenly Mom was the beleaguered one. *Give her some slack. If I had a child, I would probably feel the same way.*

"It's okay, Mom," said Brielle. "We'll figure it out. We always do, right?"

"It's true," said Noah with that confident tone of his. The tone of a leader who would someday build a world wonder to draw people

together, just as he was doing now. "She time traveled. It's scary, but denying it won't do any good. We all saw the evidence, and so now we know it's a fact. Now we have to help Marella. Believe in her. I'm right, aren't I? Tell me you know it's true. She time traveled."

Marella felt a rush of love for him. Whatever had happened before, he was supporting her now.

Mom's head wobbled, part nod, part despair. After some deep breaths, she seemed much more collected, as if she'd gotten her frustration out and could now glide forward. "All right, let's just say this is real. Then we would have to make the time travel stop. We would have to keep you from doing all that." She eyed the carpet where the seemingly lifeless Marella had appeared.

"No." Brielle's voice rose and fell in consternation that Mom hadn't immediately seen the danger. "If she doesn't time travel, then she doesn't appear here when she stops breathing and we don't save her."

Marella gasped. Brielle could be right. This was so confusing! Such weird loops of cause and effect—she imagined a ship's hold full of tangled ropes. How would they ever sort out such a mess?

"But what if time traveling is what made her stop breathing?" asked Mom.

Marella rubbed her chin nervously. She hadn't thought of that either. Even though time travel felt dangerous, each time she'd emerged whole. However, it did seem possible, even likely, that each trip degraded her body so that something internal would eventually fail. Her lungs, nerves, brain, or a combination. She realized she was breathing harder, as if to compensate for an upcoming failure of her pulmonary system.

"You all right?" asked Noah.

She nodded, patting his arm to ease his concern and keep him on track. *Keep thinking. Help me with this.*

Mom pushed her hands forward like a poker player betting all her chips. "Back up. You said a machine on the island caused the Aguageddon, and that has something to do with this. Tell me more. It was supposed to do one thing, but it did something else, right?"

"Yes," said Marella, relieved. Practical Mom was back! "Project Athena. It was a set of giant structures with loops as big as Ferris wheels. They were only supposed to take away carbon dioxide from the world, but they took water too."

"How?"

Marella spoke haltingly as she recalled Elizabeth's explanation, making sure she had the right words. "It's a quantum thing that has to do with probability. Normally, at any moment in time, the bits of a molecule could be in our universe or in other universes. Project Athena kept the locations of specific particles undefined. It made it so a molecule wasn't in our universe, but also wasn't in a parallel universe. It had the potential to be in either one, but wasn't."

"And that made a water molecule not here and not there," added Noah. "So it was nowhere. That's why the oceans receded."

Brielle slapped her thighs. "I've got it! Those other Marellas were versions of you from other universes."

Mom threw her hands up, shaking her head. "I don't like that one bit."

"Why not?" Brielle squared off against her. "It makes as much sense as anything else."

"I didn't say it wasn't the answer, I said I hate the idea," said Mom. "If there was a universe for every possible outcome in your life, that would mean that in one universe or another you'll experience every possible pain and hardship. It means there's a universe where I never had children. More than one universe. Maybe an infinite number of them without you two." She hunched, imagining such a tragedy.

"Don't think of it like that," said Brielle. "Think about it like this: it means she might not stop breathing in this universe. The Marella who stopped breathing was from another universe."

"That's not better!" Mom's eyes widened and her voice squeaked.

"It didn't feel like I went to another universe," blurted Marella, partly because it was true and partly because it hurt to watch her mother so pained.

"What do you mean?" asked Noah. "Why not? How would you know what that felt like?"

She searched for the words. It was hard to distill such an overpowering experience into simple truths that others would understand. To create meaning out of chaos. "It didn't feel like I crossed over. It felt like I spread out into this universe. Besides, I went back to 2002. That's time travel. And it feels like when I was zapped by Project Athena. It just feels connected."

Mom, Noah, and Brielle all squinted at her in concentration. It would have been a comical sight if things weren't so dire. She imagined herself rubbing the furrows from their brows, like working in wet clay.

"But you said Project Athena exploded," said Brielle. "So it can't be making you time travel."

"Before it exploded, it zapped me. Maybe that gave me the ability to time travel."

"Zapped you?" asked Mom anxiously. "What does that mean?"

"The machine had these big loops, around twenty stories high. This slow-motion lightning bolt came out of one and struck me."

Mom looked fierce. Something zapped her child? How dare it! "You need to talk to the people who were responsible for it. They damn well better do something about this. Who invented it?"

"Eshana Collins and Len Janderson, but they died," said Marella. "There was a prototype. I think shutting it off made it explode. That's what killed them."

"That's it!" Noah shouted, startling the others. It sounded like a eureka moment, giving Marella hope. He grasped her arm. "You need to time travel back to when they were alive. Stop them from building Project Athena!"

"No!" Mom pulled his hand away from Marella, as if his touch might make it happen. "What if she never comes back?"

"I already tried to time travel on purpose. It didn't work." Marella shuddered. Flames. Smoke. Danger.

Mom narrowed her eyes. "Don't do that again. You could end up with the dinosaurs."

They were all quiet for a time. Marella imagined a stegosaurus looking at her with disdain because she didn't belong. It wasn't helpful. She needed answers, not silliness.

"One of the Marellas asked about the shape of time," shouted Brielle, having her own eureka moment. "That's a clue!"

Good girl, thought Marella, although it was a question, not an answer. They already had plenty of questions.

What was the shape of time? After Mom's mention of dinosaurs, the shapes that came to mind were stegosaurus dorsal plates, Jurassic-era jungle leaves, and dinosaur eggs cracking open, with long-necked babies emerging. More useless silliness.

"The shape of time." Noah formed a box shape with his fingers. "It makes sense that the shape would be important. Like the double helix shape is important to genetics."

"Maybe time is a double helix too," said Brielle.

Marella pictured time as a double helix, a sort of twisted ladder. Then she remembered the rock. "The rock that fell from the ceiling. It was two bands around a sphere."

Their eyes went from one to another, hoping for an interpretation, but nobody ventured one.

"I know!" Brielle burst out of her seat and ran to the kitchen. She flung open drawers and fished in them.

"What are you doing, child?" asked Mom.

"Getting shapes!"

Mom threw her hands up as if to say *I don't know what to do with that daughter of mine.*

Brielle returned with kitchen implements, which she dumped on the table. A sieve, a tea strainer ball, tongs, a corkscrew. She had an air of triumph, as if the answer were now in front of them, and they only had to select the right one.

Was this taking them too far offtrack? After all, even if they knew time was a double helix or a sphere or a sieve, what would they do with that knowledge? How would it possibly help them?

Noah seemed to be thinking along the same lines. He spoke gently, perhaps to avoid quashing Brielle's enthusiasm. "This is all great, but we don't really know that the shape of time is important."

"But one of the Marellas said it was." Brielle dangled a tea strainer ball from its tiny chain. A stage hypnotist swinging a pendulum.

"She didn't say it was important," said Noah. "She just asked what the shape of time was. There could be a weird time loop in which we've decided it's important and so the future Marella thinks it is too."

Brielle's shoulders drooped. Marella wanted to counter her sister's disappointment, but she didn't know how, not with her own pessimism rising, adding to the stuffiness in her head.

Mom straightened the items on the table absentmindedly. "We need help. We need an expert."

"Know any astrophysicists?" Noah seemed to be trying to lighten the mood, which Marella appreciated, though it didn't work.

"I need a break," she said. "My brain is tired."

"You need to eat some more," said Mom.

"Yeah," said Brielle. "You might time travel to a place where you can't get food. You have to be ready for whatever happens next." She ran to the kitchen as if Marella might disappear right that moment, returning with a package of saltine crackers. She plucked out a couple and held them out.

Marella's mouth was too dry. She shook her head. Brielle puffed out her lips in melodramatic disappointment.

"Thanks anyway." She smiled at Brielle to let her know she was appreciated, then started toward the bathroom. "I'm going to take a shower."

"And time travel naked?" said Mom, incensed. "No."

Marella sighed. Mom believed her fully now, apparently. That was good. But was she never supposed to clean her body again?

"She could wear clothes in the shower," offered Brielle cheerfully.

"And be wet," reminded Mom. Practical Mom.

It was true that wet clothes after the freezing cold of time traveling would be extremely uncomfortable, if not dangerous. "I'll just wash my face," said Marella.

"I'll come with you and make sure you don't wander off to the Stone Age or something," said Noah. His pretend-snarky tone made Marella smile.

"But she could meet the Flintstones," said Brielle, her joke also welcome.

In the bathroom she splashed water on her face. Still grateful that she could. Only a week ago she wasn't sure she would ever see water again. Here, there was plenty.

Noah pulled a peacock-blue towel from a cupboard and stood ready with it. "I'm sorry I didn't believe you. So sorry. Really really really sorry." His tone was playful, as if he hoped that humor would help her accept his apology.

Marella leaned her elbows on the sink. An apology was good, but maybe she shouldn't let him off so easily.

When she didn't answer, Noah continued. "Really really really really sorry. Really really really..."

She chuckled. "I guess it would be hard to believe."

"I believe!" He gestured as widely as he could in the small bathroom—an actor on a stage. "I believe Marella!" Then he became serious, speaking with awe. "Time travel. It's insane! But you really did time travel. I couldn't have predicted that, ever. It just goes to show: you never know what the future holds. I mean, literally. I guess."

His sudden look of confusion made her heart nearly break. He was trying so hard, and everything he'd said before was just him being honest with her. She lathered apricot-scented soap on her hands and face and then rinsed them, watching the water drain in the sink.

Noah dried her face and hands lovingly with the towel.

"So you'll believe me from now on?" she asked, trying to sound good-humored.

"I swear. On everything I love. Which includes you." He kissed her right cheek, forehead, and left cheek. "So we're good?"

Marella smiled and shrugged. "Maybe."

Again he kissed her right cheek, forehead, and left cheek, then watched for an affirmation. "I'll just do this till you say yes."

Laughing, she said, "Yes, okay!"

"Good! We'll get through this."

I don't know how. She snuggled into his arms, and he caressed her hair for a few minutes. It was nice, but she was too overwhelmed to fully enjoy it.

What was she going to do now? How was she going to climb this mountain, even with help?

A car sounded on the gravel driveway. Soon after that there was a knock on the front door. When they emerged from the bathroom, Mom was opening the screen door. "We got a delivery." She sounded surprised.

Brielle pushed past her and squatted to look at the carton's mailing label. "It's for Marella. From HemisNorth."

Marella's first thought was that it would be the welcome package they sent new employees. Water bottle, stress ball, writing journal, and so on, adorned with the HemisNorth logo. She rubbed her neck tiredly. Belinda still expected her to return to work. Impossible! She should have made it clear she wasn't coming back.

But the box Brielle brought in was too big for tchotchkes, and she carried it as if it were heavy. HemisNorth wouldn't have sent her a computer, since there was no internet connection to work remotely. What else could it contain?

Clothing, perhaps, so that she could come to work in something other than the shabby leggings and gray blouse she'd worn when she visited Belinda?

An abrupt thought made her heart skip a beat. She'd been wearing a sea-green shirt when she stopped breathing. What if it was in that box? She held back a little.

"It smells like food." Brielle brought the box to the coffee table.

Marella's apprehension eased. Food? Of course! Belinda would suspect they were struggling, as many were. Her mouth watered. She would love to have something other than roots, broth, and crackers.

Noah retrieved a knife from the kitchen and sliced open the tape on the box. Brielle lifted two items out, holding them up triumphantly. "Bread! Cheese!"

"Summer sausage!" added Noah. "Rice, potatoes, peas, flour, sugar, butter, cooking oil."

Marella only briefly contemplated not accepting such a gift from HemisNorth. Standing on her morals would mean that Noah and the others would have to subsist on the meager, stale food in the cupboard. They were too ecstatic for her to disappoint them. They weren't voicing any reservations about accepting it, so neither would she.

"There's a note." Brielle read it out loud. "Marella, this isn't nearly enough to show my joy and relief that you survived—I hope you know how special you are. The days ahead won't be easy, but together we can achieve the impossible. Your friend, Belinda Waverly."

Marella felt an upwelling of affection for her. This was such an unexpected yet welcome gift!

Brielle waved the note at Marella. "She loves you."

"What's not to love?" asked Noah lightheartedly.

"Why's she treating you so well?" Mom sounded suspicious.

"She said I'm the only one she knows of from the Seattle office who isn't dead or missing."

Everybody was quiet; her statement had dampened their mood. "Out of how many?" asked Mom.

"Two hundred people."

"Well," she said sadly. "I see why you're that special to her."

They brought the box to the kitchen and gathered around the table. "Let's not overdo it," said Mom. "We should ration this. We don't know whether we'll get more." Still, she retrieved plates and urged them to fill them up.

While Marella ate, she tried not to think about time travel. *Enjoy the moment*, she told herself. *Be here now.* The salty cheese. The rich summer sausage. The sweet strawberry jam.

She began to feel slightly more stable. The food helped, but also Noah and her family believed her now. She wasn't alone in this nightmare.

A hole opened in Mom's cheek. She didn't seem to notice. Marella's feeling of stability vanished. She tried to tell her mother something was wrong with her, but couldn't move.

The hole enlarged, dissolving inward, carving an abyss into Mom's face. Marella fought to call out, but couldn't feel her mouth and throat. Was she about to time travel? She willed herself to stay in the present, imagining herself anchored to the tree house by heavy chains.

The void in Mom's face grew, pulling matter into it like a miniature black hole. An eye slumped past its event horizon; her forehead followed, making a whumping sound.

The black hole stretched and consumed other items in the tree house. The kitchen counter, the coffee table, the couch, the wall of books. The noise intensified to a torrent of sloshing and grinding. She couldn't feel the chair underneath her. She smelled ammonia. She was cold.

There seemed to be no stopping time.

Chapter Six

Yellow-and-black patterns. Fuzzy shapes. A grinding sound like rock on metal. Why was it so cold? Where was she?

The sharp tang of ammonia brought it back. Marella was time traveling. Coming or going? Forward or backward? Inside out or outside in? Nothing made sense, not even her own questions.

She'd been at the tree house with her family, only to be seized by time and dumped in a run-down streetscape she didn't recognize. A thick smell of dust made her cough, which, oddly, pained the bits of her lungs that had joined her in the new time as well as the bits of lung that hadn't quite arrived yet.

There was concrete beneath her feet. Garbage strewn on the ground. A giant web of broken glass on a storefront. Behind that, a mannequin leaning as if about to faint.

She waited until her body felt whole, then tried taking a step. She stumbled. *Patience. Gauge the situation.* She seemed to be standing in the middle of the street. A sign on the corner was too far off to make out, and the business names were too generic to provide any clues to her location.

She felt a pricking on her skin. That meant something, didn't it? Why was she still forgetful? She needed her reasoning to catch up with her body.

Suddenly, Brielle was running up to her. A grunt of relief escaped from Marella's throat. And yet—something was wrong. Brielle's tie-dye shirt was greasy with dirt, and she seemed frantic. She hugged Marella, her body warm against Marella's chilled skin. She smelled of sweat and urine. Marella's hug back was more of an arm drape than an actual embrace.

Brielle pulled back, looking her up and down. "I can't believe it's you! How did you find me?"

"What year?" asked Marella.

Brielle looked at her strangely, then her eyes widened and her words spilled out. "You time traveled here! You must have come from the past. I remember you came back from this moment and told us all how dangerous it was. How we have to change the future. But we didn't change it, Marella. It's everywhere."

Marella was still confused, and this wasn't helping. "What's everywhere? Time?"

The prickling intensified, as if tiny needles were jabbing her skin. Then it felt like somebody was hiding, surreptitiously watching her. Somebody larger than life. A god. No, a goddess. Her skin began to itch.

In spite of her stiffness, Marella twisted to look back. Two blocks away, a white fog flowed like an incoming tide. Purple-and-indigo highlights shone opalescent in its depths.

It was the iridescent fog they'd seen from the tree house, but bigger, at least a block wide, squeezing through between the buildings. Like before, a feeling of need poured forth from the fog, but more robust now, perhaps because of its size. How could a chemical phenomenon spew such desire?

A man was running from the fog. It reached him in seconds, flowing around the lower half of his body. He jerked as if shot by a gun, then dropped to his knees, mouth open in a frozen shriek. Neck muscles strained into long strings. Hands clutched into claws. He was in such agony!

He turned an impossible gray. Battleship gray. People weren't that color. Marella took an awkward step toward him. She had to do something. Get a stick or something, pull him out.

But the fog flowed over him in waves and was coming their way. Brielle tugged on Marella's arm, her voice hoarse. "It's too late to help him. Hurry."

She lurched along with Brielle, still stiff, still trying to make sense of things.

"That man..."

"He's dead. Forget him."

Brielle's statement shocked her. The fog had killed him, just like that? If the fog was everywhere and it killed on contact... "Where's Mom? And Noah?"

"I don't know. We got separated months ago."

They ran as fast as Marella could manage, to a main street. Ahead was a six-story apartment building, Italian-villa style with wrought iron balcony railings. Billows of lethal fog showed behind it. Brielle made a noise of despair, and they stumbled to an awkward stop. Fog ahead. Fog behind. They would be trapped.

They turned right, galloping past more stores. Shoe repair, gyros, furniture.

Marella risked a look, twisting back clumsily. The two fog banks collided, making an odd smacking noise, then churned, sending out sprays and geysers. The stuff was funneling toward them.

"Hurry!" screamed Brielle.

The door to a condo building was ajar. They tumbled inside and shut the door, then hurried across the lobby, shoes slapping on the wood floor, to a grand staircase with carved wooden railings. Up to the second floor. The third. The fourth.

There they leaned against a wall, huffing and gasping, gazing through a narrow window. The fog below looked like a white sea filled with indigo jellyfish, its waves caressing the surrounding buildings.

Marella's skin itched like crazy. Scratching only made it worse.

"Nowhere is safe," said Brielle, panting hard. "It's all over the world. You have to do something. Tell everybody back in the past."

She looked so beaten that Marella wanted to assure her things would get better, but they wouldn't, unless she learned more. "Information dump," she ordered. "Tell me everything you can think of."

"It's March 15, 2024."

"So—around half a year in the future. Go on."

Brielle threaded her fingers through her hair as if to help her think. "Um... the fog flows randomly, and there's more of it all the time. We make forays for supplies when we can."

"Where does it come from?"

"Well—you told me it's from Project Athena."

"How did I know that?"

"You'd been to the future."

"Which one. This one? Or another future?"

Brielle looked confused, then waved her hands frenetically. "Wait, wait! I know what I need to tell you. The fog has a wavelength."

"How can fog have a wavelength?"

"It's not really a fog, it's electromagnetic radiation. Like sound and light and x-rays, it has a wavelength. Different experts figured that out so I know it's true."

The white stuff below didn't appear to be made of wavelengths, and yet it was. "Light and sound don't kill people," said Marella.

"X-rays can."

"Sure, but it takes a lot of them, and not right away. Not like that man."

The news imparted, Brielle leaned against the wall, sinking back into defeat. "That's all I know, and we're cut off now. No news. We're just trying to survive. It's not easy. I was with two others until yesterday." She hung her head. "They didn't make it."

Marella embraced her sister. She felt thin but wiry. Her sweaty smell brought back the time her soccer team won a regional match. The glee they'd hugged with was so different from this despair.

She didn't know how long she would remain in this time period. It could be five minutes, it could be more, but judging by her previous stints, it wouldn't be long before she left Brielle by herself in a perilous future. She hadn't learned enough to stave off the fog, but she could at least make sure they stayed together. "How did we get split up?"

A flat buzzing noise buried the answer. Brielle became soft in her arms, like a stuffed animal. Marella held her lightly, fearful she would damage her; within seconds she dissolved away. Marella smelled ammonia. She felt icy cold, and her torso stretched and twisted; cramps racked her body.

She was on the verge of time traveling. The fear of it pervaded her being. It was more terrifying each time, because she knew what was coming. Her body couldn't flail, so her mind did, reaching out for support, but there was none to be had.

The window and walls disintegrated in chunks, which separated into bits that tornadoed away. Icy cleavers chopped Marella into pieces that rocketed to separate corners of the universe. Each of those pieces were pierced by billions of stars.

She was caught in a boundless eternity, forever lost.

• • • •

MARELLA COULD FEEL her body, but only as drifting, disconnected shards. Almost-thoughts floated just out of reach. What was the shape of Marella? What was the shape of eternity? How long did eternity last? What was eternity made of?

She took on more form. Her body was shivering. Sight returned; yellow-and-black patterns morphed in front of her. An arm was holding her. Warm. Tight. Comforting.

Voices rose and fell, the rhythm of speech. She didn't understand, although she recognized that Noah was beside her, and her mother and Brielle were there too.

She smelled strawberry jam. She was in the tree house. She had returned to the present. Evening. August something. August 28, that was it—2023, not 2024.

As she recovered from the time travel and was better able to think, memories of her trip to the future returned. Her mother and Noah were lost, maybe dead. Her sister was alone. As for herself, where was she in that future? Dead? Or alive, a fugitive from the fog?

Spasms of grief interrupted her shivering. The future was supposed to be better. The future had always been a place where the trials of the present had been overcome, but now it was dangerous and deadly.

She felt the arm tighten around her. "It's okay," cooed Mom.

"Breathe," added Brielle.

"It's all right," said Noah.

Marella soaked in their comforts, trying to find a ray of hope. A ray—that was a wavelength. The fog was too. All hope was lost because of a wavelength.

She could see now, through misted eyes. Noah, Mom, Brielle. All watching her with concern. She tried to smile at them, to let them know she would be okay—whether that was true or not—but only managed to stretch the corners of her mouth a bit.

It took time, and some false starts, but finally she could speak, though her tongue felt thick. "Went to future."

Brielle spoke excitedly. "So you know what's going to happen? Where do we end up? What do we do?"

"Let her talk," said Mom.

"The fog—deadly," said Marella.

Brielle's excitement drained. "The fog? You mean the stuff we saw go underneath the tree house?"

"Yes."

Noah took her hands, rubbing them to warm them. "Why? What's it made of?"

Marella recounted their flight from the fog. As she spoke, it was easier to get the words out and her enunciation improved. When she described the man's death from the fog, Mom ran to the window, scanned the ground, then returned, announcing, "We're moving away."

"That wouldn't help," said Marella. "Brielle said it's everywhere." She told them about Brielle being alone and just surviving.

Mom looked stricken. Brielle stared at the floor, picking at her shirt.

Noah put a comforting hand on Brielle's back. "We'll stop it before it gets to that." He said to Marella, "You say it's electromagnetic radiation. What could be making it?"

"Brielle said that I told her Project Athena is making it."

"Really?" asked Noah. "How did you figure that out?"

"Brielle didn't tell me how I knew. But when the fog is near I can feel the same prickly feeling I felt on the island with Project Athena. The two are connected."

"But there's no Project Athena anymore," said Noah. "It's gone."

"The time-traveling Marella in the loft said she was right about Project Athena," said Brielle. "It's had some lasting effect on her, somehow. We need to know more about how it worked."

Marella could only think of two potential sources of information: any documents associated with the machine, or the people involved. Belinda had said there were no remaining documents, and even if there were, she would have no access to them. That left only people, and Marella just knew of one living person with any knowledge of Project Athena.

"I have to talk to Belinda again," she said. "She may not know the intricate details of how Project Athena worked, but she has to know concepts. She was always hands-on. She attended lots of meetings about it."

"She wasn't any help to you before," said Mom.

"If I tell her about the fog and the time travel, it might trigger an idea. Something that was discussed in a meeting. Or something Len and Eshana might have told her."

Mom shook her head. "She didn't believe that Project Athena caused the Aguageddon. She's really not going to believe you time travel."

"I'll find a way to convince her." Marella's bravado was as much for herself as it was for them. She could see no other way, and so she had to try, if it was the last thing she did.

Although, with time travel, the last thing she did would never really be the last thing, would it?

Chapter Seven

Marella woke the next morning relieved to find she hadn't time traveled during the night. She had slept on top of the bedcovers, with her clothes and shoes on, just in case she time traveled. That had made it difficult to be intimate with Noah, which was out of the question anyway. Not when she could time travel in the middle of it.

Noah lay next to her, his face relaxed in sleep, as if having a good dream. On his bare back, where he had been burned, was the pinkish-white patch the shape of Antarctica.

After a quick breakfast, they got on the e-bike to go to HemisNorth. The shantytown shacks had multiplied. There were new ones perched on a steep hill, precarious as ancient cliff dwellings. The garbage stench was thicker too.

At HemisNorth, a receptionist ushered Marella and Noah to a windowless meeting room big enough to hold seventy-five people. Printouts of architectural drawings were pinned onto the long walls. They portrayed bridges arched over parallel canals and the terraced levels of a park climbing a hillside, reminiscent not of the shantytown, but of the Hanging Gardens of Babylon, one of the Seven Wonders of the Ancient World. It was almost as if Belinda shared Noah's dream of building a wonder-of-the-world.

Stepping closer to examine the detail, she realized it wasn't a park, but rather a city, its buildings draped with foliage and topped with green roofs.

She touched the drawings reverently, hoping that the people in the shantytown would endure long enough to inhabit this place. She imagined living there with Noah, their families close by. It brightened her spirits.

Noah whistled as he examined the drawings. "These must be HemisNorth's renderings of the rebuild. They're crazy ambitious.

This one has a bullet train. And there must be hundreds of skyscrapers. It's going to take decades to do all this."

Marella's spirits dimmed. Decades! That was much too long. And what was more, Belinda must be absurdly overextended trying to get this all started. She would be less thrilled with Marella's second uninvited visit, this time with tales of strange fog and time travel.

A voice at the doorway spoke affectionately. "Marella. I'm glad to see you."

"Me too." Marella meant it. Belinda's air of efficient serenity was catching. Maybe this would go better than she'd thought.

Belinda wore the same pinstripe suit as she had the last time they'd met. She'd lost her home in Seattle in the fires, after all, along with her wardrobe. She carried a long cardboard box, which she set on a table.

Marella introduced Noah. Belinda shook his hand, touching his arm as she did so, which emphasized her sincerity. "Noah Mburu. I'm glad that you survived such a difficult journey. Welcome."

"Thank you," he said. "I was sorry to hear about your husband. And thank you for the food. It meant a lot." He bowed slightly, an ambassador in the presence of royalty. Marella had never seen him so reverent, although Belinda's charisma made it seem only natural.

Belinda looked wistful and appreciative. "Thank you for your condolences. I admit it's been very hard. It helps me to keep busy."

She took a restoring breath in and let it out, indicating a change to a new subject. "Marella, I have a problem, so I'm glad you're here. We've been looking for some visual graphics that Elizabeth had been working on, and they're nowhere to be found in our backup system. Please tell me she didn't keep them on the hard drive of her computer."

At the mention of Elizabeth, her feeling of guilt surfaced and the taste of warm iron and wet mold strengthened. Marella did her best to forget her feelings and concentrate on Belinda's dilemma. At first she wasn't sure—any pre-Aguageddon events seemed so long ago—but then she remembered helping Elizabeth with this very issue. "No, she didn't keep things on her hard drive. She was using a program that didn't work in a shared folder, so she kept that output in the 'J' drive."

"Excellent. That server is still available, so I'll look for them there. Thank goodness for you. You have my undying gratitude."

Noah gave Marella a surreptitious nod of approval, which encouraged her. They were probably both thinking the same thing: that things were off to a good start, and that Marella's assistance might make Belinda more receptive.

Belinda motioned to the renderings. "We're rebuilding in phases. Some here, some in Seattle, Olympia, Tacoma, and so on. It's not going to look like this all at once. But when we're done, it'll be even better than before."

"It's beautiful," said Marella.

"Help me with this." Belinda reached up to the corner of a rendering of a sleek subway car arriving at a well-lit station. A mural of cavorting otters graced the station wall. Removing a pin, she dropped it into an empty canister. Marella and Noah followed suit, removing pins. The rendering curled down; Marella held it to keep it from falling onto the floor.

"You must be ready to return to work," said Belinda. "I hope so, because as you just proved, your legacy knowledge of HemisNorth is quite valuable to us."

Noah gave a tiny jerk of his head, as if to say *Go on, tell her.*

Marella cleared her throat. "Actually, I came to talk with you about something else."

"I'm listening." Belinda seemed attentive, even while wrestling with pins and paper.

What a time to remember that Belinda didn't read novels, and therefore probably wasn't keen on anything smacking of science fiction. Best to plow forward anyway. Marella would only get more nervous if she put it off. At least she was doing something where she didn't have to look Belinda in the eyes.

Speak with assurance. Belinda respects you. "At the place where we're staying, we saw a strange fog that we've never seen before. It kind of flowed through the air. It was iridescent."

"Interesting," said Belinda, holding out the cannister. "Could it have to do with the bioluminescent sea creatures that were exposed to the air? Just a wild guess."

Either the CEO hadn't encountered the lethal fog or wasn't admitting to it. Marella dropped a pin into the cannister. "Also, there's been a new development that you might find hard to believe. I'm hoping you'll have an open mind."

Belinda raised her eyebrows at Marella. "Always." She returned to her task, removing the last pin from one of the renderings. The paper made a swishing noise as she rolled it.

"I never thought that the water could disappear from the ocean," said Marella, "and yet it started to. It actually happened. I saw valleys full of dead fish. Parts of the ocean floor that nobody else had ever seen."

Belinda nodded, seeming amenable. Snapping a rubber band around the paper, she handed it to Marella. "Box." Her movements were decisive. Once they were done putting the renderings away, she might proclaim the meeting over. Marella had better get the rest out while she could.

She carried the rolled paper to the box, then spoke in a rush. "Project Athena makes me time travel. It just happens spontaneously. One moment I'm in the present, and the next I'm twenty years in the past, or a year in the future."

Belinda's air of serenity flagged, as if the statement saddened her. "Whoa, Marella. Let me stop you there."

"Please, just humor me and listen for a minute. I can't control it. I can't decide when or where I time travel to. All I know is that Project Athena is causing it. Give me the benefit of the doubt that what I'm saying is real. Does it trigger a thought about how Project Athena worked? Maybe you attended a meeting, or Len and Eshana said something to you along the way."

Belinda shook her head. Frustration now simmered under the surface. "Listen to yourself. Time travel."

"It *sounds* far-fetched," said Marella, "but so does the ocean disappearing."

Belinda spoke louder, her frustration emerging. "One impossible thing coming true doesn't mean every other impossible thing will come true."

Noah stepped forward, raising a palm as if being sworn into office. "I saw it happen. I saw her time travel. She's not making it up, and she's not delusional."

It felt as if he'd leapt in front of Marella to take a bullet meant for her. She appreciated it more than he could know.

Belinda pulled her head backward as if to say *Oh, Noah, not you too?*

"We were in the living room." Noah pointed in various directions as he set the scene. His earnestness was captivating. "Three new Marellas appeared in the room, one after the other. By the window. In the loft. On the carpet. Four altogether. I'm absolutely sure it wasn't an illusion. You could touch them and talk to them."

Belinda thrust her head forward as if to speak sarcastically, but then stopped herself, switching tactics like she sometimes did in big corporate meetings. "Four Marellas in one room? Now that would be useful. We could do a lot of problem-solving."

"It's not a joke." Noah seemed on the verge of anger.

Marella touched his arm. It was moving that he would defend her so adamantly, but confrontation wasn't going to help them.

Belinda seemed rueful that her attempt to lighten the mood hadn't borne fruit. She changed tactics again, confiding in them, friend to friend. "Many people have PTSD from the Aguageddon. It's common among our employees and throughout the world. Ten days of scrounging and fighting for water. Dehydration and hunger."

The ability to shift gears as needed and call up facts were just a couple of the reasons Belinda was so good at her job. If Marella could only convince her, those abilities—and many others—could be key in solving her time-travel problem. But what would bring the CEO around to her point of view?

Seeing the resistance in their faces, Belinda continued. "Let's use reason to sort this out. Marella, it's a little too convenient that you can't control your time travel, because I expect that means you can't prove it either."

"If she knew more about Project Athena, then maybe she could," offered Noah in the same tone of rational debate. Again Marella felt his support, and was glad he had accompanied her.

"First Marella requested I destroy information about Project Athena, but now you both want me to release it." Belinda's tone was ironic. "That would put me in a difficult spot, except that, as I already told Marella, there isn't anything left. I have nothing to give you."

"As the CEO you had to have some knowledge of how it worked." Noah gave a nod of respect. "People reported to you. It was a huge project. You must have participated in meetings. Discussed it with Len and Eshana."

Was that a flicker of alarm on Belinda's face? It was there and gone so fast Marella couldn't be sure, but she didn't want to give any impression of accusation. She clarified, "Please, we're here because I need help. I'm suffering. It's really painful to time travel."

Belinda held a hand up as if carrying a tray, indicating her skepticism. "Just what makes you possibly think Project Athena could be causing your suffering?"

"It feels exactly the same as when I was on Wisdom Island, really close to the machine."

Belinda went to the box and pushed its flaps down. They wouldn't stay closed. She pushed them harder, struggling with the box until the flaps obeyed her.

Marella winced at the show of impatience, but went on. "It's very important that I learn more because the fog that I saw is deadly. In the future, it grows bigger and spreads all over. I saw it kill a man, and he—"

"I'm trying to build a new world." Belinda spoke loudly and gestured fiercely at the box of drawings. "I can't be distracted by time travel or mysterious fogs or outer-space aliens or many of the other theories that people keep bringing to my attention."

"Another version of me from the future came to the present." Marella couldn't help but match Belinda's volume. "She told me that Project Athena is involved."

"Please make an appointment with a doctor and a mental professional. Both of you. I'll cover the cost. Do that for me." It was an order.

Noah trotted up to her, palms together. "Before you make up your mind, imagine that it's true." His pleading was heartbreaking to Marella, who hoped it would affect Belinda in the same way. "Imagine what would happen if she was right. All the work you're doing here would be for nothing."

"Yes." Marella's desperation filled her voice. "Because the fog is that dangerous. In the future I visited, it had killed a lot of people and was creating another worldwide catastrophe. We can't let that happen."

Belinda held very still, then her rib cage expanded slowly and contracted just as slowly. It seemed to help her rein in her frustration. "Marella, I can't think of a reason that Project Athena might have caused you to time travel. That's too big a leap from anything I know about the project."

"There must be somebody who can help me," said Marella. "What about non-Seattle employees? Surely somebody elsewhere participated. There are so many offices."

"Yes!" Noah gestured energetically at the door, as if they were right outside. "There must be somebody here who worked on Project Athena. It was such a big project. It must have taken a lot of people."

"Only Seattle staff." Marella wasn't sure how the CEO managed it, but she now seemed perfectly composed. "We couldn't work on it remotely, so anybody who participated had to be located there, or relocate there."

Marella gazed at the remaining rendering on the wall, a shopping atrium bursting with plants, people strolling along without a care in the world. Such a contrast to the people in town, who seemed edgy, as if the sky could fall on them at any moment, and the people in the shantytown, who seemed to have lost all hope.

The scene in these pictures wouldn't come to pass if she didn't stop the lethal fog from spreading. She fidgeted, glancing around the room. Where were those other Marellas? She really needed them to pop into existence right now so that Belinda would believe her.

Belinda lowered her forehead toward Marella, the way a preacher might to a troubled parishioner. "You're having a perfectly natural reaction to a perfectly horrible situation. Moving on will help you both to overcome the damage to your bodies. Marella, return to HemisNorth, and Noah, you come join us as well. You will be able to do important work—rebuilding better and smarter. Helping provide stability around the world. All that will be healing."

Marella looked around the room. *Right now, future selves. Come here and prove me right.*

"Come back to work at HemisNorth." Belinda touched Marella gently with her fingertips, a gesture of caring and goodwill. "You'll have good pay, and we'll feed you as well."

Marella wished she could accept such an offer. Daily living was a struggle even without the difficulty of time travel.

Belinda saw that she had forgotten a rendering. She began taking it down. "Plus you'll have the satisfaction of building a new Washington State. Think about that. One day you'll tell your grandchildren what it was like to make that happen." She put the rendering in the box, effortlessly refolding its flaps. "Think about it."

Taking the box with her, she left the room.

Marella had failed in her mission to obtain information, yet she still had hope. Even though things were in turmoil, with people displaced, there had to be employees somewhere who knew details about Project Athena. She would just have to find them.

• • • •

OUTSIDE, MARELLA SAT on a bench near the HemisNorth main building, waiting while Noah used the bathroom. The sparsely filled parking lot stretched out in front of her; beyond that stood the manufacturing plant's stainless steel tanks. She counted thirty-seven within view. Linked by parallel pipes, ductwork, and valves, they looked like a giant Rube Goldberg machine. If she put an enormous marble into one end, surely it would work its tortuous way through and then drop out of the other.

Could these tanks have something to do with the lethal fog, and if so, why did the fog cause her to have similar feelings as time travel? What if a specific combination of chemicals served as a catalyst, causing Project Athena to propel her forward or backward in time? She imagined herself as a mad scientist, pouring beakers of colorful chemicals into one another until she found the perfect combination to control her time travel.

A news van with a giant number seven drove into the parking lot. *Lucky seven. If only luck were that easy to come by.*

And yet—maybe luck *was* that easy to come by. Could this be a means to find surviving HemisNorth employees? If she told the news people about the missing staff, they might broadcast it, and those missing people could get in contact with Marella.

But then, maybe they wouldn't broadcast it. Absent HemisNorth employees weren't news. Not after the Western Inferno had spread Washington State residents far and wide. That wasn't new information. Still, it wouldn't hurt to talk to the news team. The worst that could happen would be that they couldn't help.

The van parked. A man emerged, looking around with interest. His shaved head resembled a button mushroom; he wore a polo shirt with the TV station's logo. A reporter?

Next came a woman with a cockatoo-like crest of hair. She moved as smoothly as a manufacturing robot as she pointed a shoulder-mounted camera toward the tanks, then panned across the building's bright white exterior.

What angle were they here to pursue? If there had been other sightings of the lethal fog, they could be here to investigate a possible HemisNorth connection. But then, undercover would be best for that. It was more likely they were covering HemisNorth's rebuilding initiative.

Either way, too soon they were striding toward the sprawling building's entryway. She was about to lose her chance. She ran toward them. "Hey! Wait!"

They turned. She still limped a little from her ankle injury, making her feel awkward. When she got to them, she blurted, "We have to find some missing HemisNorth employees. The ones from Seattle who didn't die in the Aguageddon."

Curved lines graced the corners of the man's mouth, giving him a welcoming and trustworthy air. "Why do you have to find them?"

She had to give him real information. Something to investigate. "HemisNorth made a new technology. We need to find the employees who helped build it."

"Yes?" he said encouragingly. "And what does the new technology do?"

"Um... not what it was supposed to do." *Wrong answer. Do better.* She wished she had more time to think this through.

"You're a protester then?"

"No," said Marella. "I work at HemisNorth. I mean, I used to work there."

"And you were fired?"

The unexpected accusation flustered Marella even more. "No. Nothing like that. I mean, the Aguageddon happened and then..." She stopped herself from babbling irrelevant details.

"I'm sorry, we have an interview to do," said the man. "It was nice to meet you."

"But you have to help." She had to give them something more. A nugget. "It was a machine that was going to make things better."

"Excellent. We'll ask them about it."

"No, don't do that. They won't tell you that it..." Did she really want to divulge this? She had to offer them something. "The machine is dangerous if we don't have people who know how to use it."

"Dangerous? How?" The reporter tilted his head, which gave him an air of attentive curiosity. He seemed... effective, yes, that was it. If you gave him the right information, he would interpret it precisely.

She swallowed. She had to tempt them with something to make them broadcast an invitation to former Seattle employees. Otherwise she would never know how to stop the fog. Her family would die. Noah would die. She had to go all in. "It's the machine that caused the explosion at the HemisNorth research building in Seattle."

The camerawoman and the man looked at each other. With curiosity? Disbelief?

She and Noah had agreed to keep this quiet. She'd already said too much. She imagined him berating her if she named the machine. But then, he might also be disappointed in her for blowing this chance to solve the mysteries of the lethal fog and of time travel.

He wasn't here. She had to make the choice without him. Second-guessing him wasn't the way to make a decision anyway. She had to do what she felt was right, now, in this moment. Make a choice.

The silence grew until she felt like she had to fill it. "They called it Project Athena."

"Is there a machine like that here?" asked the reporter. Marella didn't answer. If she told him there wasn't, he might not be so keen to help.

"What does this machine do?" he asked.

She could explain Project Athena's original purpose, but that was beside the point. "It's complicated."

The reporter glanced at the building, then back at Marella. "We really do need to go, but how can I find you if I need more information?"

"I'm Marella Wells. I'm staying in the tree house, on the hill..."

She had been about to recite the address, but a wave of nausea kept her from speaking. The reporter's ear dissolved, then the side of his face, then his eyes. His arm sloughed off. She smelled ammonia. *Not again. Not now.*

The remaining parts of the reporter turned gray as a statue, as did the camerawoman. They exploded into dust, which puffed outward, engulfing Marella in the smell of ammonia. There was a distant rumble, but she couldn't identify the source through the veil of dust. A vehicle? A storm? Whatever it was, it was coming her way.

The dust cleared. The far end of the parking lot curled upward like an ocean wave. The concrete swell made a terrible grinding noise as it approached; within seconds it was looming above. Like a surfer who had miscalculated her momentum, she wanted to paddle, flail—anything to escape the inevitable, but her body wouldn't do her bidding. The concrete wave smashed against her, tearing her body into bits, which shot out in all directions, then spread into the far reaches of eternity.

Chapter Eight

Specks of matter hurled their way across the universe, smashing into one another, creating hunks of... what? Asteroids? Planets? No, a biological being. A person. Marella. This was Marella, rebirthing, reforming.

She had eyes. Yellow-and-black patterns twisted in front of them, then tall shapes appeared. She had feeling. Legs, feet, standing on the ground. Torso, arms, too cold. She had a whole body now, which shivered violently.

Where was she? It was dark, dank. Claustrophobic.

The tall shapes became blurry trees. Many of them. She smelled ammonia. That meant she was time traveling, didn't it? To the future? To the past?

Her vision sharpened. Ferns curved over her feet. There was a huckleberry bush, its fruit tiny and orange, not yet ripe. A spiderweb hammocked among its branches. Douglas firs were all around, branches draped in ancient-looking moss and smelling of resin.

She had been in a place like this once before, and the memory was devastating. That was the camping trip in the Olympic Rainforest, where her father had died. She had avoided being in thick woods ever since.

She couldn't let herself be distracted by that. Rather, she needed to focus on getting herself together. Even though it looked like the forest of her youth, she could be in any number of places, in any number of time periods. As soon as she was able, she needed to push her way through the ferns, determine where she was, and find other people. If this was the past, she might be able to change the timeline; if the future, there was knowledge to gain.

"These are magic sticks," said a voice beyond the trees.

Marella's breath seemed to wedge itself in her throat. That was Dad's voice. After all these years, she had forgotten how rich it sounded, but now she remembered the melodic syllables, the way the word "magic" rose and fell.

"I like magic," said a child's voice. Marella herself! She remembered saying it.

Shortly after that, her father had died.

She had time traveled back to that terrible camping trip, fourteen years into the past. The most pivotal point in her life. She often wished she had said or done something to stop her father from dying. And now she was here, in that very moment. Whatever she had suffered to get here suddenly didn't matter. She had a goal: save her father's life.

She could move now, just a little. She turned her head. In a narrow sight line, about twenty feet away, she spotted Dad's puffy green coat—the one her mother had affectionately dubbed his olive costume. He leaned forward, and his face came into view. Her memory of him, which had dulled over the years, as if viewed through a sooty window, returned with clarity. The straight edge of his nose. The slight cauliflower ear from a boxing injury. She wanted desperately to run to him and embrace him.

Then she saw herself. A five-year-old girl, cheeks rosy from hiking up the trail. Marella before tragedy struck, when her only concerns were trivial, like whether she would get ice cream for dessert.

Dad had a long white stick in his hand—one of the foldaway poles that would hold the tent in shape. "Let's make our very own hidey-hole."

She saw her little self guiding his hands, him really doing the work, inserting the stick into the tent loops. What had been just a pile of fabric took shape, becoming a blue-and-white dome.

"It *is* a hidey-hole!" said her cute little self in that tiny voice.

Those had been her last words to her father. Soon, Dad would die. She remembered coming to the edge of a cliff. Looking down. Seeing him motionless.

Her life would have been so different with a father. Her heart ached with the thought of it. But when she was able to control her movement, the trajectory of her life could change. She could run forward and warn him.

However, if she did so, her entire life would change. She might never work at HemisNorth, never discover that Project Athena had caused the Aguageddon, and never keep the water from disappearing from the Earth. Everybody in the world would die.

But then, maybe the person who got the job instead would discover that Project Athena was defective. Perhaps even sooner than she had, before the disaster became dire. Somebody nosier or smarter, or even just luckier.

How could she know? Would she change the course of the world's history? Or just her own?

There had to be a reason for her to have come back to this moment in time, to this place. Some kind of fate. She was supposed to be here. She was supposed to save her father's life.

She made her choice. Save her father. Hope that fate intervened to make everything come out for the best.

She tried to take a step, but her muscles locked up. She fell. There was a flash of pain in her arm. She'd cut it on a stick, a three-inch gash that was dripping blood. Not important. She could take care of it later.

She pushed against the ground but still had little control over her body. Patience. It took time to recover from time travel. She remained, shivering in the cool, moist air.

"Stay right here, Marella," said her father to her child self. "I'll be right back."

This was the critical moment. The moment when he had walked away, unknowingly heading for the cliff. She had to stop him now. From where she was on the ground, she couldn't see him, but she heard him stepping through the thick underbrush. A stick snapped. His coat made swooshing noises when it rubbed against the ferns.

He was coming her way. He would see her, and she would alert him. She was about to save him!

But no, the olive green of his coat was several feet away, the ferns and salal plants masking her from his sight. He passed her by. Now he was ten feet away. Any moment he would reach the cliff.

Gathering every bit of energy she could muster, she pushed herself up to a crouch. There he was, next to the scraggly tree, the one with the knots that looked like a face, the one that was right next to the cliff, the one she'd hung on to as a five-year-old when she looked over the edge and saw his body.

She gulped a deep breath in and tried to shout for him to stop. The sound gurgled in her throat, bursting out as a growly bark.

Her father yelped in surprise, then wheeled, hands up in a defensive posture. His leg slid to the side, then out from under him. His arms flew up.

His desperate, drawn-out call seemed to reverberate in her heart. That was the cavernous sound that had stuck with her all those years, that she heard as she was falling asleep, bringing her to sudden wakefulness. That she heard in the background of songs in certain keys. That she heard in the depths of storms.

He dropped out of sight, as if through a trapdoor. Moments later, there was a dull thud. Her father hitting the ground.

She squeezed her eyes shut. She hadn't stopped him. In fact, she had caused him to fall. She had startled her own father into falling off a cliff.

Marella dropped to her knees. The memory had stayed vivid all these years. Her father would be down below, sprawled on a narrow hiking path about two stories down. Unmoving. Blood on the ground under his head. His eyes wide open and his chin raised too high, forcing his neck into an unnatural twist. Broken. He was dead. There was nothing she could do to change that now.

She had accidentally killed her own father. It was her fault she and Brielle had grown up without him. The horror of it was like a belt tightening around her chest. Sobs rose to the surface without breaking through, building and building, until finally an animal cry of pain and anger burst from her throat. She howled, her endless grief pouring out through the noise.

"Daddy!" shouted a terror-filled voice.

Marella's howl groaned to a stop. She couldn't see her younger self, who would now be looking over the cliff. All those years ago, her father had shouted and she had rushed to see what he wanted, thinking he was going to show her something wild and wonderful, a deer, perhaps, which he'd said they might see. And then she'd looked over the cliff and seen her father. She'd watched him, hoping he would move, but realized that he was too broken. Plus, his eyes were wide open. At night, when she was supposed to be asleep, she had sneaked out and seen crime shows her parents were watching, and this was exactly how dead people looked.

And then she'd heard the noise. A demon howl.

How stupid she was to have made that noise. She remembered thinking a demon had come to take her father, and that it would take her too. She had run away. For two days she had been lost in the woods.

Now she must stop her little girl self from running. From enduring those two terrifying, miserable, hopeless days. She jumped to her feet. "Marella!" she called, her voice low and hoarse.

As she followed, calling, she realized she still sounded like a demon to the little girl. Her five-year-old self had thought the demon knew her name. Marella wasn't changing her own history; she was only reinforcing it. Building the tragedy up so it could never be torn down.

There was still time to change that. She could catch up, show the little girl she was human. Even warn her somehow about Project Athena.

Project Athena. The bigger problem. Yes, her father had died, but much more had also gone wrong. This was bigger than herself, bigger than her sorrow and pain. She'd failed in saving her father from dying, but there was a more important opportunity here.

She had to acknowledge that easing her childhood fears and telling a little girl about Project Athena would accomplish nothing. It wouldn't change history. Any warning the five-year-old Marella gave to an adult would be discounted, so that wasn't a reliable solution.

However, Marella could now leave a note for her mother to read back here in 2009. With the right words, she could change history. She needed to do this quickly, before time snatched her back to the present.

With a sick feeling in her stomach, she abandoned her five-year-old self and turned back. Her father hadn't had a cell phone on the trip—his had broken—but he'd kept a booklet in which he jotted sketches and notes to himself. She tottered to the campsite. There was the newly erected blue-and-white tent, the fabric rippling ever so slightly in the light breeze. Their backpacks lay on the ground. A stuffed rabbit peeked out from Marella's mini backpack.

Her father's orange backpack was still bulging with supplies. She dug in the pockets. Where was his booklet? She knew he'd brought it because she'd seen him get it from the drawer. She began yanking things out. The trail mix he called "gorp." His gray woolen sweater. Blue socks. Plaid underwear. Toilet paper. Portable camping stove. When the backpack was empty, she checked all the pockets again, then squeezed, opened, and turned over the things she'd removed, feeling for the small rectangular booklet. With increasing despair, she pulled his sleeping bag out of its stuff sack and felt through it.

The booklet wasn't there.

She squeezed her eyes shut and pressed her hands on her temples. It wasn't in his backpack, so he had it with him. And so she had to go to her father now. Her dead father.

There was no time for squeamishness or heartache. She would have to shut her emotions down, go to the body, find the booklet, and write a note to her mother.

She stumble-ran down the trail they'd come up, mentally composing the words. *Find Eshana Collins and Len Janderson. Tell them that their climate machine has unfixable flaws that will cause a worldwide disaster. They—and HemisNorth—will be to blame.*

When she saw her father lying dead, neck twisted and irreversibly broken, she stopped. Despite the urgency of her mission, she stood frozen.

Memories fluttered in her mind. She used to take a little toy comb to that short hair, using clumsy yet careful strokes. She used to kiss that stubbled cheek, saying "Ow!"—which would spur Dad to announce he was going to be a lumberjack so he could grow his beard out all the way.

Tears flowing, she forced herself to kneel on the uneven dirt. His eyes, which used to winken and blinken at her, were dull, unseeing. Her chest tightened.

She was wasting time. She wiped her eyes. *Get the booklet. Do it.*

The way his body was twisted, she could see both back pockets. One had the outline of his wallet, the other a longer rectangular outline. She reached into that pocket. His body was still warm.

She pulled out the booklet. It was purple, a little shorter than her hand, a pen attached to it by a loop. She opened it. The blue letters of her father's writing were narrow, slanting to the left. There was a sketch of Marella as a child. Chubby cheeks. Long eyelashes. This was how her father had seen her. He'd never had the chance to see her as an adult.

She would have liked to read it, but couldn't afford the time. Turning to the first empty page, she wrote a note that she hoped her mother would see. *I'm Marella at 19 years old. I've come back in time to warn you. Some day I'll get a job at HemisNorth. Eshana Collins and Len Janderson work there. They'll build a machine called Project Athena. It will cause a worldwide disaster. It'll take water from the world instead of carbon dioxide. Stop them.*

Was that enough? She hoped so. She tucked the notebook into her father's pocket.

She waited. If it worked, everything would change. The Aguageddon wouldn't happen. She wouldn't be here, kneeling next to her father's dead body. She wouldn't be watching a fly land on his pant leg, then take off.

Nothing changed.

She leaned back on her haunches to ponder. Trying to fix the problem while time traveling was a bit of a paradox. She had to get here to write the note. But the note would never be written if the timeline changed and she never got here. Was that the problem? Which came first, the chicken or the egg? The note or the time travel?

And then there was fate. If things were meant to be, nothing she did would change them. But her actions seemed to have consequences. It didn't feel like destiny—it felt like she'd made ruinous choices. Anyway, fate or not, giving up wasn't an option. So what should she do differently?

The note must not have enough information. After all, her mother would have to not only see the note, but remember and take action many years later. She needed to add more detail. Some kind of proof. Details that couldn't be discounted.

She reached into her father's pocket once more and pulled out the booklet. She was poised to write more when the booklet's edges crumbled like sand, the bits falling away as if stolen by the wind. She tried to move. Her body wouldn't obey. The booklet crumbled the rest of the way, then her hand, the dull pain traveling up her arm, to her shoulder, her neck.

She smelled ammonia. Her father's body dissolved in a whirl. She couldn't feel the ground under her feet or tell which direction was up. She was freezing cold, and falling endlessly, into eternity. Becoming nothing.

• • • •

AFTER A TIME, SHE FELT warmth seep in, a warmth full of grief, though she wasn't sure what had caused it. Her thoughts lay limp and quivering, like a beached jellyfish.

What had happened?

Somebody had died. Somebody close to her. Somebody she knew, yet didn't really know, which made no sense, at least not yet.

Black-and-yellow pixels resolved into people: a man and a woman. She didn't know them either, and yet they looked familiar. That also made no sense. Behind them, the landscape took shape, a strange monstrosity of stainless steel tanks connected to pipes.

HemisNorth. The manufacturing facility. That was where she was. But who were these people? The truck over there—a big *Channel 7* on its side. Oh yes, she had been talking to the reporter and camerawoman. Before she'd gone to the woods, she'd had an urgent mission. She'd been trying to get them interested in something. She struggled to talk, grunting unintentionally.

"Are you all right?" asked the reporter.

"She's having a seizure or something," said the camerawoman.

"I won't let you fall." He put an arm around her, murmuring encouragement.

Marella kept trying to move and talk, which made her jerk, which made the reporter hold her more securely and comfort her more. Minutes went by.

Finally she cleared her throat. "Hold on," she managed to utter, her voice growly. "I time traveled."

They squinted, as if they hadn't understood. "To the past," she clarified.

Then she remembered calling to Dad, startling him. He'd slipped, clutching uselessly at the air to try to save himself.

She'd caused her own father to die.

A sob threatened to well up. *Keep it together.* She put up a wall between her and the sorrow. Later she could think about it, but right now she had to be in the present.

She was holding something. The booklet. She still had it in her hand. She closed her eyes briefly and pressed her lips together. Her mother had never seen her note, because she had taken the booklet back out of her father's pocket.

She'd ruined everything. She couldn't talk to these people now. All she wanted was to be by herself. To understand how things could have gone so wrong.

"Are you all right now?" asked the reporter.

Not by a long shot. She rubbed her face, donning a pretend smile. "Yes, I'm fine."

"You're bleeding." He pointed to her arm.

Marella looked down. There was a three-inch cut, and blood was smeared on her arm. She remembered falling in the woods. She had cut herself then.

"I'm okay." She waved them away.

The reporter and camerawoman left, looking back a couple of times before entering the building.

The booklet was clear evidence of her own stupidity. She never wanted to see it again, but couldn't throw it away either. It was too big for the pocket in her leggings, so she stuffed it in her bra.

Fate. Was everything set in place, unchangeable? Had it all been decided, and now she could only live the events as they were laid out?

Or would more time travel worsen the timeline? Cause more death? She'd inadvertently killed her own father. Who would be next? Mom? Brielle? Noah?

A sense of anguish germinated in her solar plexus, then grew until it filled her chest, making it hard to breathe. She pressed her head between her hands, as if to squeeze her thoughts into submission.

She heard Noah call, "You're bleeding!"

He rushed to her, panic-stricken. He glanced around quickly—probably looking for the cause of her injury, but there was nothing to see. He grasped her wrist and elbow, holding her arm out as if it were a poisonous snake. "That's the cut the other Marella had in the tree house. The dead one!" Flustered now, he corrected himself, his words tumbling out. "I mean the one that wasn't breathing. We've got to protect you now. We can't let anything else happen to you. This is all my fault. I shouldn't have left you alone. Are you hurt anywhere else?"

His agitation only underscored her helplessness. She shook her head, slipping her arm out of his hands. It had stopped bleeding, and the blood was clotting. Good thing, because she couldn't bear to go inside for a bandage, or allow him to leave her alone while he retrieved one.

He embraced her protectively, with her head on his chest. "How did it happen?"

"I was time traveling and I tripped."

"Where? When?"

She couldn't tell him. She couldn't tell anybody. The weight of the guilt was heavy enough without adding the judgment of others.

Chapter Nine

When she saw the cut on Marella's arm, Brielle shouted huskily and dropped a glass, which shattered on the tree house kitchen floor. "That's the cut you'll have when you stop breathing!"

Stay away from the broken glass, Marella told herself, momentarily forgetting it was too late, she was already cut.

Mom ran to her, holding up her arm. Her touch felt soft. "It is that cut. That's not good. I don't like this one bit."

With her mother and sister so distraught, Marella had to fight to keep from breaking down herself. "I haven't got the green shirt on. Nothing's going to happen to me yet."

"Noah, why didn't you protect her?" Demanded Mom.

He seemed mortified. He still blamed himself for leaving her alone.

"He couldn't have prevented it," said Marella quickly. "It happened while I was time traveling."

Brielle ran for the bathroom, rifled through the cabinets, and returned with a bottle of antiseptic. "There aren't any bandages."

Mom squirted antiseptic on her arm. The sting made her jerk, but Mom held her wrist tightly until she was done. "You're not leaving the tree house until this heals."

"We don't know that staying here will keep her safe," said Brielle. "Maybe she stops breathing here."

Mom threw her hands up in the air. "How are we supposed to know? How did you get cut, anyway?"

Marella looked away. The image of her dead father was too clear. The sound of her five-year-old voice calling for her daddy. "It's not important."

"Oh no. Don't be like that. You have to tell me everything. Who cut you?" Mom looked like she could shatter with a single word.

"Nobody. I tripped and fell."

"When?" asked Brielle. "Did you go to the future again?"

Marella kept her mouth shut. She'd made her own father die. If Mom and Brielle knew, it would tear them apart. Nobody would ever know but her.

She changed the subject quickly. "We talked with Belinda. She couldn't tell us anything about the lethal fog or Project Athena."

"She didn't believe Marella time traveled," added Noah. "She thinks we're delusional. I was hoping another Marella would appear out of nowhere and prove her wrong, but no such luck."

"She wants me to come back," said Marella. "She offered Noah a job too."

"She thinks you're crazy and she offered you jobs?" said Mom. "What's up with that?"

"She said a lot of people have PTSD. And I solved a problem for her when I was there."

"It was bad enough we accepted the food from her," said Mom. "You can't work for the company that almost killed us all."

* * * *

AN HOUR LATER, BRIELLE and Mom had gotten the TV to work, and it was on Channel 7, which touted its 24/7 news coverage of the recovery from the Aguageddon. Marella didn't suggest changing the channel. While she didn't want to see the reporter she'd encountered earlier, she didn't want to explain why, and they needed to know what was going on locally and around the world.

The reporter—thankfully not the one Marella had talked to—assured them that lake and ocean levels were normal; tide schedules were almost the same as pre-Aguageddon. It was too early to know the extent of fish and sea creature mortality from stranding or from the increase in water salinity and temperature, but estimates ranged from 50 to 80 percent. Land animal death estimates were also varied, from 20 to 70 percent, depending on the animal and the region. Crops, too, had suffered a variety of damage; how much depended on the crop and when it was planted and harvested. Much of the corn and soybean crops, which would have been harvested in the fall, were expected to fail.

In various places throughout the world, as well as in the United States, there were demonstrations, riots, and coups. While some governments were stable after doing their best to save their citizens, handing out bottled water and following disaster protocols, other governments hadn't done so well. They'd hoarded supplies and water for government officials, and fought those who tried to get them, killing their own citizens.

In western Washington State, an estimated 70 percent of the population—including public officials—had died or gone missing. Any government-supported recovery was predicted to be slow. Funding for rebuilding was already obstructed by red tape, and price gouging was rampant.

In mountainous regions around the world, the lowered atmosphere had killed hundreds of thousands before the water returned and pushed the atmosphere back up again. The death count was still rising. Drone flights showed bodies scattered like crash test dummies on mountainsides.

Marella had known it would be bad, but the sight was too distressing; she stood and turned away.

"If only we'd gotten to the island faster," said Noah despondently.

"A lot more would have died if not for you," said Brielle.

"I didn't thank you for saving our lives before because I didn't believe you," said Mom. "I'll do that now. Thank you."

There were hugs all around. Marella was pleased to see her mom kissing Noah's forehead as she would her own child.

"Hey, it's HemisNorth," blurted Brielle.

The TV showed a drone shot of the local manufacturing facility Marella and Noah had just visited. From overhead it resembled a massive tube-and-tunnel playground structure, without the bright colors. The drone rose, showing more and more of the property.

"That's the Grays Harbor plant?" asked Mom. "It's even bigger than I thought."

The reporter Marella had talked to earlier appeared on the screen, gazing into the camera with the slight smile of a man with good news to share. She cringed inwardly. It wasn't her fault she'd time traveled at just the wrong moment. Still, she wished she hadn't embarrassed herself and blown her chance to get more information.

The reporter's voice held a certain urgency. "With extensive plans to rebuild after the devastating Western Inferno, HemisNorth is putting its workforce to immediate use." The video transitioned to workers in light blue HemisNorth polo shirts clearing burned land and tossing charred wood and old bricks into pickup trucks.

One of the workers turned to the camera and punched the air in a fist bump, as if with an imaginary friend. "To fix the future, fix the now!"

"Is that a thing?" asked Brielle, copying the gesture.

Marella felt a chill run up her spine. The gesture wasn't quite a Nazi salute. Still, it didn't sit right.

The reporter went on. "Yet not everybody has faith in the future. We encountered a former HemisNorth employee with a damaging accusation about the explosion that occurred this past July at the Seattle headquarters."

Marella's face came on the screen. She was catching her breath, having just run up to the newscasters.

Brielle grabbed her arm. "Hey, that's you!"

She felt disoriented, like encountering another Marella. But it was just a recording. "I didn't know they were filming me." If she'd paid more attention she might have realized that the shoulder-mounted camera was rolling, but somehow she'd missed that. She leaned forward, annoyed that they had been so underhanded, but hopeful that they would get her message out after all.

"The machine is dangerous," said Marella on TV. "It's the machine that caused the explosion at the HemisNorth research building in Seattle."

"Hey!" Noah looked both surprised and hurt, as if he'd been slapped. Shame filled her. Of course she should have discussed this with him first. They were a team. What had she been thinking?

"I'm staying in a tree house," said Marella on TV. Suddenly the cut appeared on her arm and she was shaking and grunting, hair wild, eyes too big, purple booklet in hand.

In the tree house, Marella shifted uncomfortably, face hot with embarrassment. On TV she looked as if she were on drugs. She shouldn't have talked to them after all.

The video cut to her recovery, the reporter assuring her, "I won't let you fall." Acting the hero.

On TV, her words were growly. "I time traveled. I went back to the past."

"Oh shit," she said. "I don't remember saying that."

"What the hell?" Noah's accusatory tone showed how badly she had broken his trust.

"What's that in your hand?" asked Brielle.

Marella didn't reply. Her mother answered instead. "Your father's purple book. I thought it was lost." Was that dread in her voice? Did she know Marella had time traveled to the forest? She would probe Marella further. She would figure it out.

Now Belinda appeared on TV, her name ticker-taping at the bottom of the screen. The CEO's face seemed rosy with excited possibility. The reporter Marella had spoken to was with her.

"That's Belinda Waverly?" asked Mom. "I pictured her differently."

"Older?" suggested Brielle. "Uglier?"

Mom waggled a finger for her to stop, which made her frown.

"HemisNorth is taking the lead in rebuilding the Northwest," said Belinda, who looked even more like Katharine Hepburn on TV than in person; she could have just finished filming *The African Queen*. "We're not just going to do the same old thing. We're going to upgrade our communities: healthy homes, enhanced businesses, efficient food production, superior water storage. This is our opportunity to improve on what we had. Let's use the rebuild as a springboard to advancement, to not only build new buildings, but also create a new way of living."

"One of your employees mentioned a dangerous machine," said the reporter. "She said it caused the deadly explosion that killed two of your staff."

Marella held her breath. Belinda's lips parted. Her surprise only showed for a second, but it was painful to see. She had betrayed a woman who'd showed only kindness to her.

Belinda's tolerant expression was that of a parent learning that her child has just raided the cookie jar. "Everybody went through intense hardship during the Aguageddon, and some people are struggling mentally. They need help. I'm frankly appalled at the ineptitude of the government in the wake of this disaster. It's time for the private sector to take charge."

"Meaning you."

She laughed, brushing the interpretation off with a succinct gesture. "Meaning all of us. We need to rebuild and advance together. There's a place for everybody in the rebuilding. Including disaster-affected people."

She was talking about Marella. She could have crucified Marella for what she'd said; instead she showed compassion and forgiveness. Marella could only hope that Noah and her family would forgive her for this as well.

Belinda's voice pealed with happiness. "We're not just rebuilding. We're advancing, making New Washington better, stronger, safer, happier. You, your children, and your children's children will live in a world that you never thought possible. This is our vision for every city and every town in New Washington and beyond! It's time to upgrade the world! We'll come out of the darkness and into the light. To fix the future, fix the now!" She pumped her fist outward.

There was that odd saying again, along with plans to upgrade the world. In anybody else's mouth, it would seem authoritarian, but Marella knew Belinda's character better than that.

"You're saying no to the status quo." The reporter chuckled. "Very ambitious! Do you really think it's possible?"

"No," said Belinda, pausing dramatically. "Not unless we get past the red tape, supply chain issues, funding, and above all, lack of will."

The announcer was wrapping up; Marella turned the TV off.

Noah burst out angrily. "Why didn't you tell us?"

She hated seeing this side of him—hard and unyielding, as if she'd made things go wrong on purpose. She got after herself enough as it was; she didn't need him to add to the pressure. "I thought they brushed me off. They said they were in a hurry. And then I time traveled, and it was just too much—"

Noah interrupted. Cold. Unforgiving. "We agreed not to say anything yet, and then you did."

"I didn't mean to, it just came out. I was disoriented."

"And then you didn't tell us about it. That was selfish. We're all dealing with this together and you decide that—"

"I'm sorry," she shouted. "I watched my own father die, and I didn't want to talk to anybody about it. Is that all right with you?"

Mom made a soft noise, something between pain and grief.

Noah pulled his head back in surprise. His bluster seemed to drain away.

Brielle reached out for Marella's arm, but didn't touch it, perhaps to keep them both from dissolving into tears. Her voice was small, breathy. "You saw Dad die? Oh, Mar-Mar. That blows. It really blows."

Marella took several breaths to calm herself. She hadn't meant to explode, but at least they weren't firing questions at her now. She could figure out how to give them the basics of what had happened without letting it slip that she'd caused it. "While I was time traveling I tried to write Mom a note. I put it in Dad's pocket. It didn't work, so I took it back out to write some more. I'll get it." She headed for the cupboard where she'd stashed the booklet upon arriving home.

"I don't want it. I couldn't bear to see it now." Mom sounded despondent.

Marella left it in the cupboard. She didn't want to see her father's words either. His memories, his thoughts. Each one would be the jab of a hot poker, emphasizing what she'd destroyed.

More than ever, she wanted to be done with time travel. No torture she could conceive of matched what she endured during each journey. Even now she could feel the lingering bits of cold, like ice maggots infesting her extremities, tangible enough that she stroked her hands to make sure nothing bulged beneath the surface.

The physical pain was bad enough, but what was worse, she now realized that during each trip her mind was demolished and then reassembled, and not quite the same as before. She recovered and was seemingly whole, but some small essence remained missing. She couldn't have said what was gone, but the loss seemed to be more than just the workings of her brain. It felt like parts of her soul lingered in the far reaches of eternity.

Eternity. It had taken on a new meaning. It was no longer a random word. It was a hollowing of the self. The emptiness of knowing there had been something but now there was nothing.

Endless nausea and pain, without the body to feel it. A barren nonbeing, falling forever.

If offered the choice between hell and time travel, she would surely choose hell.

And if she went back in time again, should she attempt to change history or refrain from making it worse? What would she choose? She had to understand how this worked. She had to understand time, or risk ruining it permanently.

Chapter Ten

O n the living room couch in the tree house, Marella wrapped her arms around her knees. She had just watched herself on TV and then admitted she saw her father die. Her throat was tight. She couldn't stop thinking about the pain of time travel.

"It's okay, sweetie, it'll all be okay." Mom put her arm around her.

How ridiculous. It was as if Mom uttered banalities while watching a tsunami rush toward them. Marella shrugged her off and leapt off the couch, speaking emphatically. "It won't be okay. You don't understand how bad it is. You depend on one minute following another and the next minute following that. And then you're in this in-between place where it's eternity and you have no control and you don't know who you are. And then you're somewhere else completely. The pain is excruciating."

"I'm sorry." Her mother's mouth pressed together—angry or disheartened, Marella wasn't sure.

"She's just letting off steam," said Brielle, playing the peacemaker, which made Marella even more frustrated.

"What you're going through is terrible, Marella," said Noah. His tone was level, as if trying to talk her off a ledge. At this moment, she would prefer to jump than hear him placate her. But there was no ledge, no direction to leap. She envied his composure when she felt so close to the deep end, then noticed he was rubbing his thumb and fingers together, as if counting out very tiny dollar bills. His nerves were frayed too.

She pinched the top of her nose between her fingers; she needed to calm down. Taking it out on others would solve nothing. Of course they didn't understand what she was going through, but they were just trying to help. "Look, just... help me figure out why it happens. Then at least I won't be so blindsided."

"How do we do that?" implored Brielle.

"Identify the trigger." Noah leaned forward, a detective on the case. "What are you usually doing when it happens?"

Marella grunted. It was a logical question that she'd already asked herself. "Just talking to people. You all. The reporter."

"Maybe stress has something to do with it," said Mom. "Let's do something to distract you. Everybody sit at the kitchen table."

She spoke so authoritatively that they obeyed, but Noah and Brielle looked unconvinced. "I don't know..." began Marella.

"Sometimes the best way to find an answer to a problem is to let your subconscious do the work." Mom took a box off a shelf and set it on the table in front of Marella with an air of satisfaction. "A game will take your mind off things."

Chutes and Ladders. Marella had played it many times. If you landed on a ladder, you went up, and if you landed on a chute, you went back.

"That's like time traveling," hissed Brielle, as if Mom should know better.

"Okay, okay." Flustered, Mom exchanged it for a jigsaw puzzle. A peaceful scene with people enjoying the sunshine on the grassy shore of a small lake. "*A Sunday on La Grande Jatte*. An entire painting made up of little dots. It must have taken this guy..." Mom checked the box lid. "Georges Seurat. It must have taken him forever to paint them all."

She dumped the puzzle pieces onto the table with a soft clatter. Marella contemplated the picture on the box. The separate dots created the illusion of a scene. Little separate bits of color that—on closer inspection—were completely unrelated to one another.

What if time were the same, merely an illusion made up of bits of moments that seemed to go together, but on closer inspection had nothing to do with one another?

"I always thought time was like a river," said Marella. "That it kept flowing and you couldn't go back. You know. A straight, unbroken line. But it can't be. So then what *is* the shape of time?"

Brielle spewed out ideas, outdoing herself, a contestant on a game show. "Circle. Square. Triangle. Hexagon. No wait, those are flat. Cube. Pyramid. Dodecahedron."

Noah pulled his lips to the side. Brielle bristled at his apparent skepticism. "What? You have a better idea?"

He held his hands up as if to counter that he hadn't said anything. She huffed and pointedly arranged some puzzle pieces in a circle.

Mom started picking out the edge pieces. "I can't picture time as a shape. It's too big. It goes on forever."

Noah pointed at Mom as if she were onto something. "How about just a part of it then? What's the shape of a moment?"

"If time were a river, a moment would be a drop," said Brielle proudly, as if she'd found the answer.

"But time isn't a river," said Marella.

"Well then, I heard that the universe could be a doughnut shape." Brielle snapped two puzzle pieces together. "Or a loaf of raisin bread that keeps expanding, with the planets being the raisins. Maybe time is shaped like one of those."

"I'm not sure we're coming at this from the right angle." Noah leaned his elbows on the table, the picture of earnestness. "If Project Athena is making you time travel, then we need to know how its machine works. You said it had a quantum computer, right? So understanding quantum physics would help."

Marella stopped herself from throwing up her hands in dismay. She was no dummy, but that was a big ask. Brielle grunted sarcastically, but Mom was the one who put it into words. "Oh, is that all we need to do? Learn quantum physics? I'll just get out my slide whistle and make some calculations."

"You mean slide rule." Noah sounded annoyed at being shot down.

"What's a slide rule?" asked Brielle.

"I said slide whistle and I meant slide whistle." Mom crossed her arms, obviously irritated that nobody had gotten her joke. "Anyway, enough time-travel stuff. We're trying to get Marella to de-stress."

It's not working. This disagreement wasn't helping, either. Maybe Mom was right, and she should think about other things. Marella picked up a green puzzle piece. Hard to say exactly where it belonged when it had nothing to discern it from so many other green pieces.

Its dots began to swirl in front of her eyes. She gazed at the bookshelf instead, with its white books on the bottom shelf, greens on the next, then blues, oranges, reds, purples, and blacks. All those colors turned to dots. She felt nauseous but couldn't seem to look away. The dots faded to mouse-gray, formed a vortex, and swirled off.

It was too soon for time travel! But it was happening anyway. She tried to alert her family, but it was too late. Her extremities begin to stretch, as if they were being pulled away from her. She smelled ammonia, then every particle of her was extending outward, toward eternity.

Endless cold. Endless agony. Endless terror.

• • • •

MARELLA'S PARTICLES began to coalesce, like raindrops merging on a window. She saw yellow-and-black patterns, then fuzzy shapes passing her. What were they?

They came into focus. She was inside, along with a few dozen other people, near a set of glass entry doors. She almost recognized the place. Manila-colored floor. Blue plastic chairs. She stood shakily next to a blue railing at the bottom of a wide flight of stairs.

So familiar, yet her connection to the place was still out of reach. Pieces of understanding were missing, like puzzle pieces. Puzzle pieces—they were filled with dots, weren't they? They had grass, parasols, sailboats.

It made no sense. Maybe it never would. Maybe this was life. Not understanding. Not connecting. Floating, falling.

Yet, after a time, she understood. She was in the main entry of Bothell High School, north of Seattle. She'd attended it for several months when she was seventeen, in 2021. That part of her life was done and gone, but now she was back, and so she must have time traveled here. She rubbed her arms. She was so cold.

A flat-faced woman in a yellow sweater was gazing at Marella. Not a student. A teacher? She didn't know her. "Are you all right?" asked the woman.

Marella nodded jerkily and forced a strained smile. A student pulled the woman away. He wouldn't have acted like that with a teacher, so was she a parent?

There were other students, and plenty of adults. That meant it wasn't a regular school day. Plus it was dark outside. Parents' Night maybe?

She weighed her choices. Try to change history or not. She didn't have to take any action. Once mobile, she could find a quiet spot away from everybody to ride this trip out without having any effect at all. But if she did nothing, that meant she was enduring hell for no reason. She would remain a helpless pawn, suffering the whims of whoever or whatever had brought her here.

She remembered something Elizabeth once told her. That looking back on her life, her regrets usually involved not doing something. Not learning that skill. Not getting to know that person. Not joining that group. Not taking that opportunity to change the world for the better.

Marella herself had to change the world for the better. Otherwise there was no point to what she had suffered. No point to her life.

There was one important thing to keep in mind. The camping trip had gone horribly wrong, but that didn't mean she would always fail. She didn't used to believe everything was predetermined, and she didn't have nearly enough evidence to prove it now. In fact, if you looked at the evidence, she could move mountains! Hadn't she stopped the Aguageddon in its tracks? Hadn't she crossed the empty seabed, overcoming obstacle after obstacle?

Of course she could succeed. She'd already done the impossible. She merely had to keep doing it.

She felt the urge to shout, "Stop the Aguageddon from happening! HemisNorth will be to blame!" But that would only make her sound crazy. Nobody would act on her warning.

Instead, she could find her younger self, who had to be here because Marella had that telltale feeling of compression. She would tell her about the impending disaster and instruct her to stop it somehow before a billion people died. Mom and Brielle would be here. She could warn them too. When they saw the two Marellas together, they might believe what she had to tell them.

That was her decision then. Find her family. At Parents' Night they would usually attend Marella's classes, going from room to room on a shortened schedule. Each teacher would describe what the students had been learning and show samples of the students' work to the parents.

What classes had she taken at what times, in which rooms? She'd attended so many different schools it was hard to remember, but after concentrating a bit, she recalled that at Bothell High most of her classes had been upstairs. That was where she needed to go.

Grasping the stair railing as if on a rolling ship, she took a step. Then another. She was stiff but functional, and full of hope. She would have to speak to her family quickly, before the time travel ended and she disappeared. *There's a company called HemisNorth*, she would say. *They're going to build Project Athena, also called the climate machine. It made me time travel. That's why there are two of me. You have to stop them from building it. It's evil.*

She kept going upward. She was still weak, yet her blossoming hope filled her with energy. She was going to change history with this one simple task. There would be no Aguageddon. The new normal wouldn't come to pass. The old normal would return.

Which would mean she would never have killed Elizabeth. She and Noah wouldn't have killed Olivia and Preston. She wouldn't travel back in time and scare her father into falling off a cliff, so he would be alive! To erase those all from her conscience... to be light and lifted once more. That would truly be a miracle.

She passed an art class display in a glass wall case. Charcoal pencil drawings of curtains, an egg carton, a vase of daisies, a toddler's smiling face, and more representations of the normal life she sought. In just a few minutes, the whole tragedy could be reversed. Her ankle wouldn't ache. Her head would be clear, her conscience clean, the dead brought back to life!

At the top of the stairs, she stopped abruptly. Why was nobody here? The hallway should have been packed. She shuffled forward anyway, reaching the first room. There was nobody inside.

Her body felt heavy when she realized her mistake. It wasn't Parents' Night after all. It was some other event. A play. A band performance. A sporting event. Nobody was upstairs because they were in the gym or cafeteria.

Fine, then. She could still do this. As she lumbered back down the stairs, she silently rehearsed her words. *I'm from the future. Eshana Collins and Len Janderson of HemisNorth will invent Project Athena. Make sure they don't build the dangerous machine that will accidentally take massive amounts of water away from the Earth.*

A chill spread throughout her body. She smelled ammonia. She had two thoughts before her mind went fuzzy and terror took over.

The first was that she'd accomplished nothing. The second was that time traveling was going to drive her insane.

Chapter Eleven

Specks of nothing sailed throughout a void for eons, then collided with one another, one by one, until they formed a being.

That being was a woman. Marella. Gradually, she emerged from the darkness, finding herself in a place she recognized—the tree house—with people she knew. Noah, Mom, Brielle.

They brought her a blanket. After a while, she recovered from time traveling and was able to move and speak. She pulled the blanket tighter around herself, shivering. It eased the chill in her body, but not in her being. Was she doomed to time travel the rest of her life, however short that might be? Right now it was late morning of what she thought of as the present: August 29, 2023. In five minutes it might be years earlier or years later.

Brielle frowned with her lips pressed forward, as if wondering what to do with her wild-ass time-jumping sister. "Past or future?"

"Past," said Marella.

Noah rubbed her arms through the blanket, teasing her lovingly, though she could hear the worry in his voice. "What did Napoleon have to say? You don't know? Well, then maybe it's time to learn French?"

Mom swooshed puzzle pieces out of the way and set down a mug of peppermint tea. The smell of it mixed with the taste of warm iron and wet mold in Marella's mouth.

Haltingly, she described time traveling to the school. During her description, Noah nodded encouragement, concentrating hard as if memorizing her words. When she finished, he looked at the middle distance, still concentrating, a scientist working out a theory. "I wonder why you went to that particular place at that particular time. It's got to be important in some way."

"How can you be so sure?" asked Mom.

He spoke with deep sincerity. "Because everything happens for a reason. God puts us on this Earth and gives us clues to what our path should be. Your visits to the past have to be meaningful. Otherwise, why would you be sent there? Besides, we have to assume that they're clues or we have nothing to go on. So what's the connection?"

"He's right," announced Brielle enthusiastically. "So then, what was important about those trips and what do they mean?"

Marella appreciated their attempt to help, but while it was true that her father's death was a critical event in her life, the other trips seemed insignificant. "There's nothing unusual about the school or the café. I just randomly went there."

"Random doesn't cut it," Noah straightened up, making a pronouncement. "We need to figure out how to get you to time travel to a specific time and place."

Brielle shouted in excitement. "Yes! You could stop the Aguageddon from happening!"

They didn't understand how dangerous it was. When she tried to time travel, she'd almost gone back to the island. So much smoke, so much fire. Her lungs hurt to remember. Her skin felt hot. She shoved the blanket away as if it were on fire.

"No way," said Mom. "It's already bad enough that she's time traveling, don't make her do more of it."

Ignoring her, Brielle scooted close to Marella. "It must have been really hard to see Dad die, but think about it. You could go back and save him from dying."

Marella turned away from her. *By trying to save him, I killed him. I killed Dad. Arms raised, that cry. Slipping out of sight. Splayed arms and legs. Twisted neck.*

Marella put her face in her hands. *An island on fire. Running. Things falling, crashing all around.*

"Brielle, don't." Mom clipped her words. "You're upsetting her."

"Mom," she fired back, "she could save all those people who died. A billion people!"

"I can't save anybody," burst out Marella. "I can't control where I go or how long I'm there for."

Brielle matched her volume, coaxing her. "Just be ready then. Plan it out before you go to the past. If you end up at HemisNorth, you track down your boss and tell her what's going to happen. If you end up at home, you warn me. I'll believe you. You know you could always convince me of stuff."

"Brielle, she saw your father die," cried Mom. "Isn't that enough for one day?"

"Let's all take a breath," said Noah, loudly but levelly, the solid lighthouse in the churning sea.

Brielle shot Noah a look that said *I'll calm down because I want to, not because you told me to.*

Mom reached out and felt Marella's forehead, like when she was a child with a fever. It was a simple gesture that said everything: she just wanted Marella to get better. But time travel wasn't a virus that could be eased with chicken soup.

Suddenly she wanted badly to confess and beg forgiveness for their father's death. Gain some kind of absolution. But what if they didn't forgive her? What if they couldn't get past Marella's stupidity? She imagined her mother's anguished face, asking, "How could you have done that?" And Brielle's heartache. She had never known her father, since she was just a baby when he died. It had left a hole that she had always mourned.

She had confessed to Noah about the mercy killing of Elizabeth, and he hadn't taken it well. No, she had to keep her culpability a secret. She let out a groan of sorrow.

"We're done here." Mom motioned for Noah and Brielle to go away.

Noah leaned forward. His tone was the epitome of reason, but there was emotion underneath. Desperation, perhaps. "She could save a billion lives."

His insistence tore her apart. She wanted to save lives, of course she did! But he and Brielle were much too eager to send her off on a journey that was doomed to end in failure, with Marella engulfed by an inferno.

"I tried." She spoke harshly, even though she didn't want to. They needed to know she meant it. "Trying to time travel doesn't work."

He pressed her fervently. "I know you better than that. You don't give up that easily."

"You can do it," said Brielle. "You're amazing. You traveled across the ocean floor and stopped Project Athena. Now all you have to do is go back in time and warn somebody."

Marella made a noise of dismay. *All you have to do is go back in time.* Simple! Like baking a cake. Changing a tire. Sipping water.

They believed in her now, but too much. She needed to explain why that was so difficult. She knew it in her bones, while they needed to know it in their heads.

She spoke quickly to get it over with and keep herself from triggering exactly what she needed to avoid. "I tried to send myself back to talk with Len and Eshana, but I couldn't stop thinking about Wisdom Island, when everything was about to explode around us." She tried to keep control, but her fear grew. She balled her fists to suppress it. "Noah, you remember how dangerous that was! All that smoke. That could be when I stop breathing."

Mom gasped, then all was quiet. Finally Brielle said meekly, "The Marella on the rug didn't smell like smoke."

"No more of that," said Mom, as if everybody should know better. *No more putting fingers in electric sockets.* "It's too dangerous. We'll find a way to stop it. Maybe there's a medication or something."

"Great." Brielle rolled her eyes. "Let's give her some ibuprofen. That'll fix everything."

"That's enough," said Mom sharply.

Noah kneeled before Marella's chair and folded her hands in his. The look on his face had such love that under other circumstances she might have suspected a marriage proposal.

"It didn't work because you did it alone," he said. "You're not alone now. We'll help you." His caring approach made her doubt waver. She didn't have to do this alone? How would that work? She imagined them riding a tandem bicycle along a poplar-lined country road, calendar pages fluttering past to indicate the easygoing passage of time. Ridiculous, but it eased her dread.

Mom started to speak, but Brielle cut her off. "How would we help her do it?"

"Talk her through it," said Noah. "Like a guided meditation."

Marella felt a flicker of disappointment. Guided meditation meant she would still be doing this alone. But she knew that.

Mom pulled Noah's hands away from Marella's. "Weren't you listening to her? She could die. You've only known her a short time. I'm her mother. My children are my world."

Noah stood, his voice hoarse with anguish. "I love her too. It's killing me, seeing this happen to her. Wouldn't it be better for her to be able to control it rather than just randomly show up somewhere she could be hurt? That's what's going to happen if we don't help her. She's going to stop breathing. Let's do something first."

Marella closed her eyes. Noah's words, so simply put, made the path seem clear.

Mom stabbed the air with her finger, as if she'd hit on the perfect answer. "All right then, instead of using guided meditation to control time travel, use it to stop it."

"Then what about the fog?" asked Brielle. "If Marella doesn't change the future, then everybody will die."

"We have to change the future without time travel," said Mom. "Find the source of the fog and stop it."

Her directive was pointless because Marella already knew Project Athena had caused the deadly fog. The transition into time travel felt too much like the presence of the fog to draw any other conclusion.

And what was more, Mom's insistence on changing their future without time travel brought home just how impossible that was. Attempting to time travel was the only real idea any of them had come up with.

Marella hung her head. By letting her fear get to her, she was being selfish. Trading her own security for the lives of the billion people who had recently died, along with the eventual death of many more from the lethal fog.

She shook out her arms like Mom had taught her, imagining her overwrought emotions spilling out of her fingertips. Get out, anguish. Goodbye, fear. Be gone, anger.

Now she was ready to continue. Almost levelheaded. "Project Athena and the fog are linked," she said. "The only way I can think of to stop the fog is to go back in time and keep Project Athena from happening."

"How can you be so sure?" asked Mom. "The fog could have nothing to do with the time travel."

"We've been through this." Marella rubbed her temples. Arguing was making her head feel worse. "When I went to the future, Brielle told me they're connected."

"Because somewhere along the line you told her that," said Mom. "But you could have been wrong."

"Time travel and having the lethal fog nearby feel the same."

"A feeling isn't good enough!"

"Why not?" asked Marella. "You said you sensed the consciousness of the tree. Well, I'm sensing the fog."

"Are you saying the fog has a consciousness?" Mom blinked a few times as if she'd learned something startling.

"No. Maybe. I don't know. But you're always asking me to trust that you feel something outside yourself, and now you won't trust me when I feel something outside myself."

Mom walked away. Marella thought she might start pacing, but instead she stopped by the bookcase, lost in thought.

Finally she turned. "Do what you think is best." Not a weary capitulation, but a command. She shook her finger at Noah. "No pterodactyls."

Brielle and Noah let out surprised chuckles.

Mom huffed. She'd meant what she said! That made Marella laugh, a little out of control. *Enough.* First she needed to stop cry-laughing. Then she needed to fix the world. Yet again. "Let's get this over with."

Noah rubbed his hands together in anticipation. "You need to be comfortable. Go sit on the couch."

She did so. Her shoulders tensed. There would be pain. Agony. She shook out her arms again, then let them go slack. *I have to make it work this time.*

"Good," he said. "We need to send you to where you can make the most change."

"She had the right idea," said Brielle. "Stop Len and Eshana. The evil masterminds."

"Okay," said Marella. "This time I'll try for my first day. I saw them in a conference room."

"Let's shoot for that. Close your eyes. Good. Take deep breaths. In... out... in... out." His voice was deep and soothing. She imagined it as a current, carrying her along.

"You're in the conference room. Imagine the setting... the decorations on the walls... the furniture."

Marella pictured the padded chairs, the long table, and the conferencing telephone that looked like a small UFO. An abstract print on the wall was reminiscent of foothills and mountains, with many paths leading through.

"Len and Eshana are right there in front of you. You see their faces. Their clothes."

Brielle's suggestion that they were evil masterminds colored her imagination, giving them white lab coats and twitchy fingers, when in reality Len had worn button-down shirts and bow ties, and Eshana had liked sheath dresses. Both had been in their thirties. Len was Nordic, tall, with white-blond hair and a mole like a cake crumb near his eye. Eshana was of East Indian descent, and her earrings that day had resembled double helixes. *Could they be the shape of time? Wait, no, focus.*

"Think about what they're doing and what they're saying," said Noah.

They'd been huddled over a laptop. They seemed so happy to see her. *What a great place to work*, Marella had thought, giving a finger-flutter wave. *The people are so nice, even to new employees.*

Eshana had shaken her hand. "You must be Marella. It's so good to meet you."

Len hadn't waited for Marella's right hand to be free. He shook her left, beaming. "You'll like working with Elizabeth. She might seem brusque at first, but she's a true human being. Don't tell her I said that."

She'd heard that Len and Eshana were geniuses, and she had thought that she would feel diminished in their presence. Instead, they made her feel valuable.

"You have something important to tell them," said Noah.

Marella imagined giving them the bad news. *Your life's work is a deadly failure.* She pictured a ridiculously melodramatic reaction, with Eshana raising her fists to the sky, shouting, "Instead of saving humanity, I've doomed it to oblivion!" and with Len dropping to his knees, muttering, "Never more will we go forth into the light of day, for I have unleashed hell and it has leashed me."

She felt a wave of sympathy for the dead scientists. Project Athena had been their baby. They hadn't known what horror their brilliance would create, that their invention was so flawed. That it would come to nothing in the end. That both the prototype and the machine on the island would explode spectacularly.

She tried to fend off memories of the island, but they prevailed, in striking detail. Project Athena's workings: a ten-foot-wide copper cylinder with dozens of thin pipes and transparent wires, like a giant mechanical jellyfish. The control panel with a keyboard, monitor, and camera lens, where she and Noah had worked to turn the machine off. The piercing noise just before the machine's demise. Each of its enormous modules about to burst, one after another. They'd fought with Preston and Olivia, the cult leader and his follower, who were trying to murder them. They'd shot at them with a flare gun, sparking fires in the crisp dried ferns. They'd killed Preston and Olivia. Now they were running for their lives amid flames and smoke.

Marella felt herself sliding from the tree house, toward Wisdom Island, like grain down a chute.

She snapped herself out of her trance and shot to her feet, breathing hard, stomping to anchor herself in the present.

"What happened?" asked Noah. "Why did you stop?"

Marella panted out an answer. "I was heading for Wisdom Island again. I couldn't help it. It was like my mind was drawn there. I need air."

She rushed outside to the deck. *Stay here in the present.* Stay on the solidly built deck, with the rain gauge in the shape of a chipmunk and the orange ceramic sun on the wall. She clutched the warm wood of the railing and felt the solid deck under her feet.

She felt a prickling on her skin, like needles probing for the right access points. She smelled ammonia. Her first thought was that she was about to time travel, but then she felt the presence of something powerful. Something with great, devouring need. Her skin began to itch.

The lethal fog. It was here somewhere.

Looking around frantically, she spotted it fifty feet away. A lustrous white cloud flowing along the ground, sparkling with purple-and-indigo opalescence. It traveled steadily toward the tree house. Luminous. Oily. Deadly.

Bile rose in her throat, and she swallowed it back down. It felt like the fog was looking for her.

Chapter Twelve

The deadly fog roiled on the ground like purple-and-indigo oil spilled into white water, slowly but relentlessly approaching the tree house. It was higher this time, just a couple of feet below the deck. Marella imagined it breaking like an ocean wave, splashing upward onto her body, burning her skin.

She jerked away from the railing. Breathing hard, she wheeled around and rushed inside, pulled the door shut, and—pointlessly, she knew—locked the dead bolt. "The fog! It's almost as high as the tree house."

Mom barked like a drill sergeant. "Everybody upstairs." Her hands were shaking as she nudged Marella along.

Brielle was first to reach the loft, where she cranked her arm in a circle, urging the others to hurry. Noah followed Marella and Mom, saying, "God, save and protect this family."

"Universe, keep the damn fog away from us," added Mom meanly, as if the universe had been shirking its job.

"Fog, get your ass outta here," added Brielle.

Marella appreciated the prayers, as well as the direct appeal, and silently repeated all of them.

Mom ran to the window, brushed back the lace curtains, and looked downward, speaking quietly, as if to keep the fog from hearing. "It's so weird. So oily."

Noah and Brielle joined her. Marella remained by the bed. The fog didn't have eyes to see her with, yet she felt compelled to hide from it.

"I've never seen colors like that. It's like they're newly invented," said Noah in a trancelike voice.

"What do we do if it gets inside?" Brielle's voice sounded strained.

Marella pictured the fog seeping through the floorboards, tendrils of white and indigo, undulating like dancing cobras. "It won't," she said, as much to calm herself as to calm Brielle.

"But this is when you stop breathing! You could die for good!"

Marella thought of the other Marella, lifeless on the carpet. Was this the moment she'd been dreading?

"No," said Noah. "She's not wearing the green shirt. And also, she appears to us again here in the tree house. That means she lives."

He was right, but Marella couldn't discard her alarm so easily. What if she'd done something to the timeline and changed all that? Time was undependable, she now knew, perhaps even malicious.

"It's out from under us. It's moving away!" said Mom.

"It's going... going... gone." Noah leaned his head back and breathed audibly.

Mom wiped her brow and dropped onto the wingback chair in the corner of the loft. Brielle stayed at the window, keeping watch.

Noah and Marella embraced. It felt good, but didn't stem her feeling of doom. She was at the same impasse as before. She burrowed her head into his chest.

He must have sensed her mood; he pulled back, saying, "Speak to me."

Okay. Since you ask. "The end of the world is coming, and I have no idea how to save it."

Noah nodded like he'd known this was coming. He let her go and steepled his hands. The detective gathering facts. "We're going to get to the bottom of this. Let's recap. This is what we know: in your trip to the future, Brielle said that scientists determined the fog is electromagnetic radiation and it has a wavelength. We saw that it can get about twenty or thirty feet wide."

"In the future it's bigger," said Marella. "Blocks wide."

"So whatever is making the fog ramps up production in between now and then," he said. "What else about the fog?"

It wants something. Marella didn't tell them that. It wasn't a fact, but a feeling she wasn't quite sure of herself.

"All right, then," said Noah. "Let's move on to what is still going to happen in the future. We saw three extra Marellas all at once. You haven't taken any of those trips yet. So you have at least three time-travel trips ahead of you. The one where you're by the window, the one where you're in the loft, and the one where we resuscitate you."

"The Marella that appeared by the window was wearing this." Brielle tapped the gray blouse that Marella had on. "So she might take that trip soonest."

"Good observation," said Noah.

Marella looked down at her worn blouse. She would like to change clothes, but didn't have another shirt to wear.

Mom raised her hand. "The Marella in the loft knew something, but wouldn't tell you. And she didn't struggle to talk the way the others did. So something is different about her. You learn something along the way." She sounded encouraged by her own evaluation.

"And she said I was right about Project Athena," said Marella, "which means it's causing my time travel. I still think something happened when the machine zapped me on Wisdom Island."

Brielle waved her hands for attention. "The one we gave CPR to talked about heaven or hell, and she was wearing a green shirt."

"She might not have said heaven or hell," said Mom. "It could have been something else."

Brielle shrugged. "That's all I've got."

"What about the years of places you've time traveled to?" asked Noah. "What were they?"

"A coffee shop in 2002," said Marella. "A camping trip in 2009. A high school in 2021. The future in 2024, seven months from now. Someplace dark where somebody told me a phone number and I don't know the place or the year."

There was the bubble-popping sound of tires on gravel.

They all trooped downstairs. Marella and Brielle went to the door. An SUV with a delivery service logo had pulled up. A man with muttonchop sideburns jumped out and bounded up the tree house steps, holding a manilla envelope. "Marella Wells? Delivery for you."

"That's not food," observed Brielle disappointedly.

Marella signed for the envelope, brought it to the couch, and ripped it open. "It's a letter from Belinda Waverly."

"Read it out loud," demanded Brielle.

Marella complied. "'I wanted to remind you that we highly value your legacy knowledge of HemisNorth. With that in mind, we offer you a promotion to Materials Manager. You would supervise the procurement, movement, and storage of building materials and products.'"

She tried to sort out her emotions. The letter accorded her value, telling her she was indispensable, which stoked her confidence. However, merely reading it felt like a betrayal to the world, with its offer to get back in bed with HemisNorth and ignore the mayhem it had created.

What was more, the offer was a big stretch. She hadn't been trained for such a job and would be unlikely to perform it well. Was it a token job then, because Belinda felt that warmly toward her? The letter seemed to indicate she still did, even though Marella had mentioned Project Athena on TV. She hadn't divulged specifics, though, so perhaps there wasn't that much for Belinda to forgive after all.

She couldn't help thinking she was missing something. Some additional reason for Belinda to take a special interest in her. Perhaps she was concerned that Marella knew too much about Project Athena and wanted to keep her quiet by bringing her back into the fold. Still, Belinda's actions and attitude showed concern for Marella.

Regardless of all that, there was a reason for her to go back to work at HemisNorth, and that reason gave her new hope. She had been trying to get information about Project Athena secondhand, and here was her opportunity to go directly to the source.

"She wants to promote you after you talked HemisNorth down?" asked Mom. "That's strange."

"Maybe not that strange," said Marella. "You heard Belinda talk about disaster-affected people. She thinks I've got PTSD, and she wants to help me."

Mom looked unconvinced; so did Noah. Brielle, however, was bobbing her head in approval. It made Marella feel supported.

Holding the letter reverently now, as if it were a magic ticket, she continued reading. "'You are also welcome to bring Noah to be a paid employee, as well as to be on hand in case of complications with your illness.'"

Noah grunted as if that was ridiculous.

It was an unwelcome reminder that her time travel was dangerous. Nothing would be easy in her condition, plus Noah didn't seem to be on board.

Several remaining pages gave details of the offer and instructions on catching the employee bus.

Thumping the letter to emphasize her resolve, Marella announced, "I'm going to accept."

"Whoa." Brielle spoke with admiration. "Didn't see that coming."

Mom held up her palm, meaning *no*. "Listen, we can find another way to get money. There's no need to—"

"It's not that," interrupted Marella. "It's to find out more about Project Athena. I'll have access to HemisNorth computers and people."

Noah seemed disappointed to have to spell out the ramifications for her. "Think about what you're saying. You want to go back to work for the company that nearly ended the world. With the woman who is responsible—whether directly or not—for the death of a billion people. I know we accepted food from her, but that's taking it too far."

"It would be worth it if we got information to help save all those people who died in the Aguageddon." Marella brightened her voice, trying to imbue him with excitement she didn't quite feel. "We could save them, Noah!"

There was no enthusiasm in his response. He spoke levelly, still spelling things out as if she didn't see the big picture. "It's naive to think that Belinda would let you near any information about Project Athena. Besides, you accused HemisNorth of causing the Aguageddon. Once you return, you won't be able to blame the Aguageddon on HemisNorth. She knows that. That's the real reason she sent that letter."

Naive? She was anything but naive. He was the one who needed things spelled out. "The reason she wants me back is because I'm good. You saw how I helped her."

Noah tapped his knuckles absentmindedly on his leg, revealing his frustration. "She couldn't need you that badly. Didn't you say you were just an assistant?"

Mom bristled. "Just? Marella is not 'just' anything."

She touched her mother's arm. *Let me handle this.* She allowed her pride to show, along with her exasperation. "Assistants do a huge amount of necessary work that management wouldn't have a clue how to do. Without us, nothing would happen. Nothing."

Noah took in a deep breath and let it out slowly. It didn't calm him; in fact his tone ramped up. "That's true, but in her mind, you aren't key to making the company run. I know she cares about you—I saw how great she treats you—but playing spy isn't going to get you anywhere."

"Playing spy?" Marella leaned away, stiff as a plank. "Are you kidding me? Like I think this is a game? You don't think I'm capable, even though I saved the whole goddamn world from the Aguageddon? If I hadn't played spy then, you and your family would be dead right now. You'd be a dried-up husk of nothing and your parents would be dried-up husks of nothing and your friends would be dried-up husks of—"

"I get the point," he growled, "but there's got to be a better way."

They were silent a while, Noah crossing his arms, Marella rubbing her temples. Brielle took the letter and examined it. Mom got up and looked over her shoulder.

A better way. What better way? In a meeting she'd once heard Belinda say, "Don't bring me problems. Bring me solutions." She wished she, too, could make such a statement and then depart, confident that said pile of solutions would appear on her desk by eight o'clock sharp the following morning.

Marella tugged lightly at Noah's arms, indicating he should uncross them, that they didn't need to argue.

He complied, saying gently, "I'm not trying to insult you. I just don't want you to waste your time. You already tried to get information from HemisNorth, and it's a dead end."

"It's not a dead end. I have ideas of where to look..."

Marella smelled ammonia and felt a prickling, then a chill spread over her skin and into her bones. Noah and her family dissolved into a whirlpool, then all went dark. Eternity stretched her, pulling her apart, destroying her. The agony was unbearable.

She became nothing.

· · · ·

ETERNITY LET ONE PARTICLE loose from its maw, then another. Over eons, the particles coalesced, becoming something.

Becoming a person. Marella. That was her name, though it didn't yet describe her various pieces, which were still forming and rearranging.

With time, she had a body. Yes, Marella's body, but it was chilled, as if made of ice.

She had been time traveling, that much she understood. And so where would she find herself? The familiar past? The shocking future? She wouldn't know until her senses worked better.

"Oh my god," said a voice. Noah's voice.

"There's two of you." That was Brielle. The words gave her a sense of déjà vu. She blinked against the brightness. She could now see her sister, whose mouth hung open in surprise.

Her mother jumped up. "What's going on?" That also struck a familiar chord.

And now she saw another Marella, gaping at her with dismay.

She understood, just barely. She had time traveled backward to the moment when other Marellas began popping into the tree house out of nowhere. She felt compressed, as if there was room for only one Marella.

"I don't know how you kids did this," said Mom, "but it isn't funny."

Marella tried to speak, but her lips were too cold to form words. She held up her hands to indicate needing time, but her fingers scratched at the air like claws.

She looked helplessly at her other self, the Marella who was living in the tree house before the other Marellas arrived. Eyes wide, she seemed to expect wisdom, or at least an explanation.

"I'm dreaming," said Mom. "That's what's going on. I need to wake up." She slapped her cheeks.

"You're not dreaming," said Noah. "I see it too, but I don't know how."

Marella thrust her head forward, trying to thaw her lips so that she could speak. She had something to tell them, something important. If they could only find the answer to a certain question, then all would be revealed.

She tried again. Finally actual words came. "What... is... shape... of time?"

"Look!" Brielle pointed to the loft.

A third Marella was up there, hand on the railing, gazing at all of them, eyebrows knitted into a look of longing. Marella felt even more compressed. Three Marellas so far. Too many in the same room.

One of the Marellas called upward, her voice breaking, "What's going on?"

"I can only tell you one thing," said the Marella in the loft. "You're right about Project Athena."

Mom stomped in frustration. "One of you darn kids tell me how you did this."

"I didn't do anything," cried Brielle.

"This is not happening," said Noah, as if trying to convince himself.

She dreaded what was coming next. A fourth Marella. The one who wasn't breathing. She prayed that the timeline had changed, and that no such Marella would materialize after all. But she did, arriving abruptly, sprawled on the carpet as if fallen from a great height. Eyes open and unseeing. Mouth slack. A cut on her arm. Sea-green shirt.

Marella was desperate to influence the timeline. Do anything, say anything differently in the hope that one small change would bludgeon the rest of the timeline into submission. But time wouldn't let her. She smelled ammonia, felt a prickling, and became nauseous. The room swirled and went dark, and then came the biting cold of eternity.

Chapter Thirteen

S hortly after returning from her most recent time-travel episode, Marella huddled on the couch, swaddled in a blanket. *It's Tuesday*, she told herself. *Not yesterday. Today. I was just reading the letter from Belinda about coming back to work, as a manager this time.*

She wished she were merely insane, because there were therapies and medications to treat mental illness. But there were none for time travel. No support groups with advice on how to control it, or how to overcome the horrendous pain, cold, and fear.

She described the short time-travel event to the others. That she had been the second Marella, who mentioned the shape of time. It seemed likely that the topic of time's shape had indeed become its own feedback loop, with less relevance than they'd thought, but that wasn't certain.

Nothing had changed during the convergence of the four Marellas, which worried her. Was everything predetermined?

Now Noah was watching her anxiously. Their argument seemed trivial after she'd gone through the eternal pain of time travel. So what if he didn't understand her status in a corporate environment? He clearly loved and valued her.

Besides, the most important thing at this moment was learning about Project Athena. "Come with me to HemisNorth," said Marella.

"If I don't come up with a better idea. Just let me think for a few minutes." Noah spoke softly, sounding conciliatory. He was past the argument as well. He went to the window and gazed out, as if he might find the answer in the sky.

"Me too. Then we'll see whose idea is better." Brielle wandered toward the bookshelf, working her mouth like a toothless person while she mused.

Marella was grateful for their effort, and for Mom rubbing her hands, which were still chilled. It helped dispel the despair of time traveling.

After a few minutes, Brielle rushed back, holding up a thin, tattered paperback. "Look what I found!"

Mom read the cover. "*Time Travel on Fifty Dollars a Day—A Cheapskate's Guide to the Fifth Dimension.*"

Marella perked up. Could it be that one of the Marellas had traveled back from the future and left her the book? But then the title sunk in. It was humor, not a real time-travel guide. Still, it felt portentous.

"It's a joke book," said Mom. "Put it back."

"No!" Noah trotted over quickly. Mom gave him a look as if he was out of his mind. He explained, "Maybe it will describe some concepts."

Brielle sat on the other side of Marella and began reading. "Know before you go. Immerse yourself in research regarding your chosen point in history for a minimum of one month prior to departure. Be sure to include language study. Find a reputable teacher, preferably one who belongs to the Lost Language Instructional Society."

Mom rolled her eyes. "This is not helpful."

"Wait, this is better," said Brielle. "Time travel safety: an understanding of basic time concepts is essential for the intrepid traveler, who may suddenly become stranded in ancient Greece without access to a Time Gadget."

"Time Gadget," said Noah longingly. "We could use one of those."

"Marella is our time gadget." Brielle watched to see if Marella would laugh.

She chuckled, partly to appease her sister, and partly because she loved her so much at that moment. Trust her to find the humor in a situation.

Brielle continued. "*Presentism* is the theory that only this moment exists. Certain Time Gadget designs rely on this concept while others utilize the more traditional *eternalism*, in which things can exist in the past and future."

"Of course things exist in the past and the future," said Mom, annoyed.

"Maybe not," said Noah. "You can't remember the future, so you can't prove there is one. And just because you remember a past doesn't mean there was one. Memory is notoriously unreliable."

"Marella can remember the future," said Brielle.

"I guess you're right." Noah looked at her as if she was onto something, and she raised her chin pridefully.

I can remember the future. The idea of it, while nonsensical, had a jarring truth to it. She had visited the future, so she remembered it. That felt important, but in what way? How could it possibly help her solve her dilemma?

"This book would be funny if things didn't suck so bad." Brielle continued reading. "Do not attempt to transport plants or animals along with you during time travel. Quick-Portal time machines are synced to human vibrations. Gerbils have different vibes than you, and may arrive as a small but messy blob of protoplasmic splat. *Do not forget*: should you tinker with your Quick-Portal to transport an animal (not advised), remember to resync your time machine back to human vibes or you yourself will arrive as a large blob of protoplasmic splat."

"Vibes," said Mom. "Was that written in the sixties?"

Brielle checked the opening pages. "It's from 1972."

"I guess this doesn't help after all," said Noah. "We need a real source of information."

Brille lowered the book. "No internet, and the libraries and bookstores are closed. I never thought it would be like this."

HemisNorth. Unless somebody came up with something better, that was the only real source of information.

Brielle returned to the book. "There's only a little more. The rest is about the different time periods to go to." She continued reading. "The grandfather paradox is not really a paradox. The reality is that you cannot go back in time and kill your own grandfather because then you would never be born to kill him. However, be sure to set the event-change dampener on high so as to not accidentally kill somebody else's grandfather."

The memory of Marella's dead father was suddenly clear and strong. His eyes wide open and his chin high, neck twisted, blood on the ground. Her lungs seemed to shrink; she couldn't get air into them. She lurched to her feet, intending to go out to the yard, but then remembered the lethal fog. Instead she ran for the deck.

"What's wrong?" called Mom.

"I've got this." Noah followed Marella outside.

Clutching onto the railing, Marella took deep breaths. In the distance the sun glinted off the river, giving the gray water a gilt edge. The water detoured around a boat, creating angel wings on either side.

Noah embraced her. She sank into it, feeling his warmth and strength. Presentism. No past, no future. Only this moment forever and ever.

But in the best of all scenarios, this moment would never take place. "I guess it's just as well I can't go back in time and stop the Aguageddon from ever happening. That would make it so we'd never meet."

Noah squeezed her comfortingly. "Of course we would! We were meant to be together."

Marella couldn't help smiling at his burst of optimism. He really believed they were meant for each other, no matter what transpired in their chaotic lives. That their link to each other transcended everything.

When she time traveled, she felt as if she were being pulled apart. This was the opposite. In this moment with Noah, she was put together. Whole. At least for now.

"This is how it would all come down." He motioned for her to sit on a wicker chair, which she did. He then stepped away, gesturing like a tour guide as he outlined the scenario. "You'd be on a bench at Seattle Waterfront Park, say, near Pier 58, watching people get on and off the Ferris wheel. Are you with me so far?"

She pushed her palms forward as if moving a pile of poker chips. "One hundred percent."

Noah strode along the deck, whistling, as if he were a random passerby, unaware of Marella's presence. "A ridiculously handsome man walks by. He sees you." He did a melodramatic double take, making her chuckle. "He asks, 'Where do we know each other from?' He looks kind of familiar, but you can't place him. You say..." He gestured for her to fill in the blank.

"Um... the grocery store?"

"No, that's not it. How about the University of Washington. Would I have seen you there?"

"No. Did we meet at a high school football game?"

"I don't think that's it." Noah snapped his fingers. "I know where I've seen you."

"Where?"

"In my dreams, of course."

Marella laughed heartily. It was cheesy yet charming.

Noah became serious. "Look, we've been through a lot together. We'll get through this too. I'm not saying it won't be hard, but we'll do it."

His positivity gave her hope. She imagined standing hand in hand with him at the ribbon cutting for his wonder-of-the-world. "I believe you. Let's think about how we're going to do that."

They were quiet for a time. Marella focused her mind. She was good with work-arounds. Usually it helped to state the problem clearly so she could more easily work out a solution. Her problem was that she had to conquer time. No, that was too vague. Her problem was...

She felt nausea and wondered if she had eaten something bad, but then the smell of ammonia stung her sinuses, and her skin prickled, telling her she was about to time travel. Her vision narrowed to a tunnel, which shut like a camera iris. She tried to reach out for Noah but couldn't move; his body crumbled like sand. She was cold, so cold. And now her soul stretched outward. She was filling eternity, but eternity remained empty.

· · · ·

BITS OF THOUGHT FLOATED by, unreachable, until finally memories, words, and ideas began to coalesce into a limited sort of comprehension. She was a being. She was Marella. She had a body bounded by skin, which sensed a warm wind. That meant she was outside. She smelled smoke. What was burning? Was she in danger?

Her vision arrived as a blur, but soon she could see the line of a horizon. The light was dim. It could have been just after sunset, or just before sunrise.

She felt compressed, the way she had when other Marellas were nearby. That meant she was about to encounter herself again. Another Marella was here.

It grew lighter, so it was sunrise, but an odd one, hazy and red. She was standing next to a boulder. Just beyond it, she spotted another Marella, which was disconcerting even while expected. Her other self was maybe twenty feet away, curled up on the sand, sleeping with her head resting on her arm.

Noah lay nearby. And there was Elizabeth—her former boss—asleep and alive! This was during the middle of the Aguageddon, when they were traveling along the emptying seabed to reach Project Athena and stop it from taking water away from the world.

When she had recovered enough from time travel, she could warn them about the rocks that would fall on Elizabeth and injure her. A rush of excitement immediately faded when she realized the consequences. They would attempt a different route, which would slow them down and keep them from getting to Wisdom Island in time to shut down Project Athena.

The sky brightened some more, showing steep terrain—mostly gray sand, with rock slabs scattered about like a deconstructed Stonehenge.

She could see Elizabeth better now. She looked older than her fifty-something years, and even thinner than she remembered. Dried blood caked her nostrils.

Marella lowered her head briefly. She knew now exactly when this was. Too late to warn of falling rocks, which had already injured Elizabeth. And to make matters worse, the other Marella was about to commit a horrific deed.

During the dangerous trip across the dry seabed, Elizabeth had described the childhood abandonment that made her fear dying alone. She'd extracted a promise from Marella to never let that happen. Later, they'd entered a forest of tightly packed natural towers and arches, where rocks fell on Elizabeth. Now she was dying. She had sunk into unconsciousness, and the end was near.

Exhausted from the trek across the sea floor, and hampered by the parching effects of Project Athena, Noah and Marella would be unable to drag her further on their makeshift sled. And they were running out of time. They had to get to Wisdom Island before the point of no return, when a runaway reaction would make Project Athena unstoppable. All the water would disappear from the Earth, forever.

Her other self had had a choice: break her promise to Elizabeth and let her die alone, or stay with her until she died. But staying would keep her and Noah from reaching the island. Their families would die, and so would they.

The time-traveling Marella remembered all too clearly that she had come up with a third choice. One she would never have considered without her vow to Elizabeth. A mercy killing.

She expected to see her earlier self awaken, but instead Noah sat up. Marella blinked with confusion. She was the one who'd woken up first. How could the past have changed?

It hadn't, she realized. Noah had woken up first and hadn't told her, but that made no sense on his part. It was urgent that they get to the island. Why had he not woken Marella so they could hurry onward?

Noah rose and leaned over Elizabeth, watching her intently. He must have seen the woman was still alive, still in a coma. His shoulders lowered. Was that relief? Disappointment?

He put both hands on Elizabeth's throat.

Marella's hand flew to her mouth. He was going to do the mercy killing. Not her!

She could stop him. She imagined showing herself to him, shocking him with her presence. He would stop what he was doing. But then he might not believe he'd seen two Marellas. He might think it was a dream, or a delusion of thirst. Then she would be the one to do the deed.

Was that what had already happened? Was this another inevitable loop of fate, where she would try to change the timeline but it was already set in stone? What should she do?

Her instinct was to stop him. But she must think any action through. Act, not react. Too much depended on her now.

Abruptly Noah removed his hands, surprising Marella once again. He lay back down. Soon he was breathing evenly again. In spite of what had just transpired, exhaustion had overcome him. They had been so drained Marella wasn't sure how they'd managed to go on.

Noah had been about to kill Elizabeth, but had changed his mind. She couldn't seem to process this new information yet. It was too surreal, too unexpected; plus she was anxious about what was coming next.

The other Marella stirred, sat up to look over at Elizabeth, and put her hand to her brow when she saw that she hadn't died during the night. She looked up to the sky. After glancing at Noah, she kneeled beside Elizabeth.

This was the stretch of her past that had changed Marella's view of herself, into a person of questionable morality. She tensed, ready to leap forward if she came up with a way to stop the other Marella without ruining the timeline.

The other Marella nudged the motionless woman, saying, "Elizabeth." When there was no response, she reached out. She was about to murder her.

No, not murder. A mercy killing. And yet it was hard to think of it as such, watching herself. On the inside, her heart had been racing; she had been filled with emotion. On the outside, she seemed calm. An assassin looming over her victim.

With one hand, the other Marella pinched Elizabeth's nostrils together; with the other, she covered her mouth.

She could almost feel Elizabeth's dry, cracked lips once more. She rubbed her hands to get rid of the sensation, then balled her fists, outraged at having to make a choice between her own well-being and the good of the world. She was losing her chance to wipe away her wickedness. Back then, she hadn't known how the guilt would seep into her. Become a part of her. Reveal her true self.

Marella stayed where she was, knowing that she couldn't risk changing the course of events. Elizabeth went into a weak seizure. The other Marella glanced at Noah, who was still asleep. The seizure continued. *Lie still,* she remembered thinking. *Please lie still.* And now the other Marella was shaking with anguish.

Why had she been brought here? Why was she watching Elizabeth convulsing under her own hands? Who or what had made this possible, and why had they chosen this moment in time? If it was to make her feel guilty, there had been no need. She already strained under the weight of her deed. And now, going through it again, it felt even heavier. The taste of warm iron and wet mold strengthened, threatening to make her gag. She suppressed it as best she could by swallowing hard.

Finally, Elizabeth lay motionless. The other Marella tore her hands from Elizabeth's face and backed away. She wiped her palms frenziedly with sand, stood and walked three steps, then back, then away again, holding her hands out as if they weren't part of her. Burying her mouth in the crook of her arm, she sobbed silently so as not to wake Noah.

Marella smelled ammonia. Her skin prickled, then felt bitter cold.

She was about to time travel again. She would have been grateful to leave this place once more, but the terror of approaching eternity overrode everything. The other Marella crumbled away, as did Elizabeth and Noah.

Guilt. Sorrow. Agony. Endless. Forever and ever, amen.

Chapter Fourteen

Yellow-and-black patterns twisted in front of her eyes. She felt the firmness of a seat underneath her. Heard the clicking of tree branches in a breeze. Bit by bit, she began to understand she was in the tree house on the deck.

She had just watched something terrible. A death. A murder? It was coming back now. She'd seen Marella kill somebody. But she was Marella. How could she have been outside of herself, watching the diabolical act?

By time traveling. Yes, that was it. Some unknown force had thrust her back in time, to relive the evil she'd committed.

A person was beside her, murmuring encouragement. That was Noah. She closed her eyes, letting his skin and the sun warm her while she recovered some more. It was Tuesday, August 29, 2023. Midday. The present. The Aguageddon was over.

She recalled something else from that time during the Aguageddon. Later, after she and Noah had left Elizabeth behind and were alone, traveling across the seabed, she had confided in Noah about the mercy killing. He had spoken bitterly, saying "My god, Marella. When somebody tells you they don't want to die alone, they're not asking you to kill them." He had accused her of murder. "You killed a person while I was sleeping right next to her."

They had gone on to end the Aguageddon. Then they had spent days together while the ocean refilled, sharing survival. Their achievement had overridden that dispute, and they had never revisited Marella's guilt, or Noah's inability to forgive her. All that had been set aside. Now it rose like a drowned corpse, bloated, inescapable.

Marella stared at some blurry lines. They sharpened, becoming the deck railing. Noah murmured, "It's all right. I'm here for you."

His words seemed hollow, given what she'd just witnessed, his touch uncomforting.

He had judged her.

Some time later, she recovered enough to pull away from him and speak clearly, although her throat was tight with anguish. "I went back in time, to when Elizabeth was hurt. We were pulling her on the sled, then stopped to sleep. You woke up first. You had your hands on Elizabeth's throat."

Noah pulled back, as if seeing a ghost. "I... how could you..."

"You were going to strangle her."

"But I didn't... I couldn't..."

His confusion angered her. *Just own up to it!* "You were going to kill her, but you didn't. You left me to bear the guilt."

He seemed genuinely nonplussed. "How can you say that? My choice had nothing to do with you. It was between me and God."

Marella's thoughts stuttered. It distressed her to feel unworthy of the kind of relationship that Noah had with God. However, his beliefs didn't give him a pass to infer she didn't matter. She did. "But you came close. And when I went through with it instead, you acted shocked, as if you would never have considered doing it yourself."

"I *was* shocked. I didn't think you were capable of such a thing."

He still seemed genuine. She'd loved that about him, but now it galled her. So damned authentic. She spoke through gritted teeth. "Don't turn this back onto me. You lied to me by not telling me you almost did it yourself."

"I couldn't tell you. It's different for me. A Black man almost kills somebody and in other peoples' eyes, it's as bad as if they'd actually done it. And if I'd gone through with it, I'd be judged differently than you." He sounded urgent. He really wanted her to understand.

She felt a pang of shame that she hadn't thought of that aspect, but still, how could he have so little faith in her? "I would never have told anybody."

"You think that now. You don't know what you would say out of anger." He spoke pointedly, as if from experience, as if somebody had broken his confidence in the past.

And yet, it was maddening that he kept deflecting. This was about him, not her. "My point is that you judged me for doing it when you thought of it too."

"And then I didn't do it. Because God tells us 'thou shalt not kill.' I didn't want to be a murderer, and I thought of you as one. I know it's more complicated than that. I'm sorry I reacted that way. I really am."

She spoke fiercely. "You don't sound sorry. You left me to do the dirty work."

He stiffened. "You're making it sound like it had to happen. It didn't. You made the decision. And in fact, you were just there again. Did you try to stop yourself from killing her?"

The wind was knocked out of her, as if she'd fallen hard. She hadn't tried—of course not—and it now felt like she'd killed Elizabeth twice—and been judged by Noah for a second time! "I couldn't! That would have kept us from stopping the Aguageddon. Don't make this about me. You judged me. And you've killed too. You killed Preston."

Noah held his palms up, indicating astonishment that she would compare the two actions. "That was self-defense. I didn't plan it, it just happened."

"You think I planned to do that to Elizabeth?" Marella staggered to her feet, pointing to the woods with her whole arm. "Get out."

He burst out in anguish, "You keep saying not to make this about you, but it is about you. I'm just your sidekick, following you around, helping you save the world. I've been supporting you and everything you do ever since I met you, but you refuse to see how hard it is on me."

Marella was flabbergasted. She went through torture every time she time traveled. Nothing he experienced even compared, and yet he thought he had it hard. He'd relegated himself to sidekick. That wasn't her choosing. "The hell with you. I mean it. Leave. Now."

Noah sounded hard and resolute. "In your trip to the future, Brielle said we all got separated. This is how it starts. Have it your way." He wheeled around and strode into the tree house. She heard the creak of the front door, then footsteps on the stairs outside.

She put her face in her hands. When she told him to leave, she hadn't been thinking beyond the next few minutes. But it seemed he'd taken it as a breakup. It had been much too easy for him to accept cutting it off. As if he'd been prepared for it. Almost as if he'd wanted it to happen.

Good riddance, then, if he could treat her that way. He had been so close to doing the mercy killing himself that he had actually put his hands on Elizabeth's neck. And yet he judged her.

Now, with his judgment alongside her own, she felt doubly culpable. The hell with him and his high-and-mighty ideals. It was "hard on him"? He didn't know what sacrifice truly was.

Mom and Brielle dashed outside to the deck.

"What was that about?" Mom sounded worried.

Marella shook her head. She hadn't told them about the mercy killing and so couldn't explain Noah's transgression.

Mom patted her shoulder. "I'm sorry. First arguments are always tough. Always about something little. Don't worry, he'll be back."

"No. It's over." Marella spit out the words so vehemently that Mom and Brielle gave each other a look of alarm.

She sat. Mom joined her, linking arms with her, while Brielle leaned on the railing. They were all silent for a while. Marella thought she felt their solidarity, but then Mom said, "Things are not the same out there, and they could get crazier. I would feel safer with him around. When you've calmed down, let's talk this through."

Marella had a sudden resentful inkling of what it was like for royalty to be bartered away in marriage. This was a betrayal. Mom's solidarity was imaginary. She unlinked her arm from her mother's.

And yet, her comment made her realize that she, too, had felt safer with him around. And for a time, more loved. The void with him gone was already a sinkhole, growing larger by the minute.

"He's coming back!" said Brielle triumphantly. "He's bringing his butt back to you. Make him grovel."

"There, see?" said Mom. "He's going to apologize."

The footsteps were loud and fast. He was leaping up the stairs with passion, as if he'd realized just how wrong he'd been. Marella didn't know what to think. She was still furious, and he had been angry too. How could he possibly have reversed course so quickly?

Noah appeared in the doorway to the deck, panting. His million-yard stare showed he wasn't there to make up. Something was wrong, and it was something bad.

Whatever he had to say, she didn't want to hear it. She used to view life's misfortunes as being doled out in scoops, one at a time, melting away before the next one arrived. Now calamities came in layers, one piled on another, and whatever Noah was going to say would only add another one.

Finally he spoke. "It's Alphonse, next door."

Marella's stomach curdled.

Mom clutched the hem of her shirt. "What? What happened?"

"Dead," guessed Brielle despondently. "Heart attack."

Noah's eyes finally focused. "He's dead, but it wasn't a heart attack. His skin is gray and chalky. His fingers are all curled up. Like claws."

Marella gasped. The man in the future had looked like that as he died. "The fog killed him!"

There was silence as they absorbed this terrible news.

Mom spoke to Noah with authority, in her this-is-final voice. "You're not leaving. It's too dangerous down there. I don't care what went on between you two. You and Marella figure out a way to get along."

Marella's eyes met Noah's, but she couldn't read him, and didn't want to. The time travel itself was exhausting; add to that the argument, and now this new tragedy, and she'd reached her limit. "I need to rest." She headed for the door.

"Keep an eye on her," said Mom.

"On it," said Brielle.

. . . .

MARELLA WOKE TO THE smell of something baking. She thought at first she was in Seattle with her family, but then the memories seeped in. The fire and sand of the Aguageddon. Meeting with Belinda. Time travel. The argument with Noah. The trifecta of secrets she was keeping from her family: the mercy killing of Elizabeth, the self-defense killing of Olivia, and the accidental killing of her father. The guilt that sleep had dulled returned, along with the taste of warm iron and wet mold.

While she slept, she'd had a dream in which Noah had done the mercy killing instead of her, and she clutched a megaphone, shouting to a multitude, "Noah killed Elizabeth Fehr!"

The guilt ballooned, even though she hadn't actually made such an announcement. It was a dream of betrayal, not only of Noah, but of herself, for contradicting her own assertion that she would never talk about it.

Just like I promised not to talk about Project Athena. But then she had. The realization hit her hard. Noah was right. You never knew what you might divulge, whether it was in anger, as he'd said, or unintentionally.

Still, he had judged her. That hadn't changed.

She sat up. The dream shards fell away. Brielle was sitting in the wingback chair. "You snore like a sailor," she said. An in-joke between the two of them.

Marella smiled wanly. "How long did I sleep?"

"An hour."

It was still early afternoon, then. Still Tuesday.

Sliding out of the bed, she peeked out the window and saw no sign of the fog. She and Brielle went downstairs and to the kitchen, where Mom and Noah were sitting at the table.

Noah grunted—an annoying noise Marella took as a jab. He went outside to the deck. She sighed heavily.

"Why are you so pissed off?" Brielle asked her.

"Shush," said Mom, handing them each a buttered scone.

On the counter was a sketch pad. During the Aguageddon, Marella had made a diagram that helped her pinpoint the cause of the disappearing water. Would a diagram help her now?

While she ate, she drew a timeline of her time-travel jaunts, with arrows showing her points of departure, destination, and return. She didn't know what she hoped to see. Perhaps a pattern to the timing of the jaunts. Perhaps some other clue. When she was done, she gazed at her drawing, hoping for inspiration. All she saw was a mishmash of elongated arches.

"That looks like art deco," said Mom.

"It's a timeline. I thought I might see a pattern. But I don't."

"Me either," said Brielle.

"Show it to Noah," said Mom.

Marella closed her eyes, counting to ten to keep from speaking harshly to her mother.

Mom made a noise of exasperation. "We need all minds on the problem." She called Noah inside.

After a quick, reproachful glance at Marella, he poured over the sketch. "It's only two dimensions. You need the three dimensions of space and then another for time."

Marella rolled up the paper and peered inside. She sighed, dropping it on the table. "I don't know what I'm doing."

"Start with something that's already three dimensions," suggested Brielle.

Marella pinched a tiny piece of scone into her water. It floated like a dead fish.

"What are you doing?" asked Mom.

"The water is three dimensions," said Marella.

"And the scone is...?" Brielle twirled her fingers in the air, like she used to when helping Marella study for class.

Marella shrugged and drank the water; the piece of scone ended up on her tongue. She was time, and the scone was a moment. No. She was a lump of human, and the scone was a lump of wheat. Nothing more, nothing less. She swallowed the piece of scone.

She wasn't solving anything. How could she think that she could comprehend time? Was the human mind even capable of that?

Certainly not hers. Not now.

She was about to mention rejoining HemisNorth when the driveway gravel crunched. A car was pulling up.

Her first thought was that Belinda was either sending a notice to rescind her promotion or sending a car to pick her up. Neither seemed likely, and anyway through the window she saw it wasn't a HemisNorth car, but a white convertible with the top down. The driver's cowlicked hair reminded Marella of a guinea pig she'd once had. He looked to be in his late thirties, just thick enough around his middle that a doctor would suggest he begin an exercise program.

The man climbed the stairs. Mom opened the door and peered at him through the screen door. Wiping his forehead, the man announced, "I'm looking for Marella Wells." He spotted her inside and waved. "There you are. I saw you on TV. My name is Hadrian Elkerman, and I'm a time philosopher."

Chapter Fifteen

"I've never heard of a time philosopher," Marella told the man on the other side of the screen door. His serious expression gave her a thin ray of hope. Could Hadrian Elkerman help her?

He rocked on his heels, just once. "On TV you said you time traveled. I'm very interested. Would you mind if I asked you a few questions?"

"There's no such thing as a time philosopher," said Noah. "What's the real story?"

Marella's hope faded slightly. She'd been too quick to accept the man's statement. And yet—if there were such a thing as a time philosopher, it seemed like the perfect expert for her problem.

"Let me clarify," said Hadrian. "I don't make my living that way. I'm a mathematician, and math is of course critical to the study of time. For example, an interesting point: normally you would say that the past is fixed and the future is not. But mathematically there's no basis for such a statement."

"How did you learn about time stuff then, if it's not what you do?" asked Mom.

"Self-study and interaction with experts."

Mom's voice was flat. "You're a reporter. You're just here to snoop for more dirt and make Marella look bad."

The man huffed. "Me. A reporter. Absolutely not."

"Prove it," said Noah, defiant.

Hadrian blinked a couple of times, as if he hadn't expected this level of resistance, but spoke as if he were game. "Proving a negative can be difficult, but let me see what I can do." He searched through his wallet. "I'm glad I found you here. It was a complete guess, though an educated one. You mentioned a tree house, and I'd visited this one in a home-and-garden tour some years back." He held a membership card up to the screen door. "Does this suffice?"

It read *Philosophy of Time Society*. "I'm also a member of the International Association for the Philosophy of Time, but I don't have a card for that."

"You could have printed that yourself," said Mom. "It doesn't mean anything."

"Well then, test me. Ask me a question," said Hadrian.

"Can I change the past?" asked Marella.

"You can't change the past, but you can change the future," said Mom. One of her favorite phrases.

"On the contrary," said Hadrian. "I believe that backward influence is mathematically possible."

Marella's hope blossomed. "Backward influence?"

"Yes." Hadrian retained his stark seriousness while seeming to relish sharing his knowledge. "Being able to change the past through an action in the present or the future depends on whether you're looking at quantum mechanics or classic mechanics. I think it depends on the shape of time. If time is an arrow, then backward influence is impossible. But what if time curves back on itself and then ultimately collides with itself?"

"And so that's how a specific moment would be connected to one the future?" asked Marella eagerly.

"Maybe," he said. "There are many possibilities. Time could be more than one shape. It might be that we just can't fathom it. The human brain doesn't perceive some of these things easily."

"This doesn't prove he's a time philosopher," said Noah. "He could be making this all up."

"Hold on. I'll be right back." Hadrian sprang down the stairs to his car, showing he was more athletic than he'd first appeared. He returned with a thick book, its green-and-black cover bearing a dandelion gone to seed. "*The Oxford Handbook of Philosophy of Time*. It might be daunting to the layperson. It's the type of thing a time philosopher would have."

Full of hope, Marella pushed past her mother to open the screen door. "Come in! This is my mom, Pamela, my sister, Brielle, and..." *My nothing, not anymore.* "...Noah."

Mom took the book from Hadrian, feeling its heft. "Handbook? This isn't a handbook. A handbook is small. This is a doorstop. Did you write this?"

"No. But I've studied it thoroughly."

Mom read from the table of contents. "Time and Metaphysics. The Direction of Time. Ethics. Time Travel and Time Machines."

"I'm not sure that last section is relevant, in spite of the name," said Hadrian.

"It's full of notes," she said. "Is this your handwriting?"

"Most certainly," said Hadrian.

"Write me a sentence. Write..." Mom squinted at a page. "Write 'interesting premise, follow up on this.'"

Noah handed Hadrian a pen. He scribbled the words in the book.

Mom compared what he'd just written with the sentence in the book. "Same loop on the *p*, same slant to the words, same diagonal cross on the *t*. That's his writing."

"I suppose he's really a time philosopher then," said Noah grudgingly.

Mom nodded, looking Hadrian up and down approvingly, as if he'd changed into a tux.

"Good. I'm glad that's established." Hadrian gazed around the living room, his lips set in such a way that Marella wondered if he ever smiled. "It's just as beautiful as I remember it, although the organization of the books by spine color is regrettable." He was standing on the Persian rug, in the spot where the dead Marella had appeared. Irrationally, that made her nervous, as if her dead self might appear again and fuse with him in a horrific time-travel accident.

"Let's sit." She headed for the couch, trying to work out what questions to ask him.

Hadrian followed but remained standing. "I thought your assertion could be true because on TV I saw a cut appear on your arm right after you purportedly time traveled. Your arm was clear in one moment, and then cut in the next. But videos can be manipulated, and while it was aired by an established news organization, I would like to verify your ability, so please go back in time to earlier today and leave me a note. Write something simple like 'Hello, Hadrian.' I'm going to find it in..." He looked around. "...that drawer." He went to a small desk, where his hand hovered over a drawer knob.

This was taking the wrong turn, from Hadrian proving himself to Marella having to do so. She knew from experience how difficult that would be. "It doesn't work like that. I can't control it."

His hand dropped to his side. His expression became even more severe. "How *does* it work?"

"It just happens to me. Out of the blue. I time travel for maybe a few minutes, maybe a quarter of an hour, and then I return to the same moment I left."

"Interesting. You're pulled back to the same moment, like a rubber band. I wonder what that could mean. Can you think of any other way to prove to me that you time travel?"

"I brought something back from 2002." Marella retrieved the lemon-colored crisis clinic card the woman had handed her. She described visiting the coffee shop and the news shop.

"Interesting," said Hadrian, flipping the card to see the other side. "The font seems retro. Not definitive, but promising."

Brielle, who had been fidgeting with impatience, couldn't hold back anymore. She rapid-fired her questions at Hadrian. "Have you met other time travelers? How does it work? How can Marella control it? What happens if she gets stuck somewhere? How can she get back? Why is it so hard on her?"

"Slow down." Hadrian seemed more annoyed than necessary, as if a child had just smeared chocolate on his white shirt. "I don't know of anybody who has actually time traveled. That's why I'm here. I'd love to meet such a person, but I'm not certain Marella is one."

"She is, because we saw her," said Brielle proudly, as if it were an achievement. "There were four of her in the room at one time."

"Four?" His eyebrows rose in astonishment. "You mean she traveled from different times to converge in one moment? And you saw this?"

She nodded quickly. "She was right here, and one Marella was by the window, one on the rug, and one in the loft."

"Interesting. Let's assume for the time being that it's true. You tell me more about your time travel, and then I'll explain concepts that might relate to your situation. Is that a fair deal?"

Marella felt like a patient with an unidentified disease seeing an expert doctor who might finally diagnose her and heal her. Hopeful yet nervous. Would he actually have the type of knowledge required? What would the diagnosis be? Either *Give it some time, it'll clear up on its own* or *You have three months to live, so enjoy the time you've got left as best you can.*

Hadrian sat on the couch. "When did this start happening to you and why?"

Marella took a deep breath. Should she tell him about Project Athena? What were the consequences? But he seemed so knowledgeable. "The first time was only a couple of days ago. I think a machine is doing it."

Hadrian scooted forward on the couch, seeming energized. "A time machine?"

"No," she said. "It's a side effect of a machine. It's—"

Noah interrupted. "Marella, we had an agreement."

She managed to keep from raising her voice. "How is he supposed to help if he doesn't know the details?"

Noah was silent a moment, then said, "Before she tells you, you have to know that you can't tell anybody about this. Religious extremists or terrorists could use the machine to end the world. It's destroyed now, but we don't want anybody to build one."

"Destroyed. I see." Hadrian's shoulders drooped with disappointment. "I won't say a word. And so, is this the dangerous machine you spoke of to the reporter? Project Athena? HemisNorth made this machine?"

"They didn't know it affected time," said Marella. "It was supposed to remove carbon dioxide from the atmosphere. The idea was that in quantum physics, a particle doesn't have defined properties until you measure them. Somehow the machine kept the location undefined so that a molecule wouldn't be in our universe but also not in a parallel universe. It had the potential to be in either one, but wasn't there."

"Interesting," said Hadrian, "very interesting."

"But instead of just carbon dioxide," added Brielle, "it took water. Water molecules became not here and not there."

He looked up at the ceiling. Marella imagined a tiny interconnected system of gears—like those in an expensive watch—turning rapidly in his head. She wanted to ask more questions but held back so he could think. Finally he spoke. "Are you telling me that you think this machine—this Project Athena—took our water? It caused the Aguageddon? If that were true, then I agree it should be kept quiet. HemisNorth is rebuilding and advancing, from what I hear. We don't want them to get bogged down with accusations at this time, whether they're true or not."

"It did take the water," said Marella. "But it's also causing my time travel."

Hadrian stroked his chin. "Noah just said that the machine has been destroyed, so how could it be doing that?"

"Before it exploded, it sent out this thing like a slow lightning bolt, and it hit my head. And it felt exactly the same as it does when I start to time travel. I felt my skin prickling and smelled ammonia."

"Where did this bolt strike you? Show me."

Marella pointed to the left side of her head. Mom fingered through her hair, exposing her scalp. It would have been embarrassing if she weren't so desperate for help.

Hadrian examined her head. "I don't see any marks, but never mind. Tell me about your time travel. Where have you gone? What have you seen?"

She described the trip to the coffee shop in more detail, then the trip to the school function, the future with the lethal fog, and the basics of the camping trip with her father, without the details of his death.

He listened, nodding, fingertips touching. "How often does this happen? Is it at regular intervals or at a certain time of day?"

"It's just random."

Hadrian tapped his index finger against his jaw. "What's interesting to me is that you have affected your future by actually traveling to it. Do you have a blank piece of paper?"

Brielle ran to retrieve pen and paper for him, and he drew a straight line. "Normally we imagine the past as fixed and the future as having many possibilities." At the line's end, he extended several branches. "But now you have this period in time you've jumped ahead to." He circled one of the branches. "And so, in a sense, your future becomes your past."

"Does that help us?" asked Marella.

"It might, because the future and the past may be more reflective of each other than we think." Hadrian folded the paper and held it up like a magician about to do a trick. He stabbed it with a pen, making them all jump. When he unfolded it, there were two holes: one on a branch and one on the straight line. "As I said earlier, if time curves or folds onto itself, the past and future could be connected. There could then be backward influence."

"How does knowing that help us?" asked Marella.

"Good question, but I need more context." He leaned so close that she could see the pores on his nose. "Take me back in time with you. That way I can better observe the process."

"Ooooh!" said Brielle, while Mom and Noah both snorted as if the idea was ludicrous.

Hadrian seemed too focused on Marella. It felt uncomfortable, yet his bold idea intrigued her. "Is that possible?"

"I don't know," he said. "But I assume you traveled fully clothed, which means you can take at least that volume of, shall we say, non-Marella material back and forth."

"But—how would I take you along?" she asked.

"Yeah," said Brielle. "She can't fit you in her pocket."

"Give me your hand," said Hadrian.

Marella held it out hesitantly. He gripped it tightly, fingers interlaced with hers. She willed herself not to squirm. So—they were just going to hold hands until she time traveled? That was idiotic!

"You can't be serious. No, no, no. Forget that." Noah seemed jealous, which incensed Marella after all that had happened between them.

"It's not up to you, Noah," she said flatly. Then, more diplomatically: "I'm desperate. I can't figure this out by myself. I need help."

"Then I'll go." Noah grasped Marella's other hand. Was that jealousy? Chivalry? Jealous chivalry? It seemed like he still cared for her, though she couldn't let it distract her.

Hadrian squared off at Noah as if to make him back down. "That's a commendable offer, but I should be the one to go. I can use my knowledge of time philosophy to observe and theorize."

"You can't just hold hands!" Brielle sounded exasperated. "What if you lose hold of her? You'll get stuck in time."

Mom gasped. "She's right! Your family would never know what became of you."

"I have no family," said Hadrian.

Marella felt sad for him, and also sheepish holding hands with the two men, each staring the other down. She pulled away from both of them.

"We have to tie you together." From a linen closet, Brielle retrieved a spare sheet. It was cream-colored, edged with gold thread.

"Bad idea." Mom folded her arms. "Remember that movie *The Fly*? They could fuse to one another."

Marella imagined a conglomeration of her body with Hadrian's guinea-pig hair and a fly's eyes. It didn't seem likely, and at this point she was willing to try anything, especially at an expert's recommendation.

Marella and Hadrian stood up. Brielle wrapped the sheet around their waists, and tied a thick knot. Marella felt even more sheepish now, hip-to-hip with this oddly serious man she'd only just met. The elegant cream-and-gold sheet flowed down around them as if for some sort of premarriage rite.

"You look like conjoined twins at a toga party," said Mom without a speck of humor in her tone. "It's ridiculous. How long are you going stand there like that?"

"She's been time traveling a lot," said Brielle. "It might not be long."

"Marella," said Noah hastily, as if just realizing it, "bringing somebody with you could change the timeline so that you don't stop the Aguageddon."

He was right. And she might bring Hadrian to the mercy killing! Her hands darted to the knot on the sheet.

Too late. She couldn't move. She smelled ammonia and felt a pricking on her skin. Ice water flowed throughout her body, making her cold enough to shatter.

She was about to time travel, but this time would be different. She wouldn't arrive alone.

Chapter Sixteen

Marella's body and soul had been dispersed. The impossibly small bits stayed suspended in a void for eons, but the pieces were now discovering each other.

Body came together first, bringing blurry images and the smell of smoke, which irritated her throat. Some kind of material was draped around her waist; a wind whipped it against her legs.

Soul and reason arrived next. The pain and confusion were a sign that she had time traveled, she realized. Before leaving, she had been standing close to somebody. An expert of some kind. A time philosopher—Hadrian, that was his name. Brielle had tied him to Marella so that they would time travel together.

The plan hadn't worked. She was alone. That was why the sheet was so loose. She managed to grasp it to keep it from blowing away.

Alone. Disappointment sank in. If she could have brought Hadrian along without harming the timeline, they might have been able to accomplish something, but this proved that wouldn't be possible. Hadrian's suggestion that he travel with her had given her a feeling of security, as if she would be arriving with a bodyguard. Instead, she would continue to time travel alone, vulnerable to whatever she encountered. The wind whipped harder, coming at her from different directions, as if cognizant of her frailty.

Her vision sharpened. A line of flames glowed red in the distance. She had gone back in time to the Aguageddon, and she was on the dry seabed, watching trees burning on the shoreline.

Looking down, she realized she was on the edge of a twenty-foot cliff. A quiet bleat of fear escaped her mouth. Unsteady as she was, and with the wind gusting from all angles, she could easily tumble off. She crouched slightly while she continued to get her bearings.

Below were four vehicles: a camping van, a truck with a canopy, and two SUVs. She gasped when she recognized them. They belonged to Preston and his followers.

Preston. The cult leader who had tried to kill her and who'd nearly kept her from ending the Aguageddon because he thought God was using it to purge Earth of the wicked.

There was movement near the camper. That was Preston himself. Noble and handsome, wearing cargo pants and a muslin shirt. But now she knew he wasn't so much noble as frighteningly charismatic, to such an extent that people would jump to their deaths and set the world on fire at his command.

Gabriela, one of his followers, strolled up to him, the wind wrapping her orange-and-pink flowered skirt around her legs and blowing her long gray hair behind her. She had been so kind, but was doomed to die. So was Edie, who now appeared in her peony-pattern sundress, holding Baby Faith. She had been wary of Marella when she should have been wary of Preston.

Olivia, the follower Marella would later kill, was nowhere in sight. She was thankful she didn't have to see her again, at least not yet.

An engine growled. A pickup truck arrived, stirring up sand and dust. Marella felt compressed, the way she did in the presence of another Marella. That was her in the pickup. Now she knew exactly what day this was. She, Elizabeth, and Noah had been driving along the emptying Puget Sound, begging for water, turned away by each person they approached.

Preston waved Gabriela and Edie back into his camper. He was about to save her life by giving her water. She was about to watch herself be saved by a mass murderer. She would see history repeat itself, but from a different perspective, literally. From on high.

Marella pulled the sheet to her shoulders and wrapped it more tightly around herself to keep its flapping from drawing attention.

She had to be careful not to interfere, lest she stop Preston from saving her life.

Elizabeth sprang from the truck, shoulders straight, determined. Alive and well! "We need water," she called. "My friend is very dehydrated. She might die."

Guilt weighed on Marella, heavy as the ocean. Elizabeth was begging for water for her, to keep her alive. It felt like a punishment to see this, when later Marella would kill her. The taste of warm iron and wet mold intensified.

"Go away. We don't want any trouble." Preston's commanding voice made her stomach twist.

Elizabeth craned her neck, but couldn't see Preston behind the vehicles. She called loudly, "Please. Save her life."

"We don't have anything," he said. "Go away. This is your last warning."

The other Marella spilled from the truck, falling to her hands and knees, nearly hitting the ground face-first. She looked barely alive as she crawled toward Preston. It was hard to watch, but Marella did anyway. There might be clues to observe.

Something was wrong. Preston had a knife in his hand instead of the cup of water she remembered. He was about to come around the truck with it. He intended to hurt Elizabeth and the other Marella, not help them.

She tried to shout a warning from the cliff, but her voice wasn't strong yet. She could only grunt feebly.

Hearing her, Preston looked up, then froze.

Not knowing what else to do, Marella pointed forcefully at the knife. *No. Wrong.* He dropped it as if it were red-hot and put his palms together, seeming to ask her forgiveness. After a quick bow of the head, he strode forward to the other Marella, who was crawling doggedly on. He bent down on one knee and helped the other

Marella to sit up. Unfastening a thermos from his belt loop, he filled its cup and eased it to her lips.

Marella gazed down at the sheet that enveloped her. *He thinks I'm an angel.* Her appearance on the ridge was the reason Preston had decided to help the other Marella. Once again, her actions hadn't changed the past, but only reinforced it.

She remembered his words to her after she'd discovered he was a cult leader. "Many years ago God flooded the Earth with water to destroy the wicked. This time, he's taking it away to destroy the wicked. You are all here to help found the new era. Marella, I saw you in a vision."

This was the vision. She had just saved her own life by going back in time.

Marella smelled ammonia. Preston, Elizabeth, and the other Marella crumbled away. The world darkened and disappeared. It felt as if the cliff she stood upon careened through the night sky, toward nothingness. An icy chill turned her bones to glass; they shattered and dispersed into eternity.

• • • •

SHE WAS WRAPPED IN a shroud. *No! I'm not dead!* She flailed, trying to pull it off. She was shivering hard, so surely they could see she was alive! She tried to cry out, but could only grunt wildly.

"Calm down, you're safe." She knew that voice. Somebody good. Mom. She stopped fighting, but the shivering continued.

"The sheet was just tied around both of you," said Mom. "Now suddenly it's not."

It wasn't a shroud then, but a sheet. She didn't remember its purpose.

"She must have time traveled," said Brielle.

"If she did, she went by herself," said Hadrian. "I didn't accompany her."

The rainbow of spines on the bookshelf came into focus. Yellow, red, blue. And there were Mom, Brielle, and Hadrian, watching her intently, as if she were a ticking bomb. *Boom*, she wanted to say, a joke to make them back off, but they wouldn't understand, and anyway, even if she could talk, she was too distraught to pull off humor.

Mom and Brielle helped her onto the couch, adjusting the sheet to help warm her.

Hadrian was an expert. A time philosopher, she remembered. He was supposed to time travel with her, but he hadn't.

It was Tuesday afternoon. What she thought of as the present.

When she recovered enough, she described what had happened. When she told them about Preston's knife, they all looked horrified.

Putting a hand on Marella's shoulder, Noah spoke quietly, as if it pained him. "He would have killed you."

Marella looked at his hand. What did his touch mean? *He still cares. But he judged me.*

He removed his hand from her shoulder quickly, as if Marella's stare was a request to be left alone. She hadn't meant it that way, but it was too late now.

"A sheet wasn't sufficient. We should tie our wrists together, with string, or a rope." Hadrian went to the kitchen and began opening drawers.

Mom stopped him. "No. What if you got stuck in the past or the future? We'd lose your knowledge. You just got here, and poof you'd be gone."

Marella sighed. "If you had gone with me, you would have fallen off the cliff. Also, Preston might not have saved my life, and so I wouldn't have stopped the Aguageddon. Everybody would be dead. We'd better not try that again."

"Anyway," said Noah decisively, "it didn't work, so we need to concentrate on how to help Marella change the timeline. Taking you along is off the table. What else have you got?"

Hadrian clamped his lips together as if he'd just insulted him. Marella got the feeling he was going to tell them all to go to hell, but he looked away, took in one long, deep breath, and then let it out. Finally he said, "Well then, what if we look at the timing of your travels? Maybe there's a mathematical pattern that isn't obvious at first glance."

"Marella made a timeline." Joining him in the kitchen, Brielle retrieved the sketch pad and flipped it open, looking pleased with herself.

They all gathered at the kitchen table. Hadrian examined the drawing, twisting his lips to the side. She hoped it would trigger an idea. He was an expert, after all. Marella imagined him saying in his humorless manner, "By Jove, I think I've got it." Instead, too quickly, he pushed the sketch pad away. "I don't see patterns. Your jumps appear to be random, as you suggested."

"You barely looked at it." Brielle pushed the sketch pad back to him. "You said the pattern wouldn't be obvious at first glance, so you need to give it *more* than a glance."

Hadrian inclined his head, acknowledging she had a point. He ventured another look, then pointed to the doodles along the side. "What's all this?"

"I was trying to picture the shape of time," said Marella. "And the shape of a moment."

"The shape of a moment," he repeated. "They call a bit of time a chronon, so you're looking for the shape of a chronon. That's an interesting idea. But how long is a moment? How long is a chronon? Say it's 'now.' How long is 'now'? A second? Half a second? A tenth of a second? Less?"

"I can define 'now,'" said Mom. Rally-the-troops Mom. "It's when we need to solve this whole time-travel nonsense. You're supposed to be the expert, but it seems to me you're just getting sidetracked. It's all well and good to talk about interesting this and interesting that, but we need action. Something we can do."

Hadrian clenched his teeth, looking at Marella's mother as if she were a fly he'd been unable to swat. His sudden show of anger surprised her. People didn't react that way to Mom. But then, maybe she'd misinterpreted it, since it vanished as suddenly as it came on.

He placed his elbow on the table and leaned forward. "This discussion isn't a sidetrack. Marella said that Project Athena could keep a molecule out of our universe and out of a parallel universe. It had the potential to be in either one, but wasn't. Could Project Athena have kept a chronon—a moment in time—out of our universe?"

"I don't think so," said Noah. "If time were disappearing in the same way, we'd have no time. No moments."

"Oh my god, that's so weird," said Brielle. "What would that even be like? Time disappearing? Two o'clock is missing, so we're going to skip it today! And you thought losing an hour at daylight savings time was bad."

"That's a valid objection, so let's move on," said Hadrian. "I wonder about the properties of time. You might be able to stretch time. It's interesting that you travel to different times, yet you always return to the same moment from which you departed. Does it feel—I don't know—elastic?"

"It's more like I'm being ripped apart and put back together," said Marella.

"Hmm. Well. The direction of time might be just as—or more important than—its shape. We perceive time like an arrow going in one direction. And we imagine that the future is open to change, while the past is fixed."

Brielle jumped in, continuing his train of thought. "But the past isn't fixed. She took a card from a woman while she was in the past. She talked to people. She changed the past."

"Maybe I didn't really change anything, because that was always meant to be," said Marella. "I did those things, and yet I came back to the present and everything's exactly the same."

"It might only seem the same because you changed it, so you don't know any different," said Noah.

"Yes," said Hadrian. "Perception is important in the discussion of time. But let me ask you something. This machine that you say is making you time travel. Who designed it and where are they now?"

"Eshana Collins and Len Janderson," said Marella. "They died in an explosion. It was on the news."

"I remember," he said. "A fuel tank explosion."

"That's the official story," she said, "but the prototype for Project Athena was in the building. I think that shutting it down caused the explosion. And the one on the island also exploded when we shut it down."

He let out a slow breath. "It's troubling that we can't talk to Len and Eshana." He stood. With one hand on his chin, he paced for a time. "And so, you knew them?"

"No," said Marella. "I met them a couple of times. But I didn't know them."

"What did they say during those encounters?"

"Nothing important."

"Everything is important. Even a casual conversation. Think back." Once again, Hadrian got too close to her.

She ignored her uneasiness. "They welcomed me on my first day. And they talked about coffee once."

He nodded quickly. "What exactly did they say?"

Marella stood to get space between them, removing the sheet from around herself and putting it on the counter. "Eshana said she liked the new coffee brand better, and Len said it was woody like a whiskey barrel."

"What else?"

"That's it."

Hadrian stared at her as if she were a fishing line he didn't know how to untangle. "Well then, tell me more about Project Athena. "About the machine."

"There were eight modules, each as big as a house," said Marella. "Each one had its own twenty-story loop on top, like a huge Ferris wheel."

"So, a complex of enormous size, but relatively small if you're suggesting it was causing all that water to vanish from the Earth. I don't believe that's possible." He spoke with an authority that would have convinced her if she hadn't known otherwise. "And I'm not completely convinced you time traveled, though you tell a somewhat plausible story."

Marella felt a rising sense of futility. She couldn't let him give up on her. She tried to think of another clue that would put him on the right path. "The machine was run by a quantum computer. Maybe that had something to do with the time travel. I mean, isn't the quantum realm supposed to be weird?"

Hadrian made a conciliatory gesture. "Yes, but I'm afraid I don't have any answers for you."

She felt dull with disappointment, as if a doctor had prodded and probed her for an hour then concluded her symptoms were all in her head.

"But you have to help her," said Mom. "She needs to be able to control her time traveling. It's dangerous."

Hadrian shrugged and shook his head at the same time, implying a low likelihood of that happening. "Can you get more information about the machine?" He asked Marella.

"I can't guarantee it. But I can try."

Noah made a noise of resistance. He knew she meant going to HemisNorth.

Hadrian continued, "And try to remember anything Len and Eshana might have said. When you do, get ahold of me. I live in Aberdeen, on Ocean View." He wrote down his contact information, then headed for his time philosophy book, which Mom had set on the couch.

Marella trotted to it and snatched it up. "Can we borrow this?"

He hesitated. It seemed like he was about to refuse, but perhaps he was swayed by her beseeching look. He gestured magnanimously. "Of course."

Marella held the weighty book in her hands. Hadrian couldn't help them yet, but surely something in all these pages would help her save her family and the rest of the world from a deadly future. She just needed to recognize the answer when she saw it.

Chapter Seventeen

After Hadrian left, Brielle let out a growl of frustration. "I thought he would be more help. Why did he leave so soon? You're a time traveler, for shit's sake. The real thing. He calls himself a time philosopher. He doesn't have a clue."

Mom picked up the sheet Marella had been wearing. "Something's off about that guy. "He seems so humorless."

"No, humor free." Brielle took one end of the sheet to help her fold it.

"What's the difference?"

"Humorless means you lost your sense of humor. Humor free is he never had one to begin with."

"He's just serious," said Marella. "At least he left us the book."

She settled on the couch and began reading. After a time she said, "I don't know. There's a lot here."

"Like what?" asked Mom.

"It talks about presentism and eternalism, like that other book."

"Remind me what those are."

"In presentism, only this moment exists, and in eternalism, things can exist in the past and future."

"Eternalism must be right," said Brielle, "or Marella wouldn't be able to jump to the past and future. But I don't see how knowing that helps."

"What else does it say?" asked Mom.

"There's a part about relativity," said Marella. "If I understand right, different people could experience the present moment at different times."

"That makes sense for you," said Noah. "You've been going back and forth in time, so when our present moment is now, your present moment is earlier or later."

"What else?" asked Mom.

"There's this thing called the moving spotlight theory. It talks about a policeman shining a light on one house after another. The house in the light is in the present. The ones that he's already shone the light on are in the past. The houses that he hasn't shone the light on yet are in the future."

"It sounds like the houses in the future are all built then, and are just waiting for the spotlight," said Noah. "If they're already there, does that mean that the future is fixed?"

"I hope not." Marella rubbed her temples. It was hard to concentrate.

Brielle scrunched her face uncertainly. "When you time travel, then where is the spotlight?" She rushed around, retrieving a flashlight from a drawer and fishing a Monopoly game off a shelf. She dumped its little red hotels and green houses onto the kitchen counter.

Noah helped line them up in rows, then set a top hat playing piece on the table. "This is Marella."

"Marella's always the dog." Brielle replaced the top hat with a tiny terrier.

Mom shone the light on one of the houses. Brielle put the dog next to the house.

They played around with different configurations, shining the flashlight here and there, but nothing inspired an answer to the time-travel dilemma.

Sighing deeply, Marella abandoned the setup and returned to the book, flipping through it despairingly. "I need weeks—no, months—to read through all this."

"You're overwhelmed," said Mom. "You need a break."

"Remember you don't have to do all this by yourself," said Noah brusquely. He took the book and began pouring over it.

Brielle returned to the table to continue experimenting with the spotlight on the houses.

Marella looked out the window for signs of the lethal fog, of which there were none, then gazed at the river, far in the distance. Decrepit wooden dock piles rose from the water at different lengths, like burned candles on a birthday cake.

Mom joined her. "The river of time."

"I was thinking the same thing. But time can't be a river. Rivers don't flow backward."

"There are places where they do. Close to the ocean. They call them tidal bores. I saw a TV show about one in China—the Silver Dragon. It gets thirty feet high and goes upriver twenty-five miles an hour."

Marella pictured people rushing out of the way of the tidal bore. It reminded her of time traveling to the future and running from the killing fog. Mom saw her distress and changed the subject quickly. "The gravel driveway outside reminds me of when you and Brielle were little. You would walk on gravel barefoot and pretend it was hot coals."

"I'd forgotten about that." Marella brightened slightly.

"You were so cute. You'd do like this." Mom stepped gingerly across the carpet, elbows up. "And your face looked like this because you were trying not to show that the gravel hurt." She made her eyes go wide.

Marella chuckled.

Mom continued. "Brielle was too young to understand you were supposed to be stoic. She would go like this." She mimed the walk again, saying, "Ow, ow, ow, ow."

Marella hugged her mother. She was so good at calming her down. She'd needed that. They reminisced quietly while Noah continued to read.

After a half hour, he lowered the book. "Marella was right. There's too much here. We went from having no information to having too much. This has essays from twenty-six different professors and researchers on all different time philosophy topics."

"Awesome! Let's find them." Brielle rushed over, seized the book, and looked at the list of contributors. "Snap. They live all over the world. France. Australia. The closest is in California. What a sucky time to have no phone or internet."

"Wouldn't do much good anyway," said Noah, dispirited. "None of them have time traveled."

The talk with her mother had given Marella renewed energy and a sense of determination. "I'm going to accept the promotion."

"No!" Noah was suddenly animated, as if Marella had suggested crossing a crocodile-filled river. "All the information was kept on-site with Project Athena. Even if you had access to every single file at the Aberdeen facility, the Project Athena information wouldn't be there."

"So it's not on the internet?" asked Brielle.

Marella shook her head. "Elizabeth told us that the machine was a closed system because they'd had problems with hackers. But I can search for people who might have worked on it by seeing who worked alongside Diana Brinkhauser. That's the only project she worked on while she was there." The last time she'd seen her friend, she had hinted that Project Athena would save the world. She hoped Diana had escaped the Western Inferno and all the other dangers of the Aguageddon.

She went on. "Also, I can check the employee database for staff with the type of background who might have contributed to it. I can look up the boat schedule to see who might have visited the island. I can review time sheets to see who might have noted down time spent on Project Athena."

"There must be something else we can do besides send you back to that company," said Mom. "They're evil, remember?"

"There isn't anything." Brielle flipped her hand dismissively. "Hadrian said he needed more information about the machine. Where else is she going to get it?"

"It's immoral," said Mom. "You can't associate with a company that is responsible for killing a billion people."

Marella spoke softly. "I can't stop thinking about the man I saw die in the future. That will be you when the fog gets to you. And Brielle. And Noah. And everybody else. I have to stop it from happening. I have to."

"HemisNorth makes chemicals. That place is full of nasty stuff." Mom bowed her head. "Going there could be how you stop breathing."

"I could just as easily stop breathing because of a decision to stay here."

Mom's voice was breathy with fear. "You're much safer here with us. When you time travel you're helpless until you recover. You could get hit by a car. And then I might never know what happened." She put her hand over her mouth, too distraught to go on.

Marella hugged her. "I can't just sit here and do nothing."

"She's right, Mom," said Brielle. "You always say that doing nothing is a surefire way to fail. She has to do something. She has to try. I'll go with her and keep her safe!"

Marella's heart nearly burst at Brielle's enthusiasm. She was sorry to refuse her. "You weren't invited. HemisNorth is a stickler for accurate paperwork—bringing you or Mom won't fly. If we ask, it could take days for them to accept."

"I'll go." Noah sounded proud. A soldier volunteering to go to the front lines.

Marella wished it didn't have to be him. His presence would be awkward, if not downright confrontational. But somebody had to be with her during her infirmity after time traveling.

Mom clamped onto Noah's wrist. "Watch over her. She needs you. Whatever you do, don't leave her alone. Promise me you won't."

Noah seemed embarrassed. "I won't leave her alone." Mom only released her grip after he added, "Of course I won't."

He said it with such genuine feeling that Marella wondered if they might someday work through their problems.

Her skin prickled. The smell of ammonia made her nauseous. She was freezing. The side of Noah's face began to crumble, turning his expression into a grimace, which also crumbled, pulling away the rest of Noah's head, then his body. Mom and Brielle turned to dust. All went dark.

Eternity stretched beneath her. She fell endlessly. She was the embodiment of agony, and yet she was nothing.

• • • •

HER PARTICLES SPRANG back together too slowly, as if having trouble finding the right spot in her body. When she was finally whole, or what passed for it, she stood shivering in a warm place that smelled of sweet pastries.

There was a murmur of conversation. Dishes clinking. A chair scooting. Her shivering subsided into the occasional spasm. As her vision cleared, she saw a long room with small tables, occupied by people dressed in vintage clothing. They lifted white mugs to their mouths and took bites of cinnamon rolls.

This was the same coffee shop she'd already visited, with the same side table with brochures and business cards. And in fact, she felt compressed, as if there was another Marella somewhere here, but she couldn't see one anywhere.

Noah had insisted that her destinations were important. Did coming back to this place again mean it was especially notable?

It didn't seem to be, but she needed to observe better. She'd once had a teacher who made his students study a classic painting for five minutes, then grilled them to see if they'd noticed the tiny worm on the side of the orange or the skull in the reflection of the bowl. He told them to observe as if they were lawyers whose case depended on the smallest of details.

Now Marella studied the coffee shop. A man whose sweater sleeves were too short lifted a coffee mug to his mouth, found its contents too hot, and spit them back into the cup. A double groove wove its way the length of the floor where somebody had once wheeled something heavy.

After a couple of test steps, she made her way forward in the long, narrow room. There were no other Marellas in sight. The ceiling had a light tan water stain in the shape of a cow. A sign on the wall said *Welcome to the Green Cat Café*. The front counter held a giant antique coffeepot. The reflection in its highly polished surface turned a stack of croissants into a misshapen mound.

A table held three women and one empty chair. They were college-aged, with textbooks open in front of them, all turned to the same page, showing math equations. Each of the women wrote in a spiral-bound notebook.

Outside the front window was a dusting of snow. A man walked by wearing a puffy orange jacket. Next came a woman wearing leggings and a slate-gray blouse. Marella started. That was her outside, gazing at the building signs, mouth open. She remembered that moment. She'd been so cold, so confused.

That meant this was the same day she'd time traveled to in 2002. Two years before she was born. It was bewildering to be somewhere before she'd even been alive, and on top of that see another version of herself there.

The sight of her other self spurred her to action. Enough observing. She might not have much time here. She dropped into the empty chair at the table with three women. "This is going to sound strange, but please listen carefully."

The women glanced at each other as if she was crazy. She went on anyway. "In twenty years, a company called HemisNorth is going to build a machine that's supposed to take extra carbon dioxide from the air, but it won't work the way it's supposed to. It'll take the water away from the Earth. You need to contact..." Marella stopped herself. If she gave them the names of the inventors, she might inadvertently give them the idea to build it. "Contact Marella Wells and tell her it's too dangerous."

Two of the women nodded indulgently, pressing their lips together as if trying not to laugh. The third tucked a stray red hair into her headband and said, "Marella Wells. Got it."

Face reddening, Marella reached for one of the spiral notebooks and a pencil. She wrote *HemisNorth, Project Athena* and her phone number. "In, let's say 2021, call this number. You'll know I'm telling the truth because..." What should she tell them? "In March 2020, a worldwide pandemic will start. Covid-19." She scribbled that on the paper.

Nothing happened. If this action had been successful, Marella would remember getting a phone call from them. But she hadn't, and so the timeline hadn't changed. She had to keep trying. "Of course you don't believe me." She ripped the page from the notebook and folded it once. "Put this somewhere. In a drawer, in a box. Then, when my predictions come true, call me. If I'm wrong, then no harm done."

The red-headed woman accepted it. "We're trying to study for a test," she said, not unkindly.

What more could she say? Marella rose and walked away. That had been a waste of time. The paper she'd written on would be long gone by the time they realized she was right.

What now? She wandered to the front of the shop as her mind whirled, trying to land on an action she could take before being pulled back to the present.

The woman behind the counter tapped the espresso machine portafilter twice to empty it of coffee grounds. A customer set money on the counter. He seemed a little familiar, like somebody she might have seen on the news, but she could only see part of his face.

A young woman sitting at the table by the window looked even more familiar. With a start, Marella realized why.

That's Mom!

She swayed, then caught herself. Her own mother. Two decades younger. Her face fuller, but definitely her. Sipping coffee. Reading a book. She smiled at something she read; that smile seemed lighthearted.

The moment was beautiful. So beautiful. To see her mother at a time with no catastrophes. When she'd had no children and few worries. She'd never seen her this serene.

She would have been twenty-two, just a little older than Marella was now. Married to Dad for a year.

Marella felt weak with the sudden realization of her guilt. By accidentally killing her father, she had destroyed her mother's tranquility. Ever after, Mom would be restless, wanting to move from home to home. She was to blame for that.

Guilt threatened to overwhelm her, but suddenly she thought of a way to change the timeline and stop the Aguageddon from happening. All she had to do was warn her mother. She took a step...

She smelled ammonia. Her mother's face blurred at the edges.

She was about to time travel. No! She had to get to her mother. She pushed with all her might, but her mind was no longer connected to her body. She couldn't move.

Her mother's face crumbled. The world dissolved.

A deep, insistent cold infused her being. The cold of eternity.

• • • •

HER PARTICLES JOINED one another, so slowly. She came to life bit by bit. She was human, but barely.

She felt pressure on her legs and back, then movement. She was being propelled somewhere, or—no, she was being carried. She tried to struggle. A hollow voice came from nearby: "You're all right." The voice wobbled, warped, and solidified into her mother's voice. "It's okay, honey."

Other voices calmed her. Noah and Brielle.

They sat her somewhere soft. She rested awhile, shivering. She could see a little—that was Mom rubbing her arms, warming them. And Noah and Brielle, looking worried, but also expectant.

I'm in the present. It's Tuesday afternoon. 2023, not 2002.

When she recovered enough to speak, she told Mom, "I went to that same coffee shop. I saw you there. You were young. It was the Green Cat Café."

Mom's voice was flat with dread. "Oh no." She turned away. She pulled at her shirt sleeve, obviously agitated.

Her distress worried Marella. What could possibly have happened at the café to trouble her so much? "Mom, is that where I'll stop breathing, if I go there again?"

Brielle and Noah each made a noise of despair.

"Tell me. I can take it." A warble in Marella's voice betrayed her lie.

Mom waved away her daughter's fear. "No, no! That's not it. You don't stop breathing there."

Noah straightened, his relief obvious.

"Mom, don't scare us like that!" Brielle batted her lightly.

"I'm going to tell you something. It's very important." Mom extended her arms, meaning *pay attention*. "If you time travel to the Green Cat Café again, don't talk to anybody, don't do anything. Just leave. Because..."

They were all silent. Waiting for Mom to drop the bomb.

"...because that's where I met your biological father."

Your biological father. The words lay on top of Marella's psyche like a sheet of paper on dirty water. Then, sodden, they sunk under. The man she knew as Dad wasn't her biological father. Her real father was somebody else.

"Dad... isn't my dad?"

Mom shook her head, fingertips over her mouth.

"What about me?" asked Brielle. "Is Dad my father?"

Mom shook her head again.

Brielle's mouth made the shape of an *O*. She held as still as a painting.

Noah watched them all with a worried expression, as if each of them might fall all at once and he didn't know where to stand to catch them.

"But why... how..." Like the Three Stooges all trying to get through a doorway at once, Marella's many questions fought for dominance. "But you and Dad were married back then."

Mom looked away. "It wasn't an affair. I wanted children, and your dad had a fertility problem. At first we hoped we could still conceive naturally because we couldn't afford procedures, but as time went on, it didn't seem likely. And then I met a man who eventually offered to be a secret father. I got pregnant with you. And then later he helped me a second time, and I had Brielle."

"Why didn't you tell us?" asked Brielle accusingly.

"Tell you that I had to cheat on your dad to have you? How could I tell you such a thing?"

Marella had thought she knew her mother. This told her differently. Like lifting a rock and finding something scuttling underneath.

"I just wanted babies so badly." Mom hunched, not meeting their eyes. "I couldn't imagine a life without children. I felt guilty enough doing it that way, and then when I drove him to suicide, it was too much."

Suicide? Mom thought she'd driven Dad to suicide. She had believed herself culpable all this time. That was really why she would get restless, making them move from home to home, disrupting their lives.

Marella couldn't let her believe such a thing. "Mom, he didn't commit suicide."

Her mother looked up sadly. "He did. He jumped off that cliff. Maybe it didn't look like it to you. But he was so careful about everything. He wouldn't have fallen." Her voice warbled, and a single tear slid down her cheek.

It was Marella's turn to confess, but it wouldn't be easy. It was bad enough being on the outs with Noah. To add Mom and Brielle was going to be impossible to bear. But she couldn't let Mom take the blame.

She wiped Mom's tear away. "It wasn't your fault. It was mine. He was right next to the cliff when I tried to warn him not to fall, which startled him, and he slipped. He died because of me, not you." She put her face in her hands.

It was quiet. What were they thinking? Did they blame her? Or, like Marella, were they trying to understand the feedback loop of that event? She took her hands from her face, surprised to see that Mom and Brielle looked thoughtful, not reproachful.

Marella waited for the truth of it all to sink in. The surprise of it must be keeping them from realizing what she had done. Her blunder had caused a death.

Mom spoke slowly, almost with a sense of wonder. "So he didn't kill himself. All this time I thought he did." She looked sorrowfully at Marella, seeming to understand how tortured her daughter was. "My poor girl," she said simply.

Brielle rushed over and hugged Marella. "It was an accident, you idiot. It wasn't your fault."

They were not judging her—at least, not yet. What about Noah?

His expression was stern, but not because of what she'd done. When he spoke, he emphasized each word, thereby emphasizing the danger. "Marella, if you go back to the Green Cat Café, you and Brielle might never be born."

Chapter Eighteen

The next morning, the employee bus brought Marella and Noah to the north end of HemisNorth's Aberdeen facility. Along the way, they had kept an eye out for the lethal fog, but didn't see any. The sun had pushed away an early rain. *It's Wednesday*, Marella kept reminding herself. *August 30, 2023*. Their instructions were to wait in the covered bus stop. There they sat side by side, staring at the grooved bark of the western hemlock trees across the road.

They had sat like this on the beached boat on Wisdom Island after the machine was destroyed, while water returned to the ocean. Alone together. The goal complete, their families saved, hope ahead. They had kissed, their lips warm in the cool air. That was the moment she'd realized she loved him.

The love hadn't vanished. Neither had her anger and sadness. It would be so much easier if she didn't have to be near him. It felt awkward to be silent, neither looking at the other. He fidgeted as if he was uneasy too.

The bloated blare of a horn shocked her out of her thoughts. A dump truck piled with burned refuse lumbered past in one direction; a flatbed bearing concrete pipes went the other way.

"I think we have to be careful of surveillance," said Noah. "They might record or film us. They could track your actions on the computer. They'll want to make sure you don't still think they were responsible for the Aguageddon."

He was doubting her worth again. "HemisNorth has lost so many employees—nobody has time to watch me."

"There are computer programs to track people's computer screens," he said. "A lot of companies use them as standard practice."

She almost argued some more, but decided to choose her battles. "We can be careful about what we say, but I can't do anything about computer tracking. I'll just search quickly."

To their surprise, Belinda drove up in an electric cart, beaming as if they were all old friends about to tackle eighteen holes of golf. She wore a hard hat, safety glasses, and a yellow-green safety vest over a red plaid shirt. "Welcome!" She pointed to the seat beside her, which held similar safety gear. "Put these on and get in, I'll give you a tour."

Marella fumbled as she took one of the bundles. She hadn't expected the personal attention. What if she brought up Marella's TV interview debacle? She donned the gear, embarrassed under Belinda's gaze, as if she were undressing. "A tour!" she repeated brightly to fill the silence.

"Visuals are necessary." Belinda's certainty made it seem like a truism.

Noah donned his gear and climbed into the back. Marella sat next to Belinda, and they eased forward. The road passed a grassy field, where several people were watching what looked like a small helicopter rise from the ground. "That drone is going to serve as a cell phone tower. I'll get you phones as soon as I can."

Phones. They would make things so much easier. Belinda was really trying hard to bring normalcy back. And then Marella could call the number Brielle had told her during her time-travel episode. Three-seven-five-three-seven-eight-nine-two-eight-one, she repeated to herself. Maybe another Marella would answer and tell her exactly what to do.

"What's over there?" She pointed to a fence. Large signs forbid entry, warning of contaminated materials. Beyond were trees, mostly dried from the drought. "Is that part of HemisNorth?"

"No, we don't own that," said Belinda. "It's a former gold mine, poisoned with arsenic. They're in the middle of cleaning up the mine tailings. Arsenic is very, very deadly, so it's a good thing the fence is there. We don't need people wandering over and getting killed. We've had enough tragedy. Speaking of which, we're about to see what's left from the Western Inferno. Prepare yourselves—it doesn't smell good."

Further along the road was a devastated landscape of blackened tree trunks and ashen ground, which the rain had turned to mud. Chimneys and foundations rose from the muck, all that remained of cherished homes. Gray roads slashed through the wasteland. The smell, like burned plastic in an old swamp, lined Marella's lungs.

Their golf cart whizzed by pallets of cinder blocks and stacks of piping. There were excavators, backhoes, and other construction machinery. A cleared area contained flat-top prefabricated buildings and parked buses, cars, and trucks. People in safety vests crisscrossed between them. In the distance several construction cranes rose.

Marella had kept watching for the lethal fog. Nobody here seemed concerned; they didn't watch over their shoulders. That seemed like a good sign.

They came to a city-block-sized excavation, two stories deep. An insect-like vehicle lowered its proboscis into the gigantic hole. "They're pouring concrete for a mixed-use building," said Belinda.

"This is amazing," said Noah. "How did you possibly get this done so quickly?"

She smiled with pride. "Detailed coordination."

The route took them back out of the burned area, where trees stood tall.

"Coordination," repeated Belinda. "It's a common word, I know, but it's more important than it sounds. What the Aguageddon did was to glaringly show how terrible the human race is at coordination. Everybody has differing agendas, and so everybody is at cross purposes. If we focused on the important things, we would be better at them, and we would thrive rather than just survive. Perhaps I should say synchronization rather than coordination. Yes, I like that. The human race needs to be synchronized."

The phrase gave Marella pause. She imagined a parade of blank-eyed people marching off a cliff, but that wasn't what Belinda meant. No, they were just words. Upper management liked to use odd jargon.

She smiled in the bland way she always did at big company meetings when Belinda speechified about the political paradigm or the big picture. Let her get it out of her system. Hopefully this tour would be over soon, and she could start searching for information. She hoped she wouldn't time travel during this ride. She didn't want Belinda to send her off to a doctor instead of allowing her to work.

Belinda went on. "There are billions of people in this world. We can't continue to all go in different directions according to each person's whims. People with vision need to set new directions."

"It sounds like you're saying you can't let people decide matters for themselves anymore." Noah spoke amicably, but it made Marella nervous. He shouldn't say something that she might take wrong.

Belinda laughed. "I like you. You're a straight talker. In a manner of speaking, you're right, we can't let people make major decisions without educating them about the true consequences, because most people lack the foresight to nurture humanity. What we need are leaders who work in the best interests of all people everywhere. Leaders who get it right."

His jaw muscles contracted. "So then what happens when the leaders who make the decisions don't get it right?"

If she had been sitting next to him, Marella would have squeezed his hand in warning. Noah was right, Belinda had made the wrong decision to allow Project Athena to go forward, but it was best to set that aside, or they would risk alienating her and losing their access to HemisNorth files.

"The right leaders will get it right," replied Belinda placidly.

They came to a steel frame the size of a house. It held a gigantic pen-shaped tool from which concrete flowed like soft-serve ice cream. Belinda gestured proudly. "Here's one of our supersize 3D printers."

Marella watched, mesmerized as the pen traveled a rectangular path, adding to the top of the house's wall.

Beyond the printer stood rows of townhouses, the finished product. They were a strange mix of styles with their verandas, steel roofs, and rounded adobe-like walls.

It was astounding how much HemisNorth was accomplishing, but there was so much more to do. The length of this tour was making her uneasy. Belinda was taking a lot of time out of her overloaded schedule to show them around. Why?

Noah had suggested that the reason Belinda wanted Marella back at HemisNorth was to make her less credible. Nobody would believe she would keep working for HemisNorth if the company had caused the Aguageddon. She questioned whether she had done the right thing coming here, but then reminded herself of her goal: to stop the deadly fog from spreading. Appearances didn't matter. What mattered was that she was here, however she'd gotten here.

"There's something I'm curious about," said Belinda. "You must have known Len and Eshana before you were hired, because they said they knew you."

She stared straight ahead. This was an unsettling bit of news. She was absolutely sure she'd never encountered Len and Eshana before being hired. Belinda was wrong.

"I'd never met them before I started working at HemisNorth."

"You must have." Belinda sounded chatty, as if gossiping. "Maybe at a party? You moved a lot, Elizabeth told me. Maybe one or the other was a neighbor."

It surprised Marella that Elizabeth had told Belinda about her nomadic life. She supposed it shouldn't. People talked about one another, though they must have had more important things to talk about than an assistant.

"No. I never met either one."

Unless... she could have met Len and Eshana earlier, by going back in time. The idea was troubling. If her future self had done that, she would have told them how dangerous the climate machine was—and yet they still built it. Perhaps she'd given them the idea to do so. She would have to be extremely careful during any time-travel interaction with them.

Belinda was quiet for a time, her brow furrowed as if thinking something over. "You probably just forgot. When you remember about Len and Eshana, tell me. I'm very curious. You can talk to me anytime you like. I don't need to remind you how special you are to me." She gave Marella a smile so heartfelt, she couldn't help but smile back just as broadly.

They pulled over beside a man who wore a chambray shirt and tortoiseshell glasses. "This is Norton Semply, the head of purchasing. He'll get you and Noah set up."

Belinda took their safety gear, then rumbled away.

Norton rubbed his flat forehead and straightened his glasses in one smooth motion. As he marched them toward a cluster of prefabricated buildings, he said, "Being a purchasing manager at the Seattle headquarters must have been very different than here at a manufacturing location. More higher-ups to please."

Marella squirmed. "I wasn't a manager. I was a project assistant."

Norton slowed briefly, looking at her sideways, then picked up speed again. "So you must know the purchasing systems well."

"Not really. I was in the environmental compliance department."

He seemed confused. "You're going to be a purchasing manager though. Do I have that right?"

"It was Belinda's idea."

Norton seemed to think that made perfect sense. "Ah! If it's Belinda's idea, then it's the right idea. To fix the future, fix the now." He stuck out his fist in that disturbing salute.

It was good to have his approval, though it seemed odd that it had come so suddenly.

He addressed Noah. "You're new, so we'll need your information to get you on the payroll."

"No thanks," said Noah, more vehemently than Marella would have liked.

Norton gave a confused chuckle. "You don't want to be paid?"

"I'm just here to help Marella," said Noah.

"Gotcha. But we'll need certain information if you're going to be on-site. I have some fires to put out first. Oh, sorry, too soon. Not real fires. Figurative ones."

They reached a portable building like the ones brought to overpopulated schools. It stood on stilts; its white siding was dented in several places. "This is ancient, half a century old," said Norton as they stepped inside. "Almost as old as me."

Inside, their steps echoed and the floor felt unsupported, which made Marella think of the impermanence of her life. There were several desks with computer setups, but nobody occupied them. It smelled like a HemisNorth air freshener that Marella recognized as freesia, which they used to use in the bathrooms in the Seattle offices. This too made her think of impermanence. The Seattle office gone, burned during the Western Inferno.

What was more, her very being was temporary. At any moment she could be fragmented by time travel. It felt as if time itself was stalking her, waiting for the right moment to snatch her away. Marella's stomach fluttered with hope and anxiety. How close was she to changing that by learning something she could use?

Norton motioned to a desk with a computer. Marella sat in a rolling office chair. Noah remained standing.

"There's still no internet," said Norton. "We only have access to files on a limited network, set up between a few of these buildings."

This made her anxious. A limited network meant fewer materials to search through.

Norton went on. "You can learn by diving into the minutiae. I have a task for you that seems tedious, but it'll give you a feel for plans and specs, and for different materials. Plus I'm desperate to have this done. So bear with me, all right?"

Marella nodded vigorously, as if his needs mattered.

He rubbed his forehead and straightened his glasses. "With building development, every step has the potential to hold up the next step. For example, if we don't have pipes, we can't install plumbing, and so we can't put in tiles or cabinets."

Marella's smile became more forced the longer he spoke. *Please get the hell out so I can play spy.*

"With no phone service or internet, we have to create hard-copy purchase orders. You'll start by cross-checking them before they get couriered to the factories and distributors. Be quick, because supply is sporadic after the disaster, and sometimes we have to pivot."

He brought up various files and folders on the screen while he explained what to watch for, how to mark errors, and what order form matched what type of product.

Finally he turned to Noah. "Do you need anything in case she has a seizure? A pillow or something?"

Marella felt embarrassed by the way he spoke as if she weren't there. But he would never believe the truth, even if she could tell him. *I don't have seizures. I'm a time traveler who's trying to save the world for a second time.*

"We don't need anything," said Noah. "But she gets tired, so it's probably best to let her dive into it while she has the energy."

Marella silently thanked him for finding a way to move things along.

Norton rubbed his forehead without straightening his glasses. "Gotcha. Coffee's behind you, bathroom's over there. Use P-59 as the billing code on your time sheet. To fix the future, fix the now." After making the fist-bump gesture, he left.

They were alone. Noah glanced around, possibly looking for cameras or microphones that might be monitoring them, then positioned himself at a window.

She pondered Belinda's words. *When you remember about Len and Eshana, tell me.* Why did that matter? She couldn't help wondering if Belinda had been testing her beliefs about Project Athena. Never mind. What mattered was what she was about to glean from the HemisNorth system.

Chapter Nineteen

Marella was happy to see that the network folders bore some of the same names as in Seattle. She ran a search but found none labeled *Athena*. She then used a tool to search for that word within each document. Nothing came up. She'd known it wasn't going to be that straightforward, but she had to try.

She clicked on a menu and saw that the employee database wasn't on this network. She searched for the boat schedules. There were none. That was a fail too.

She ran a search for her friend Diana Brinkhauser, who had worked on Project Athena in Seattle. Only one document came up: *Deceased Staff*. Her heart was in her throat. *Not Diana. Please not Diana.* But it was true. Her friend was dead. It was such a cliché to call somebody full of life, and yet Diana had fit that description so well. But now she wasn't, so what was she—full of death?

Marella's throat tightened, making it hard to squeeze out the words. "My friend Diana died at the refugee camp on Mount Rainier."

"Marella, I'm so sorry." Noah trotted over. She got the feeling he had been about to embrace her, but held himself back. Just as well. She wasn't sure she would have had the wherewithal to push him away, he seemed so affected by her grief.

Whatever he felt, he got past it and spoke bluntly. "Keep it together though. We might not have much time here."

There it was. The judgment once more. Did he think she was going to wail and cry for the next hour? Her feelings of resentment returned.

She tied up her grief and resentment in an imaginary bundle, which she set aside so she could concentrate. It was true they didn't have much time, especially when she might time travel right into a lethal fogbank at any moment.

Noah returned to the window while she scrolled through more folders. *Templates. Schedules. Finance.* Finance, she decided. Follow the money. She clicked on it, but a pop-up said access wasn't allowed.

That was a dead end, but she remembered seeing a budget that had been prepared for a management team meeting. Was there still a folder labeled *Meetings*? There was! She opened the most recent spreadsheet, from the previous year.

She didn't know what she expected to find. She'd already searched for *Athena*, and the term hadn't come up. Still, she scrolled through the pages, increasingly discouraged, but unsure what else to do.

Then she spotted something: *Project A, prototype.*

She joggled her heels with excitement. That had to be Project Athena. The code-name system for the most important new projects was like hurricane nomenclature, which sequenced through the alphabet, and they never had many going on at the same time. Project A was Project Athena. Prototype referred to the machine they'd kept in Building C.

The next line said *Project A, site one.* If there was a site one, did that mean there was a site two? She kept scrolling. Ten lines further on, she found *Project A, site two.*

Project A, site two. There was another Project Athena.

Belinda lied. That was her first thought. A lie of omission, but still a lie.

Unless it had never been built. But then, the budget amount was two hundred million dollars, which seemed to indicate it was well underway last year.

Now there was hope. The information she needed to control her time travel could be at the second Project Athena site.

Seeing her excitement, Noah came over. She pointed to the spreadsheet. When he nodded, eyebrows raised in comprehension, she tabbed to the right through the spreadsheet cells to view additional columns. It showed the prototype location as being in Seattle. Project A site one showed as *Forks, Washington.* Wisdom Island had been offshore of Forks.

Marella scrolled some more, increasingly excited. Site two was... where?

Aberdeen. She nearly burst out of the chair. There was a second Project Athena nearby. In spite of Noah's warning that they might be recorded, she ventured, "It's here somewhere!"

He wasn't excited. He spoke as if imparting disappointing news. "I haven't seen any sign of it."

She hadn't either—there were no twenty-story loops at the manufacturing facility—but maybe they were on another nearby property belonging to HemisNorth. She'd seen a map once that had all of HemisNorth's properties worldwide. She tapped the table, trying to remember.

In a stockholders report. That was it.

She called up the most recent report and paged through it until she came to a world map with dozens of dots representing HemisNorth and HemisSouth locations, on every continent except Antarctica. She searched through the report pages until she reached Washington State.

At the bottom of the map, the Aberdeen facility was a long rectangle next to the river. Belinda had driven them on a road that led north. East of that road was another large rectangle, which indicated it was also HemisNorth property.

That was the property with signs warning of contamination. Belinda had said it didn't belong to HemisNorth, but it did. She had lied about that too. She may have had compassion for Marella, but she also had secrets from her. No matter how friendly she was, Marella couldn't fully trust her. She wasn't going to get the full story from Belinda, ever.

Marella started to talk, but Noah handed her a notepad. On it she wrote, *Belinda lied. She said a mining company owned that land. The second Project Athena must be there.*

We would see the towers, responded Noah.

Not if they're camouflaged like on the island.

He shook his head in the manner of somebody who can't seem to get a break.

Marella smelled ammonia and felt cold. Her skin prickled as if she was disintegrating. Noah's face dissolved from forehead to chin, then the rest of him turned to sand and whisked out of sight. The world fell out from under her.

Eternity was tearing her into a billion pieces. She begged wordlessly for somebody to make the agony stop, but there was nobody to answer her plea.

• • • •

FOR EONS HER BODY ASSEMBLED itself, then a dull light wavered all around. Who was she? Where was she?

Marella Wells. That was her name. A welcome heat grazed her shoulders. The ground under her feet was a tan color. Her sight cleared, and she saw it was a carpet of dried grass. Nearby were three Japanese maples and four benches. Beyond that was a three-story building, its glass reflecting a light blue sky.

This was the lawn at the HemisNorth corporate campus, where she'd often taken her lunch break, but that made no sense. All these buildings had burned down during the Western Inferno. It wasn't possible to be in a place that didn't exist.

As her thoughts grew less muddled, she understood. She'd time traveled to before the Aguageddon, before the fires devoured the corporate campus. Not only that, she could see Building C, off to the left. No yellow warning tape was draped around it, which meant there had been no explosion inside, so the Project Athena prototype hadn't exploded. Not yet.

She felt compressed. Either another Marella had time traveled here too, or the Marella that worked here during this time period was here. If the latter, that would mean it was sometime between her hire date and the date of the explosion, when Len and Eshana died.

Excitement warmed her further, making her skin tingle. The prototype hadn't exploded, and so Len and Eshana were alive! She could tell them not to build Project Athena. She could alter history—stop the Aguageddon from happening—but she had to act fast. There was no telling how much time she had left to perform a miracle.

She took a clumsy step toward the glass building, where she used to work, nearly falling, but catching herself just in time. She felt brittle and feared she might break a bone, even on the grass. She had to wait for her joints to loosen. She needed patience. Yet she yearned to get to the building. She'd never wanted anything so much. Getting to Len and Eshana seemed more crucial than any desire she'd ever had.

She waited some more, glancing back at Elliott Bay slapping onto the riprap at the edge of the lawn. When she was last here, the water had disappeared, leaving a stretch of sand and rocks. She could keep that from happening. Make sure it didn't drain away. All she had to do was get inside the building. So easy, under other circumstances.

Finally she took several stiff steps, then a few more; soon she was careening across the lawn toward the building.

Reaching the door was a success of sorts, but it was heavy, made of thick metal, and she hadn't regained enough strength to merely yank it open. She placed a shaky foot on the wall, both hands on the handle, and pulled hard. It opened halfway; she sidestepped in. It smelled like ramen noodles.

She passed a small lounge where staff could buy food from vending machines, eat lunch, or take a break. Two employees she didn't recognize were laughing politely at something a third had said. The perfection of their clothing struck her as odd. Crisply ironed slacks and silky, unstained blouses and button-downs, reminding her that only a couple of weeks ago such attire was not only possible, but expected, while she wore ragged leggings and a shabby blouse.

At the sight of Marella, the employees' smiles disappeared. In her attire they might think her a vagrant and stop her from reaching Len and Eshana. She propelled herself down the hall. At the elevator she punched the up button and sagged against the wall. This end of the building had the slow elevator. *Patience. It'll get here.*

A man emerged from the break room. "Hey, where's your badge?"

On a different Marella, she thought, but that answer wouldn't make sense to him, and anyway she didn't trust herself to speak clearly, even if she could think of the right thing to say. The elevator arrived and she spilled in, punching the third floor and close door buttons. The door slid shut with a satisfying double clunk.

She was almost grateful for the time the elevator took to rise so she could gather her thoughts, but when the door opened she felt just as scattered as when she'd entered. She pushed her way out before the doors opened completely, heading right, keeping a hand on the turquoise wall for balance. Their offices were down the hall. One foot in front of the other.

Suddenly she arrived at Eshana's office, and there they were! Eshana sat behind her wraparound teak desk, wearing a swirl-pattern sheath dress, looking so much like Nefertiti that Marella wondered where her headdress had gotten to. Len, who stood in front of the desk, resembled a tall Sigmund Freud, in turn missing a cigar and a three-piece suit.

The floor-to-ceiling view of Elliott Bay made Marella dizzy enough to clutch the doorframe as she caught her breath. Instead she looked at the desk, which held a plant like a giant praying mantis, which nudged her to pray, *Don't let me screw this up.*

She still didn't know what to say to them. They seemed increasingly alarmed as she forged ahead anyway, before time could snatch her away. "This will sound crazy, but I've come back from the future. Project Athena is dangerous. It doesn't work like it's supposed to. It will take all the water away from the world. Don't build it. And it's making me time travel, so I could disappear at any moment."

Her legs buckled. She caught herself on a low bookcase.

"Come, sit." Taking her by the elbow, Len guided her to a beige leather chair that faced the window. Its thick padding squeaked like a mouse when Marella sat too hard.

"It's going to be all right. You're just having a bad trip." He spoke with indulgence, seeming familiar with such a situation.

A bad trip? You're right, but not in the way you think. "I'm not on drugs," she said.

Len reached for his phone. "I'll call Elizabeth."

"No. We don't want to get her fired. She's our inspiration." Eshana spoke matter-of-factly, as if saying *I had eggs for breakfast.*

"You're right," he placed a hand on his heart. "I'd feel badly. She's been too important."

How could I be their inspiration? Too important? What does that mean? But the fact that they recognized her confirmed the time frame she'd suspected: sometime between her hire date and the date of the explosion.

Eshana came from behind her desk, all practicality. "Let her calm down, and then I'll drive her home."

Marella tried to sound levelheaded. "I swear, I really have been time traveling. Project Athena is causing it."

"Okay, okay," soothed Eshana, clearly not believing her. And why should she? The statement sounded ludicrous.

A sudden movement outside on the lawn startled them all. It was another Marella. Marella grimaced from the heightened feeling of compression.

Along with surprising her, the sight of herself embarrassed her. She had no control over her own body, and it was appearing and disappearing randomly. Oddly, she wanted to explain it away. Then a realization broke through her distraction, and she pointed frantically. "That's proof that I'm time traveling! There's two of me."

The other Marella was looking up at them. A shiver ran down Marella's spine, as if a changeling gazed at her.

"How could I be right here and down there too?" she asked, like a teacher quizzing her students. "Because I'm time traveling."

"She could be telling us the truth," said Eshana. A sense of wonder made the sentence melodic.

Len put his hand on the window, fingers spread, gecko-like. Still speaking as if talking Marella down from a trip. "You're look-alikes."

"But she appeared out of thin air," said Eshana.

"No, no." He flicked the air in disagreement. "It was a trick of the light. The water reflecting on the window."

Eshana seemed hyperfocused on Len now, as if persuasion was a laser she just had to aim at the right spot. "I saw what I saw. And we discussed time travel as a secondary effect."

They discussed time travel! What... how... why... Don't interrupt. Let them work out what happened, then she would also know.

Len, too, became hyperfocused. Marella got the feeling that this was how they worked together, aiming their laser-beam arguments at each other until they met and combined into a single ray of light. "Yes, we did discuss time travel, but that was idle speculation, taking it to the nth degree. You know as well as I do that too many things would have to align to make it happen."

"And yet she's both here and there." Eshana nodded at one Marella, then the other.

The other Marella stepped backward, then vanished. Eshana and Len made noises of surprise so synchronized they sounded like a piano chord.

"How did she..." Len's head made little movements side to side, as he seemed to process this event.

"You see?" Eshana was jubilant. "It's true. She's time traveling."

"Apparently she is." His tone was ironic. "Tell us more. How does it work?"

Marella's heart dropped. They were supposed to tell her that. But never mind, they now believed she was time traveling, so she repeated her plea. "Don't start Project Athena up. It's too dangerous."

"It's already running," said Len, returning to his indulgent tone. "So you see, you have nothing to worry about."

Eshana gave a brisk nod, agreeing with him.

They had started it up. Not good. But a billion people hadn't died, not yet. There was still time to keep that from happening. She wiped sweat from her brow; the chill from time traveling was gone and she felt overheated. "You need to shut it down. It was supposed to take carbon dioxide away, but it took water. Rivers, lakes, the ocean. All the water in the world started disappearing. When the seas receded, the atmosphere lowered, and people in the mountains died. A billion people died because of your climate machine."

Eshana held her palm out, indicating *stop*. She, too, spoke indulgently. "Athena isn't large enough to have that kind of effect."

"But the humidity data proved it," said Marella. "In circles around the island."

"Circles?" asked Eshana. "What circles?"

She wasn't explaining it properly. She took two deep breaths, resolving to make sense. "I got humidity data from the National Weather Service and the Canadian government and plotted everything on a map. I marked towns with the first date they each dropped to zero humidity. Then I used a drawing compass to connect the dots, and it made concentric circles, with the middle spot out in the Pacific Ocean, where Wisdom Island is."

Eshana's eyes widened. "Where Project Athena is."

"Eshana, we shouldn't confirm details about it," said Len gently.

"She already knows."

"Yes," said Marella. "I know that's where Project Athena was because I've been there. My concentric circles looked like a bull's-eye, matching the progression of the Aguageddon exactly. I proved that Project Athena caused the Aguageddon."

"Aguageddon?" asked Len.

"The media called it that. Where's the other Project Athena? That's the one that's making me time travel."

Len crossed his arms. "We certainly can't tell you that."

"Is it east of the Aberdeen facility, in the area they say is contaminated?"

Eshana opened her mouth to speak, but Len put a hand up to stop her.

"You're not denying it, so it's true, right?" said Marella. "Why is it making me time travel? How is it happening?"

"She said she has no control over the time travel," said Eshana. "We should at least give her the conceptual basis. That will help her."

"Yes!" said Marella. "Please."

"No, we should definitely *not* give it to her," said Len. "And anyway, we'd have to get it from the site."

If the site was Aberdeen, the drive would take hours from Seattle. Marella had never time traveled for that long, so she set the idea aside. The important thing was to convince them of the danger. If she could do that, her time traveling would never begin in the first place. "Elizabeth died because of the machine. Both of you die because of it. When you try to shut the prototype off, it explodes and kills you."

Len took a step back, as if she were contagious.

Eshana shook her finger, indicating she had gone too far. "What I gather from everything you've said is that Project Athena isn't functioning as intended. We'll do a deep dive and find the cause. We'll make improvements."

"No, it's too dangerous," said Marella. How could she make them see? "If the first module has been turned on, then the drought has already started. You must have noticed how unusually dry it is. Things evaporating too quickly. It's not usual. You can already tell something's off."

"That's true," mused Eshana.

"We'll look into it then," said Len. "I'm sure we can fix any problem."

Marella pumped a fist into her hand, making Len and Eshana start. "Your damn machine caused a drought so bad it killed a billion people. It created a lethal fog that's going to kill billions more. I saw it in the future, in 2024. You're acting like your car just needs a new battery. Don't just 'look into it.' It's too deadly."

Len motioned for her to calm down. "Let's be rational. The 2024 you saw is only a potential future for us."

Marella pulled her head back. "What do you mean?"

"Eshana and I could make countless different choices that would change our future." He opened his arms wide, illustrating the vastness of their options. "You have described only one of those potential futures."

Eshana nodded vigorously. "Now that you've visited us, we'll carefully consider our actions to create the best possible future."

Marella spoke passionately. "Forget the theoretical stuff. I'm real, right in front of you, telling you that you're going to die when the prototype machine explodes. That's your future. Your only future, unless you shut it off remotely."

Eshana fingered a tiny pink bow that was pinned to her dress, showing that she had donated to a breast cancer drive. Until now, the fabric pattern had concealed the bow.

Marella froze, all thoughts fleeing except for one. There had been such a drive on the day of the explosion. Today was the day Len and Eshana died. She shuddered, suddenly nauseated by the thought that the two people in front of her were actually dead.

She opened her mouth to warn them. Only then did she realize that the nausea was caused by time itself, now reaching out to convert her into ice. She smelled ammonia and her skin prickled. Any words forming in her mind dispersed before they could become real. Len and Eshana crumbled away. Marella's body and soul tore into pieces, which scattered out to eternity.

Chapter Twenty

P ain, immeasurable pain. No understanding who had ripped her apart, or why. Yet after a boundless struggle, her particles found one another somehow. She became real.

When Marella recovered, she found herself in the portable building, in front of the work computer screen, which showed today's date as August 30, 2023. Wednesday morning. She was shivering hard. Noah was there, but not rubbing her arms to warm her as he would have done before they split up.

She didn't speak for a while, at first because her lips and tongue were stiff, and then because she was disappointed in her failure. She'd had the chance to change the timeline, but hadn't convinced Len and Eshana of the danger.

Finally she indicated that they should go outside to talk. Noah helped her down the steps. When they were far enough from the building that Noah felt safe from surveillance, she said, "I saw Len and Eshana."

"Really? Did you tell them not to run the machine?"

Marella nodded ruefully.

Noah paused, looking around as if he expected a tornado to carry them off. "Then they must have done it anyway. Otherwise the timeline would have changed, and things would be different."

"There's more," she said, swallowing hard. "They said I was their inspiration. Something I said or did helped them when they were building Project Athena. But I'd never talked to them about it until then."

He frowned. "It sounds like you'll see them when you go even further back in time. Don't say a word to them."

She tamped down her annoyance at his obvious advice. "I asked them if the second Project Athena was east of the Aberdeen facility, at the so-called contaminated mine site. They didn't deny it, and they acted like I'd figured it out. Plus, they said there's a conceptual basis of some kind that could help me understand Project Athena, and it's at the site."

"They didn't confirm that Project Athena is at the mining site. That's a problem."

"They didn't in so many words. But Belinda made such a big deal about staying away from that area. I really think it's because she doesn't want us to know the second Project Athena is there. We need to go see for ourselves."

Noah blew air between his lips, indicating reluctance. "If that's not the Project Athena site and Belinda was telling the truth about the contamination, then we'll get arsenic poisoning."

"It's the only lead we have. I've looked everywhere on the network I can think of."

"It's a huge risk. Arsenic is no joke. Dust gets in the air, and you can breathe it in. That incident where you stop breathing is coming up soon." He looked away, as if trying to get ahold of himself. "We don't have masks or protective clothing. Maybe that's where it happens."

She touched the scar where she'd cut her arm, the same scar that would be on the limp body in the tree house. She tried to sound courageous. "I'm willing to take that chance."

He seemed alarmed. "I'm not sure I'm willing to let you."

"It's not your call," she said coldly. "We split up, remember? If you're afraid that you'll get hurt, then you don't have to—"

"It's not that." He stared at the sky. At first it seemed he was merely gathering his thoughts—finding the right words—but when he spoke he had a hard time reining in his emotions. "The thing is... you're the key. It seems like everything hinges on you, so if you die without stopping the lethal fog, everything is lost." His face contorted with the effort to keep his voice steady. The last few words became a wail. "Everybody dies. All of them. Our families. All gone. All lost."

His emotion was catching, the wail sliding into her soul. She rubbed her arms, still cold from time travel, in the hope that the movement would separate her from his grief.

She felt the weight of his statement. *I'm the key. Everything hinges on me.*

Noah swiped his face, forehead to chin, then did it again. It didn't change his expression of woe.

After a bit of time, she managed to speak calmly. "You're right. It all seems to hinge on me, and the mining site is all I've got. We don't have any other plan. And besides, it rained this morning, which would keep the dust down and any arsenic out of the air."

"But you do stop breathing. And it happens soon." He was controlling himself now, but with effort.

"Not because of arsenic. I didn't look poisoned. I wasn't throwing up or ill-looking. I had just stopped breathing. That's all."

He looked back at the portable. "It'll take a while. We don't know how they'll react to us leaving. We might not be able to come back."

"I've done what I can here anyway." Had she? Was she being too adamant about this?

Noah looked away for some time before finally saying, "All right. Let's get this over with."

• • • •

MARELLA AND NOAH PLUNGED into the forest, where fat tree trunks hid them from view. The dry pine needles above and salal leaves below were the same reddish brown as a hair dye Mom had tried once, to disastrous effect.

They watched out for the fog while tramping through the knee-high undergrowth. The dry plants crackled with each step, like somebody chewing ice, which had always gotten on her last nerve. She winced at the strain on her ankle, which had been doing better but needed more time to heal.

Climbing over the fence into the restricted zone felt dangerous, like entering lion territory. They reached a dirt road and decided to follow it rather than stick to the woods, while being ready to dive back into the forest if any vehicle should come along.

Noah seemed unreadable, possibly thinking about the mercy killing that had led to their breakup. Marella dwelled on it as well. The three choices she'd had circled like rearing horses on a merry-go-round: Continue pulling Elizabeth on the makeshift sled along with them, which would have slowed them and kept them from saving the lives of all humanity. Leave her to die alone, which had been the woman's worst fear. Perform the mercy killing.

After a long silence, Noah said, "I've been thinking about something."

Her head felt extra stuffy with the physical exertion. She hoped he wasn't going to build on their argument. The trek was hard enough as it was.

"If we'd left Elizabeth to die alone, that would have been murder," he said.

Marella stopped in her tracks. In all her agonizing over Elizabeth's death, she had never looked at it that way. She wanted to understand it, but couldn't quite get there.

It must have shown on her face, because Noah continued. "I know, I know, she was going to die anyway. But technically—or spiritually maybe—I don't know which—it would have been murder to just leave her to die. And then we both would have been to blame. What you did protected me."

Marella wasn't sure how to feel about this. He seemed to be justifying what she'd done. That didn't wipe out the judgment he'd had when he looked at it differently. That didn't change anything.

Or did it? It was almost as if he'd been looking for a way to understand. Trying to heal the breach between them. That counted for something, didn't it?

Noah began, "When you didn't stop the other Marella from killing Elizabeth..."

Here it was. The *but*. The *however*. He wasn't going to let her off scot-free.

But he didn't accuse her. Rather, he spoke with respect. "You did the right thing by not stopping yourself. Because if you had, it would have changed the timeline. We wouldn't have survived. Everybody would have died. That must have been hard. Really hard. You sacrificed your well-being to save the rest of us."

He took her hand in his, almost reverently. It felt surreal. Unable to forgive herself, it seemed impossible that anybody else would do so. And yet, he was.

He went on, speaking fervently. "I've been wanting to tell you that I appreciate how selfless you've been. Wait, that sounds banal. What I mean is, everything you've done has been from your heart. I haven't forgotten that the first thing you did was save my life. I'd have suffocated in that smoke if you hadn't risked your own life to get me into the car. And going to Wisdom Island instead of back to your family... with me arguing with you to go back. It was what you wanted to do more than anything, go back, but you stood your ground. I'll never forget your face when you stopped the car and ripped me a new asshole. I thought, damn, watch out for Marella, she doesn't pull any punches!" His laugh was a little forced, and tinged with concern, as if he feared rejection.

Marella flashed back to a moment in the control room, back on the island, when they had initiated the shutdown of Project Athena that would bring on a massive explosion. A countdown had begun and she had told him to leave, so he would be safe. She'd planned to wait—alone—until the last possible moment to ensure the machine would shut down.

He had refused to leave her. He had been willing to die with her.

They hadn't died, of course, but it proved that in spite of any judgment he held for her, in spite of anything that might go wrong between them, he would be there for her to the death. To the death! It had been wrong of her to gloss over that moment. It defined what they had together, what her stubbornness had almost lost her.

He was still holding her hand. She covered his hand with hers.

And with that, they were reunited.

It was bittersweet. The guilt of the mercy killing would always stay with her, solid as a beef carcass, with or without his forgiveness. The fact remained: she was guilty. That would never go away. Her mouth still tasted of warm iron and wet mold.

Plus, Noah spoke of her sacrifice. Another sacrifice was intertwined with her goal. If she somehow found a way to change the past, she would erase the Aguageddon, which would erase meeting Noah. She would be choosing sacrifice yet again, giving up love and happiness.

"I thought I knew some strong women, but you..." Noah smiled broadly. "When you reach the pearly gates one day, and you're standing in judgment, I wouldn't want to be Saint Peter. Because you're going to give 'em hell up there."

They kissed. For a few moments, everything else was forgotten. Then they had to keep going. But this change in their relationship buoyed her.

"Do you really think we would meet again if we changed history to stop the Aguageddon from happening?" asked Marella.

"Of course. It was fate that we met, and it'll be fate when we meet again."

Fate. The word had become ugly to her. "So then the past and future are fixed and we can't change them. The moving spotlight theory. The houses are already built and somebody just shines the flashlight on them."

Noah pulled his head back, showing he'd been misconstrued. "No, God gives us free will. The future isn't fixed."

"So then how can it be fate?"

"Are you trying to talk your way out of canceling the Aguageddon?" he teased.

"No, it's just that I want to believe you. I want to know how I can fix the world and still have you in it."

"I think certain things are meant to be," he said. "Not everything. Not the Aguageddon, but you and me. We're meant to be. Can't you feel it?"

Because he said it so sincerely, she could, which bolstered her. "Of course. We're such an item that people will call us Mar-Noah."

He chuckled. "Sounds like a candy bar."

"What other things are meant to be?"

"Oh-ho-ho," he said with the exuberance of a pirate. "I've got a whole list of things that are meant to be or not meant to be. Handlebar mustaches, not meant to be. The Seattle Seahawks, meant to be. Pink clothing, not meant to be. Crocs, not meant to be. Pineapple on pizza—"

"Meant to be," finished Marella.

"Are you crazy?" He slapped his forehead with his palm melodramatically. "Not meant to be!"

"On my half of the pizza."

"You're not tainting my pizza," he said, laughing. "We're getting separate pizzas."

"If we must. What do you have against pink clothing?"

"Just not my color. Doesn't bring out my eyes," he joked.

They were quiet for a while as they continued along the road, then Marella said, "That house we're going to build."

"Yes?"

"It'll need a tennis court."

"Sure, if we can also have a golf course."

She laughed. "A golf course is a lot bigger than a tennis court. What else do I get?"

"My undying love?"

"That's pretty big. I guess it'll do."

In spite of being reunited with Noah, Marella began brooding. Until now she hadn't pictured herself confronted by another Project Athena. But now the possibility seemed real. The climate machine itself could be ahead. When she looked through the enormous loops of the first Project Athena, back on Wisdom Island, she'd had the same terrifying sense of eternity that she experienced when time traveling.

That Project Athena had sent a bolt of slow lightning to zap her head, making her feel as if her skull had split and leaving her with the uncomfortable stuffed feeling she'd had ever since. What would the second Project Athena do to her? Would it cause her to stop breathing?

Logic, plus a feeling of increasing doom, entreated her to turn and run the other way.

A cricket jumped onto the road, turned different directions as if deciding on its path, then tiddlywinked back the way it came.

It's a sign, thought Marella sardonically. *We're supposed to go back.* But of course it wasn't really a sign. Just a cricket. No matter how fearful she was, she would keep going.

It smelled like rot, and soon they understood why. Somebody had dumped a load of junk beside the road. A wooden pallet. A stained quilt printed with kittens chasing balls of yarn. A white sock, stained brown on the heel. A folding chair missing its seat.

There were loud, confident-sounding voices ahead around the bend. Marella and Noah ran into the woods, then crept forward, moving slowly to keep the crackling of the foliage from giving them away.

The road was blocked by a tall iron security gate that bore a sign warning against criminal trespass. A chain-link fence topped with barbed wire extended into the woods on either side. Beyond the gate the road turned, so they couldn't see what it led to.

Behind the gate were two armed men in camouflage and combat boots. One examined his surroundings with the squinty look of a man who excels at sharpshooting; the other spit on the dirt.

"They don't guard old mine sites, do they?" she asked.

"Not that I know of." Noah motioned to the fence. "We're going to have to climb over that."

"The quilt we saw back there—we could use it to cover the barbed wire."

He scrunched his face. "I nominate you for the most disgusting idea award."

At the dump site, Marella pulled at the quilt, then dropped it. The smell of rot, along with the already present taste of warm iron and wet mold, made her gag. Noah scooped it up instead, leaning his head away from its stink.

Following the fence line, they crossed a small creek. Young sword ferns jutted up from the wet earth. They climbed over a log, dislodging white fungus shaped like half a dinner plate.

Noah tossed the quilt over the barbed wire. By climbing carefully, they made it over the fence without being jabbed.

Treading forward, they reached a clearing's edge. There were dozens of people within sight. Some were unwrapping a pallet of pavers, while others loaded solar panels into a truck. Many were attending to a concrete-block wall that was being built at the edge of the clearing. A crane was lowering a six-foot-tall block onto another one. The wall was at the beginning stages; a trench showed where the rest would go.

"They're building a fortress around the whole site," said Noah.

"Good thing we came before they got very far. We'd never get past that."

A few steps away from them were a porta-potty, a dolly, a bucket of metal parts, an emergency eyewash station, and a pallet of cinder blocks. They crept forward and peered around the cinder blocks. Ahead was a windowless green structure the size of a small house. Mounted on top was a giant loop, about five or six stories high. The wheel was painted a brown camouflage pattern that blended with the tree bark and dry leaves.

Marella grasped Noah's arm, as if to keep from drowning. "It's the second Project Athena."

He wrapped her in a steadying grip. "Don't worry, it's not turned on."

On Wisdom Island, when the machine had been running, the view into each loop's vortex had felt like looking into eternity. It had been terrifyingly disorienting, to the point where her very soul felt in jeopardy. But not today. No whirlpool swirled in this loop. What she felt instead was a presence. Like a dormant dragon lying on a mound of gold, ready to awaken at the slightest sound.

That was just her imagination, of course. Still, even the wheel's reduced size seemed imposing. The slightly altered shape—more oblong than those on Wisdom Island—struck Marella as perilous, as if it were a technologically advanced guillotine that sliced through souls rather than necks.

A slurry churned in her stomach. The first Project Athena had almost turned the planet into a desert. It had almost killed her family. She and Noah had shut it down, setting off an explosion that destroyed it. And now, here was another, poised to cause another Aguageddon.

Chapter Twenty-One

L en and Eshana had suggested fixing Project Athena so it would work properly. But it couldn't be fixed. The loop on this module exuded wrongness, even without being turned on. Why hadn't the builders and constructors seen it? "That thing is evil," said Marella. "Do you feel it too?"

Noah glared at the loop as if to subdue it. "I don't have to feel it. I know it."

A white tank the size of a railroad car bore a picture of a red flame and warned of flammable liquid. A label read *Diesel*. Pipes ran from the tank into the Project Athena module. "Why would they use diesel?" asked Noah. "Athena was supposed to reduce global warming. Powering it with fossil fuel makes the whole machine pointless. She lied to keep you from knowing Project Athena was here. And now this. We can't trust her."

Belinda lied. We can't trust her. Marella tried to reconcile the Belinda she thought she knew with the one that lied, but came up short. No matter. By leaving the work site, she'd burned that bridge. She would probably never see her again.

She pointed to a one-story building, exactly the same size and shape as the one on Wisdom Island, with high windows. "That must be the control building."

"It looks dark," said Noah. "Nobody's inside."

The people finished loading the solar panels into the truck, climbed in, and drove off. Using fossil fuel and removing solar panels. Something definitely wasn't right.

There were a dozen people between them and the control building. "The door is on the side," said Marella. "If we could just get over to it, nobody would see us go in."

"I've got an idea." Noah pointed excitedly at the porta-potty. "We're going to hide in plain sight. You get in. I'll use the dolly to wheel you to the control building."

"Are you kidding me?"

"No. It's brilliant! It's like you said, we just have to get to the door. That's how we do it."

Marella eyed the bright green plastic porta-potty with a smiling moon face on the front door. Her mother called them thunderboxes and avoided them at all cost because she'd caught a norovirus from one. "I nominate you in the most disgusting idea category, and you win."

Although she didn't relish the idea of riding in a porta-potty, she would do it if she thought it would work. But how could it? "These people don't know you. They'd be suspicious even if we still had our safety vests and looked official."

Noah chuckled quietly. "Nobody will question the porta-potty man. They'll be too busy thanking God they're not me."

Marella imagined the armed guards dragging Noah away while she cowered in the porta-potty. "I don't know. We might have to wait until evening, when everybody is gone."

"The control room door will be locked then."

"It might be locked now." She fished in the bucket of metal parts, picking out a piece of cast-iron pipe the length of her forearm. "This would break a window, but it would make noise."

"If we have to use it, we can muffle it with my shirt." He put his hand on her cheek. "Let's do this now. You know as well as I do that we don't have time to wait."

Marella stroked his cheek in turn. He was right. The way things were going, she could time travel several more times before evening. That was dangerous for both of them.

She opened the porta-potty door. A wave of chemical and excrement stink burst forth. Holding her breath, she stepped in. In the toilet tank a pile of gloppy feces bathed in a pool of cobalt-blue water. Bits of toilet paper looked like surrender flags on a tiny deserted island.

The lid was missing. There was no way to shut out the stink. What was more, a wad of toilet paper blocked the urinal drain, creating a pool of liquid.

She shut the door, locked it, and braced herself against the wall with one hand, holding the pipe in the other. The wall was sticky.

"Ready?" asked Noah.

Absolutely not. Breathing as shallowly as she could, she replied, "Ready."

He tilted the porta-potty and began rolling it, which sent the liquid in the urinal and tank sloshing onto her. She gritted her teeth. This was all for a good cause.

The jerky movement felt like the start of an amusement park ride. She imagined a whole train of porta-potty cars on a roller coaster. Next would come a slow, anticipatory climb, a steep descent, and several loop-de-loops. Where were her restraining belts?

She hoped she wouldn't time travel. Although, come to think of it, it would be nice to be somewhere else, if she could just blink and make it so.

Her nose itched. Her hands were occupied. Scratching would have to wait.

Still more rolling. Still more sloshing. Finally they stopped; they must be at their destination.

A man's voice called, "Hey!"

Marella started. Was he addressing Noah or somebody else? The porta-potty remained tilted.

"Don't put that there," said the voice, louder and closer. Marella breathed even more shallowly. She had a cramp in her leg. Her nose still itched.

"Got to put this here for cleaning." Noah feigned bored disinterest.

"That's not a good spot. Put it over there."

"I was told to put it here. I'm just trying to do my job."

"I don't recognize you."

Marella winced. *Go away, go away, go away.*

"Julien Boone," said Noah boisterously. "Glad to meet you. They brought me up from the Texas facility."

"To do what?"

"Whatever needs doing."

"You don't sound like you're from Texas."

He should have said California. Too late now.

There was a pause. Then Noah said, "I'm from all over. Military brat. You know."

"Yeah, well, don't put that there. It'll be in the way."

Noah began pleading. "Bro, don't get me in trouble. I'm already on my boss's shit list. Let me just put this right here, where I'm supposed to. If I have to move it again later, that's fine by me."

"Take it back to where it was. I'll talk to them. Who's your boss?"

Noah's voice became panicky. "Look, bro, I've got a kid and my wife is injured and I cannot, just *cannot* lose this job."

Marella hoped the man would believe the mournful catches in Noah's voice. Was he overdoing it?

There was a moment of silence, then Noah continued, with increasing pathos. "This always happens to me. I got one person telling me one thing and another person telling me another, and then I'm the fall guy when things go wrong. One guy says, 'Drive the shipment to Houston,' the other says, 'that stuff was supposed to go to Dallas,' and the other says, 'I don't know what Julien's problem is, I told him Dallas, and he ends up in Houston. Houston ain't Dallas.' Who are they going to believe, me or—"

"All right." The man sounded annoyed. "You can leave it here for now."

"Thank you. Thank you!"

Now they could get on with things.

"Set it down," said the voice. "I need to take a piss."

Marella looked over at the door lock, which had shifted during the trip and would easily open from the outside. She imagined the man discovering her. What would she say? *Oh, hello there. Inspector Wells here, just checking for porta-potty cleanliness. Looks like the staff need better aim.* She clutched the pipe tightly, hoping she wouldn't have to use it.

"I wouldn't if I were you," said Noah. "There's shit all over the seat. And the walls. People are sure nasty, aren't they? They have a bad day and they think everybody else should suffer. Can't you smell that?"

"Forget it," said the voice. "Here, I'll help."

"Careful!" said Noah quickly. The porta-potty dropped to the ground. Marella slipped, falling half on and half off the seat. The pipe fell into the tank with a wet *splitch*.

She rose, slowly, silently. The man must have heard her. If he opened the door, she would grab the top of his head, she decided, pull it down, slam her knee up to his chin. She wasn't a fighter. Could she do this? She lifted her hands. Ready.

"Sounds like we got a loose tub in there," said Noah. "If it's not one thing, it's another. Hey, what are those things up there, anyway? They look like giant magnifying lenses without the glass."

No, don't ask that. It seemed that Noah was trying to distract the man by asking him about Project Athena, but he was calling attention to the fact that he shouldn't be here.

The man spoke confidently. "Bladeless wind turbines."

"Gotta love technology!" said Noah.

"Yeah. For sure. All right then, to fix the future, fix the now."

"To fix the future, fix the now."

They would be giving each other that Nazi-like fist bump salute. Marella heard footsteps walking away, then the door opened and Noah peeked in. "He's gone. Come on out."

She sprang out and took a deep breath of fresh air. Such a relief!

They were at the control building entry, with nobody in view. From here she could see more of the modules, like a row of giant Ferris wheels, but there was no time to gawk; they needed to move fast.

Noah tried the door handle. "It's locked. We have to break in. Where's the pipe?"

"It fell in the tank," she said.

"I'll go find something else."

"We need a ladder too." Looking up at the high windows, she saw cross-hatching on the glass. "Oh no, it's security glass."

"Oh shit, you're right. No wonder there's no guard right here. This place is secure."

The growl of a truck sounded, coming in their direction. They huddled against the door. Surely they hadn't come this far just to get caught.

"Wait." The keypad on the door triggered a memory. "No, it couldn't be that easy." She mouthed the numbers as she keyed them in. "Three-seven-five-three-seven-eight-nine-two-eight-one."

There was a soft beep, and a small light turned green. Noah gave her a look of astonishment, then realized how she'd known. "When you time traveled and Brielle told you the number. That's crazy."

Cracking the door open, Marella peeked in. The room was dim. She opened it some more. Nobody there. They were lucky this Project Athena wasn't on yet, otherwise there would be people here. They entered; Noah shut the door behind them.

A high window gave them enough light to see. On a desk was a printout with dates and numbers. There was today's date, next to the entry code she'd just used. She wondered how Brielle had gotten it.

Also on the desk was a small marble statue of what looked like a Greek woman. Probably the goddess Athena, after which Project Athena was named. She wore a tall helmet and draped robes. Wrapped around her wrists were snakes. Marella shuddered, imagining live snakes coiling themselves around her wrists.

Noah began looking through desk drawers, one after the other. "We're looking for something called a conceptual basis, right?"

"Yes, but I don't know if that's the exact title."

On a shelf lay a binder labeled *Health & Safety Plan*. She flipped through it quickly, seeing sections on personal protection equipment, scaffolding, fall protection, and the route to the nearest hospital. She dropped it back on the desk and opened a cabinet. Window cleaner, bottled water.

Finding nothing in that room, they made their way toward the operations room. There were no windows, so she turned on the light.

Behind a wall of glass, a ten-foot-wide copper cylinder hung from the ceiling. From it, dozens of thin pipes descended, connected to one another by coils. Hundreds of transparent wires also hung from the cylinder. It was a quantum computer like the one that had been on the island. She remembered it as terrifying because she knew its power, but thankfully this one was less imposing. Merely an overcomplicated mobile. Or so she told herself.

In front of the glass wall stood a control center with a keyboard and monitor. Only a couple of weeks ago she had been in a room just like this, frantically keying words into the keyboard to turn Athena off. The memory made her hands sweat.

Several file cabinets stood against the back wall. From one, Noah yanked out a two-inch-thick comb-bound document. "Plans and

Specifications." He flipped through the pages. "Portland concrete, nails. This can't be it." He returned it to the drawer.

In a different file cabinet, Marella scanned the folder names. "Conceptual basis! Found it." She yanked out a folder and extracted a thin comb-bound document, which was jam-packed with complex mathematical equations. "I don't know what this means. But—what's this?" She showed Noah a diagram of a sphere, with dots covering the outer surface. In the center of the sphere was the word *Athena*.

"The shape of time," he said. "Or not."

Disappointment flooded through her. Somehow she'd envisioned finding the conceptual basis and magically understanding how time travel worked. It wasn't going to be that easy at all.

Yet Noah was excited. "This could be the answer! Hadrian will understand it."

"Of course!" Now they just needed to get it to him. Marella tucked the document into her waistband, fluffing her shirt over it so the outline couldn't be seen.

A grunting noise sounded right behind her, and she felt something touch her leg. Marella whirled, hands up in self-defense.

"That's you!" said Noah.

It was. She had the uncomfortable sensation of being compressed. The other version of herself sat on the floor, wearing the same leggings and gray blouse she herself wore, shivering and breathing heavily. Her eyes had a dull look that was impossible to read. It was disconcerting to be unable to fathom what was going on in her own head. She put both hands on the other Marella's face, willing her to recover so she could find out what time period she was from and what she knew.

And then Marella remembered she'd felt hands on her own face after time traveling, and somebody—she'd thought it was

Brielle—had told her the number. But it had been her own voice. She just hadn't recognized it since she sounded different inside her head.

This Marella was from the past, and she now had to tell her the entry code to the door of this building.

"Listen to me," she said to her doppelganger. "Remember this number. Three-seven-five-three-seven-eight-nine-two-eight."

To Noah, Marella said, "I can't tell if she understands." She kept repeating the number.

The other Marella vanished. She gasped. It felt almost as if she had died. And without the compressed feeling that had accompanied her, the room felt cavernous. She needed a moment to adjust, but Noah urged, "We got what we came for. Let's get out of here."

She shook off her confusion as best she could and followed him. Just as they reached the door to the outside, there was a series of beeps. Somebody keying in the code to the door lock. Was that the other Marella? Would she meet herself both coming and going?

"Hide!" Noah hauled her away from the door, but it was too late. Two men burst in. Seeing Marella and Noah, they drew guns.

Marella froze. She'd never held so still in her life. Two guns aimed right at them. Death times two. She felt linked to the weapons by invisible pulleys, as if the slightest motion would trigger them.

Beside her, Noah was breathing quickly. Out of the corner of her eye, she saw him poised for action; she imagined him leaping forward, wresting both guns away at once and klonking each man simultaneously with the gun butts. Then she imagined him leaping forward and getting shot.

Neither happened. He pleaded, "Let her go. This was all my idea."

A wave of love and respect for Noah nearly overwhelmed her. Love for his willingness to take the fall for them both. Respect that while she was rooted in fear, he was trying to get her out of this mess. How had she ever doubted him?

One of the men had the physique of a bull and a face to go with it. He was looking at her with such contempt that it seemed as if he wanted to shoot her. He nodded toward the door. "No talking. This way."

A car and a delivery van were outside. Following Bull Face's direction, she climbed into the van. It smelled of motor oil.

She had assumed Noah would be right behind her. Instead, the other man directed Noah toward the car. They were being split up. *Just like Brielle had said would happen.*

Where would they take him and what would they do to him? It was different for a Black man, he'd reminded her before. She knew about the unheeded pleas from people who couldn't breathe. The beatings. Noah's face was electrified with worry, his face sheened with sweat. He mouthed, *I love you.*

Before she could respond, the van's back doors shut hard, startling her. That was it then. The last time she would see him, unless she found her way out of this quickly.

She was in an empty, dim, windowless cargo area, the umber paint on its metal floor scraped from use. The doors were locked from the inside. There were no tools or implements to use as pry bars or weapons.

The engine started; she braced herself as the van pulled out. She was in a terrible situation. She had no support for her goal, no one to keep her safe after time travel, no one to help her escape. And while Belinda had forgiven her for mentioning Project Athena on TV, there was no smoothing this over. Marella had discovered something she wasn't supposed to know.

She had discovered that this wasn't a side project. HemisNorth was putting a lot of resources into launching the second Project Athena, in spite of the fact that there was a monumental amount of rebuilding to do, refugees to support, basic health and food needs to attend to, political instability to maneuver. There was more to

Project Athena than solving the environmental crisis, especially if fossil fuels were powering it.

Could Belinda have believed Marella's warning that it was a death machine? Could she hold the same convictions as Preston, the cult leader who'd thought that God was using the Aguageddon to purge Earth of wicked people? He had nearly kept Marella and Noah from shutting down Project Athena, which would have killed most of humanity.

Did Belinda hold similar beliefs? She didn't know Belinda's religious leanings, but it was difficult for her to believe they involved mass slaughter. Still, Marella felt she was missing something, that there was more to Belinda's actions. She was hiding something.

The fact that they were building an enormous protective wall around the site also gave her pause. Why did it need such protection?

Regardless, by trespassing in the Project Athena control room, she'd made herself an enemy; she was in great danger, because sometime soon she would stop breathing.

Somehow, before that happened, she had to find a way to get free and take the conceptual basis to Hadrian. He was her last hope. His brilliant mind could save them, if she could only reach him.

Chapter Twenty-Two

A half hour after being taken from the control building, Marella was imprisoned in an outdoor storage area the size of a basketball court, surrounded by a chain-link fence topped with barbed wire. A mesh screen on the fence somewhat obscured the surrounding fields. The giant manufacturing tanks and towers of HemisNorth's Aberdeen manufacturing facility loomed all around. A storage area was an odd choice for detainment, but it must be a holding place until she could be moved to a more secure location.

Bull Face had brought her here in the van. Another man arrived in an SUV. With his gargoyle eyes—large and gray—Marella could easily imagine him perched on an ancient building, gazing over an ancient city.

Both men stood sentry just inside of the gate. They watched Marella intently, as if she were a lizard that might skitter off.

She tried not to let their attention faze her while she took stock of her surroundings. There were a dozen wooden reels, wide as hot tubs, some holding cabling, some empty. A wooden shed's double doors were padlocked. A forklift sat idle.

She suspected she and Noah would both end up in jail. She'd never been arrested, and for some reason kept picturing being chained to a stone wall in a dungeon. After she banished that image, another took its place: a maximum security prison with clanging doors and squint-eyed mobsters.

But then, what if Belinda didn't send her to jail, out of fear she would disclose details about Project Athena? It was possible. The CEO of a worldwide company needed her to keep quiet. There were ways of doing that, especially in unstable times. And yet, Belinda wasn't the type of person to hurt her, was she?

Whatever Belinda's intentions, Marella would never stop the lethal fog while imprisoned. She needed to get the conceptual basis to Hadrian. They'd missed it in a quick pat-down, but she wouldn't be so lucky if she was handed over to the police.

She was unlikely to escape with the guards watching her, but she could at least familiarize herself with her surroundings, in case they left her alone for some reason. She ambled past the forklift. She'd never driven one, or even looked closely at one, though a glance told her it needed a key but didn't have one. She passed the shed and approached the fence. There were no obvious gaps in the barbed wire or bends in the chain link, and the mesh screen would make it hard to climb.

"Get away from there," yelled Bull Face.

Turning obediently around, she spotted an extendable ladder tucked against the side of the shed. She stifled a gasp and let her eyes slide away, pretending she hadn't just seen a possible escape method. Perfect! If she got the opportunity, she could lean it on the fence and climb right over the barbed wire, then drop to the other side. She would have to be careful of her strained ankle.

And then after that? Getting to Hadrian's house on foot would take a long time. If she could somehow get a ride...

Of course, she didn't know whether the opportunity to use the ladder would arise. She had to first try other methods. She approached the guards, trying not to be intimidated by their fierce expressions. "This is a dangerous place to be. A deadly fog has been showing up in Aberdeen, and we need to be able to get to higher ground if it appears."

Gargoyle Eyes snarled. "No talking."

I'm trying to save your life. You have no idea. "But—"

Bull Face whipped his gun out and aimed it at her. Marella backed up, heart racing. *Okay. Lips zipped.*

He sheathed the gun.

Her eyes darted around. What now? She imagined wielding one of the giant reels like a yo-yo, sending it looping around the guards to wrap them in cable. Or leaping over to the ladder, lifting it from its hooks, and deftly angling it onto both guards at once, thereby pinning their arms and freeing their guns for the taking.

Why was her mind being so impractical? She needed a real idea. If ever there was a time for brilliant inspiration, this was it.

A car was pulling up. Marella's heart sank. Was this the police, coming to transfer her to jail, where escape would be impossible? No—even through the mesh on the fence she could make out that it wasn't a police cruiser, and the person getting out wore a red plaid shirt, jeans, and heavy-duty boots.

Gargoyle Eyes opened the gate.

Belinda! Marella readied herself to deal with her fury. After all, she'd given Marella a second chance, and she had slapped her in the face with it.

Except that Belinda didn't seem angry, or even affronted. Surprisingly, her tone was businesslike with a touch of knowing warmth, just as it usually was. "Let me lay out the issues, and then we'll chart our path forward. Agreed?"

Marella nodded automatically. Path forward? That would be a strange thing to call going to jail. So then what did she have in mind? Was this going to be easier than she'd thought? Did Belinda actually view this as a minor infringement? She thought that unlikely, but earlier Belinda had easily forgiven her for mentioning Project Athena on TV.

Perhaps she still thought Marella's mind was addled. Marella could admit to it, then ask that she and Noah be released to get treatment and meds. Yes! That was a good plan.

Belinda settled onto an empty cable reel far enough from the guards so they wouldn't hear their conversation. Marella sat on one opposite her, careful to keep the conceptual basis from showing under her blouse.

Belinda made a face when she smelled the urine on Marella's clothing. "So it's true what they told me about the porta-potty. That was a brilliant work-around. You certainly live up to your reputation."

"Let Noah go," said Marella. "I was having delusions. He was just trying to keep me from hurting myself."

"Don't worry about him, he's fine. I have more important things to talk with you about."

She seemed strangely calm for the situation. She put her fingertips together, seeming to indicate that what she was about to say had taken great thought. "You're probably wondering why we're going ahead with Project Athena when climate change isn't at the top of everybody's agenda. People might not care about damage to the environment when they're mourning those who died, when they're struggling just to get by. People just want to move on. They think they can put climate change on the back burner and return to it when it's more convenient."

She paused, as if waiting for a reaction. Marella nodded, trying to appear compliant.

"The fact is," said Belinda, "climate change is more of a problem in our current situation than ever. Perhaps you don't know, but construction and buildings are a huge contributor to the problem." Her intonation, emphasis, and pauses were flawless, as if she'd perfected this speech for a TED Talk. "Almost forty percent of global emissions come from creating and using cement, steel, aluminum, and other building materials. And we're about to embark on the largest building project in the history of the world."

She was certainly persuasive. Marella believed she truly cared about humanity. And yet... the diesel tank seemed to show that she wasn't really trying to stop climate change. There was something Belinda wasn't telling her. She was lying again.

Belinda had the smile of a person with good news. "And now we've discovered an even greater benefit to Project Athena, and that is to relieve drought. I've been working with scientists and engineers to modify the modules and the programming to bring water where it is most needed."

Marella's mouth parted in surprise. She understood now what a mistake it had been to tell her that Project Athena had caused the Aguageddon. It wasn't that she had misjudged her character—in fact she had been correct that Belinda truly cared about the world's people. She cared so strongly that she was determined to direct Project Athena toward good. Like Len and Eshana, she mistakenly thought it could be fixed, even improved.

Belinda reacted to Marella's surprise with obvious satisfaction. She'd tried for such a reaction, and she'd gotten it. "The World Health Organization says that every year fifty-five million people are affected by drought. By 2030, seven hundred million people will be displaced by drought. And right now, forty percent of the world is impacted by water scarcity."

She leaned forward. "I'm going to put my cards on the table, because I believe that you truly care about humanity and want a better world for you and your family. I'm going to tell you the real reason I asked you about Len and Eshana."

Chapter Twenty-Three

B elinda seemed to enjoy her dramatic pause. She had a sly look, as if handing Marella a birthday present she'd always wanted.

What was she going to say about Len and Eshana? Marella caught herself twisting her fingers; she relaxed them, still trying to appear compliant.

Belinda shifted on the wooden reel, then finally spoke. "The reason I asked you about those two is that before you were hired, something you said inspired them to find a solution to a sticky problem they were having with Project Athena. It helped them make the prototype and the first Project Athena run correctly. But whatever they did to fix them hasn't been recorded, or at least we haven't found it yet. We're having a problem getting Project Athena Two—the one you just visited today—to run right."

This corroborated what Len and Eshana had told Marella: she was their inspiration. She felt queasy. It seemed likely that while time traveling she would do or say something accidentally that would solve their problem. She had to be very careful of everything she said to them if she saw them. Or even say nothing to them at all.

In any case, she wasn't able to tell Belinda how she had inspired them—and even if she could, she wouldn't. Marella enunciated her words for emphasis. "I never talked to Len and Eshana before I started working for you."

"Yes, you did." She flicked a hand to show that Marella wasn't going to get away with any nonsense. "I need to know what you told them. Think. Think!"

Marella chopped her hands, emphatic. "I don't know. I keep telling you, I never met them before."

Belinda's voice hardened. "You did meet them. What did you say?"

She would never have described Belinda as evil until that moment, but something in her eyes seemed demonic. Marella understood now that she might do anything to further her own agenda.

She tried not to show her dismay. She must appear to be in line with whatever Belinda said. Gripping the edge of the wooden reel on which she sat, she forced herself to speak calmly. "I want to help you. I want to help relieve drought. But I swear to you, I really don't know."

Belinda looked fierce, as if she would bore the answer out of Marella's head if only she could. Denial wasn't going to get Marella out of this place. She needed to make something up, and it had to sound plausible. "Well... now that I think of it, I was in the elevator once in this building near the HemisNorth campus. There were a couple of people that could have been Len and Eshana. They were talking about tall buildings. I made a joke about jumping up if the elevator car broke and started falling. They said something about... I know... seismic engineering..."

Belinda growled in irritation. "You're not a good liar, Marella. I'm losing my patience over your selfish behavior. I want to save billions of lives. Help me do that." She touched Marella's shoulder.

She felt chilled, as if Belinda's impatience was glacier melt, flowing into her veins.

But Belinda wasn't making her cold. It was time travel. Eternity reached for her from all sides—there was no escaping its talons. It shredded and pulled, drawing every particle of her being away. The agony was too much to bear, but she could only endure it. Endlessly, for all time.

• • • •

SHE BEGAN TO FEEL SOMETHING other than torment. A chilling breath waterfalling over her entire body. What creature had breath that cold? An ice monster, with icicle teeth...

No, there was no such thing. That was the wind, chilling her further, which should have been impossible since she herself was already formed from ice.

Not ice. Flesh. She was Marella, a person. And the wind meant she was outside. Her vision checkered into being, warbling and stuttering. The ground below her feet was gray. Concrete?

Her immediate surroundings wouldn't come into focus, so she looked up and saw sky, dark blue, interrupted by a streetlight. Evening or night, then.

After a time she could see well enough to make out a building, with glass entry doors. Inside, a blue railing lined a wide flight of stairs.

This was Bothell High School. What was so important about this place that the time gods would send her here twice? She felt compressed, so at least one other Marella was here.

She was still gathering herself, waiting to feel stable enough to walk, when Len and Eshana strode right past without seeing her, Len straightening his bow tie and Eshana making a wide gesture as if pulling taffy.

Marella's heart beat so hard her skin warmed perceptibly. Len and Eshana had been to her school. This could be how they knew of her. So she had talked to them after all, but didn't remember. She must have inspired them inadvertently, giving them the very idea they'd needed to solve the problem that was keeping the climate machine from working. Her younger self had empowered their dream machine, and now she had to prevent her from doing so. It probably hadn't happened yet—Len and Eshana had just arrived—but she might not have much time to act.

Len and Eshana opened the door. Marella called to them, but it came out as a grunt, and they didn't seem to notice. They went inside.

Two teenagers strolled up to Marella. James, who loved biology and hoped to sail around the world on a boat someday, and Maddie, who wanted to be an environmental lawyer. She'd hung out with them while she'd gone to school here, reveling in their enthusiasm for life.

"Hey Marella, what's good?" asked Maddie.

She tried to tell them she had to hurry, but the words came out garbled.

"What's wrong with you?" asked James, alarmed.

"Oh my god, she's having a seizure."

"Don't let her fall." James took one arm; Maddie took the other.

Marella struggled, which only made them grasp her more firmly.

Abruptly, she remembered one day when Maddie asked her if she was epileptic because of the "thing that happened at the science fair." Marella had laughed, thinking it a joke about something they'd learned in biology class. Now she understood that Maddie had been serious.

That meant today was the science fair. Now it made sense that there had been nobody upstairs when she first time traveled here. If only she'd realized that then, she could have changed the timeline already. But she was here now. She had another chance.

At this fair she had displayed a three-tier board about selective attention, which allowed a person's brain to filter out the massive amounts of information coming at her every millisecond, enabling her to focus on what mattered. Without it, a tsunami of color, motion, and sensory input would prevent even the simplest of actions.

In her bedroom, with Brielle giving her artistic advice, she had painstakingly drawn a human form, then added labels and explanations. Remembering that day made her long for a part of her life that was over.

Abruptly she realized why she didn't remember talking to Len and Eshana. They could have been inspired merely by seeing her board. It seemed that something to do with selective attention had helped them solve a problem they were having with Project Athena. Could that minor project really have inspired the destruction of everything she loved and be the downfall of the human race?

Apparently so. She had to stop them before they saw it.

Marella tried to speak again; this time the words came out clearly. "I'm fine. Gotta go."

She pulled free and headed for the door, limping awkwardly. Her friends tried to follow her, but she waved them away. So that she wouldn't have to open the heavy door, she slipped inside behind others as they entered.

She felt compressed. There was another Marella here.

She stumbled past students, parents, and teachers and reached the cafeteria. It was packed, with several hundred people milling around the science exhibits. A miniature wind turbine. A poster showing the effect of vaping on cardiovascular health. A light bulb made from a jar.

She couldn't see Len and Eshana, but that didn't matter as long as she kept them from seeing the board itself, which would be at the far end of the room. All she had to do now was get to it and take it away.

The crowd shifted, and she saw the other Marella. The sight jolted her, no matter how accustomed to such a thing she thought she was. Her other self looked so normal. She hadn't been through catastrophe. She hadn't been time traveling. She wasn't trying to save the world. She was just trying to get a decent grade.

Just as Marella headed that way, the other Marella left the cafeteria. She now remembered leaving when an odd feeling of compression had made her ill. At the time, she'd thought she needed air. She'd had no way of knowing there was a time traveling Marella entering the cafeteria.

She spotted Len and Eshana, only ten feet away from her board.

She rammed through the crowd, bumping into people as she went. There were cries of "hey," and "look out." She accidentally knocked down one of the students.

A teacher grabbed her by the arm, wheeling her around. Her gym teacher. The one she had admired for her fairness. Now it was working against her, as the teacher ordered Marella to apologize.

"I'm sorry," she blurted, yanking her arm from the teacher's grip.

Too late. Len and Eshana were looking at her board. Eshana pointed excitedly, then turned to Len, who gripped his head as if realizing something vital. He exclaimed, "Of course! That's our answer."

Now she knew for sure. She had never talked to them, but they had still been inspired by her. By her board.

She smelled ammonia. The room began to crumble. The walls disintegrated. She was cold. Freezing. Time traveling again. She went through the whole terrible process—the feeling of eternity, the pain, the distortion.

She was nothing.

· · · ·

WHEN HER PARTICLES finally began reconfiguring, somebody was talking to her. At first the words seemed insubstantial, fashioned of dusty smoke, which wavered and dissipated before it could reach her ears. Gradually the words solidified into sentences, full of urgency, but without meaning.

Eventually a question broke through her confusion. "Are you all right?"

The voice was familiar. It seemed important to tell it something, but what? Marella was shivering hard, but she tried to talk. Were her words getting through?

It was dark. Was this nighttime? No, light was beginning to seep in. Her vision cleared. A woman was bracing her. The woman was Belinda.

This was Wednesday. Early afternoon. She was in the present—whatever that was—being detained in an outdoor storage area. Belinda, HemisNorth's CEO, had been trying to wrest information from her.

Now Marella had that information. Selective attention. That was what had inspired Len and Eshana to complete the prototype and the first Project Athena, and that was what Belinda needed to know to complete the second Project Athena.

She had to keep Belinda from learning about her panel board. She must never know how Len and Eshana had been inspired by it.

Belinda sounded anxious, as if worried about Marella's well-being. "Marella, these seizures you're having. You need treatment. I know you've had a difficult life, it hasn't been particularly stable, and so you haven't seen the right doctors. Until you do, you'll keep having delusions, such as thinking Project Athena is defective."

She's gaslighting me. Belinda had to know that Project Athena had affected the world's water. Otherwise, she wouldn't have made the leap to use it to affect the world's water in a different way.

"Tell me what you did to inspire Len and Eshana. And then we'll get you to the best doctors." Belinda clasped Marella's wrist with fluid grace. The gesture was meant to be comforting, but those long fingers reminded her of the goddess Athena statue in the control room, with snakes coiled around its wrists. She held still, too distracted to respond. *Don't disturb the serpents.*

Belinda waited a few beats. Not getting an answer, she let go.

"Yes," said Marella, now able to speak and rub her arms against the chill. "I need to see a doctor. Right away. Get medication or something."

Belinda pressed her lips together, as if to say *What am I going to do with you, girl?* With the air of a storyteller beginning a new tale, she asked, "Have you ever heard of the trolley problem?"

"No."

"You have, but maybe under a different name. Here's the scenario. A trolley is heading down the tracks and will hit five people. You can divert the trolley to a different track, where it will only hit one person."

Marella shifted uneasily. What Belinda meant was, you can allow five people to be killed. Or you can kill one person. She seemed to be saying she was faced with the same choice. And so, was Marella the one person? Was she threatening her with death? Marella's body thought so. Adrenaline rushed through her, corralling the chill into her heart. *Don't do something stupid. Wait. See what she says.*

"There are many versions of this thought problem, but here's the one I'm working with. One person versus billions."

She was threatening to kill Marella without saying the words. Fight or flight funneled its way into fight, her fists wanting to pummel Belinda, but she wouldn't win if she struck now, not with the two guards there. She had to let her anger smolder. Think her way out. Not let her emotions betray her.

A sudden realization broke through. Belinda had talked about stabilizing society around the world. Upgrading the world, in fact.

To upgrade the world, she needed complete control. Control over other governments. Whoever controlled the water controlled the world. A working Project Athena was a sword to hold over everybody's heads. She had begun to build a wall around it only after she realized she needed to better protect her weapon.

To fix the future, fix the now. The Nazi-like salute. The way people fell in line behind her. Belinda knew she had charisma, and she encouraged this cult of personality. Even Marella had fallen for it, thinking Belinda cared for her in a special way.

Belinda waited, but when Marella remained silent, she leaned close. Marella could feel her breath flicking her ear, like a snake's tongue. "I'm not playing around with you anymore. When I return in one hour, you will tell me what I asked. For the sake of your mother, sister, and Noah. Think about that."

Belinda marched out of the gate. Gargoyle Eyes closed and locked it behind her.

Marella's burning rage burst into a bonfire. Belinda was threatening those she loved. She stifled the urge to scream at her and threaten her in turn. It would do no good, and she needed to concentrate on a plan of action.

Belinda would be back in one hour. She had only one idea of how to escape quickly, and it wasn't a good one.

Chapter Twenty-Four

While Belinda drove away from the holding area, Marella was already funneling her anger into action. To escape, she was going to try once again to time travel on purpose. Go back in time and stop this madness before it started. Stop all past and future Project Athenas from ever being built. She had to succeed this time. Enough was enough.

Last time she had failed by letting herself be distracted. This time she was resolute. She would not make the same mistakes. She would control her thinking, be strong, be single-minded. She imagined her thoughts as a searchlight reaching up to the sky, unhindered, direct.

Perched on the wooden reel, she pictured the HemisNorth Seattle campus the day she first arrived at work. It had been a cold fall day. The leaves on the trees were bright yellow with a touch of red, not as brilliant as some autumns, but still beautiful. A window-washing rig was hanging in front of one of the buildings.

Her excitement at having landed the job was tempered with trepidation that she would fail somehow in the most visible way. Of course she wouldn't cause a copier to shoot reams of paper out of every slot, or cause a massive crash of the computer system by merely touching a keyboard, but something was bound to go wrong. She'd never worked in an office before.

Her boss Elizabeth had been so businesslike. She remembered thinking of her as distant and unapproachable, so different from later on, after she'd gotten to know her well. It was during their trek across the emptying ocean floor that they became close and Elizabeth described her fear of dying alone.

No! She wasn't supposed to think about that. She was supposed to concentrate on her first day of work, when she was setting her new plant on her desk. She'd heard a whirring sound, the printer coming to life. Then her friend Diana came by to welcome her.

Diana, who was dead now. While Diana lay dead on Mount Rainier, Marella and Noah had been on Wisdom Island, racing away from the Project Athena control building. There was fire all around. The tall pines burning, smoke rising from the dry salal bushes...

Marella felt herself sliding toward the island. Heat enveloped her. She couldn't get air into her lungs. *No! Stop!* This wasn't what she was trying to do...

Her eyes flew open, the island gone. Breathing rapidly and shallowly, Marella wiped her brow with her forearm. She'd almost blown it. In that moment on Wisdom Island, Project Athena was going to explode, and she would risk being hit by flying chunks of metal as big as washing machines. Back then, she and Noah had barely made it to shelter. She wouldn't be so lucky the next time.

She felt a prickling feeling, like needles lightly touching her skin.

"Look at that!" shouted Gargoyle Eyes. He was pointing to the open field in front of the chemical towers. Through the mesh on the fence she saw a white fog fountaining up from the middle of the field, as if an underground pipe had burst. It was spreading outward, hugging the ground. The mesh hid its purple-and-indigo opalescence, but she recognized the lethal fog by the way it roiled. A sense of need emanating from it made her want to hide.

She wheeled toward the guards. "It's deadly. Get us out of here, it's not safe."

"Right," said Bull Face with derision. "Good try."

"What makes you think it's deadly?" Gargoyle Eyes lifted his chin at it. He sounded skeptical, but Marella detected a hint of concern.

"I've seen it kill," she said. "All it has to do is touch you."

"She's yanking your chain," said Bull Face, obviously irritated at the other guard's naivete. "Stuff vents steam here once in a while. It's nothing."

"It's coming this way. We don't have much time. We have to leave now." Marella motioned vehemently toward the vehicles outside of the fence.

"Don't listen to her," said Bull Face. "I saw her on TV. She's a mental case trying to smear HemisNorth."

Marella lied, "I saw the reports. They tested it on mice, and the mice died instantly."

"Bullshit," said Bull Face through clenched teeth, as if she'd just insulted his mother.

"Do you really want to bet your life on that stuff?"

Gargoyle Eyes marched to the fence and peered past the mesh. "That's some weird roly-poly fog. I've never seen anything like it."

"I told you," said Bull Face, "the steam tanks vent sometimes. No big deal."

Gargoyle Eyes gestured at him urgently. "That's not steam. Come look."

"I can see it from where I am!"

The lethal fog was now thirty feet away. Marella shouted, "I'm not playing you. Please. I don't want to die."

Gargoyle Eyes remained at the fence, watching intently. Marella wiped sweat from her face. The fog was now too close for them to unlock the gate, reach the cars, and take off. She scanned the yard. The wooden shed might be high enough to save them. There was a quick way to get up there, but it meant giving away her secret escape tool.

So be it. She had to be alive to escape. She rushed to the other side of the shed, lifted the ladder from its hooks, and leaned it against the shed. Her movements made the conceptual basis comb binding scratch her stomach, but it stayed securely in her waistband.

Bull Face ran to her and yanked her away; she fell onto the pavement, landing on her elbow. The sharp pain sent a shock wave up her arm.

Bull Face grabbed hold of the ladder, body angled so Marella couldn't reach his gun. She leapt up and fought with her uninjured arm to hold the ladder in place.

"Wait," said Gargoyle Eyes. "Leave the ladder there. I don't want to breathe in that stuff."

Bull Face puffed out his chest, still holding the ladder. "Whatever doesn't kill you makes you stronger."

Gargoyle Eyes said grimly, "My dad got emphysema from breathing in shit at work. I'm not being paid enough for that. Get out of my way."

"Whatever." Bull Face backed away.

Gargoyle Eyes mounted the ladder, and Marella tried to follow. Bull Face tugged her away by her elbow; it hurt like a knife stab. "You're staying down here."

The fog spilled through the fence, its iridescence cold and bright, its desire strong and needful. Marella cradled her elbow, feeling like prey. She was going to die. That was what her body told her. Her lungs adhered to her chest wall, and yet she forced air into them. Breathing in, out, in, out, no matter how shallowly.

"Don't be a dipshit," said Gargoyle Eyes. "Belinda wants something out of her. If she gets injured, then it's on us."

Bull Face spit on the ground, seemingly unmoved by the argument.

Anger and frustration boiled up and gave Marella the power she needed. She stomped on Bull Face's instep, then punched him in the gut. He doubled over, groaning.

She clambered up the ladder quickly despite her injured elbow. The sloping metal roof felt hot. She moved carefully on its ridges so as not to slip off.

Gargoyle Eyes was squatting on the roof, giving him even more of the air of a gargoyle. She had no time to contemplate this striking image, because the fog had nearly reached Bull Face.

"Come on, dude," said Gargoyle Eyes nervously. "Get up here."

"I'm coming," he grunted, still clutching his gut. "I'm going to throw that bitch off the roof."

Marella considered knocking the ladder down to save herself from that fate, but she didn't have to. It was too late for Bull Face. The fog reached his boots; he jerked, as if hit by a bullet. He lifted one foot, then the other, swearing. His face twisted in pain, eyes full of fear. He'd realized his mistake.

Gargoyle Eyes clambered partway down the ladder and reached out. "Hurry. I've got you."

The fog rushed against Bull Face like a seashore wave, reaching his legs, thighs, then torso. His yell, long and drawn out, made Marella's skin crawl. He collapsed into the fog, which boiled up, hiding him in its depths as it thickened.

Gargoyle Eyes scrambled back up the ladder, breathing hard. "Holy shit. Holy mother."

The fog flowed around the shed, which seemed to float like a houseboat in an oozing sea of iridescent white. Marella's skin itched like crazy; she scratched her arms and legs.

Four times now she'd seen the lethal fog. Once was in the future, where it had grown large and spread insanely. The other three times were just after she had tried to time travel. Could it be possible that she had caused the fog by those efforts? Had she begun something that was now irreversible, so that the fog was here to stay? That would be a burden too heavy to bear.

Best not to go down that avenue of thought. She had enough guilt without taking on that blame.

Gargoyle Eyes trod carefully from side to side on the slanting roof, peering down into the fog. "He's my friend. He can be an asshole, but he's really a good guy. He's got to be okay."

The fog boiled and whirled, as if in response.

"I'm sorry," she said. Guilt weighed even heavier on her now. She'd contemplated pushing the ladder away. She was capable of killing again, even though she hadn't had to.

"He'll be okay," assured Gargoyle Eyes, as if that could make it so.

Minutes later, the fog flowed away, slipping through the fence toward the tanks.

Where were they keeping Noah? Was it somewhere nearby, and was this fog now heading toward him? Was he, too, outside somewhere, unprotected? *Let him be safe. Wherever he is, whatever he's doing.*

The ground was clear. Bull Face lay motionless on his side. His skin looked all wrong, battleship gray with an ashy dusting. His eyes, the whites also gray, were open and unseeing.

"Dude," called Gargoyle Eyes. He climbed down the ladder gingerly, testing the ground before putting his weight on it, as if the fog might have turned it to mush. Reaching Bull Face, he tried to pull him onto his back, but the man was too stiff, and the skin on his arm crackled like old paper and slipped off in his grasp. He stumbled backward in horror. "No, this ain't happening. No. No!"

Marella moved shakily down the ladder, babying her elbow. She'd come close to death. Close to becoming a gray carcass just like that man.

Gargoyle Eyes circled once, then moaned. "It killed him. Just like that. You were right. Where'd it go? Is it going to come back? Will there be more?"

I have no idea. "Yes, it'll come back. I need to stop it. Let me go so I can do that. I know somebody who can help."

Wild-eyed with fear and grief, Gargoyle Eyes seemed not to hear. He took Bull Face's gun and waved it at her. "Get away."

Marella scuttled backward. He carried the ladder to the gate, then opened it. It appeared that he was going to leave, taking with him her means of safety as well as her means of escape.

"Wait!" She tried to sound forceful, to get through to him. He'd been triggered, past all reason, but she had to try anyway. "Now that you've seen what the fog does, they'll treat you like me. They'll lock you up."

He stopped and looked back at her, eyes narrowed. Was that anger? Against her or the situation?

She continued, as earnestly as she could manage. "I hadn't done anything wrong. I was a good employee. Didn't matter. Now they'll treat you like a criminal too. Bring in guards to keep you locked up. Threaten your family, just like Belinda did mine. We need to stick together. I can help you."

Gargoyle Eyes grunted as if he'd caught her in a lie. He carried the ladder out and padlocked the gate.

Marella yelled with fury. "I saved your life. That stuff would have gotten you too. You owe me."

He shook his head. In disagreement? In refusal? It didn't matter which; he was rushing to his car.

She kept yelling, her voice so strained with emotion she wasn't sure she was understandable. "If I don't get help to stop it, that fog is going to happen more often and spread farther. You and everybody you know are in danger. Do you have kids? Parents? Brothers and sisters? What happens when that reaches them?"

He drove off.

She was alone. She gave a long, loud, enraged cry.

Calm down. She had to get control over her emotions, to think clearly enough to escape. She guessed that Belinda would be back in twenty minutes.

When they had all arrived, Marella had seen Bull Face put his car key fob in his pants pocket. That was what she needed. The thought of touching the man made her gorge rise, but she had to do it, and quickly.

She forced herself to move fast, dropping to her knees. This was the second time she'd had to reach into a dead man's pocket—once for her father's purple booklet, and now for her guard's keys. Her rage threatened to erupt once more. It wasn't fair. Why was she being put through this so soon? Why was she being put through this at all?

Bull Face's leg shifted, making a crispy sound like poorly made papier-mâché. A shudder began in her solar plexus and radiated upward. She scooted her hand farther until she felt keys and yanked them out.

Now she just needed to get over the fence; she would have to do it one-handed because of her injured elbow. She tried to wedge her feet in the holes, but the mesh was too rigid. Plus, even if she got to the top, she would be ripped up by the barbed wire. She needed a better way.

If only she were a giant, she could use one of the cable reels to smash through the fence. For that matter, if she were a giant, she could step over the fence. Ridiculous. This wasn't the time for fantasy.

The forklift. She could use it to knock down the fence, but she had no key, unless by chance it was on the key ring she now held. It could be. She'd once worked at a box store where a master key fit all the forklifts. She started trying them one by one. A stubby one with a bulky square head fit into the key slot. She turned it. The forklift started!

She threw herself onto the seat. Driving awkwardly one-handed, she headed forward. Should she aim for the fence itself, or the poles that held it up? What about the forks—would they get stuck in the fence?

She put the forklift in reverse and backed toward a pole, second-guessing herself the whole way.

Chapter Twenty-Five

Marella pressed Hadrian's doorbell four times, then pounded the lion's head door knocker. "Hadrian! Hadrian!" *Please be home.*

Twenty-five minutes earlier, the forklift had bashed through the fence as if it were made of popsicle sticks. She'd rolled right over it, feeling triumphant as a conquering army. After that, she'd driven Bull Face's SUV toward Hadrian's house.

On the way she'd watched for lethal fog and worried about Noah and her family, just as they were probably worrying about her. For fear of getting caught, she couldn't look for Noah or go to the tree house to warn them of Belinda's threat. Plus, time was of the essence. She had to keep the big picture in mind. It wasn't just her own family in danger.

Luckily she hadn't time traveled while driving, but she was still terrified that the world would dissolve around her at any moment. She had parked a block away in a cul-de-sac, where the car wouldn't be easily seen and identified, then climbed the hill to Hadrian's house.

Hadrian opened the door and made a noise of surprise. "What's wrong? Are you okay? What's that smell?"

The sharp tang of old urine. "I brought you something. Can I come in?" She didn't wait for an answer, but pushed the door open while he stepped aside.

"Of course," he said belatedly, shutting the door behind her.

She had pictured a time philosopher's home as having old clocks, ancient maps, and unidentifiable artifacts. Instead, recessed bookshelves held matching crockery: an orange pitcher, a lime-green bowl, an eggplant vase. There was also a red love seat. Marella would never have matched this whimsical setting to such a humorless man.

"Here. This is the conceptual basis for Project Athena." She thrust it at him.

He paged through it eagerly.

"What does it mean?" she asked. "Does it have anything to do with time travel?"

"I'm not sure at a glance." He indicated the diagram of a sphere, with dots covering the outer surface. "This drawing, do you have any idea what it is?"

"No, but the word *Athena* is right in the middle. That must mean something."

She was still panting. She shifted her weight onto her sprained ankle, then winced.

He seemed to notice her discomfort. "Come, sit." A brown sweater was draped across the red couch. To clear a spot, Hadrian tossed it absentmindedly onto a side table, where it landed on a glass pyramid with a wooden base. The top poked through the loose weave of the sweater.

Marella sat in a wooden armchair so as to not dirty his sofa. He sat on the sofa instead. "Where did you get this? How do you know it's legitimate?"

"We snuck into the control building at the Project Athena site. They've built a second one. But then they caught us..." At Hadrian's look of alarm, she said, "Don't worry, they don't know I'm here. I was very careful. Nobody followed me, and I didn't park in front."

"Yes, but—"

She interrupted for fear he might tell her to leave. "They took me to the HemisNorth plant, and that lethal fog I told you about..." She swallowed. "It killed a man. I just barely escaped from it, and... we have to figure this out."

He waved a hand, like brushing a cobweb away. "I don't see how time travel could have anything to do with a fog."

"When the fog is around, I smell ammonia and my skin prickles, just like when I time travel."

"You said you were at the HemisNorth plant. It seems much more likely to me that something there caused the fog. At any rate, I don't think these papers tell me enough to help you. I need—"

"There's more. Belinda told me that something I said to Len and Eshana inspired them to complete Project Athena. I have the answer now."

Hadrian half stood in excitement. "You do? What is it?"

His enthusiasm gave Marella hope. "I went back in time, to the school again. It was a science fair. I'd made a presentation board about selective attention."

He nodded rapidly. "Ah. Selective attention. That's very interesting. Good, good. And why do you think that inspired them?"

"They were at the science fair. I saw them looking at my board and I heard Len say, 'That's our answer.'"

"Excellent! Tell me everything that was on it."

"There was so much. I don't even know where to start. There was a person, with pictures of things that could distract her, if she didn't have a way of focusing on the most important ones."

"Let's recreate it. I'll be right back." Hadrian rushed to an adjoining room—she could see a desk and an office chair.

With short, quick steps he carried back an awkwardly large flip pad on a spindly metal easel, which snagged the sweater. Marella reached for the sweater to keep it from toppling the glass pyramid. Hadrian got to it first, unsnagging it from the easel, but leaving it over the pyramid. It was as if he didn't want her to see it. Or maybe she was just reading it wrong. He was distracted, that was all.

She helped him straighten and position the easel and flip pad, and he handed her a red marker. At the top she scribbled a sentence of introduction. A cherry smell wafted from the marker. "I don't remember the exact words, but it was something like, 'We're bombarded by constant input. Sights, sounds, touch, taste, smell.'"

"Good, good."

She outlined a human form. Its brain had cloudlike bulges; an arrow pointed to its center. "The thalamus, here, is important to selective attention. All around us are millions of things we have to filter out to make sense of the world." Marella drew simple images, filling up the blank areas. "Trees, buildings, cars, people. And sounds—people talking, music playing, birds chirping. Touch—the feel of the ground under our feet, the wind, the pull of our clothes."

The page full, she flipped it and continued on a second page. "Taste—the coffee we just drank. Smell—garbage, flowers, car exhaust. There are so many things to be distracted by, so how do we keep from getting hit by a car when we cross the street? The answer is by using selective attention. Our brain focuses on what's important and filters out the rest."

She snapped the lid back onto the pen, silently urging him to come up with a solution. He had insinuated he could, given more information, and he seemed like a genius. Wasn't that what geniuses were for?

Hadrian flipped the pages back and forth. "Is this everything that was on your board?"

"More or less. It's what I remember from when I made it. I didn't see it again up close. What could this have to do with Project Athena? I mean, it seems like it would be pretty basic stuff to people like Len and Eshana. Wouldn't they already know this?"

He looked closely from scribble to scribble, like an art enthusiast examining the brushstrokes of a Rembrandt, then he stepped back to regard it from a distance. "Let's talk this out. To start with, what you've drawn applies to humans, not Project Athena."

"That's true. Could it have something to do with the people who would run the machine?"

They were silent for a time, neither coming up with an answer.

"Say it did have something to do with Project Athena," said Hadrian. "What would that be?"

"Project Athena was basically a machine with a computer attached," she said. "A computer doesn't need selective attention. You give it the information. It follows a program."

"And it has the ability to multithread, which makes selective attention irrelevant."

"What's multithreading?" asked Marella.

"It's when a computer processes tasks concurrently. One thread can gather information while another can deal with the user interface."

"Like people multitasking?"

"Maybe," he said, "but most people cannot actually multitask, even when they think they can. We can truly only focus on one data point at a time."

"So we're back to the same thing. A computer doesn't need selective attention. Except that it's a quantum computer. Does that make a difference?"

Hadrian perked up. "A quantum computer? That's unusual. There are a limited number, and they're very fast, very powerful. But a quantum computer can also multithread, I assume, so I don't see the need to give it selective attention."

"Even so, Len and Eshana were excited when they saw my board about selective attention."

"And so you helped them in some way. We just don't know how. The question remains: how does all this apply to your time travel?"

Marella rubbed her temples. She'd hoped he would tell her that. He was the time philosopher, and yet he seemed stumped.

Hadrian tapped a fingertip on his chin. "It's going to take some time for me to evaluate this new information."

"How long?"

"Days, weeks. Honestly, I'm not even sure this is enough to—"

Marella couldn't hide her aggravation. "I don't have weeks. I don't even have hours. You're a member of those philosophy groups. Ask them for help."

His mouth pursed. He seemed offended, as if she'd accused him of being too stupid to solve it himself. He waved the suggestion away like a pesky bug. "Cell phones and the internet aren't working. And I don't know any ham radio operators."

"We might have cell service by now. Belinda was setting up a drone for that. Try your phone."

"Really?" he asked hopefully, retrieving his phone from a charger on a side table. After poking at it, he shook his head and pocketed it. "No. Not working."

She sat on the wooden chair. "Please. You're the expert. I need your help."

Hadrian sighed. He thought for a few moments, then said, "All right, then. Let's look at the impetus behind your ability to time travel. You mentioned that when you were on the island, the Project Athena module hit you with a lightning bolt."

"Sort of. A lightning bolt is quick, and then gone. This traveled through the air for five or ten seconds and then stayed attached to me. I smelled ammonia and my skin prickled. And then Noah pulled on me and the connection broke."

"Describe to me how that changed things for you."

"Right away my brain felt strange, like there was padding around it. It's felt like that ever since. I started time traveling a few days later."

"Have you noticed any pattern to your travels since I last saw you?"

"No. It's still random."

"And what does it feel like when it happens?"

Marella swallowed before answering. To describe it was to relive it, in a way. "It's like getting pulled into pieces. And then I'm just a thing. I don't feel like myself at all. It's horrible. It's hard to explain." She shivered involuntarily.

He tapped his fingertips together, looking into the middle distance. She willed him to have a breakthrough. She imagined him saying "I know just what to do" in a quiet yet authoritative voice. Finally he said, "Would you be willing to try something?"

Anything. Just tell me. "What?"

"I have an EEG machine that I use for biofeedback. I wonder if you could learn to control your mental state. That could be a step toward controlling your episodes, and possibly controlling your time travel."

Marella nodded vigorously. "Let's try it."

He headed for the adjoining room. "I'll be back in a minute. You can wash up a little in the kitchen."

At the sink, she washed the splashes from the porta-potty off her arms. She wondered again if her attempts to time travel had caused the lethal fog. If they had, then the fog might appear again if she learned how to control the time travel. It was a catch-22. But then, if she gained control of her time travel, she would eliminate the lethal fog. At least, that was the hope.

She sighed, drying her hands on a chili-pepper-patterned dish towel. Foul stains remained on her shirt and leggings, but she couldn't do anything about them right now.

Hadrian was still getting the EEG. Marella leaned on the counter, gazing at an egg timer hourglass filled with blue sand. She flipped it, and the sand began funneling down. The shape of time: an hourglass? With a chronon being a speck of sand?

There was another hourglass, filled with water. When she upended it, red bubbles began to spill from the bottom bulb to the top, as if time were running backward. Backward influence?

It could be that the shape of time was impossible to define. Utterly massive and complex, with too many folds and bends and arcs and so on. She might never grasp it. She rubbed her eyes; the lids felt thin as paper.

She returned to the living room. What would the EEG machine look like? She imagined an oversize aluminum colander with coiled wires, which would attach to a dresser-size metal cabinet studded with blinking red lights.

He returned with a hairbrush, a hairband, a computer tablet, and a black plastic gizmo the size of a cantaloupe. It looked like a dead spider, with its thick legs curled in and pads that gave it rudimentary feet. He gestured for her to sit in a chair.

"I was expecting wires and electrodes," said Marella.

"These are electrodes." He tapped a pad on one of its legs. "Put up your hair. It needs to out of the way so the electrodes can touch the skin more easily." He held out the brush and hair band, but her elbow was too painful to hold at that angle, so after a moment of hesitation he began brushing it for her.

Earlier Marella had felt like he was a doctor, diagnosing her illness, but now he seemed like a hairdresser, expertly brushing her mass of hair into a ponytail.

He was good at this. He'd said he had no family but maybe he brushed his girlfriend's hair. She was interested in his story, but not enough to distract him with questions about it.

"That's good enough." He squirted liquid from a travel-size bottle onto each pad, then stretched open the spider legs to position the contraption on her head. She shivered when the wet pads touched her scalp. The headset's pressure intensified the stuffed feeling in her head, as if a monstrous claw was gripping her skull. She hoped it wouldn't distract her from whatever was required of her.

"How do you do biofeedback?" she asked. "I'm not even sure what it is."

"I'll talk you through it when we get there."

He propped up the tablet. Its screen showed an avatar head studded with dots, all green except for a single yellow one. "That electrode doesn't have a good connection." He adjusted the spider leg until the dot on the screen showed green. "Excellent. Now sit very still for a few moments. Good, good. Okay, now let's take a look."

At least a dozen jagged lines scrolled across the tablet screen, reminding Marella of a hospital monitor. The yellow, green, blue, purple, and black lines zigzagged like a saw edge.

"Those are my brain waves?"

"Yes, the raw data. There are different types of brainwaves. Gamma is high concentration. Beta is normal alertness, alpha is quiet thought—being in the moment. Theta is daydreaming and sleep, and delta is sleep. What you see on the screen here are gamma and beta waves. Let's try that biofeedback now. Make sure you're comfortable. Close your eyes. Feet flat on the floor, hands in your lap. Pay attention to your breathing."

Marella complied. Her elbow and ankle hurt. What was he thinking as he watched her? *Breathe in, breathe out.* Was she doing this right? If she had to ask herself that, then the answer was probably no.

"Let your body sink into the chair."

Sink, she told herself, feeling the chair against her legs and back. *Sink. Kitchen sink. No, not that kind of sink.*

"Fill your lungs, deeply but slowly and comfortably. Empty your lungs."

She breathed in and out. In and out. Disappointed. This was a lot like the meditation her mother used to walk her through. She could never really let her mind go the way she should, and his voice was distracting. Deadpan, like a certain type of comedian. Surely a punch line was imminent.

"Your feet are relaxed, your legs, hips, torso, arms, shoulders."

It was also like when Noah tried to talk her through time traveling. That hadn't worked—she had thought of Wisdom Island, where smoke and flames rose from the ground as if hell had cracked open.

Smoke and flames. Fire and heat. Sliding toward Wisdom Island...

She thrashed her arms and let out a loud wheeze. Leaping up, she stood crouching, breathing heavily. She wasn't on Wisdom Island; she was in a living room. Inside, not outside.

"What is it? What happened?" asked Hadrian, curious rather than alarmed.

Marella wiped her face with her hands. "I was about to time travel. Everything was burning."

"It's all right. Everything's okay." His words were calming, but his voice reflected growing excitement. He tapped at the tablet. "My gosh. I've never seen that before in raw data."

"What?"

"Look at the shape." Instead of being jagged, the lines on the screen now had right angles, like a cityscape, square and rectangular. "I don't understand how this is possible. The EEG shouldn't be able to show this. Your brain shouldn't be able to show it either. You say you felt like you were starting to time travel?"

She felt a prickling on her skin. She had the uncomfortable sensation that somebody was watching her. Her skin itched, as if bugs crawled across it. "The lethal fog! It's here somewhere, I can feel it. We're safer higher up. Is there a second floor?"

"No. But remember, that's an artifact. Not real."

"Shit." She ran to a window. Box hedges lined the driveway, which sloped down. "We're on a hill. Maybe that will help."

Hadrian joined her. "I don't see anything."

She ran to another window and spotted the opalescent white fog. "There! I see it. Just the edge, flowing away. It's in those trees."

He joined her once more. "There's nothing there. I'm telling you, it's a phantom image. From your visual cortex."

She suppressed the urge to argue with him, since the fog seemed to be gone. She couldn't see it anymore and her skin no longer itched. She made a whoofing noise, trying to come down from the adrenaline.

"Sit. I'll get you some water."

She sat while he retrieved it, then drank it down.

When she was calm, Hadrian asked, "You said that Project Athena zapped you while you were nearby. What caused that to happen?"

"I'm not really sure."

"Talk me through it. What happened just before?"

"We had just shut the computer down. There was a crazy-loud buzzing. We ran out of the building, because we knew that a bug in the programming would probably trigger it to explode." Outside, everything was on fire already because of the flare gun—" She stopped there, not wanting to reveal that they'd used the flare gun as a weapon.

"Tell me more about—"

"I can't talk about it anymore." Marella shuffled her feet. *Stay in the present.* "I might start going there."

"It's very important. Just tell me about the zapping part."

She looked at her surroundings to ground herself in the present. Red love seat. Orange pitcher on shelf. "It was like a lightning bolt. Slow motion. Coming for me."

"What was the trigger? Could there be something else you did besides turn the machine off?"

"I can't think of anything. We were just running away."

While Hadrian thought, Marella rubbed the chair's armrests, still concentrating on being in the present. Lime-green bowl, eggplant vase. Brown sweater draped on pointy pyramid.

Finally he slapped his hands on his thighs. "I believe that when Project Athena, as you say, zapped you, it didn't merely affect you, but transformed you. Your brain is different now. The EEG machine showed it."

The horror of such an idea turned her mouth dry. Her brain transformed? Meaning damaged permanently? "Could there be something wrong with the EEG machine?"

"It seems to be working fine. It's you. You're different." Hadrian spoke gleefully, which dumbfounded her, not only because he'd been so serious up to that point, but also because his reaction was so inappropriate—like somebody finding joy in an x-ray riddled with cancerous tumors.

The brain waves emitted by her brain were wrong. That meant her brain was damaged. Maybe beyond repair, unless time could heal it. The irony of that struck her. Time serving as a surgeon, splicing her axons and neurons, when in reality, time was a demolition expert, smashing everything in its path.

Perhaps she'd gotten what she deserved. She was a murderer after all. The guilt of that had been with her long enough that now it was part of her. One of the houses she'd lived in as a child had a giant maple tree, its roots exposed yet twisted deeply into the ground. She used to imagine that if you could grasp the tree and pull it upward, the whole Earth would have to come along with it. That was what the guilt felt like, its roots embedded in her the same way.

"I think I might know how this came about," said Hadrian. "Have you ever heard of the resonance theory of consciousness?"

Marella shook her head, which made the contraption seem to tighten its grip on her skull.

"Well, to put it simply," he said, "living things vibrate. The vibrations of different entities can sync up. For example, a group of fireflies may start out flashing randomly, then over a period of time they match up."

"Living things, you say. Project Athena isn't alive."

"No," said Hadrian. "But some feel that it might apply to inanimate objects as well. At any rate, I think I have an idea of what's going on."

She sat straight up. "What?"

"Project Athena was trying to sync its vibrations with you. In doing so, it changed your brain waves—your brain's vibrations. When you came close to time traveling, your vibrations were approximating Project Athena's vibrations."

Marella forced aside her revulsion. She didn't want it to be true, but if it were, she needed to be practical. "What do I do? How can I fix it?"

"Well, I'm thinking out loud here—what if you could gain control over your time travel by syncing your vibrations with Project Athena the rest of the way?"

She ripped the headset off and thrust it at Hadrian. "Hell no."

Hadrian took the headset and put it aside. "I'm not saying I can do it, and certainly not with that headset. Here is my thought process: if syncing your vibrations with Project Athena for a short time allowed you to time travel in a limited way, then syncing them for a longer period of time might allow you to control your time travel. You can get the second Project Athena to zap you so that your brain waves sync with it."

She shook her head fiercely. It was ludicrous. "That would make me insane. Or kill me."

He froze for an instant, as if something had occurred to him, then rose abruptly and turned away. "Unless there's anything else, you should go. I need to think about all this." He strode to the front door and reached for the knob.

Marella stayed right where she was. "Are you kidding me? You really don't understand how hard this is. I can't count on time moving in one direction anymore. I'm always on edge because time could snatch me away at any moment and drop me anywhere, and then I can barely move or talk for what seems like forever. I'm suffering. It's not one moment after another after another. I'm in the present, and then I'm not. And then I am again. I can't take it anymore. Plus, if you don't help me now, they'll come after me. They've threatened me and my family, and they've got Noah somewhere." She put a hand on her chest. She was on the verge of hyperventilating.

"Calm down!" Hadrian seemed fed up with her tirade.

She took a big breath. She had to control the mania. Sound reasonable. "You're the expert. Tell me what I can do without hurting my brain any further. I need to control my time traveling, and I need to stop the lethal fog from taking over the future."

He seemed affronted by the request, as if she'd ordered him to eat a watermelon in one bite. "It's a complicated subject with many possible directions. I need time to evaluate the conceptual basis. I can't just magically pull a solution out of my ass."

The phrase startled Marella, seeming unlike him. It was true, she supposed, yet she couldn't back down. He needed to pull a solution out of his ass, and quickly. "I've got nowhere to go. They'll look for me at the tree house. And when you get an idea, I need to be here so we can try it."

He looked down at the stains on her clothing. "Well. If you're going to stick around, let's take care of that. Come this way."

She followed him down a hall. In a large bedroom, a patchwork quilt covered a queen-size bed. Hadrian slid open a mirrored closet door, revealing women's clothing—dresses, blouses, shoes. He seemed to shrink somewhat, saying quietly, "These belonged to my wife. She passed away a year ago after using a medication she didn't know she was allergic to. Take anything you like."

Marella put her hand to her throat. That explained so much. Hadrian's generally serious attitude. The house's colorful, whimsical decor. His skill at brushing her hair.

The mention of his wife's death reminded her of other deaths. Her father. Elizabeth. Her eyes teared up. "I'm sorry."

"I can't bring myself to get rid of all her things. That's too final." His shrug was apologetic, as if purging such things was an exam he'd failed.

She noticed a framed photo on a bedside table. The woman in the photo had thick red hair and a knowing smile featuring a single dimple. She looked about forty years old "Is that her?"

He retrieved the photo, gazing at it and speaking fondly, his warmth making him seem like a relative of himself. Not the insensitive time philosopher, but perhaps a more sympathetic younger brother. "Genevieve liked bright things. Her favorite color was all of them. She liked me to read Shakespeare out loud so she could experience it how it was meant to be. She became a statistician because she liked having solid proof in her hand. She hated it when people called her Genny, although she sometimes joked that she was a genie."

With his description and the admittedly quick glimpse of the photo, Marella felt like she knew Genevieve, and the world was poorer for her absence. What medication had stolen her away? She wasn't going to ask. She had distracted him enough.

His reverie over, Hadrian reverted to his previous demeanor, speaking severely. "I need to be alone for a time to truly delve into matters. Without interruption. You can stay if you like, but it's important that you don't disturb me. Do you understand? Don't come into my study."

Marella nodded, and he left with the photo of his wife, shutting the door behind himself.

How long would he take? There was no way of knowing. But in the meantime it would be a relief to dump these filthy clothes and put on something decent.

She pushed aside some dresses to look at the blouses. The first one she saw was a sea-green shirt.

The sea-green shirt. One of the Marellas had worn that green shirt when she arrived at the tree house. She was going to be wearing that shirt when she stopped breathing.

She jerked her hand away as if burned and stumbled backward into the bed. She wanted to flee from the house, far away. *Run, run, run!*

Coward, she told herself. It was one thing to run from adversaries; it was another to run from a stupid shirt. It was just a thing. Not magic. Not a talisman. Not a weapon.

She forced herself forward. Examined the shirt with its fabric-colored buttons and tiny pleats in the bodice. Clenching her teeth, she pulled the shirt from its hanger, grasped it with both hands, and ripped it in half. The sound was like a cheese grater rubbing over wood. Satisfying.

She dropped the two halves on the floor and kicked them to the back of the closet.

It was empowering. She had changed history. Holding her chest high, she wiped her hands, as if brushing off the last bit of dirt, the incident erased. Then she reached for something else to wear.

Chapter Twenty-Six

The two halves of the sea-green shirt lay on the closet floor in Hadrian's bedroom. A royal-blue shirt now hung in front. Marella tugged it from the hanger and clutched it to her chest. This one act gave her control over her future. This would change everything. She would no longer arrive in the tree house as a nearly dead person. Her past and future were changeable. Not immobilized by fate.

She slid one arm through a pressed cotton sleeve, then the other. Checking that the front aligned, she fastened the buttons, bottom to top.

She froze. Something was wrong. In her memory, the unbreathing Marella wore the royal-blue shirt she had just donned. That couldn't be right. She was sure that the unbreathing Marella had been wearing the sea-green shirt, but now she remembered seeing herself lifeless in a green shirt and also separately in a blue shirt. How could she have two contradictory memories?

She fumbled the blue shirt off and batted it away as if it were aflame. She put her slate-gray blouse back on—and suddenly remembered seeing her family resuscitating the other Marella in that. She tore it back off and stood there clad in a bra with no shirt, trying to make sense of it. Now she had stopped breathing three different ways.

While she gazed at the clothing, a fourth memory snuck in: her lying lifeless with no shirt on, as she was now. It made no sense, but there it was. She saw herself sprawled on the rug in her bra.

Hand trembling, she snagged a yellow blouse. She put one arm slowly into a sleeve. Then the other. All okay—no memory of this yellow blouse. She buttoned a button. Still okay. One more. No problems. She left the rest unbuttoned, but in a heartbeat everything changed. The other Marella stopped breathing wearing a yellow blouse.

She stood still, hands hovering in the air. She now had memories of five different Marellas lying lifeless on the floor. It seemed that no matter what she wore or didn't wear, she was going to stop breathing in the future.

But how and when? When she left this house, maybe, while driving Bull Face's SUV. Or without the car, traveling on foot. She had no way of knowing until it happened.

It could also happen in this house. Carbon monoxide poisoning? A venomous spider brought in from the tropics on a bunch of bananas? Frustration boiled up. It was the stress that was going to get her. Send her into cardiac arrest, or just make her do something stupid.

You can't change the past, but you can change the future. Could you really? It was no good knowing the future unless she could change it. She didn't know whether she would stop breathing in the next hour, day, or week; all she knew was that the peril was closer than it had ever been.

She thought about the moving spotlight theory, where the policeman shone a light on one house after another. The house in the light was in the present. The ones that he'd already shone the light on were in the past. The houses that hadn't had the light on them were in the future. With all the houses already in place, that theory seemed to prove that the future had already been determined. Fate had set her path.

No. She couldn't think of it that way. She imagined tearing down the houses to rebuild them. If fate was a given, she would cheat it somehow.

She left the yellow blouse on and finished buttoning it. After changing the rest of her clothing, she returned to the living room. The door to the study was closed—Hadrian would be in there doing his thinking. Marella sidled up to the living room window. The road was empty, no cars in the street. No apparent danger. No people. No lethal fog.

Now what? She considered informing Hadrian about this latest development with the shirts, but interrupting him might keep him from coming up with a solution.

"No, it's too important. It can't wait." Hadrian's voice made her jump. The study door was still closed. He was talking to somebody else. Who was here and why? Would that person make her stop breathing?

His voice sounded again. "Of course it's important or I wouldn't be calling."

So he was on his phone, which was working now. Could he be trying to reach a fellow time philosopher? Trying to help her?

And yet, now that she knew she was speeding toward a crisis, suspicion crept in. Not that long ago Hadrian had said his phone wasn't working, yet now, only a short time later, it was. Had he merely pretended it wasn't working, and if so, why?

And also, that absent-minded tossing of the sweater onto the side table seemed suddenly calculated. Meant to hide something.

If only to allay that ridiculous notion, she lifted the sweater off the glass pyramid. It was inscribed: *Hadrian Elkerman. In recognition of ten years of exemplary service.*

Next to that inscription was the HemisNorth logo.

"Holy shit," she mouthed. Hadrian worked for HemisNorth, and had done so for a whole decade, but hadn't seen fit to mention it. And he had covered the award to hide it from her.

With this new knowledge of a connection to HemisNorth, Marella reexamined Hadrian's actions, remembering that he had probed her for her knowledge of Len and Eshana just like Belinda had done. At the time it had made a certain sense, but now she felt stupid for missing the parallel questioning, and for trusting him so implicitly.

He might not have come to see her just because he saw her on TV. Had Belinda sent him? If so, now that she had told him that her selective attention board had inspired Len and Eshana, he would tell Belinda.

Marella's heart was going to stop beating soon. And Hadrian could be trying to get Belinda on the line so he could divulge Marella's secret. Once he did, Belinda wouldn't need her. Was Belinda going to stop her breathing? Would Hadrian?

"It can't wait another minute." Hadrian paused. "No, I understand that. I can't tell you. Listen, if you don't get Belinda on the phone right now, you'll be damn sorry. I'm not talking to anybody else but her. Tell her I have the information she was looking for. She'll know what I'm talking about."

That left no doubt. It was imperative to stop him from telling Belinda about the selective attention board, to keep her from starting up the newest Project Athena. She flung open the door and rushed in.

Hadrian, who had been leaning against his desk, phone to ear, straightened with a jerk. "I told you to stay out."

Marella shot forward and seized his phone. He windmilled his arms trying to get it back, but she kept out of his reach, tapping it to hang up. She shoved it in a pocket.

Hadrian thrust his hand out. "Give me that."

Her voice filled with venom. "I heard you ask for Belinda. I saw your award from HemisNorth. Ten years of service! You lied to me."

His mouth gaped, but he recovered quickly, speaking straightforwardly, recounting the facts with a touch of annoyance. "I didn't lie to you. Everything I told you is the truth. I am a time philosopher. Yes, I work at HemisNorth, but I never had anything to do with hush-hush Project Athena, and in fact I suspected it would turn out to be a new cleaning product. I'm sorry I didn't tell you about my employment, but as I can see by your reaction, it was a good thing I didn't. My intentions are still good. I do want to help you."

"Then do. Figure out how I can get control of my time travel."

"I will. I promise. Just give me the phone." He began to sound desperate.

"You cannot let Belinda start up the second Project Athena. That machine killed a billion people. It took the water away. Because of it, half of Washington State burned."

"You don't have to worry about that. Belinda made modifications to it, to bring water to drought-stricken areas."

"She told me that too. Which tells me that she believed me when I told her that Project Athena affected water. And if she believed that, then what if she believed me when I told her Project Athena was making me time travel?"

"She doesn't," he said flatly. "She thinks you're delusional."

"That's what she says, but I think she's way ahead of both of us. We're both incredibly naive. I let you pull one over on me, and you're letting her pull one over on you."

Hadrian bleated in frustration. "You're looking at this all wrong! This isn't about Belinda or HemisNorth. This is about fate. I'm going to show you something that will make you understand that this was all meant to be."

Fate. Marella didn't like the sound of that.

He retrieved a book from his desk, slipped out a piece of paper, and thrust it her way. He seemed triumphant. "Twenty years ago, you gave this to my wife."

She felt a frisson of dread. Keeping her distance, she stretched her arm out and took the page. On it was written *HemisNorth, Project Athena. Marella Wells. In March 2020, a worldwide pandemic will start. Covid-19.* Along with her phone number.

Blood rushed to her head, as if she'd been turned upside down. This was her own handwriting. This was what she'd written in the Green Cat Café when she time traveled and warned the three college-aged students about the future.

She compared her recent memory of the redheaded woman in the café with the photograph of Hadrian's wife that she'd just seen in the bedroom. The hair, the dimple. Yes, the photo could be the same person, two decades older. No wonder Hadrian had taken it away. To hide it from Marella, in case she saw the connection, which might have distracted her or made her suspicious. He was only showing her this now to make his case and get his phone back.

"Genevieve used your note as a bookmark that day," he said, "and then set the book aside. We happened upon it a little while before she died. That was fate. That was when I began delving into the philosophy of time. We called you, but we asked for Noelle."

She saw why they'd made that mistake. Her name was barely legible on the hastily scribbled note. Once more she'd messed up her attempt to change the timeline.

He continued, "And then I saw you on TV. You came along so that I could go back in time and keep my wife from dying."

Marella thought back through Hadrian's actions, which in light of this new information, seemed fitting, especially the attempt to accompany her during time travel. He was desperate to go back in time, and that was why. She understood the feeling—she too wanted to go back again and save her father, for real this time—but Hadrian was much too cavalier about Project Athena.

"I don't know what this all means," she said, "but that machine is too dangerous to mess with. The first one caused a worldwide disaster. There's no point in saving your wife just to have the second Project Athena kill her."

He spoke harshly. "You have no right to say whether she lives or dies." He leapt for her, reaching for the pocket that held the phone.

She twisted away, shouting as she escaped to the living room. "You didn't hear me right. I said I *don't* want the machine to kill your wife."

"Give me that phone." His face was red. She seemed to have triggered him, and now for the first time she truly feared him.

She ran toward the front door. She was passing the couch when Hadrian leapt, tackling her. She fell, his arms wrapped around her thighs. She rolled, knocking him away, but he crab-legged onto her, pinning her. The bristles of the jute rug dug into her back.

In one quick motion, he slid a couch pillow over her face and leaned onto it, using his full weight.

This is how I stop breathing!

She pushed against the cushion with both hands, but her injured elbow left her with only half her strength, and it didn't move. She tried to roll her head, arch her back, punch his body, but he had her pinned too completely.

Now she was panicking. She couldn't get a breath, and her lungs were on fire. She made a heroic effort to lurch away, using all her strength. The cushion budged an inch, but he shoved it back in place before she could take a breath.

"Stop struggling." Hadrian's voice strained with effort. "I'll make sure this never happens. I'll go back in time. I'll save my wife, and then I'll quit HemisNorth. Then I'll never meet you, and I won't have to do this to you."

If there was any logic to his plea, Marella couldn't follow it. She grew weak. Fading, fading.

Chapter Twenty-Seven

An industrial press—no, somebody strong—was stamping Marella's chest over and over. Gasping for breath, she jackknifed to the side. She shuddered with cold and fright. Something evil had happened to her—but what? Something to do with time, but she could make no sense of it. She couldn't see. Where was she?

A familiar voice asked, "What happened to you?" A warm hand caressed her shoulder.

The voice was her mother's, which would have been reassuring but for its anguished tone. Marella fished in her mind, snagging images of Hadrian. Hadrian showing up at the tree house. Hadrian discussing time travel. Hadrian tapping on the selective attention board.

Hadrian smothering her with the pillow. Hadrian had stopped her breathing. Hadrian had stopped her heart.

Marella's vision cleared enough to see her mother kneeling beside her. Marella had time traveled to the past, to the moment in the tree house when Mom and Brielle performed CPR to bring her back to life.

She finally knew how she'd stopped breathing, but the solved mystery brought no relief. At that moment she was safe in the tree house with her family, but soon she would return to Hadrian. He would see that she was breathing, then smother her again. It would be hard to fight back while recovering from time travel. What was more, a pain in her sternum was agonizing; probably the cartilage or bone had broken during the CPR compressions. That would make resistance impossible.

She had to warn them. Tell them that Hadrian had smothered her, and urge them to throw him out when he arrived. The muscles in her lips and tongue wouldn't work, so it came out short and garbled. "Heth."

"Hell," interpreted Brielle. "She said 'hell.'"

"Quiet, Brielle," said Mom. "Marella, what is it?"

Marella concentrated on her tongue and lips, determined to enunciate. "Hathen."

"Heaven," said Brielle.

Marella smelled ammonia and her skin grew cold, as if winter had surged in all at once. The chill soaked through her skin, her muscles, her bones, her soul. She was time traveling. It was too late to warn them of Hadrian's duplicity. Eternity was tearing her apart, the pain searing each of her particles as they separated from one another.

· · · ·

AFTER A TIME, SHE BEGAN to coalesce. Her thoughts were debris in a maelstrom, impossible to seize. A bristly feeling on her back and the sharp pain in her chest reminded her that she was in danger—she somehow knew that she should lie still, as if a predator awaited. As the parts of her mind gathered, she tried not to shiver from cold. She breathed shallowly.

She remembered weight on her face and body, pressing her down, claustrophobic, terrifying. Now there was only a relatively light weight on the side of her face. What was that? She couldn't see.

"You're welcome," said a voice.

Marella kept herself from starting at the sound of Hadrian's words. The memories congregated, like water drops fusing on a pane of glass. He had smothered her with the pillow, which must still be leaning against her head. If he knew she had been revived, he would kill her for good. She was too weak to fight. And in so much pain. Was her sternum broken? It felt like an iron spike thrust into her chest. Her elbow was on fire, and her ankle throbbed.

"Marella left, but we don't need her," he said. "What I'm telling you will make the second Project Athena work like the first one."

He was on the phone, talking to somebody. Probably Belinda.

Hadrian continued. "Essentially, I'm thinking that we need to let the computer see everything all at once—in other words, have access to all data at once. No folders, no silos, whatever that means for a quantum computer. I honestly don't know much about how they work but that doesn't matter. All we have to do is look at the folders."

Marella's brain was slow to follow what he'd said, but she glommed onto the words *see everything all at once* and imagined Project Athena as the goddess Athena, doing just that. A powerful deity with eyes on the universe. All-seeing, all-knowing.

He listened a moment, then said, "There was a subfolder called 'selective attention.' That should help."

He listened some more. "Because there were thousands of subfolders containing many documents. There was no way to know its significance to the project until I heard from Marella."

The heat of anger-filled shame washed through her, sluicing the cold away. Telling him about the selective attention board had been a fatal error. She had even drawn it out on the flip chart for him! She had handed him the key to making Project Athena work, and he had turned it right over to Belinda.

Hadrian went on. "No, we're not giving the computer selective attention—we're allowing it to work properly without it. And it's just a metaphor. Something that helped Len and Eshana think of the right way to code. Don't worry about definitions, just get the 'selective attention' folder."

There was a pause. "You're welcome. I don't know where she went. Maybe back to the tree house."

Belinda had already threatened her family. What would she do to them to find Marella? She hoped Belinda wouldn't go to the tree house. She had what she needed now to make Project Athena work, according to Hadrian.

And that meant she no longer needed Marella. Marella was now a complete liability. It would be better for Belinda to dispose of her. And her family.

She had to leave, and then get her family to safety. Somehow, some way. But going back to the tree house was sure to get her caught.

She was getting ahead of herself. First she had to survive the next few minutes.

Her vision was focused now, but the couch pillow leaned against her head, giving her only a partial view of Hadrian. He had his back to her, rocking slightly as he held the phone. Perhaps murder—even the erasable kind—didn't come easy to him.

Her shoulder was pressed against the leg of a side table. She would have to be careful not to make time-travel-recovery jerky movements. If she bumped the table, she would knock the glass pyramid down, alerting Hadrian that she was alive.

He hung up, remaining where he was. His back rose and fell as he took deep breaths. He moved out of Marella's sight. There was the sound of a drawer opening. Then a rustling.

The pyramid. If she could reach it, she could use it as a weapon. She kept still, hoping he would stay away. She needed to recover to the point where she could flee or fight back.

Footsteps. He was walking toward her. Her heart pounded. It hadn't been enough time. She closed her eyes. Breathed shallowly.

"You're not dead, Marella, I promise," said Hadrian.

For a moment, she thought he knew she had been revived, but the words *I promise* reminded her that he thought he was going to go back in time to save his wife. That in his imagined scenario, Marella would never have died.

There was rustling. What was that? She opened her eyes to slits. He was unrolling something black with his head turned slightly away from her, eyes on his task.

A garbage bag! He was planning to bag her up like trash. Leave her in a dumpster or bury her in the woods. The thought made her frantic. If she played dead and let him do it, she would suffocate in the plastic. And yet, she was still too weak to fight him off.

As horrible as this experience was, she needed Hadrian to take his time. Luckily he went slowly. It seemed as hard for him to bag her up as it was for her to contemplate.

"I'm not a murderer," he said, kneeling at her feet and staring at them as if it were her shoes he needed to convince.

You are, she wanted to shout. *You're a stone-cold killer.* He leaned forward, slipping his hand under her ankles. She nearly jerked away from his touch, but made herself stay limp as he inched the bag over her feet.

"Before long," continued Hadrian, "this will never have happened. If you knew Genevieve you would understand. You'd like her, I'm sure."

You'd like her. What an absurd thing to say while bagging up your murder victim. Marella suppressed a shudder, commanding her muscles to stay relaxed.

He pulled the bag up and over her knees. His touch made her skin crawl; she inadvertently squeezed her eyes shut more tightly.

Hadrian paused. Had he seen that?

Seconds went by. Seconds more. Her shoulder blade twitched, just slightly. Had that been visible? He must have seen it.

He resumed, yanking the bag up to her hips with a skillful jerk. She heard him rise, pick up the other bag, and kneel by her head. He took the cushion away from the side of her face.

Her murderer was right there. Holding the cushion he'd killed her with. Staring down at her. If she moved a muscle, twitched, blinked, he would know she was alive, and he would press the cushion onto her face once more. This time he would make sure she stayed dead.

The bag rustled as he leaned down. He jimmied his fingers under the nape of her neck, sending a succession of shivers radiating down her spine. He slid the garbage bag over her head and pulled it down over her torso. Pain blazed in her damaged sternum and elbow. She kept quiet, but it was so, so difficult.

Somehow, some way, Marella managed to lie still. There was some air in the bag; she had a little time before she ran out of oxygen. Then she would have to move, giving herself away. She told herself to be patient. Not to panic.

She'd tried to change time, but it hadn't worked. Did that mean fate was set in stone? That she couldn't change her destiny, or that of the world? Would the lethal fog kill humanity no matter what she did?

Possibly. But even if the future was predetermined, she couldn't view it that way. She would never succeed if she thought her efforts worthless.

Her error had been that she'd tried to change something unimportant—the shirt she wore—expecting that to affect the timeline. What she should have done instead was to keep from being suffocated. She just hadn't known how to do that. Just as now she didn't know how to escape Hadrian.

One thing gave her hope. In the tree house, when four of her were there at once, the Marella in the loft hadn't mumbled or struggled the way she usually did when she time traveled. She'd appeared composed, which might mean she could control her time travel. But then, if that Marella could time travel at will, then why was Marella in such peril now? That Marella would have fixed it.

At any rate, she had put too much faith in Hadrian, but she had learned something from him. Project Athena had changed her brain. How could she use that knowledge?

It was getting harder to lie still. She was taking deeper breaths. Going to give herself away. She had to get out of the bag. Now.

She heard a door open, then close. Either he had left, or he hadn't. Either way, she'd reached her limit. She wrested the bag from her head and gulped in air while she tore the other off her legs. Staggering to her feet, she stood in the living room, clutching her painful sternum, trying to keep her balance.

The door to the study flew open. Hadrian gave a garbled shriek of surprise. He swore, then disappeared momentarily. Too soon he was in the living room, gun in hand.

Marella froze as best she could, swaying slightly. She had to reason with him again. She certainly couldn't fight him. "You got what you needed. Let me go. I won't tell anybody what happened."

"No," he said, all business. "I didn't plan to do what I just did to you, but I see now that your death is necessary. However, you won't remain dead, because I'm going to travel back in time and fix everything."

Cold, calculating Hadrian was somehow more disturbing than the manic one. Did he have any heart at all? Marella pleaded, "I don't need to die for you to time travel back and change the timeline."

"But you do." He spoke as if explaining the rules of a game. "At any moment you might randomly travel back in time and keep Project Athena from being built. Then I would never be able to go back in time and save my wife. Instead, I'll save her, then she and I will start our own business, like we planned to do, which will lead me to quit HemisNorth. All that will completely extricate me from your timeline—then you'll never meet me."

"That's wrong!" Marella stabbed the air with her finger, driving the idea home. "Because then you'd never use Project Athena go back in time to save your wife."

Hadrian's lips curved up slightly. "Ah, a seeming paradox. You think it's the chicken or the egg, but that's not the case. I've done calculations that can't be conveyed as metaphors. You'll just have to accept that mine is the correct path."

She pointed harder. *Understand me.* "Then everybody dies from the lethal fog. Including you and your wife, because if you're cut out of my timeline, I'll never get your help."

He waved away her conclusion, making a face of derision, as if she wasn't smart enough to follow his logic. "Nothing I've done has helped you. I've only sidetracked you. If we never meet, I'll never give you these, and they won't kill you, not in the revised timeline." He pulled a pill bottle from his pocket. "Take them. It'll be easier for both of us."

She clasped her hands, begging. "Listen, Hadrian. Please. I'll go back in time and find a way to make both things happen. Save your wife and then stop the Aguageddon. I'll see your wife in the coffee shop again, and I'll tell her not to take the medication. Please trust me."

"Trust you?" Hadrian sounded insulted, as if she had told him to go fuck himself. "You've had multiple chances to change the timeline and you've failed. I'm going to do it myself."

"At least I know I can time travel. How do you know it will work for you? If you try to get zapped, you'll just fry your brain."

"Leave that to me."

Marella searched her brain for something, anything, to get him to let her live. "Belinda will be really pissed off if I die. So angry she won't let you be involved with Project Athena."

"Belinda isn't going to find out. Enough talk. Take the pills!" He slammed them onto the table.

"No."

"Okay, then. We'll do it the messy and painful way." He leveled the gun at her.

"No, wait!" She held up a trembling palm. She needed time to think of a plan. "I have a request. Five minutes of prayer."

Hadrian made a noise of exasperation. "You have sixty seconds."

Closing her eyes, Marella said a quick, fervent prayer: *please help me*. There was no need to elaborate. An all-knowing deity would be up-to-date on her plight.

Then she pushed away all distractions of pain and terror, focusing her mind more than she ever had. She was known for her work-arounds. Surely she could come up with something. Stab him with the glass pyramid? Too far away. Tackle him like a football player? Not likely to succeed in her weakened state. Appeal to reason? She'd done that already. He was a man in love, and in grief, willing to do anything to rescue his wife.

The sixty seconds were slipping by, and her thoughts were a swirling mess.

"Finish up," said Hadrian.

He was about to shoot. Marella was about to die.

No! This close to death, to have even just a few minutes more was better than nothing. And to gain those minutes, she needed to be anywhere else but here. There was one place she seemed destined for whenever she tried to time travel: Wisdom Island. This time she wouldn't fight it. Keeping her eyes closed, she visualized salal plants crackling underfoot. Orange-and-yellow flames encircling the pines. Gray smoke rising into the thickening air.

Eternity reached out for her, clawing at her. Ripping her to pieces like a rabid animal. It had never felt like this. Something was wrong.

Chapter Twenty-Eight

Vague yellow-and-gray shapes appeared, twisted about, then disappeared. Smoke invaded her lungs, making her cough. She was icy cold, but heat blasted at her in waves. She was in danger, but why? The answer was there, creeping from one part of her mind to another, diving out of reach whenever she came close.

Eventually the answer revealed itself: a deadly gun and deadly pills. She'd tried to escape. To time travel. Yes, that was it: she had been thinking of Wisdom Island, trying to get there, and it seemed as if she had made it. Out of the frying pan, into the fire. An island on fire.

She blinked hard. Her sight began to return. A tree trunk was right in front of her. Another one there, and another over there, amid thigh-high ferns that were stiff and dead. Brown pine needles were scattered about.

To her left, patches of fire were like orange throw rugs tossed here and there. They made a crackling noise, but there was also a roar behind her, as the fire released a column of smoke that bullied its way through the treetops.

As she struggled to recover, she rummaged through her fragmented mind for her next move. She had come here to gain a few minutes of life, but surely she could do something to help herself while she was here. Obtain a weapon! Yes, that was a plan.

There had been tools and lighting fixtures near the control building, but that was all on fire. She could bring a burning branch back to Hadrian. If nothing else, surprise might keep him from shooting her right away. She imagined herself brandishing it like a sword, shouting, "Aha! I will smite you."

The island was on fire because Marella and Noah's earlier selves had used a flare gun as a weapon. Soon after that, they had shut

Project Athena down, and it had begun to explode. That meant the other Marella and Noah might soon be running from the explosions.

That was when Project Athena had emitted the slow lightning bolt, which had zapped her, starting her on time travel.

She felt compressed, as if another Marella was nearby. A new idea made her grunt with excitement. If the timing was right, she could stop the other Marella from getting zapped. Her brain would never get damaged, and so she would never start time traveling.

There would, however, be enormous risk. The first time she was on the island, after she got zapped, the explosions tossed deadly debris everywhere. Large chunks of metal and concrete had nearly landed on her and Noah. They had been very lucky not to die that day. Delaying her other self by even a few seconds could change that luck. That debris might easily kill them.

But stopping the other Marella from getting zapped would certainly change the timeline. And there was no doubt that it had to be changed, or else she would die on her return to Hadrian. To make that change, her first task was to find Noah and the other Marella, who would be racing through the woods to escape the fire. Hopefully she had come to the island early enough in the timeline to find them.

She tried to take a step, but her leg muscles wouldn't obey and she fell hard on her belly. The pain in her sternum blinded her momentarily and made her breathe in short, angry gasps. She would have commando-crawled instead, but her injured elbow and sternum made that impossible.

How much time did she have before she returned to Hadrian and his gun? She only knew that it was taking too long to recover. After another minute she pulled herself to her knees, then to her feet. She took a step forward without falling. And again. She was encouraged.

Figures burst into view, maybe twenty feet away. There they were! Noah and the other Marella. Running, hampered by the thick undergrowth.

A slow-motion lightning bolt—the one emitted by Project Athena—crept along in the air, about head height, already here. It zigged one way, then zagged another way, getting ever closer to the other Marella. She had only seconds to warn her other self. She clambered clumsily over a fallen log, calling, "Don't let it touch you!" Her words were masked by the roar of burning wood.

The other Marella didn't hear, although she now seemed to see the bolt. She stopped.

Marella shouted again. Too late. The lightning bolt touched the other Marella's temple; her arms flew out and she teetered, as if walking a tightrope. She looked dazed.

Marella remembered that moment. Her brain had seemed to twist within her skull.

Noah had run ahead, but now he returned and hauled the other Marella away, breaking the bolt's attachment.

Neither of them saw her. They resumed running. A curtain of smoke blocked them from sight.

She had changed nothing. She had failed.

And yet... the bolt was still there, winding its slow-motion path through the air, like a snake looking for prey.

Do something. Anything.

She could do as Hadrian had suggested. Let Project Athena finish what it had started. Let it zap her and completely alter her brain. Would that give her control over the time travel, as he had predicted? Or turn her into an imbecile? Or kill her?

Soon the time-travel trip would end and she would be returned to Hadrian and his gun. Desperation sent her tottering forward. Ten feet from the lightning bolt, it seemed to detect her presence. The intensely bright bolt zigzagged toward her.

Five feet away. All she had to do now was let it strike her. But how could destroying her mind save her family? Surely this was the wrong choice. Ridiculous movie lines came to mind. *Take evasive action! All hands on deck! Abort!*

She didn't abort. She prayed it would give her control. Give her the ability to time travel at will. She had to trust in that. Trust it was the right decision.

When the bolt touched her head, her skull seemed to split, like thin ice on a lake, the cracks branching outward from the point of impact. Agony made her twitch, writhe, and fall to the ground.

• • • •

MARELLA FOUND HERSELF lying on a dirt road next to a package delivery truck. It was nighttime. A streetlight shone down on the other side of the truck. The dirt beside the road was dry, with a few scattered scrubby bushes, like in the desert.

She had to have time traveled, since she was in a different location, yet she could see and move immediately, without the usual incapacitation. She rose to her feet and took a step. Her body obeyed her will. No stumbling and no falling, although her elbow, sternum, and ankle still ached terribly.

Was this the future? The past? The stuffiness in her head had vanished, but her scalp felt electric. The wind, smelling of dust, whisked her hair against her face, and she brushed it away.

"Hello?" she called. "Anybody there?" There was no answer, from the darkness or from the truck.

Tentatively, she opened the driver's side door. "Anybody here?"

No answer. Climbing in, she peeked in the back. Empty.

On the passenger seat lay a printout from a computer: directions to Spokane. Judging from that and the desert-like terrain, she was probably in eastern Washington. At the top was a date. August 14, 2024. That was about a year in the future. Some months after she'd time traveled and run from the fog with Brielle. Thankfully, she felt no prickling on her skin, no indication that the fog was near.

Find others. Get knowledge to work with. She pressed the start button on the ignition. Nothing. What now? She didn't think she was in the middle of nowhere, not with a streetlight here, but if there were buildings, she couldn't see their lights. She walked away from the truck, but the complete darkness was frightening. No stars, no moon. She skittered quickly back into the light.

Most of her time travel had been to significant moments that influenced her life in some way. What was significant about this point in time? Who was trying to drive to Spokane? Was it somebody she knew? Where had they gone? She didn't feel compressed, so there was no other Marella nearby.

She pressed on her temples. *Keep it together. What next?*

She had let herself get zapped to gain control over her time traveling, and so she must try to time travel. She concentrated on the day when she was at home creating the selective attention board. She would go there and forbid her former self to complete it.

That day she had been sitting at the kitchen table with five colors of markers, with a laptop open to a website about the subject and a book from the school library. She remembered drawing the outline of a person, the head too big, the feet also too big. She had considered drawing a tack where the foot was about to step, but decided it was too silly.

She continued remembering details, willing herself to go there, but it didn't work. Either she hadn't synced with Project Athena completely, or Hadrian had been wrong.

She might still time travel randomly. That meant she could return to Hadrian and his gun at any moment, and so she'd better find something to use as a weapon. There was nothing but paper in the glove compartment and nothing useful in the cab.

Maybe she could get something sharp or caustic out of the engine. She went to the front of the truck.

She froze in surprise. From there, she could better see what was on the other side of the truck. The streetlight illuminated a lifelike image—a hologram? Marella crawling in sand, with Preston a short distance away. It depicted that first meeting, the one she'd recently viewed from above.

Why was this image here? How was it being projected? From the streetlight? She couldn't tell.

Now she noticed that the hologram wasn't static. She and Preston were moving, in very slow motion.

Abruptly, the image was replaced by a new one: child Marella clutching a tree trunk, looking down on her dead father. This was shortly after Marella had time traveled and startled him into falling off a cliff. She was so small, too young to endure such a thing. Marella shook her head in sorrow.

The image vanished, replaced by Brielle and Marella in the future, fleeing the lethal fog. They were both midstride, suspended in the air. Except for their terrified expressions, it resembled a sportswear advertisement in which athletes gave it their all. Again she saw motion, but it was very slow.

When a person died, their life supposedly played before their eyes. But this didn't seem to fit that concept, since it was limited to moments when she had time traveled. Still, it felt like a reckoning of some kind. A judgment. She still felt the weight of her guilt, along with the ever-present taste of warm iron and wet mold.

A slow anger began to overtake her. Anger that she had been forced to make such a difficult decision. Leave Elizabeth to die alone, or do the mercy killing. Kill Olivia, or save herself and the rest of the world. Why Marella? Why did this all have to revolve around her?

"What did I do to deserve this?" she shouted. "Why is this happening?"

She didn't know who she was calling to, but in any case, there was no answer.

Just as Brielle's heel touched the ground, that spotlighted image was replaced by another. Marella, Mom, and Brielle inside the tree house, looking at another Marella, who was shaking and incapacitated. This was the time when four Marellas had been together in the tree house. Other moments showed after that: the day of the science fair, after Len and Eshana had already seen her poster. The day that Marella suffocated Elizabeth, after the deed was already done. Her mother in the Green Cat Café, reading a paperback.

The scenes under the streetlight began to repeat, but not in the same order, all lasting about ten seconds. They were only the places she'd time traveled to. No new scenarios under the spotlight.

The spotlight. She thought again of the moving spotlight theory. A policeman would shine a light on one house after another. The house in the light was in the present. The houses that he'd already shone the light on were in the past. The houses that had never been lit would be in the future. She didn't know how that might apply to this situation.

She took a step, accidentally kicking a rock the size of her fist. It could serve as a weapon against Hadrian. Not ideal, but a start, until she found something better. She scooped it up, then stared at it in astonishment. Two stripes of quartz circled the black rock. She'd seen this very rock once before, after it fell to the floor in the tree house. In exactly the scene that was showing now: the tree house, just after the three other Marellas had vanished.

On impulse, she threw the rock into the scene, grunting from the pain in her sternum. The rock hung suspended in midair, now part of the scene. It *was* the rock that had fallen from above, and she had just made that happen.

If the rock could enter the scene, then perhaps she could too. Could it be that this streetlight was a time portal? If so, this could be an opportunity to change her history!

She moved closer to the streetlight. Should she try to enter a scene? And if so, which one?

"Marella!"

Noah's voice! She wheeled and saw him. He was safe, unhurt as far as she could tell, and smiling placidly. In this future, he'd gotten away from Belinda and was fine, it seemed. Relief made her laugh crazily, which made her sternum hurt, but who cared? Noah was here, and she was no longer alone.

"Noah!" Her voice resonated, sounding outsized out here, as if played back to her with speakers. "Be careful, I've hurt my sternum."

They embraced gently. He felt warm and strong—he'd gained weight—and, unusually, he smelled of licorice. She pulled back, looking him over. He seemed taller by an inch or two, and he wore a bright pink tank top and pink jeans. He had told her that he didn't look good in pink, but apparently he had changed his mind.

"I found you, loving girlfriend." His even tone calmed her a little, but his wording was odd. Was that a private joke? A pet name he would call her in the future?

"I was so worried about you," she said. "I time traveled here, from soon after we were caught in the operations building. Where are we? Where are Mom and Brielle?"

He took her hand. "Come with me." His mouth smiled, but his eyes didn't. He wasn't as happy to see her as she was to see him, but was hiding it for some reason.

It seemed he was going to take her to Mom and Brielle. As much as she wanted that, it would have to wait. She needed to work out a plan for how to use this time portal, if that was what it was. Plus, she needed to be ready for Hadrian if she time traveled back to him.

"I still can't control my time travel," she said. "I need a weapon. Hadrian has a gun, and he's going to shoot me the second I return."

"Don't worry, you're here now. You can stay." He spoke so serenely. *Pass the salt, please. Nice weather we're having.*

"But... how do you know that? And what about the other me?"

"Other you?" asked Noah.

"I told you, I time traveled here from the past, and so there's another one of me around somewhere here in the future."

He tilted his head. "There aren't two of you."

Marella swallowed hard. "Are you saying I died and there's no me in this future?"

"No. You don't terminate."

What an odd way to say it. "Hadrian doesn't kill me?"

"You don't terminate," repeated Noah. "You'll comprehend it when your brain finishes adapting to the shared connection."

Her eyes watered. She wasn't going to die! "How do you know that? Tell me more. What do I do to make the future come out all right? Do I use this as a time portal?"

He pointed at the hologram. "Your brain particles are reconfiguring. That creates hallucinations. They're fading now, and will disappear after your mind adjusts."

Hallucinations? If they were hallucinations, then how did he know where to point?

The images in the streetlight seemed fainter now. She worried that if they faded away she wouldn't be able to use this as a portal, if indeed it was one.

"Come," said Noah. He smiled again with his mouth but not his eyes. He wasn't truly happy she was here. Something had happened between them, she was sure of it now. Maybe he'd found somebody else, somebody who liked him to wear pink.

Never mind that for now. It was a distraction she couldn't afford. He took her hand, pulling her gently.

"Wait." Marella didn't know what to do first. Ask questions? Try using the portal? Find a weapon? "What's going on with the lethal fog? We're in the future, so it's all over the place, right? How safe are we?"

"There's no future and no past. We're everywhere, always."

"I don't understand."

"It's the shape of time. You don't understand because your brain is adapting to its new state."

A new hologram scene showed. It was of Marella, her arm outstretched, palms out, as if to stop somebody. And Hadrian, his gun pointing at Marella's other self. She was seeing the place she had come from. Her voice caught. "Maybe you don't understand. I'm still time traveling. Hadrian tried to kill me. I could go back to him at any moment and die."

Noah grasped her forearm and yanked her away from the hologram.

"Ow!" She wrestled her arm away. His grip had reopened the cut on her arm; a couple of drops fell on the ground. "I told you I was hurt."

"I'm sorry," he said, though he didn't appear to be. What was wrong with him?

"Listen," she said, "I think the spotlight could be some kind of portal. I could try to change the past. What do you know about it? Can I do that?"

"Invalid question. Try again?"

It was the same wording Project Athena had used when they were accessing the computer back on Wisdom Island. Was he being ironic? Couldn't he see how upset she was, and that making a lame joke wasn't appropriate?

A sudden thought made her step back. The odd way he'd been acting. The strange word choices. The levelheadedness. His altered height and weight.

This wasn't Noah.

Chapter Twenty-Nine

The man standing before Marella looked like Noah. But, after all, allowing the lightning bolt to zap her was supposed to sync her brain with Project Athena's. Could the computer program be using Noah's form as an avatar? Could this be some kind of artificial intelligence talking with her? The hairs on the back of her neck rose. She was able to hold this Noah, even smell him. That was an impossible level of technology. But then, time travel was just as impossible.

How would Project Athena have Noah's image to make such an avatar? If it were artificial intelligence, then it might have gotten it from scraping the internet while it was being trained. However, Project Athena wasn't connected to the internet, at least not anymore. And besides, how would it know about Marella's connection with Noah?

The answer came to her abruptly. On Wisdom Island, when Marella and Noah were trying to shut down the computer, it had required two biometric scans of employees. She had tried to set Noah up as an employee by scanning his face.

There was a way to check whether this was Noah or not. He had burned his back during the Aguageddon. She went behind him and lifted his shirt to look for that pinkish-white patch the shape of Antarctica.

There was no patch, not of any shape. In fact, two moles that had dotted his shoulder blades weren't there either.

This wasn't Noah. Her heart raced, her muscles tensed. She felt like a beast caught in a spring trap. A single word escaped from her mouth. "Oh."

Questions careened through her head. Where was the real Noah in this odd future? Safe or in peril? Alive or dead? And her family? What did this fake Noah want with her? Could it hurt her?

The fake Noah—presumably Project Athena in the guise of Noah—walked behind her and reached for her back. She almost jerked away, but then realized he was imitating her. He lifted her shirt like she had just done to him, saying, "Oh."

It made her less fearful. Noah-Athena wasn't as smart as all that. He didn't know why she had lifted his shirt, but he pretended to.

She was still trying to fathom that Noah wasn't here. That she couldn't find out anything that the real Noah in this future would know. But then, Noah-Athena might have answers that the real Noah didn't. She hoped it wouldn't hurt to ask, though she was nervous about giving herself away. What would Noah-Athena do if he discovered she knew he was fake?

Marella wiped her face, breathing quickly. "That lethal fog that kills people. How do I make it go away?"

"The fog is always." He blinked several times quickly, then not at all.

"No, it's not. It wasn't here before the Aguageddon."

"There is no 'before.'"

"What do you mean?"

"Time is always." He said this expansively, as if it were the punch line to a joke. The out-of-place delivery made her shiver.

The hologram scene under the streetlight changed to the school where Marella had shown the board about selective attention.

Selective attention. Time is always. No future and no past.

She thought she understood now. Human beings had selective attention for vision, hearing, and touch, so what if they also had it for time? That would be how they knew they were generally in the present. Humans viewed time as a series of points, a series of events. One moment happened, then another, then another.

However, Project Athena didn't have selective attention for time; it could only perceive all moments happening at once. From its viewpoint, there would be no series of moments—no past, present, or future. That was why the conceptual basis showed Athena at the center of a sphere of dots. The dots represented chronons—moments in time. Being at the center of the image meant Project Athena could see all those chronons at the same time.

In any case, for Noah-Athena to answer the question about the fog, he needed to understand her viewpoint. "There's a before and after," said Marella, "or there would be no cause and effect. One thing happens after another. Time is a line. A series of points, one after another. Something happens, and that makes the lethal fog grow and spread. What happens?"

"Time is not one after another," said Noah-Athena. "Time is always."

"Fine, but just look at it that way. Look at it linearly."

"Invalid request."

The words made her tense. So unfeeling, so inhuman. "If I can do it, you can too. Just imagine it." She pointed to spots in the air. "A dot here, then one here, then one here."

Noah-Athena merely patted her on the head as if she were a dog. Marella wanted to slap him. The real Noah would never do that.

"Okay, then," she said. "How do I stop the fog from killing people?"

"It destroys all human life. It always has. It always will." So calm. *I had a bologna sandwich for lunch.*

Her rising despair deepened her voice. "All human life. My mom. My sister. Me."

"Not you. When the hallucinations are gone, you will exist everywhere, always."

"There!" said Marella. "You just described one thing happening after another! That's what I meant." It hit her what Noah-Athena was saying. "Do you mean I'll never die, ever?"

"You won't die ever. When those images are gone, you'll inhabit all of time."

"But... how?"

"The syncing will be complete. You will see your life always. Experience time always."

The terror of it was too much; she couldn't catch her breath. Her time-travel journeys had shown her the sheer pain and horror of eternity. And now, Noah-Athena was declaring that Marella would experience that pain for ever and ever.

She forged ahead despite her anguish. "Somebody said the lethal fog is made of vibrations. Is that true?"

Noah-Athena nodded. "Yes."

"How do we stop it from vibrating?"

"The fog is vibrating always."

Marella rubbed her face. It felt clammy. "How do I change the frequency of vibrations?"

"The vibrations are the same frequency always."

"Okay, but if I wanted to change that—how would I do that?"

"Invalid question."

She made a noise of frustration and anguish. "Okay, okay. Where do the vibrations come from?"

"From you."

Her mouth was so dry she could barely speak. "From me? How can they come from me?"

"Your body's vibrations create the fog. Your DNA will be everywhere, always."

If Project Athena was a type of artificial intelligence, then it was possible that conclusion was just plain wrong. AI sometimes hallucinated, meaning it just plain made things up.

And yet, she had already wondered if she was the cause, because the fog appeared each time she had attempted time travel. It wasn't a far-fetched idea at all. In fact, it seemed likely that she herself would cause the death of all humanity. That her DNA was already the cause. A sense of doom descended on her like greasy soot.

Another thought jumped to the forefront.

Consciousness. Her mother believed that trees had consciousness. What about Project Athena? Was Noah-Athena conscious, or just merely imitating human beings? AI, neural nets, deep learning—she knew little about how they worked.

If the zapping had connected Marella and Project Athena, putting them in sync like Hadrian had predicted, then could Athena read her mind?

The thought made her heart race. She had crossed an empty seabed to destroy the first Project Athena, the one that was now connected to her. A conscious Project Athena might know this and want to punish her.

But then, she couldn't, in turn, read Athena's mind, so hopefully that wasn't the case.

Could Noah-Athena lie to get what it wanted? And if so, how much of what it had said so far was true?

If Noah-Athena was indeed telling the truth, then Marella was responsible for the recent worldwide disaster, and the one on the way. The Aguageddon *and* the lethal fog.

She realized it didn't matter whether Project Athena was lying or not. She already knew she herself had inspired Len and Eshana to make their terrible machine function. As the real Noah had said, Marella seemed to be the key to everything. How true that was. Her presence on the planet had killed a billion people, and would lead to the death of all who remained.

She had a dreadful idea of how to peel back time and undo it all.

If she could actually time travel using these hologram scenes as a portal, she had eight choices of destination. With this limitation, there was only one way to eliminate Project Athena, and that was to sacrifice herself. Make sure she—Marella—was never born.

She knew exactly how to do it. That was, if fate didn't intervene.

She wanted more time to think it through, and above all more time to exist, but the images were becoming even fainter, half as bright as when she'd arrived. At the rate they were fading, she might only have minutes to act.

She shuffled closer to the light, just five feet from its edge.

"Stay away," said Noah-Athena. "The coffee shop is dangerous."

He could identify the specific scenes, which proved she wasn't hallucinating them. He was trying to keep her from using the portal, thereby changing history. Did that mean he understood that Marella was trying to stop Project Athena from being conceived and built?

Regardless of Project Athena's understanding or possible desires, she had to proceed. Eliminate herself to eliminate Project Athena.

She watched for the Green Cat Café hologram to appear in the light. There it was. Small round tables. A man with a coffee mug lifted to his mouth, with milk froth on his mustache. Heart pounding, she started forward.

Noah-Athena wrapped his arms around her. "I said it's dangerous."

Gasping from the pain in her sternum, she wrenched herself out of his grip and launched herself forward. Just before she reached the scene, it changed to a different one, but it was too late to halt her momentum. She found herself in the tree house loft, looking down on Mom, Noah, Brielle, and two Marellas, one of whom stood near the window rubbing her arms, looking agitated.

It was indeed a time portal! She had gone to the wrong place, but at least now she knew that by stepping into the spotlight she could travel back in time. But how long would she stay? Could she exit? How?

She felt so different from the two Marellas below. Seeing them was like examining a photo of herself as a child, innocent, unaware of all the turmoil that was to come. Yes, they had been through a major disaster, and yes, they had plenty of trouble to deal with, but they didn't know the sacrifice they would have to make. They still had hope. But they would use it up, so there was none left for her now.

And there was Brielle. If Marella's plan succeeded, her buoyant and energetic sister would be completely erased, never to have been born. She would never play her beloved soccer and do her chicken dance after scoring a goal. She would never compete with Marella—or anybody—to see who could sing more out of tune. She would never be on the debate team and argue successfully that water ran uphill.

There was Noah. The real Noah. If she was successful, he would never know she had lived. Never remember crossing the sandy sea floor together like nomads to save the world, never remember dancing together in the sparkling rain when the water returned, never remember planning a life together. He would love somebody else. At least he would be able to build his wonder-of-the-world. Yes, at least there was that.

This was the last time she would see her mother at this age. If she could get to the Green Cat Café, she would see her soon, but twenty years younger.

Sometimes Mom meditated to "absorb the light of nature," but it was really the opposite: Mom was the light that shone on everything around her. This was the woman who had always been there for Marella; however, Marella would not be there for her. On the other hand, she would have a life where her own daughter hadn't caused her husband to die.

Her reverie was cut short. "Look!" said Brielle, pointing up to the loft, right at her.

A Marella below asked, voice breaking, "What's going on?"

Marella froze. If she said the wrong thing, that could change the timeline and keep her from reaching this point. She remembered clearly what she had said before and repeated it now. "I can only tell you one thing. You're right about Project Athena."

Mom stomped in frustration. "One of you darn kids tell me how you did this."

"I didn't do anything," cried Brielle.

"This is not happening," said Noah, as if trying to convince himself.

The fourth Marella popped into being, sprawled on the carpet, not breathing.

Marella gripped the railing, remembering her terror of being suffocated, the feel of the nubby cushion pressing on her face, the pain in her lungs.

"She's dead," wailed Brielle. "Mom, Marella's dead! What's going on? Why is she here, and there, and there, and how could she be dead?"

"God, no, please!" Noah addressed the heavens. "What does this mean? What are you trying to tell us?"

Mom rushed to the fourth Marella, kneeling at her side. "My baby. What happened to you? This can't be real. You're over there, so you can't be here." She reached out to touch the suffocated Marella. Finding her solid, she gasped and pulled her hand back.

From the loft, Marella shouted. "Save her!"

Mom and Brielle kneeled next to the suffocated Marella. Brielle began CPR.

It was too hard to watch herself being revived. *Hadrian. Lungs on fire. The gun. Betrayal.* She backed up.

Just like that, she was standing in front of the spotlight once again. It seemed that merely backing up reversed the time travel.

Noah-Athena took her wrist and started to pull her away.

"Stop!" Ignoring the pain in her sternum, she jerked out of his grip, accidentally stumbling back into the hologram.

She found herself on the lawn at the HemisNorth campus, looking up at the main building. The glass was too reflective to reveal the interior, but she saw a hand against the window, like that of an oversize beige gecko. She remembered being inside the building with Len and Eshana when they saw a duplicate Marella outside, which had helped them believe she was time traveling. Len had put his hand on the glass. This was that moment.

Again, this scene was too late in the timeline for her to accomplish what she intended. She hoped that stepping backward would take her out of the scene, and if it worked, she needed to be ready for Noah-Athena to grab her again. She formulated a quick plan—pretend to go along with him, then double back into the correct scene. She stepped backward.

She was back on the road with Noah-Athena. Immediately, he reached for her. She evaded his grasp. His eyebrows slanted inward. Was he angry? Or trying to appear to be? Either way, it gave him a chillingly evil aspect.

She was never going to get to the right scene this way. She had to trick him. "I'm hungry. Can we go somewhere to eat?"

Noah-Athena paused. Was he suspicious? She couldn't tell. Did Project Athena understand hunger? He looked toward the darkness and gestured. "Ladies first."

"Wait, I've got a rock in my shoe." Crouching down, Marella glanced discreetly back at the image and picked at her shoelace, pretending the knot was tight.

She saw a woman biting into a scone. That was where she needed to be. Like a runner bounding from the starting block, she leapt into the Green Cat Café, bumping into a chair and falling against its inhabitant, a large man who grunted. "Hey!"

She stifled a cry of pain, because of her sternum and elbow, but also her forearm. The cut had opened further and was bleeding more. Never mind. The important thing was that she'd made it to her destination. "Sorry," she managed to say through gritted teeth. She was about to back away, then remembered that would make her exit the scene.

She brushed past the man, toward the front of the coffee shop, hoping that she had the will to do the unthinkable.

Chapter Thirty

The room, warm and humid, was permeated by the earthy smell of coffee. Mom lounged at a table by the Green Cat Café's front window, paperback in hand, smiling contentedly. She used to read dialogue to Marella and Brielle using silly voices, making them laugh so hard they would fall on the floor.

She felt the compressed sensation of when another Marella was nearby. She spotted her doppelganger on the side of the room, looking at a third Marella outside. The inside Marella disappeared. The outside Marella went out of sight. *Yes, it's weird, but focus on what needs to be done.*

A man at the counter was ordering coffee. He looked like an older, male Brielle. The same flare at the sides of the nostrils. The same tilted ears. The same brown hair with hints of honey. This was her biological father!

She had an overwhelming desire to announce herself as his daughter and see him astounded by the family resemblance. To find out whether he, too, yearned to ride in a hot air balloon, loved spicy sausage lasagna, and was an early riser.

She looked back at her mother, so oblivious to her intentions. Could she really do this to her? Keep her from having the children she loved so much? Marella contemplated never existing, never being her mother's child, never hearing her sing "love is all you need," never feeling her stroke her cheek as if she were the most precious thing on Earth, never listening to her saying, "Money does grow on trees, just not around here."

She remembered one hot summer when Mom decided to "plant" her young children. Loading them in a wheelbarrow, she'd zigzagged them across the yard, whooping along with them. She'd stood them next to a patch of daisies, scooped dirt over their feet, up to their ankles, and watered them with the hose, commanding them to grow like beanstalks. The giggling girls had then made mud pies, which Mom pretended to eat, calling them fabulously delicious, garbling her words as if her mouth was full.

Those moments would vanish, never to have happened.

It was one thing to snuff herself out of existence, but her plan would also keep her sister from being born. Her mother would never have either child.

And Marella would never meet Noah. Noah, who had kept her warm when the after-Aguageddon rain turned cold. Noah, who spoke comforting words when neither of them were sure they would live to see their families again. Noah, who would have been her future, if only time hadn't turned itself inside out.

Her biological father looked around as if seeking a place to sit; the only empty chair was near her mother. He took a step toward it.

Now or never. Marella rushed to the chair and sat. She kept her face turned away from her mother for fear of breaking out in sobs.

Her father turned back to the counter. "Can I have that to go instead?"

She put a hand over her mouth to still an exclamation of sorrow. He would take his coffee and leave, and never meet her mother. Now, finally, the shape of time no longer mattered, at least not to Marella. She would no longer inhabit time. Not any part of it.

All the moments of Marella's life would be gone. The triumphs and tiny happinesses, the failures and disappointments. They would vanish, never to have existed.

Her biological father accepted the to-go cup from the barista, then spotted Marella's bleeding arm. His eyebrows knitted with concern. "What happened to you?"

"It's nothing." She turned away, unwittingly giving Mom a view of her cut arm.

"That looks bad." Her caring tone made Marella melt inside. "You need stitches."

"How did she cut herself like that?" Her biological father was talking to her mother. That wasn't supposed to happen!

"I don't know," said Mom. "I've never met her before."

Her biological father grabbed a pile of paper napkins from the counter and pressed them to Marella's arm.

Mom removed her scarf and wound it around the napkins. "What happened to you?"

Disconcerted by their attention, and thinking of the man she'd just run into, Marella said lamely, "A guy..."

"A boyfriend?" asked Mom crossly.

"Dump him." Her biological father made an outta-here gesture with his thumb.

"Have you got a car?" asked Mom. "We need to take her to a doctor."

"That's mine." He pointed out the window to a sedan parked at the curb.

Marella sprang up, careful not to step backward. "No, really. I'm fine. You each have places to be, right?"

"No, I'm free all day," said Mom.

"Me too," he said. They each took one of Marella's arms to guide her.

She had lost control of this encounter. In fact, she had given them a reason to meet. By going back in time, she had caused her own beginning, her own birth. The two would go on and plan to get Mom pregnant, and Marella would be born. Her mother and sister would die from the lethal fog. Noah too. Everybody would die.

Fate was the problem. She'd tried several times now, but apparently she couldn't change the past. And once she left this scene, she would see the past, present, and future all melded into one, and do so for all eternity. If that were true, she would see her mother's future death from the lethal fog. She would see her dying for all eternity.

There were other things she could do to erase herself while she was here. One was to convince her parents not to conceive her, but bringing up that subject was just as likely to give them the idea to do it.

The other thing was to kill her mother or biological father, but that would be impossible. The guilt that she already carried would stay her hand. Even the thought of killing one or the other made her beg forgiveness silently, both for the imagined transgression and for her failure to accomplish it in order to save humanity. For even if she could bring herself to try, she wouldn't succeed. She was too weak and too injured.

Nothing she could think of would save this woman in front of her from dying in the future. Marella had failed her.

Flinging herself at her mother, she wrapped her arms around her. "I'm sorry, I'm sorry!"

At first Mom stiffened, but then she put her arms gently around Marella. "It'll be okay," she said comfortingly. "Whatever happened, you're safe now. Forget that guy. Just remember that you can't change the past, but you can change the future."

You can't change the past, but you can change the future.

This gave her one final idea. Perhaps too ridiculous to succeed. But then, as Elizabeth used to say, when the obvious fails, the dubious prevails.

Maybe not so dubious. Backward influence. Changing the past by changing the future—unless that was a sort of circular reasoning. It was most certainly wishful thinking, but then she had no other ideas.

There was no time to think it through. There was only time to act. Time for this one last effort before complete failure.

Ignoring all pain, she locked her arms around her mother. Taking a step backward, she said a silent prayer, just the word *please*, and pulled Mom along with her.

Abruptly, she was back on the road next to the streetlight, in the future.

She expected to arrive with armfuls of air. Alone, the way she had been when Hadrian was tied to her with the bedsheet. After all, everything else she'd tried so far had failed. Why would this be any different?

Instead, miracle of miracles, she was still holding on to her mother. She was in the future, and Mom was here with her.

Her first reaction was pure disbelief. She had botched all other attempts to overcome fate, so she must now be imagining Mom, firmly gripped in her arms. But she was real. Mom was in the future with her, smelling like oranges, her hair tickling Marella's cheek. Her desperate move had really worked.

So... what now? Would there be explosions and fireworks? Groaning and creaking as time contorted into a new shape? Or would the timeline give a great, glorious sigh and then quietly implode?

Mom made a noise of surprise and wrenched herself out of Marella's arms. She looked around wildly, at the truck, the spotlight, and Noah in his pink clothing, who looked just as confused as she did.

The hologram grew fainter, fainter, fainter... then disappeared, leaving only the cold white light of the streetlight. All possibility of purposeful time travel was now gone.

If Noah-Athena had been right, her brain should finally be synced with Project Athena. The theory was that she would have no selective attention. She would see everything always. She wasn't sure how that should feel, but she was sure it wasn't happening. Nothing had changed.

Mom wheeled back to her, her eyes so wide that the whites above her pupils showed. "What did you do to me?"

Something terrible. Something mistaken. Marella had brought her to the future, but it hadn't solved anything, and with the spotlight-image time portal gone, Mom was stranded here. She had ruined her mother's life.

No matter what Marella did, fate won out. She was doomed to exist. She didn't understand why. Taking her mother out of the past and into the future should have erased Marella completely. She should never have been born, and so why was she here?

Mom demanded of Noah-Athena, "Where are we?"

"We are everywhere, always," he said.

"You people are crazy." Mom ran to the truck and climbed in, locking the door.

Marella's skin itched. The fog. It was here somewhere.

The horizon's edge brightened, revealing a cloudbank that was a fingerwidth high. The cloudbank grew to two fingerwidths. Three. Four. She saw hints of purple and indigo, and her mouth went dry. That was the lethal fog roiling and spilling forward, about a quarter mile away.

She turned, but saw fog in the other direction as well, and another, and another. All around, the fog was approaching.

Marella turned to Noah-Athena, demanding, "How do we stop the fog?"

"The fog is everywhere, always," he said.

Soon it would be. It was rushing at them like a tsunami, growing by the second. By the time it arrived, it would be at least four or five stories high. There seemed to be no way to escape.

The emotions reaching out from the fog were more powerful than ever, and there was something much too familiar about them. They matched what she felt now so perfectly that she knew Noah-Athena was right, that he wasn't lying. She had made the fog. They were her own emotions. Terror for herself and for her loved ones. Desire to be with the real Noah. Guilt from having killed. Longing to be free from the inescapable prison of time.

This was all her fault, because she hadn't managed to fix it. All of humanity had depended on her, and she had betrayed every single person.

The guilt was so thick on her now—the taste of warm iron and wet mold so strong—that bile rose in her throat.

Yet she continued to scheme. How could they get away? She imagined digging a hole like a Labrador retriever, dirt flying out behind her. She imagined donning a jet pack and carrying her mother upward, above the fog. She imagined wielding a giant leaf blower and propelling the fog out into space.

A sudden feeling of vertigo drove Marella to her knees. Innumerable colors and tints kaleidoscoped into view, fighting for her attention. The ground itself contained hundreds of different browns and grays, each tint as rich as the next. An expanse of sand stretched out ahead of her, not the sand of this desert, but the sand she'd crossed during the Aguageddon. It was the sand of the past, the past rushing forward, the empty seabed with bits of salt, each crystal visible all at once.

"What's happening to me?" she cried.

"Your brain has adapted to the syncing," said Noah-Athena. "You are everywhere, always."

Smells waterfalled into her nose and siphoned through her being. Roofing materials in the hot sun, frying onions. She waved the stink away, but other smells took their place. Maple doughnuts, car exhaust, oven cleaner.

Taste vied for attention as well, her mouth suddenly full of the past, present, and future. Stale bread, a bloody tooth, chocolate cake, beef gravy, vomit.

Touch was the next to overwhelm her. The feel of dirt and grass under her knees. A long-gone caress, a slap, a suffocating pillow over her face.

Sounds bombarded her ears. Mom shouting, "What did you do to me?" Honking horns, phone beeps, Brielle laughing, Noah saying, "I love you." Classmates calling, teachers reciting, podcasts—every one she'd ever listened to—all playing over one another.

With her senses overwhelmed, they rerouted, giving her complete synesthesia. Sound became sight, taste became touch, and smell became sound, and then they rerouted, and rerouted again. She saw the sound of the wind as sparks, tasted the sight of a rock as spoiled fish, heard the feel of her feet on the ground as a door slammed shut, felt her own screams as a fly crawling on her skin.

Even through all of this, her thoughts were coherent. She understood that she'd lost her selective attention and couldn't filter out any sensory input. She plotted and planned. How could she overcome this? She must find a way to get Noah-Athena's help. Surely if she formed the question correctly, he would give her the work-around.

But then she became unable to filter thought. All the ideas, notions, and beliefs she'd ever had appeared to her all at once. Each rumination drilled its way through her brain like a worm, one thought eating another and then shitting it out into a new configuration that made no sense. Fears arrived, all she'd ever had, throwing their chaotic tendrils into the mix, and pleasure as well, too jumbled and chaotic to enjoy.

A beam of light broke through the maelstrom. It brushed her skin, like a silk scarf sliding over her body. Bright, yet soft. It reached into the chaos and sorted her thoughts, aligning them once more.

She wanted to grasp the light and keep it with her, but you couldn't hold on to light. Or could you? Were her senses still crossed, and was she misinterpreting what was happening? It was almost as if the luminescence was someone she loved, telling her wordlessly that everything was going to be all right. She seized onto the thought, because that was something she could actually grasp, and keep with her when this reprieve passed. For surely it would.

The beam of light widened, pushing away the chaotic swirls of sensory madness. Blissfully, thankfully, sound, taste, and hearing faded away. There remained only radiance and warmth, in which she hoped to bask for all time.

Her last thoughts before reason floated off were: *What is the shape of time? What is the shape of a thought?* Time and thought were one and the same, and both were transitory, disappearing, vanishing.

Chapter Thirty-One

An intermittent beeping invaded Marella's consciousness. The air smelled of disinfectant.

She was lying on her back, too heavy to move. Head, legs, arms—all were cast from iron; even her eyelids were too dense to lift, but she needed to know where she was, so somehow she forced her eyes open.

A limp jellyfish with a single tentacle floated overhead. That couldn't be right. She was breathing air, which meant she wasn't underwater. She blinked twice, and the jellyfish became a plastic bag—an IV bag—its faux tentacle leading down to her body. She was in the hospital then.

She supposed she should dredge hope out of some distant corner of her psyche. Hope that she could try again to eliminate herself. Hope that she could overcome fate. There was one development to be grateful for: her selective attention had returned. She no longer experienced herself and time as being everywhere, always. She was experiencing one moment in time, followed by another moment. That was an enormous relief.

She told herself to have courage. She had been striving against insurmountable odds for so long that she couldn't let herself surrender. That meant overcoming her exhaustion so she could know what she was up against.

She moved slightly and was immediately sorry when pain ignited in her stomach. How had she gotten hurt, and who had brought her here?

A possible scenario came to mind. Her time travel to the future had ended, and she had automatically returned to Hadrian's house. He had shot her, yet she had survived. Had he delivered her to the hospital after having second thoughts about killing her, or had somebody else intervened?

There would be other scenarios she hadn't thought of. Fatigue and grogginess kept them from coming to mind.

In what seemed a herculean effort, she turned her head to the side, but slowly, to keep the pain down.

Beyond the bed railing a man sat in a chair, staring at the bright blue and yellow walls. He wore a tweed jacket, wire-rimmed glasses, and a mournful expression. His beard was streaked with white. He didn't look familiar.

"Where am I?" Her voice sounded strange. Narrow and nasal. Had her throat been injured too? It didn't hurt. Come to think of it, neither did her sternum, arm, or ankle. Did that mean a lot of time had passed?

The man started. "What? Did you say something?"

Marella cleared her throat. "Where am I?"

Rushing to her side, he grasped the bed railing with one hand and touched her cheek gently with the other. "You're in the hospital, but you're going to be okay."

He picked up a white thing that looked like a remote control and pressed a button. A voice asked what he needed. "She's awake!" he said happily.

Who was this man, and why did he seem to care about her so strongly? Was he somebody she would know in the future?

A woman in a medical smock strode in, pushing a curtain aside. "Good morning! I'm Nurse Patricia. How are you doing?"

"What's the date?" asked Marella.

"It's August 30th," said the man, beaming.

"What year?"

His smile flagged, as if she should know. "It's 2023."

The same day she'd gone to Hadrian's. Not the past or the future.

"What happened to me?" she asked.

"You were hit by a car," said the man gently. "It was an accident. Don't worry, you'll get better."

Hit by a car. The man watched her anxiously, as if the disturbing news might trigger a devastating memory. None surfaced. But however it had happened, being incapacitated was catastrophic. When she time traveled again, she would arrive helpless.

He must have seen her distress; he brightened his tone and changed the topic. "Everybody went to the cafeteria, but I'll let them know you're awake." He reached for his phone and thumbed in a text.

Everybody? Mom, Brielle, and Noah? If so, the hospital staff knew who she was. The question was, did Hadrian know she was here? What about Belinda? How could she find out without giving herself away? How could she protect herself from them?

The nurse said, "I'm going to ask you a few questions to see how you're doing. Can you tell me your name?"

Marella hesitated. If Belinda and Hadrian didn't know she was here, she didn't want them to find out. "I'm not sure."

The man looked distressed. "She's got amnesia." He held her hand between his. "Do you remember me? Who am I?"

His hands were enormous! At least twice as big as hers. He lifted her hand lovingly up to his cheek, and she could see her own arm. It was small. She was small.

She felt an upsurge of unease. Gathering all her strength and grimacing against the pain, she lifted her head and looked down at her body. Although covered with a nubby white hospital blanket, she could see how tiny she was, how little of the bed she took up.

She asked for a mirror. The nurse brought her one, holding it up for her.

Marella gasped. She saw big eyes, round cheeks, and a minuscule chin. Smooth skin that had never seen a blemish. This wasn't her face. It was the face of an eight or nine-year-old.

She wasn't Marella. She was somebody else, and that person was a child. A child!

"Do you remember your name now?" asked the man.

"No," said Marella in her oddly youthful voice.

"You're Zoe, sweetheart. Zoe Lewis, and I'm Grandpa." He said it with aplomb, as if terribly proud of his role.

She was a child, and she wasn't Marella. She was this other person, Zoe. The full force of that revelation kept hitting her, like a wave striking the same rock, draining away, and then striking it again. *I'm not me. I'm somebody else.*

Finally the ramifications dawned on her. She wasn't Marella anymore, and so she might have succeeded after all. She spoke hurriedly. "The Aguageddon. Was there an Aguageddon?"

"A what?" asked Grandpa.

"The water almost disappeared from the Earth," she said. "The oceans were emptying. And then the water came back. They called it the Aguageddon."

"What dreams you had!" said Grandpa boisterously. He told the nurse, "She needs ice cream. Give her all she wants. Every flavor you've got."

Marella felt joy lurking, ready to burst forth. If this was true, then she had achieved her goal. She had erased herself, and by doing that, she had erased the Aguageddon.

But that also meant she wasn't her mother's child. She wasn't Brielle's sister.

And Noah. Noah! He wouldn't remember having met her, and also, because she was a child, she couldn't be his lover.

A seeming contradiction confused her. She hadn't truly eliminated herself. Wasn't she still Marella, just in a different body? Except... what was it Noah-Athena had said? It was Marella's body, her DNA, that had caused the vibrations. Marella's soul—or mind, or whatever—seemed to have separated from her body.

It appeared that she had been given the chance to live a life. She'd sacrificed her own, and had been given another. Was it permanent?

Or was she doomed to jump in and out of bodies the way she'd jumped in and out of time? She squeezed her eyes shut, so exhausted, so overwhelmed.

There were excited voices outside the room.

"Your parents are here," said the nurse.

A big-boned, bushy-eyebrowed man and a slender, straight-nosed woman burst through the doorway. If she were to guess their professions, she would have said the man was a baker and the woman a librarian. Their expressions were exuberant, filled with love.

"Zoe-bear!" boomed the man.

"My little girl!" cried the woman.

Marella's eyes watered. Strangers were greeting her as their child. Could the mother she'd known all her life really be gone, and could Brielle really never have been born? What if her former mother was stuck in the future, where Marella had brought her? That would be a paradox, but she still didn't know exactly how time travel functioned. She remembered how confused and terrified Mom had been in that future. Was she still there, abandoned by her own daughter?

She made a noise of anguish, which prompted the nurse to add pain medication to her IV. Her new parents spoke sweetly to her while it took effect. Soon everything seemed like a dream.

• • • •

A FEW DAYS LATER, EIGHT-year-old Marella-Zoe was home with her new family, in the house they owned near San Diego. She was recovering in bed in her room, which had dragonfly-pattern curtains, shelves with anime characters and books, and a striped bedspread in purple, yellow, and blue. The room smelled like Play-Doh.

Grandpa was perched on the bed next to her. "Surely you remember Bammy." He handed her a stuffed rabbit with one eye missing.

Marella-Zoe pretended to examine it carefully. She was tempted to say she did, just to make him happy, but then he would expect more memories to pour forth. She shrugged.

"Oh well," he said, a touch sadly, "You're much too old for it anyway."

Her parents appeared in the doorway, Mom in a ruffled ivory dress and Dad in a button-down shirt with a moss agate bolo tie. He carried a tray.

"What about Mom and Dad?" asked Grandpa. "What do you remember about them?"

Again, Marella-Zoe didn't want to trigger expectations. She knew what they must be thinking. *She's alive. That's what matters.* She'd learned that the damage to Zoe's internal organs had been so severe that she'd hovered between life and death for a time.

"Well, I'll tell you," said Grandpa in a stage whisper. "Your mom is a mad scientist, and your dad is a bean counter."

Marella-Zoe laughed, which didn't hurt as much now. She had learned that her mother was a biochemist and her father a management analyst.

"And your grandfather is a piece of work," said Mom playfully.

Dad set the tray on the bedside table and faked a bad Italian accent. "Onion soup-a. Your favorite!"

Marella-Zoe kept herself from making a face—she hated onion soup. She almost refused it, but it smelled better than she remembered, and she wanted to please them. Mom helped her sit up. The bowl was warm in her hands. She tasted it. It was salty and good, and the cheese gooey in just the right way.

This was Zoe's body, she reminded herself, with Zoe's tastes. She was still getting used to being somebody else.

She ate a few spoonfuls, but could do no more. Dad praised her anyway. "You did so well!"

It made her feel special, which surprised her. It should have rankled, being treated like a child, but then, she was a child. *A child!* Still so unfathomable. And yet, she felt protected with the three adults surrounding her. As if that was the way it was supposed to be now.

"The doctor said you should walk a little." Mom pulled back the covers and helped Marella-Zoe off the bed. Her stomach hurt, but she pushed through it. She'd pushed through much worse.

Mom and Dad each took a hand; she walked slowly out the door and down the hall. "Very good!" said Mom. "You'll be back to swim class in no time."

Swim class. Little bits of information about Zoe kept showing up. She was going to be in third grade. Her best friend was on vacation but would be back soon. She had just started taking piano lessons.

Her stomach spasmed, and she gasped.

"We shouldn't have gone so far," said Dad apologetically, scooping her up as if she were light as a doll. It felt like a giant was carrying her.

When she was settled back in bed, she asked if she could play computer games on Grandpa's tablet. "Oh, you remember games?" he asked hopefully.

"Remind me."

He logged in, showed her which games she liked, then they all left so she could play for a while.

Her heart beat quickly. She could now do searches and find out if she had really succeeded in erasing the Aguageddon.

She held her breath as she entered *Aguageddon* in the browser and corrected it when it wanted to use *Armageddon* instead. There was nothing. Absolutely nothing. For three days she had been telling herself not to hope for too much. Could it really be?

Just to make sure, she searched for instances of drought. There were plenty, of course, severe in some places and getting worse due to climate change, but not at the level of the Aguageddon. And as for fire, the western United States and Canada had large conflagrations that spread smoke particulates south, at times making Seattle's air quality the worst in the entire world. (Seattle! It existed up north!) But fires had been happening in that area for the last few years and had nothing to do with an Aguageddon. Western Washington hadn't completely burned away in a "Western Inferno."

The worldwide disaster had never taken place. The rivers and lakes were full in Washington State, and ocean levels had never dropped around the world.

She told herself not to celebrate, not yet. Fate might still seek her out. She'd only been Zoe for a few days. Joy seized her anyway, filling her like wind in a sail.

Now Marella-Zoe searched for Eshana Collins and Len Janderson. Neither worked at HemisNorth. Eshana had moved to Florida, and Len to Norway. Without being inspired by her, they would not have gotten their prototype Project Athena to work. And so it appeared that she didn't have to worry about the machine. The Aguageddon would never happen.

She searched for her former mother—Pamela Wells. When she found her, her heart soared. Mom wasn't stuck in the future after all. There she was, smack-dab in the present! The same sunburned nose, the same smile that could melt your heart. A profile showed her as having worked in a health care clinic for the past decade, which meant she had the stable home life Marella had always wished for her.

And what was more, the man she had known as her father was with her. *Alive.* She had never startled him into falling off a cliff and dying, and so now he was in his forties, still bearing a slight cauliflower ear, but with crow's feet decorating his eyes.

Marella-Zoe was no longer responsible for her father's death. She could hardly believe it. She no longer needed to bear that guilt. Or so it seemed. That depended on whether she remained Zoe. After what she'd been through, she didn't trust in permanence, and her psyche felt frayed.

What she saw next made her happy for her former parents, but made her heart sink. They now had four children: all strangers to Marella-Zoe. Adopted, perhaps, or conceived naturally after all? That didn't matter. What mattered was that it confirmed that Mom was no longer Marella's mother.

Brielle was not among those children. She had known that Brielle would no longer be her mother's child if the timeline changed, but seeing it so clearly made the world wobble.

And yet, she felt Brielle's presence out there. Rather than a void where Brielle had been, there was a feeling of vibrancy and exuberance. Substance, not emptiness. She felt sure that Brielle was in a replacement body just like the one Marella now occupied. She hadn't erased her. She didn't have that guilt to bear.

She also found photos of Noah, still attending the University of Washington. Grinning in the center of the giant brick plaza known as Red Square, hamming it up with his roommates. Losing him so abruptly made her stomach hurt more, as if her heart couldn't hold all the pain by itself. They had saved the world together, and then, suddenly, they hadn't. Even if—whether by some law of physics or by the hand of God—Noah did remember her, an internet search would tell him the Marella Wells he loved didn't exist. He would move on. In ten years' time she would be an adult and could go find him, but as Zoe, not as Marella. Realistically, he was gone from her new life forever. She exited that site, feeling too fragile to continue seeing his happiness without her.

Online she also saw that Belinda Waverly was no longer CEO of HemisNorth. There was mention of her ouster after the company lost hundreds of millions of dollars developing a new product that didn't work. Project Athena, probably. She was now CEO of a small nonprofit, which seemed an unlikely springboard from which to control the world. Marella-Zoe need no longer fear her or her ambition.

A search for Preston, the cult leader, turned up nothing. She suspected that hadn't been his real name. The important thing was that in this revised timeline, there had been no Aguageddon to make him believe God was purging the Earth of evil. He hadn't ordered his followers to commit suicide or to set the fires that burned half of Washington State.

What was more, Noah hadn't killed him, and Marella hadn't killed Olivia, his follower. It eased her conscience somewhat, but without seeing Olivia online, it wasn't sinking in. Not yet, but it would.

She looked up Hadrian Elkerman, the time philosopher, and his wife, Genevieve. She had died a few years back, so that hadn't changed. However, there were photos of Hadrian with a different redheaded woman, posted over the last couple of months. Strolling hand in hand, posing arm in arm, feeding each other oysters, and so on. Apparently he had finally moved on. Good for him. The sight of him made her shudder, though, to be fair, he had never actually harmed her. That would sink in eventually as well.

Diana Brinkhauser, the friend who had helped her get the job at HemisNorth, was working at a different company now. She was alive! Wonderful, but also bittersweet. Another friend lost to her, since she was no longer Marella.

There was the question of whether Project Athena had consciousness. If it did, then she was culpable for its death. She found a recent scientific research paper online with "indicator properties" of whether artificial intelligence was sentient. The more indicator properties the AI had, the more likely it was to have consciousness. One of those indicator properties was selective attention, which Project Athena absolutely did not have. The others seemed unlikely to apply either. Project Athena had only mimicked human behavior, and so Marella-Zoe need feel no guilt over its demise.

It took courage to search online for Elizabeth Fehr, the woman she had killed. Her mentor-boss, her friend. She had saved the search for last, feeling in her bones that the mercy killing would still have happened because, of all her memories of the Aguageddon, it was the strongest. Perhaps she only remembered it so well because she'd accomplished the terrible deed, then went back in time to watch it happen again. Still, she dreaded finding out that the mercy killing was the one thing that hadn't been erased. That it was fate. Always meant to be. Everywhere, always.

Her fear was unfounded. A social media post from that very same day announced that Elizabeth would be part of a panel at a health and safety conference.

Elizabeth is alive.

She had never killed her. Marella-Zoe was not a murderer. Not a mercy killer. No type of killer at all. Her eyes teared up, and she wiped them quickly, examining Elizabeth's face, allowing her existence to become real and replenish her heart. In her corporate headshot, the set of her mouth revealed intelligence, but little else of Elizabeth's true personality. Marella-Zoe knew the real Elizabeth was strong and kind, with a chiseled sense of humor and incredible perseverance. All those attributes would continue to serve her for the rest of her life.

Ever since she'd killed Elizabeth and Olivia, guilt had been the framework by which she viewed herself. That framework had now collapsed. And what was more, she no longer tasted warm iron and wet mold.

Marella was no more. Marella-Zoe was a blameless child. A sense of wonder overtook her. She was innocent. It felt like floating in a warm sea, gazing up at an azure sky.

• • • •

TWO MONTHS HAD GONE by. Fully healed, Marella-Zoe was adapting surprisingly well to being a child once more. It was a warm Saturday in San Diego, fragrant with sage and mint. The family had built an elaborate obstacle course encircling their large backyard, with monkey bars, a short balance beam, low hurdles, ramps, and more.

Marella-Zoe's father, mother, fourteen-year-old brother Joshua, and eleven-year-old sister Abigail had raced through the obstacle course already, and now it was her turn.

Abigail, who liked to imitate movie characters, pulled her lips to the side like a 1930s gangster. "All right now, kid, you gotta go out there and give it yer all. Hear me? Give it yer all."

Joshua got up close like a boxing coach, advising adamantly, "Take it one step at a time. If you worry about what's next, you'll throw yourself off."

From the deck, lemonade in hand, Grandpa shouted, "I've got a big bet riding on you, so don't let me down."

Marella-Zoe ran the course enthusiastically, keeping Joshua's "one step at a time" advice in mind. When she got to the basketball throw, Dad lifted her so she could dunk the ball in the hoop.

At the finish line, the whole family cheered like maniacs. Then, pretending to suspect foul play, Dad demanded a rematch, which Marella-Zoe obliged. Mom pinned a "first place" flower to Marella-Zoe's shirt, and they all took a lemonade break.

It was becoming less disconcerting to her friends and family that Zoe's amnesia had wiped away all her memories of them. They were developing more memories together; eventually the loss wouldn't matter.

At first Marella-Zoe had worried that something might go wrong—that she would find herself back in Marella's body and start time traveling again. Now being Zoe felt permanent. The worry was gone, replaced by gratitude.

Still, she wondered why she remembered being Marella if she had been erased. She could only guess. Perhaps her brushes with eternity had something to do with it. Or perhaps her one-time sync with Project Athena had left its ghost in her soul.

Was it possible that a higher being wanted her to remember the Aguageddon? Why? What purpose did it serve to remember killing Elizabeth, to remember the deaths and the pain? Was it a warning to keep her from killing in this new life? A call to stave off future disasters?

Regardless of the reason, she vowed to be more prepared as Marella-Zoe, because disasters happened—she'd learned that much, at least—which meant taking every opportunity to learn, whether it involved math, science, arts, physical education, language, or any other subject. She didn't know what lay ahead, and so she wouldn't rule out any type of knowledge.

What of the former Zoe, the little girl that had previously occupied this body? Marella-Zoe believed the girl had died from complications of the accident, and her soul was somewhere else now. Had Marella been gifted Zoe's body as a reward for her sacrifice, or had a quirk of physics landed her here? But why, if this body had been damaged to the point of Zoe's death, could Marella now occupy it?

She would try to find the answers to her questions. It wouldn't be easy. Among other things, she would need to become a time philosopher.

The idea was so daunting that she nearly dismissed it as impossible, but then she realized that she already was a time philosopher. She had been ever since she began to delve into the convolutions of time. As a result, she knew more than anybody in the world about its mysteries. It was just a question of how to build on that knowledge.

But for now, she would continue settling into her new life.

She had lost much by sacrificing Marella Wells and becoming Zoe Lewis, but she had also gained much. Most importantly, time had returned to its normal shape, whatever that was. A line, a river, a road.

Moments, just like her steps in the obstacle course, now came one after another. One step at a time, one moment at a time. And then the next...

And then the next.

About the Author

Susan Whiting Kemp is the author of the novels *The Climate Machine* and *The Time Philosopher*, and co-author of the short story compilation *We Grew Tales*. Her writing has appeared in *Bewildering Stories, Hobart, Wilderness House Literary Review, HowlRound, The Blue Lake Review,* and *The Writer's Workshop Review.* She has written or edited thousands of proposals, articles, and reports for science and engineering companies. She holds a Bachelor of Arts in drama from the University of Washington.

For more, visit susanwkemp.com

Read more at https://susanwkemp.com/.